Lily
Beach

Lily Beach

A NOVEL

JENNIE FIELDS

ATHENEUM
NEW YORK 1993

MAXWELL MACMILLAN CANADA
TORONTO

MAXWELL MACMILLAN INTERNATIONAL
NEW YORK   OXFORD   SINGAPORE   SYDNEY

Copyright © *1993* by Jennie Fields

Atheneum   Maxwell Macmillan Canada, Inc.
Macmillan Publishing Company   *1200* Eglinton Avenue East
866 Third Avenue   Suite *200*
New York, NY *10022*   Don Mills, Ontario M3C 3N1

Macmillan Publishing Company is part of the Maxwell Communication
Group of Companies.

Library of Congress Cataloging-in-Publication Data
Fields, Jennie.
Lily Beach / by Jennie Fields.
p. cm.
ISBN 0-689-12176-8
I. Title.
PS3556.I4175L5   *1993*
813'.54—dc20   92-26822

10 9 8 7 6 5 4 3 2 1

Printed in the United States of America

FOR CHLOE

May you always have as many wishes
as there are wishbones.

I'd like to thank Linda Yellin, Michael Brennecke, and Gayle Keck for their early readings and invaluable comments. And special thanks to Susan Zigouras, without whom this book might not have been written.

Lily
Beach

Andres Pulaski is a tormented man. The famous Paraguayan print-maker has discarded a wife he hated, has escaped the murderous regime of General Stroessner, and now, in 1960, is living in a white Victorian house in Iowa City, Iowa. He should be savoring his fame: Museums are calling to view his prints even before he finishes them, paying ridiculously high sums. His American wife has given him three American sons. And the University of Iowa has become, because of him, a mecca for print students.

But he is suffering. Each season, it seems, he has become infatuated with one of the coeds. Most years, these infidelities add glamour to his already plump life, but this year he has discovered a girl unlike all others. A girl that haunts him, diminishes him to one of the hollow-eyed people that live in his prints.

Almost all the American women he's known before are about texture: rubbed with lotions until their skins are like suede, hair stiff and lac-quered like spun candy, nails painted glossy, lips painted sticky. They are fitted out, dressed up, and presented as untouchable dolls. But this one is what the other students call Bohemian, her clothes always black or the color of bruises, wrapping her body with easy intimacy. Her hair is loose and long. And maybe she is a little bit wild, a little bit morally undisciplined. This is what he's come to expect from girls like her.

But he has never encountered a girl quite like her. For he has never seen a person so incandescently alive. When she comes into a room, it makes a mockery of his own gray aging self. He feels he is drawn merely in pencil, while she is engraved in the total spectrum of his inks.

He has tried to draw her naturally full and rougey lips, tried to find their coral equivalent in his inks, but he is at a loss to capture her, for despite her aliveness, which seems to stir the air when she enters a room, what is most appealing is her sadness. It veils her enormous dark-lashed eyes. He has never seen the like before in a girl her age. What does she know that's so painful? He needs to discover it and plots daily how to approach her. He is known to be gruff, morose, never allowing anyone into his studio. Certainly not his pretty indiscretions.

But so many times he has imagined bringing this delicate girl, this Lily, to his barnlike room in the art building, which smells of dust and ink and his own sweat, and sharing with her his new prints. She will understand them. They alone might make her love him.

On election night in November 1960, and restless because of her, he comes to the art building. He has forgotten a print he's promised to show a prospective buyer in the morning, and while his wife eats a sandwich in front of the television and squeals as the states' results roll in— Kennedy and Nixon running neck and neck—he crosses the campus in the dark to retrieve it. It has been a searing day, ridiculously hot for November, and the air in the art building is heavy with the scent of turpentine and acid, almost flammable. Up on the second floor, where he has his studio, the pipes drip, rusty with humidity. There's no one in the building at all—it is nearly midnight—and he finds himself afraid. Uneasy fears that remind him of his last harrowing weeks in Paraguay, politics, the death of the people he most loved. When he hears a noise on the top floor, he presses himself against the wall, sidles up the stairs quietly so no one can possibly hear, and with aching slowness, allows himself to look.

And there she is, in the print lab all alone. Lily. He will never forget it—his entire life feels altered—for in the heat she's taken off her shirt. Sitting with her back to him, in the shadows, she's naked from the waist up. Her hair is drawn up to allow her neck to cool, the wet hairs clinging to the slender stem of her spine. Her shoulders are like peaches. And her back, slicked with sweat, has a fluidity that makes his heart pump painfully. When he shifts his weight and the floor creaks, she pulls on her linen shirt with a panic of movement. She's intended no one to see her. It's only because Andres Pulaski still moves like a man who faces death that he's been granted an indelible view of life.

PART ONE

Iowa City

Chapter One

The night air of Iowa City smells of apples on this first cool night in a week. And once again, Lily Beach shares her bed with a stranger. She cannot imagine that this man will be different from the others. She tends to choose nice, remote men who make no dent in her life. Her evenings with them later feel no more meaningful than if she'd stayed home alone, watching Ed Sullivan.

Now twenty-one years old, glad that nothing in her life is permanent, she raises herself on an elbow to look at this man. In the shadows, his face appears young, though he is four years older than she. She discovered this at the party where they met, and little else, except his name, which is Will Sternhagen, that he is engaged to a woman in California and therefore what she thinks of as "safe."

Lily sits up. The record player has finished its stack of 45s and is playing over and over the top record, "Are You Lonesome Tonight?" Elvis's deep, echoing plea fills the room, is only interrupted by the occasional cranking sound of the arm moving away and back again.

This room, where Lily lives as a graduate student, where she engraves her prints, smells not just of her metal plates and waxes and resins but of the flat smokiness of their discarded clothes—everyone at the party seemed to chain-smoke except her and this man. Perhaps it was only this that drew her to him. Or his beautiful teeth. She remembers how she watched his pure smile across the room, his pretty, bruised-looking mouth. She leans over to look at it now, but it is hard to see anything but the soft, dark stain of his lips against her pillow. She looks at his hand, which is near her face. It is gently shaped, and as she puts her cheek close to it, it smells faintly of ink. She lies down again, quietly for a while, thinking about him, wondering about him, listening to Elvis's sad whine. She does not feel special about this man or the way they made love. She cannot know that from the moment she brought this man to her bed, her world has been fully staged with the people who will most affect her life. She cannot know that this sleeping man will dent her as she hopes no man ever will. She thinks only of their tired and boozy lovemaking, kind enough, gentle enough. But, in the end, lonely. She thinks of her stepfather and what he would think to find her here with this man, who may or may not know her name. In the cool dark, the corners of her mouth curl into a pleased smile, thinking of her stepfather's hot discomfort. When she gets out of bed and goes to the window, the man awakes.

"Where are you going?" he asks. "Lily?" She likes his voice. It is soft, instantly intelligent, and he has remembered her name, after all.

"I'm going to see what's going on at the Pulaskis' house."

"Really? Can you see it from here?"

"There." She points as he comes up behind her. Andres Pulaski's beautiful old mansion spills light onto the backyard of Lily's rooming house. At night, when she's lonely, she stares at this house, filled with family life: Andres's children, his large, shirtwaisted wife, and Professor Pulaski himself, who, rumor has it, has propositioned every pretty graduate student in the department. She has become obsessed with watching, waits for lights to go on or off, for a face at a window, wonders how long they will stay married.

"I feel sorry for his wife," she says now. "I think Professor Pulaski likes me."

"Does he?" the man says. "Has he said anything to you?"

"No. It's just the way he looks at me. Creepy." She stares at this man, tries to see into him, into his eyes, which are somewhere, murkily, between green and blue. "Are you going to do that to your fiancée when you're married? Look at young girls, want other women?"

"You're already doing it to your 'steady boyfriend,' aren't you?" he asks. He smiles lazily.

She has told this man little about herself, only that for the last two years she has been in love with a man who's gone off to Europe on what he calls "a junket."

"It's different. I haven't made any commitments to Ted. He's in Paris for a year or more."

"Well, as for me, I'm engaged. I figure until I marry, I'm still fair game." The man draws the covers up to his chin. "I'm not sure I want to be the perfect example of husbandhood, anyway," he says, flopping back on the bed. "I don't want anyone mistaking me for 'Father Knows Best.' "

"Don't worry," she tells him. "It's not too likely."

Lily gets out of bed naked and walks to the corner of the room she calls the kitchen. "You hungry?" she asks.

"Kind of."

"I'll make popcorn."

"You're beautiful, you know," he says. She doesn't think of herself as beautiful, but she is of an age that later she will envy. Nudity is easy for her now. She is all liquid in her bones and skin. Still, she is flattered by his compliment.

"You're nice," she says, stopping by the record player to lift the stack of 45s again.

"Nice? I'm thoughtful, charming, maybe. But don't call me nice. Pat Boone, now there's a nice man," he says, wrinkling his nose.

He sits down on a chair by the little table where she usually eats her dinner. She takes in the blond hair on his legs, his knobby knees, his thin but appealling shoulders and chest. And his face: It is such a simple face, his eyes pale, his nose slender. Blond hair that darkens at the ears, a high forehead, a perfectly square chin. Like a child's drawing of a man. Even, but not terribly remarkable or handsome. It is his mouth that draws her. Almost feminine. A mouth for kissing, loving, whispering. She longs even now to kiss it again.

"Nice is boring. Stultifying," he goes on. "My fiancée is nice."

"Your fiancée is boring and stultifying?" she asks, pushing aside her desire for him.

He looks bemused, shakes his head. "Safe," he says finally. "Can't wait to be a housewife. She would rather watch TV than go out for a fancy dinner. And she was a staunch Nixon supporter. She thinks Kennedy might as well be a Communist. You don't, do you?"

"A Communist? If she calls Kennedy a Communist, what is she? I voted for Kennedy. I even leafleted for Kennedy."

He smiles at her. "Me, too."

"You're that far apart politically? You sure you want to marry this woman? You say she's safe with such . . . pleasure. What do you need to feel safe *from*?" she asks him.

"Wild girls like you." She turns and looks at his eyes, which twinkle now with renewed desire.

"I don't ever want to be a housewife," she says. "I don't think I want to get married for a long time." She pours the kernels into a pot.

"Why not? Most girls your age are married already."

"Half the girls my age, in fact. I saw it in *Life* magazine last week."

"So? Why are you different?"

"You don't think I'm different?"

"You went to bed with me willingly, without so much as a commitment for dinner. That's pretty damn different. And not unappreciated."

"I suppose that makes me fast," she says. "A slut. Right?"

"Is that what you think you are?" he asks her. He gently takes Lily's elbow in his hand, but she starts to shake the pan across the hot plate, shrugging him off.

"I suppose you think I'm a slut, too," he says, shouting over the sound of the pan. And then he mimics a silly, almost effeminate sigh. "It's so embarrassing." She laughs, is almost discomfited with how comfortable he makes her feel.

"So what do you have against marriage?" he says, stilling her hand for a minute.

"Don't," she says. "You're going to burn the kernels. My mother and father divorced when I was ten."

"People make mistakes."

"They always hated each other. My mother must have had impaired judgment when she married him. Then she remarried. You don't want to know about *that* marriage." It is just a rote answer, and absurd, shouted against the new and intermediate sound of popping. It doesn't contain in it the agony of the marriages she's known or what in the end happened to her mother.

"So, your mother has bad taste. What else is new? Is she still married?"

"Actually . . ."—Lily shakes the pot even faster, so that the noise is deafening—"actually, she's dead," she nearly whispers.

But she knows by the surprise in his eyes that he's heard her. "Oh . . . God. Sorry."

Lily shrugs. She doesn't want to tell him how bad it really is, that since what happened to her mother, she is weary and trying to drown the pain in the noise of men like him. She can't tell him that sometimes, alone at night, she feels her mother is there—the delicate touch of her mother's hand, her scent. She can't tell him that since her mother's death she feels distant from everybody, as though she is shrouded in batting.

"Are *your* parents still married?" she forces herself to ask, to make herself stop thinking.

"Nope. I'm the poor child of an ugly, ugly divorce. Just like you. Aren't we the modern ones? My father's remarried. He left my mother when I was twenty, bought a Corvette, and married my kindergarten teacher. Yup. It's true. Don't look at me that way. I think they'd been having an affair since I was in kindergarten." As the final kernels explode in the pot, they don't speak, but Lily can feel Will's presence behind her, knows he is watching her.

"Maybe I don't want to marry," she says, "because I don't want to get divorced."

"Yeah," he says. "I have sympathy for that." She turns off the hot plate and transfers the popcorn to a bowl. Amid the smell and steam of the hot kernels, he turns her around and kisses her. His mouth is more than pretty. She feels excited in a way that almost scares her. She feels he is more like her than anyone she's known.

"Come back to bed with me," he says.

"What about the popcorn?" she asks.

"The popcorn? Well . . ."

He grabs a handful of popcorn, then lays her down on the bed and plants the kernels, two in her hair, one on her neck, one in her pubic hair, one in her navel, and eats them off of her with the barest touch of his mouth. In the middle of it all, she turns her head and sees the lights go out at the Pulaski house.

In the morning, when Will Sternhagen leaves, Lily lies in bed for a long time. His fruity scent stays behind him. The scent, the feel, the sense of him, are so different from her boyfriend, Ted, who, each time they part, kisses her pristinely, leaves her feeling safe and untouched. Now that Ted is gone, each week, Lily receives a letter from him, from Paris. It is filled with cool endearments. Ted is a quiet man, a man who knows very little about women, and in some ways, little about her.

Lily met Ted two summers before her mother died. He was everything she thought she should want: Harvard educated. An MIT postgraduate. He worked so hard in school, he had no time for women. She was struck with his innocence. His interest in her is still like a clean slate.

The first night they met, at a college friend's house on New Year's Eve, he asked her endless questions about what it was like to be a female college student. About what girls did to their hair and nails, about why she smelled like almonds. He seemed overwhelmed and fascinated by the difference between men and women. And a little scared of women. He put her on a pedestal. Look but don't touch. Even now, when he knows the most hideous things about her life, he still thinks she's a virgin. And how he reveres her mythical virginity! He won't allow her to breach it even with him, though she's tried. "We're going to wait," he tells her.

He is the sort of man who apologizes when he swears, who kisses her gently and somewhat fearfully, who is more comfortable with his books, his research, his hopes for the future, than his sexual feelings for her. Maybe, Lily sometimes thinks, that is why she chose him. All the men in her mother's life had been angry, distasteful, filthy men. And Ted seemed so pure, so untouched.

Then he had to see the ugliness behind her mother's death. She could not have survived it without him. But in the end he did not stay with her after what happened. He ran away to Paris. And though he said it was just some time he needed after his degree, before he committed himself to a life of paychecks, science grants, and aerospace engineering, though he said that he still loved her, she knows it can't be true. He is not the sort of man who runs away. He is purposeful and predictable. Once a week he writes. An old Harvard chum has a studio apartment on the Left Bank. They roam the bookstalls. They go to the beatnik coffeehouses, where the music is magical. He says he's coming back. His letters are his best attempts at warmth. But she thinks he is afraid of what he knows about her. She thinks he has gone to Paris to escape the disease that is her life.

Will Sternhagen doesn't call Lily all week, and she goes about her life with a listlessness because of it. She works, shelving books at the math and science library. She spends her obligatory hours in the print lab, pressing together again and again the inked copper plates, the heavy sheets of rag paper. The roller squeaks; the inks smell of sweat and oil. And up from the paper come diaphanous shadows of sad women she etched at home into wax with the dental tools she found long ago at a country fair. Most of the art she does involves a loneliness, a dejection that reads in the faces she draws, no matter how abstract, in the stance of the women's bodies she cuts into the wax—their bodies shrug no matter how hard she tries to make them look sturdy or certain.

Lily has been told that she is very talented but can't help feeling she is fooling everyone. When something comes out well, she thinks of it as a happy mistake. Other people in the print department praise the work she takes off the presses, have even asked to take pressings she throws away, say her shapes and colors taste of Matisse, of Klee. But their interest in her makes her want to step back from them. She doesn't really know anyone well, has made no real friends in this first year here. It is as though she is too tired. When she tries to compliment someone or ask someone a question, the art lab seems too noisy, too impenetrable. Though many of the students are also new, she feels they are part of a group of which she will never be part. Especially the women, in plaid skirts and bobby socks, the men with their Brylcreemed hair. She envies their clean-cut images. But she might as well be watching them on television, they seem so distant and different from her. In a different plane, parted from her by a screen of glass.

But Will is like her. She can't stop thinking of how easily they talked, how sweetly he made love to her. There is another man she's been occasionally sleeping with, a clarinetist with the university symphony, something of a beatnik, with a beard and a cool, dry way of speaking that offends most everybody over thirty. She is supposed to see him this week. For a few hours she plots how she's going to turn him down. She doesn't think she wants to be with anyone but Will, but in the end she makes herself see him. Why should she get involved with Will Sternhagen, anyway? She has Ted. And besides, Will hasn't called. In bed with the clarinetist, she alarms him. "What's gotten into you?" he asks her. Lovemaking with him is usually precise, pared to simplicity. But she is wild, restless. And in the end she gives the musician quite a rousing night. "Hey, cool. I didn't know it could be like this," the clarinetist tells her, exhausted and shaken. She's enjoyed it, too. She always enjoys it and then has to face the emptiness alone.

• • •

Lily is ashamed that she likes sex so much, that she knows she needs it, that life seems incomplete without it. She thinks that other women are not like her at all: all the pretty little coeds in their matching sweaters and bubble haircuts. The women who say no even if they would rather say yes.

Lily lost her virginity her freshman year in college to a male ballet major. He was very handsome and very sweet and respectful, but it wasn't because of his assets that she slept with him or even because she knew he needed her to prove his masculinity, uncomfortable with his choice of being a ballet major. It was because she realized, in one hot, lustful moment, that this was the pleasure that made adulthood worthwhile, that this was the ecstasy that replaced childhood surprise.

She could not have known that in the fateful moment she said yes, she would alter herself forever, that once called up, her desire would never retreat, that it could be a burden, that it could run her, decide for her. Pandora's box. Oh, those long nights she has regretted opening herself to the man in the pink tights! He showed her the way to pleasure and left her in its hold. And since her mother died, her desire is worse, gluttonous, needy. All the passion she had before for her art, the hopes she had for her life, are dulled, as though she is looking through sand-blasted glass; but the one time she feels alive, aware, is when she's making love to a man. Then, for a moment, she feels lucid, entirely there, her senses thrumming. It is like being pinched awake from a dream. Love me. Love me, each meeting of their flesh says, and this is as close as she can come to feeling any kind of love at all.

Will Sternhagen finally calls on a Thursday night. "I've been thinking of you," he says.

"Want to come over for some popcorn?" she asks.

Later, when she opens the door for him, his smile makes her step back with understanding. It was most definitely the smile that intrigued her at the party. There is in his smile a perfect mixture of vulnerability and knowingness. There is, in his smile, a mirror of the qualities Lily attributes to herself. And as soon as his coat is off, she finds herself kissing him, hungry for that mouth, that incredible mouth—and drawing him to her bed. This time, they do not speak or try to get to know each other. The fury that he took so long to call obliterates the tenderness of her lovemaking. Just like with the clarinetist, she is wild. But Will doesn't seem to notice or desire to slow her down. Men never notice or care when she's feeling like that. They revel in her insatiability, her drive, and see none of the pain that fuels it.

"God, you are astonishing," he says two or three times. "Could you teach my fiancée a few lessons?" he says afterward, in the dusky silence.

"I don't know what came over me."

"Whatever it is, don't lose it," he says. He looks at her, holds her face in his hands. His touch is gentle, almost feminine. She reads respect in it, and tenderness.

"Do you sleep with your fiancée?" she asks him.

"Yes. We have." She feels somewhat relieved that simple, "normal" girls also share her vice. But then he adds, "I'm not sure Sandra likes it much . . . yet."

"I'm sure she'll learn to," Lily tells him politely.

"Do you think so?" he asks, the merest shadow of worry in his voice. "Can women learn to like sex?"

"With someone like you they might," she says, and she wonders if she sounds too starry-eyed or interested, if he will interpret her answer as liking him too much.

Obviously, he doesn't see her sweetness toward him as a threat, for the next day he calls and comes over again. And the next. And the next.

This is how Will Sternhagen comes into her life. Like an accident, like a gold coin gleaming out of a drawer filled with pennies. The only problem is, all she is really looking for at this time in her life is pennies. She has Ted and her odd commitment to him. And her new feeling for Will weighs on her, more sometimes than she can handle. Still, after their second time together, the time of her angry lovemaking, she finds a kindness in herself for him, a givingness. There is no more teeth grinding. Each time, there is less pushing away emotionally. And yet there is still a fire, a passion in her that never seems to stop surprising him. If he hesitated calling her after their first time together, that hesitation is gone.

Lily writes to Ted in Paris,

Sometimes I can't walk away from what happened to my mother. Will you ever be able to see me without the truth of that time blocking me? I can't help feeling it's why you left so quickly, because for you I don't exist anymore. For you I am a bad memory.

And Ted writes back:

You mustn't think of what happened to your mother. I can't believe it's good for you. The weather in Paris is beautiful this time of year. But I find it hard to relax here. I keep thinking about opportunities back in Chicago. Chin up, now. With love,

Lily hates his letters. Never reads them more than once. But she cannot imagine losing contact with the one man who knows everything, with the one person who remembers it all. One day, when she gets out of the shower, she sees Will reading one of Ted's letters. He drops it as soon as he realizes she is watching, but he looks at her curiously later. "You love this guy Ted?" he asks.

"Do you love Sandra?" she asks.

One day, after Lily and Will have made love, Will asks, "Is it just physical between us?"

"Physical? I don't know. I like you," Lily says.

"Don't you get the feeling there could be more between us?"

"Well, there's two things between us right now," she says. "Ted and Sandra."

He nods. "You know, if it wasn't for that, I might even fall in love with you."

"God," she says. "Do you have to say stuff like that?" She sinks into the pillow with worry and deep satisfaction. Indeed, after they make love, they talk like true friends. They cuddle; they laugh. They talk about what makes them laugh and about what worries them. Lately, Lily's been worrying about fallout shelters, school basements, pyramidal stacks of canned goods, and metal tanks of water. All that stands between Iowa City and slow death by radiation poisoning. Lily has nightmares about running for the fallout shelter, about the bombs, about the flash of light so bright; the light alone burns you.

"What would we do if we were in a fallout shelter together?" she asks him.

"Make love for two weeks straight," he says.

"Would you tell me you loved me, I mean, knowing we were going to die?" she asks him.

"If you would tell me first," he says.

They talk about sit-ins in the South. "Can you imagine if they wouldn't let you eat at a smelly old lunch counter just because of the color of your skin?" he asks her.

"Would you want me if I were black and you were white?" she asks.

"I'd flaunt how much I want you. I'd walk down the street holding your hand. I'd threaten whoever wouldn't let you go where you'd want to go," he says, warming her heart.

Once he tells her, "Lily Beach. Your name sounds like a beautiful, sheltered place. The kind of place a person goes to escape the world. I feel that way with you."

In his arms, Lily feels safe, too. Will is her equal, her partner. When they lie in bed together, they don't talk about owning each other or jealousy or commitment, because there is no question they belong to others. Sometimes Will tells her about his fiancée, Sandra, and Lily thinks she sounds foolish. She is studying to be an elementary-school teacher, which is fine, Lily supposes, but it is what all bland, silly girls do in this era, when what they really want is to marry and have elementary-school children of their own.

"Maybe you're living out your father's fantasy," Lily says. "Marrying a kindergarten teacher."

Will is silent for a while. "I never thought of that," he says.

"I was only teasing."

"It hit a nerve," he says.

"Maybe I don't want to get married, after all," he says one morning, kissing her neck.

"So don't," Lily says, and finds her heart thumping.

"But I'm committed."

"So do," Lily says, and finds her heart thumping even harder. "Why is the question coming up?"

"No change of heart," he says, his voice solidifying, closing her off. "She's just asked me to take some teaching courses next semester," Will says. "You know, to teach high school."

"Who asked you?"

"Sandra."

"But you're a good printmaker. I've heard your name mentioned in the department. I know Pulaski thinks you're tops. You should be able to be a printmaker. Make money off your prints. Or at least teach college."

"You can't make money being a printmaker," Will says. "Almost no one makes real money. Even people with galleries in New York. Sandra says, 'At least there's a need for teachers.' "

"Well, Professor Pulaski makes money. Scads of it, from what I hear," Lily says. "Anyway, I hope you and Sandra enjoy being teachers. Send me a postcard from hell. I'd rather be a welder. Teaching is so compromising."

Will rolls away, is silent for a long time. When he makes love to her, it is with anger.

"I wish I'd never met you," he says, and then kisses her passionately. "Why?"

"Everything was clear before I met you. Maybe we should stop seeing each other. I think we should stop seeing each other."

Later, when he's gone, Lily cannot sleep and hates that she ever went to bed with him. She sits down and writes a passionate letter to Ted, more passionate than she's ever dared commit to paper.

I can't help thinking of you. It torments me not to be with you. Just to touch your hand would save me, I think sometimes.

The next day, Will comes back to Lily as though he'd never said anything at all. Lily mails the letter, anyway.

Lily has been drawing and painting all her life, as far back as her memory goes. She remembers poster paints at the kitchen table, her mother's impatience with paint on the kitchen chairs, on her clothes, on her hands. She remembers the smell of her mother. Her breath resembled the scent of burning leaves, spicy and autumnal. Back then, Lily didn't mind the burr of smoke knitted deep into her mother's sweaters or its sour remainder on her irritated, constantly smoking hands.

"Must you paint again?" she'd ask so wearily. How impatient her mother always was. How vaguely sad she always seemed. The more distant her mother became, the more Lily lost herself in paint and colored pencils, charcoal sticks and turpentine.

Now, in the art building, Lily works with layers and layers of paints, experimenting, trying things she's been told she can't do. The paint must be channeled, directed, and yet it moves its own way, and this is what excites her. Such a delicate balance. The challenge elates her. Hours have passed, and she is working slowly, not caring at all about the time. At the next easel, a girl she hardly knows is chattering with another woman she doesn't know at all. It is after hours. Free time. Anyone in the art department can use the tables and easels. On some nights, there is a nude model, sitting with goose bumps on the gray metal stool. So odd, Lily thinks, that the men all wear loincloths and the women are always naked, as though the university is trying to protect the female students from something they must not see. But tonight there is the standard still life of draped cloth, bananas, grapes, an old coffee grinder, and a mirror. Lily is lost in the mirror, the slight, grayed adjustments she must make to create the world reflected in glass, the subtle distortion, the thin line of fluorescent green along the mirror's edge.

"He told Erich he's having doubts about marrying her," Lily overhears. "He says he wonders if he really loves her, after all."

"What does Erich say?"

"Erich says he thinks there's someone else in the picture, but Will's kept things very quiet if there is. But I've figured it out. I know who he's seeing."

Lily feels her breathing thicken. She pulls her brush slowly from the canvas.

"I can't see Will Sternhagen being with anybody. I tried to get him interested in me once, and he pretended he could see right through me. Of course, I could take it as a personal insult. But I'll bite. Who is it?"

Lily glances over at the woman speaking. She has one of those bubble haircuts, so dark it looks dyed, and too much makeup, which makes her eyes look Egyptian.

"Louise Lewis. I saw them talking the other day on the quad, and he was twisting her hair around his finger."

"No."

"Yeah, really. Then he kissed her. And she got all rag dolly. Then they walked off."

Lily swallows hard and tastes such a rush of jealousy, she has to leave the room for air. She's never before felt jealous about Will. After all, Sandra found him before her. And she has Ted. But she knows Louise Lewis. A silly, flirty girl from California who reveals her deepest family secrets within seconds of meeting you. "My sister was wearing that very perfume when she committed suicide," she actually told Lily, much to her horror. "I had to identify the body. She was wearing way too much of it. But it's nice on you."

Louise Lewis. Lily realizes that at least on campus she feels she owns Will. Since that second time they were together, Lily's given up everybody else, except Ted, of course. She gathers her paints, her unfinished and promising painting, puts them in her locker, and sets out for Will's. She's never been to his place before. She knows where he lives, though, in a rooming house that prohibits women from visiting. She once knew another man who lived there, dated him shortly and remembers saying good-bye on the Victorian porch, remembers him entering the lopsided screen door hanging from one hinge.

When she pulls it aside tonight, the door makes a cracking noise. It is cold out, and inside Will's house, a rush of heat hits her. The entrance hall smells of bacon and sweat socks. She sees Will's name on a mailbox with his room number below and climbs the stairs to find the white door with his number on it. It isn't until she hears the sound of her knuckle thunking against the wood that she wonders what she's going to say to him.

When he finds her there, his eyes open wide. He's wearing a blue bathrobe too small for him, naked underneath; she can see a peek of skin, a flash of his sleek penis. He pulls her in from the hall and closes the door.

"I'll get kicked out if Mrs. Semple sees you," he says. "What's wrong?"

She just shakes her head. What right has she to be jealous? They don't own a particle of each other.

"What's wrong?" he asks again. In his voice she can read a perfect mix of anger and concern. When she starts to cry, he draws her to him so tenderly, it injures her heart.

"Oh, darling. Something's happened," he says. "Tell me."

In a silly blur she begins to tell him about the woman at the easel, about the woman's suggestion that he's sleeping with Louise Lewis.

"You're not, are you? You're not, are you?" The way he holds her in his arms, she knows that he cares for her in a tender way she never suspected. He nuzzles his face against her neck. When she looks at him, there is a strange, worried look in his eyes.

"I slept with her once," he says finally.

Though she came to accuse him, she hardly believes it. She realizes she has come only for him to tell her it simply isn't true. "Why did you sleep with her? When?"

"Last week."

"But why?"

"Because you confused me."

He sits apart from her on the bed, doesn't look at her. He is ashamed. She sees this in his hands, which twist at the pillow he's picked up as a shield. She sees it in his lips and eyes. She turns her face away, cannot look at him now. As she stands to leave, she feels no searing pain, just a nothingness. Her heart is as bloated and empty as a balloon. Still, she can't leave just yet. Her legs have no strength; her bloated heart is slamming. She glances around the room. It is pale blue, filled with books. His sheets are neatly made. There are two beautiful paintings on the wall: oils of models perching on stools. He has turned even these student exercises into something special, the tender, blue-shadowed bend of their backs, the subtle flush of their skins. The room smells of Bartlett pears, which sit in a blue glass bowl by the window. It is the room of a man she realizes she cares about deeply. Finding her last bit of strength, she moves toward the door.

"Don't leave before I explain," he says hoarsely.

"If I don't leave now, I might knock your head off," she says. Her voice is so weak, she wonders if he's heard her. She finds the stairs with her feet, but not her heart. It stays in the room with Will as she runs across the pentangle in the dark. It stays in the blue room with his beautiful paintings, his bruised mouth, his desire for her, and she wonders if she can get it back.

Professor Pulaski sees Lily Beach hurrying across the campus, rushing, as if in fear or pain. And he wants to stop her and put his arms around her. Someone, he thinks, has broken her heart. He follows her for a while, but his legs, his heart, cannot keep up. Later in bed, he thinks of his next print, a woman running in the night, half in an unflattering lamplight, half in the fearful dark. And a man, well behind her, in the shadows, running, too, but with no chance of catching her, a man who wants to save her.

Chapter Two

Lily does not see Will Sternhagen for nearly two weeks, will not see him, though he comes daily to her door, calls, waits for her outside classes. He has betrayed her, and she did not expect it of him. Even though there was no commitment. Even though he plans to spend his life with Sandra, she cannot bear the thought that she was not enough to satisfy him, for whatever reason. Lily knows betrayal. Her own father left her when she was ten years old to start another family, forgot to ever send her a birthday card and eventually even an address. He is lost to her forever, and it is a loss she will never free herself from. She has considered sending detectives to find him. Now that her mother is dead, she feels more need to confront him, to know why she and her mother weren't enough for him, though she remembers life with him being even more lonely and painful than without him.

The only family Lily has left is her stepfather, Jack. He adopted her when he married her mother. Lily hates him. Once, she was glad her mother married him. Once, at the age of twelve, she liked his strong hands, his sandy eyelashes, his ability to balance their lives with his maleness. She remembers the first time he touched her. He put his arm around her shoulder. They were at a restaurant. She was wearing a peppermint pink taffeta dress with puffed sleeves. He put his arm around her and squeezed so that the sleeves crackled. "My new daughter," he said very loudly. How she loved the encouragement of that touch. To think someone actually wanted to be her father! Her own father never did. Now the very thought of him touching her turns her to ice.

Now she knows. Jack is a brutal man, narcissistic, impatient with women, precisely like her father. Both are men that broke her mother's spirit and then lost interest in her. And there is the way Jack feels about Lily. He is a man who doesn't know that some feelings are, will always be, inappropriate.

Lily knows Jack wants her to feel indebted to him, so she intends to make something of herself, to be independent. With her own money, she feels safe from Jack; she feels she need never see him again. She is going to graduate school entirely on scholarships and on money she earns at the math and science libraries, where she works every afternoon of the week except Sunday.

There, in the stacks, Will finally corners her.

"You have to listen to me," he says. She fills her arms with books, trying to ignore him, but she's gathered too many. She tries to shelve them—math and science tomes weighing easily ten or more pounds a piece—but they fall noisily from her arms. He bends down with her and helps her gather them.

"Please," he whispers.

She nods but won't look at him.

"You scared me," he says quickly. "I have to marry Sandra. I have to. You scared me. You made me think I couldn't do it anymore. I had to be with someone else to get free from you."

This all comes out so rapidly, his voice so high pitched she is sure others have heard.

"I never told you not to marry Sandra."

"I have to marry Sandra."

"Fine. Marry her."

"You don't understand."

"You have to marry Sandra. I understand perfectly. I never told you not to marry Sandra. I'm in love with Ted. I've absolutely expected you to marry Sandra. I just didn't expect you to sleep with Louise Lewis."

"It was a terrible mistake, okay? I can't stand her. I probably picked someone I purposely can't stand."

"You're hideous," Lily says. She pushes the library cart through the stacks. He follows behind.

"You don't get it, do you?"

"I'm trying," she says, and turns to him. Again, it is his mouth that undoes her. It looks so sad, so frightened. His lips are bitter with held-back tears. She likes that he is able to cry. She never expected that of him, either. She touches his mouth with her fingertips.

"Okay," she says. "I'll see you when I'm out of here. Meet me at my room." He takes a deep breath, nods, and disappears down the long corridor of stacks.

He is waiting outside her rooming house when she arrives, hunched over in the cold, leaning against the porch railing. She opens the door, and he comes in behind her, spilling cold from his coat, hair, and hands. His Scandinavian cheeks are blotchy red.

"How long have you been waiting?"

He shrugs. "Too long."

She makes him tea, and he shivers in the rocking chair as he drinks it. She puts a quilt around his knees that her grandmother made when she was being courted by her grandfather in Chicago. She is glad he is in her room and feels more tender toward him than she planned.

"I have to marry Sandra because the wedding invitations are chosen and the silver pattern is chosen and because I broke off another wedding once and the whole family hated me for it. Besides, I do love her."

"What wedding? What are you talking about?"

"I was engaged to another girl in college. Lisa Rudolfo. In the end I knew it was a mistake, so I broke it off. Her two brothers came to my door and offered to beat the shit out of me. Her father made threats you wouldn't believe. And they made me pay for part of the catering, the band—"

"How close to the wedding did you break it off?"

Will smiles now, a childish smile. "The night before."

"Jesus!"

"I know. It was immature. It was unthinkable. I've heard all the words. God, I'm freezing," he says, still shivering, pulling the quilt up now around his neck. "I was only nineteen."

"Why did you think you wanted to marry her in the first place?"

"Because she told me she loved me."

"That's all it takes?"

"No one ever told me that before."

She comes close to him now, sits by him. She has missed his voice, his hands, his scent.

"I'm not going to keep you from marrying Sandra. Just stay with me until the school year is out. Just don't be with anyone else until then," she asks. She is giddy with his need to explain to her, with his need for her approval.

"Would *you* marry me if I asked you?" he whispers, so sweetly that she has to take a deep breath before she can answer, and then her voice comes out too harsh, too censorious.

"Why are you so crazy to marry? It's almost like you'd marry anyone."

"You know that's not true. Would you marry me?" She thinks for a moment, and tries to imagine them together at an altar, on a honeymoon, in a tiny apartment with frilly pink curtains.

"No. I don't want to get married for a long time."

"I really do love Sandra," he says.

"Stop it, I know you do."

"I just don't want you to think I don't. She's a good person. She's a kind person."

Lily can't help but laugh at him. At his insistence, at his need to convince himself. He is not a cynic, after all, she now knows, but a romantic.

"Come on," she says. "Get in bed with me where I can warm you up." In bed, she wraps herself around him. Skin to skin he is the most delicious man she's ever known. She cannot be close to him without desiring him. She burrows under the covers, which are warm now, scented with his unmistakable fruitlike aura, and takes his cock in her mouth. In moments it is huge and silky. She explores every soft fold of it with her lips and tongue and teeth. When he pulls away and stretches himself above her, when he presses its thick sureness into the wet center of her, she forgets Ted's leaving her, and her own father leaving, and the emotional or physical flight of every man she's ever known.

For many days, she and Will Sternhagen are inseparable. They paint together at night in the free room, walk home and sleep together, eat all their meals together from her little hot plate, even though he has a contract at Mrs. Semple's. He waits for her at the library, at her classes.

It is nearly the holidays, and each week, Ted's letters are filled with talk of her joining him in Paris for Christmas. She does not want to spend the holidays with Jack, her stepfather. But she has no money to join Ted by plane. There is no time to take a boat. And Will is flying to California to be with Sandra.

She wonders what it is like when Will and Sandra make love. She cannot imagine anyone sleeping with Will but herself. She wonders if Sandra is silent and sweet and nonparticipatory. She wants to think so. Will is excited about seeing Sandra again. He tells Lily. He counts the days with her. But he seems, strangely, to make love to Lily even more lovingly than usual, for he is filled with anticipation and joy. It is nice to make love to him when he is so tender, but she knows he is withdrawing, preparing for his trip. Perhaps he really *does* love Sandra. He talks about how simple her tastes are. How innocent and unschooled she seems to him, for she mostly reads popular books, likes to watch television. He speaks of her ordinariness with reverence. "She's all prepared for Kennedy to ruin the country," he says with awe.

As the holiday approaches, Lily thinks often of Ted. She cannot see him clearly in her mind, and that makes her long for him. At night, in bed, even when Will is there, after they make love, when he is sleeping, she thinks of Ted. It is not erotically, as she often thinks of Will. But it is a hurt, a need for him that makes her uneasy. She feels abandoned by him and bonded to him in what they both know. And she is jealous, too, that he might have found someone in Paris. An innocent, like him.

"I just can't get the money together for Paris," she writes to him. "I'd love to. Do you still think of me?"

"Of course I think of you," he writes. "Even when I try to think of everything else. You would love what I am seeing. You would love it all."

She often worries that what he loves in her is artifice, a sham. He loves her for being the pure, vibrant little virgin she shows to him. She often thinks that if he can love her without the sexual side of her, he is snowblind, that except for the sex there is such an emptiness, that only a false front could make her appealing.

She tries to tell Will about Ted. Will can't believe that Ted hasn't slept with her, doesn't apparently want to.

"He thinks people should wait until they marry," she explains. "Or he thinks I want to wait until we marry."

"But doesn't he try anything? Anything at all? How could he look at you and not want you? He must be crazy." When Will tells her things like that, she kisses him; she can't bear the thought of losing him. His disdain for Ted's passivity draws her to him.

The night before Will leaves for his trip, their lovemaking is different, intense. They are not strangers in any way now. They are lovers that have turned a corner, unafraid, willing to risk all to know each other more. Murmuring to her, whispering to her, her name, his feelings, he enters her slowly, reverently. "Do you feel it?" he asks. "Oh, Lily, Jesus! We create so much heat." He is biting his lip, closing his eyes, touching her in dizzying, faster circles, calling to her: "Sweet girl, darling, honey, beautiful, oh, beautiful. Look how excited you are. Look how you are arching. . . ." She is stretching her fingers over the globes of his buttocks, reaching under him to tenderly squeeze his warm, full testicles so that he calls out more. And when the pleasure comes, it is silvery, it is gripping. He is at first gentle, then thrusting. She feels impaled, owned, overwhelmed, released. No one has ever excited her this much or made her feel so loving. No one.

Lily spends the holidays alone, though it makes Jack angry. He tells her he's worried people will say he's not doing his job as a stepfather if Lily doesn't come home to Winnetka for the holidays. But she will never go back there. How could he expect she would?

"Fine. Don't spend the holidays with me. You *are* ungrateful," he mutters.

"What do I have to be grateful about? I'm paying my own way through school. I'm not making you stuff a turkey for my Christmas dinner. I don't ask for clothes or money. I owe you nothing. And I intend to keep it just like that."

"What about all those years I did pay for you?"

"You only did it because mother insisted. You never wanted to."

"Yeah, she sure did insist. In her own way, she twisted my arm for everything she wanted."

"Don't say things about my mother. Not after what happened."

"All of that was your fault," he says so coolly she must close her eyes to shut it out. "You couldn't even face what you wanted."

For Christmas dinner, Lily eats oatmeal with a whole box of raisins poured on top. She eats it slowly, drawing on a sketch pad next to her plate a picture of a cat stretched out in front of a fireplace. Oatmeal specks the drawing. She is wearing her mother's old chenille bathrobe. She feels washed out, ugly, lonely, and angry. She is glad when it's time to go to bed. In bed, in the dark, she thinks, Someday I will have a family to share Christmas with. And she imagines a man, not a bit like Ted, nothing like Will, someone strong and assured, in a flannel suit, smoking a pipe. Gregory Peck is his closest equal. His voice is as deep, too. He has feet and hands as long and thin as a Giacometti. He holds the children in his lap. A girl named Susan and a boy named Daniel, both with eyes puddle-dark, endlessly, noisily, glad that Lily is finally home.

Will calls the very Sunday he has arrived back in town, though it is late. Lily speaks to him on the hall phone in her robe, with other people from the rooming house milling around, waiting to make calls. She is conscious of being in her robe, wonders why he felt free to call so late.

"Can I see you?" he asks, sounding breathless, urgent.

"It's late," she tells him.

"I'll be there fast," he says.

When he finally arrives, she lets him in. She's been too tired to put on clothes, feels vulnerable in her robe. He barely lets her open the door to her room before he is embracing her, snuggling her.

"I missed you," he says.

"Did you?" She is surprised. Surprised at how tender he is looking at her, surprised at how he draws her into his lap in the rocking chair.

"Did you have a nice trip?" she asks.

He shrugs.

"It wasn't nice?"

"I guess we were both tense," Will says. "So many plans to make. So many obligations. I felt like I barely got to see Sandra without one of her aunts breathing down our necks or her mother asking us to choose ornaments for the wedding cake."

"I guess that happens to people about to get married," Lily says.

"And when we were alone, Sandra was sort of preoccupied."

"Did you get to be alone?" Lily asks tentatively. She is not sure she wants to know. Worried that what he tells her will wound her more than she's guessed.

"You want to know if we made love," Will says.

"I didn't ask that."

He smiles at her and draws a finger along the line of her cheek.

"Did you think of me while I was gone?" he asks.

"Of course."

"Did you think of the way we made love that last night?"

She finds herself blushing. "Yes," she says softly.

"We have something incredible between us, Lily," he says, kissing her cheek, her ear. "I hope you didn't worry about fallout shelters while I was gone."

She feels like a little girl in his arms.

"Were you lonely at Christmas? Did you share Christmas with anyone?"

When she shakes her head, she can't look into his eyes.

"I should have stayed with you," he says. "I wish I'd never left your side after that last night. I have a present for you," he says.

The package is lumpily wrapped. Inside are blue coral beads, smooth and feminine, clasped in silver. She puts them on, luxuriating in the cool bite of them at her neck.

She has only bought him a book, but he says he likes it.

He insists on spending the night, though he doesn't always, especially when there are classes the next day. But tonight he tells her he needs to hold her, that he's been away from her too long.

As the spring comes on, once again, she and Will spend all their time together. So much so that people are talking. All around her, people are asking if Will Sternhagen's no longer engaged to that girl in California. "Are you dating Will?" they ask, and the word "dating" makes her smile, seems so archaic for what their friendship has become. Now it is a season of reading books, talking, sharing ideas, more than it ever was before. They read *Franny and Zooey* side by side. They wonder at Salinger's obsession with religion. They both feel they have none. A religion for life, they say. That's what we have. They critique each other's prints and paintings. Will says he's impressed with Lily's, especially her nudes, but he speaks quietly when he tells her so.

"I saw Pulaski watching you the other day," he says. "I think you're right."

"About what?"

"That he's interested in you."

"Do you think it's my talent?" she asks.

Will is silent for a moment.

"Your talent for what?"

She hits him. For the first time, she realizes that when it comes to art, they are competitors.

"I'm just teasing you," he says.

"I don't like to be teased," she tells him. And he is very solicitous for a few days after.

As weeks go by, there is a sweetness that grows between them. They go to restaurants, to the town's greasy spoons, and to the Amana colonies, where every restaurant serves plates of fried chicken, smoked pork chops, bowls of farm-fresh cottage cheese, beets, potatoes. They eat so much their stomachs ache. Sometimes they drive out to a farm field at night and make love among the rows of last year's stalks, dry and noisy as crinoline, the Iowa moon as liquid as a calf's eye in the warming night sky. Sometimes they do nothing at all in Lily's room, hang around in their ink-stiffened clothes, and enjoy the ease of it.

Then a period begins for them of sexual abandon so intense and varied that Lily herself feels shocked. Each day, there is a new reward for their mutual adventurousness. One day, Will spreads towels on her bed, pulls out a bottle of cooking oil, and stripping her, laying her down on the towels, pours the smooth oil over every inch of her nakedness, then slides on top of her until the thin gloss of oil heats between them, makes their slipperiness fiery.

For a few weeks, he brings her different sex toys: badly packaged, made of hard, colorful plastic. Together they laugh at the false penis, at the one that looks like a baseball bat, the one that resembles a nun, and yet he can work her into a lather with them every time, making her beg to put the toys away and satisfy her. After all the teasing, he's the real thing. Her desperation for him makes him feel powerful, and he teases her, withdraws, prolongs her desire. There is humor in all of this, and fear. Lily has the vital impression that nice girls don't do things like this. And if they did, they would never enjoy it all as much as she does. How can she ever pretend innocence with Ted after this?

One night he brings in a brown paper bag, a thick, soft cotton cord, binds her wrists and ankles, and draws it down under the feet of the frame of the bed, then for hours teases her into a flurry of passion so dark and without control that she finds herself begging in the most intense terms for him to come into her, release her, consummate the promise.

From the back of a liquor store on the edge of town, he brings home pornography, which he reads to her, slowly, suggestively, touching each sensitive inch of her until she is so excited, she comes, when, strangely, he is not even touching her. And once he makes her go with him to the liquor store and cajoles her to go to the counter and ask for Marie.

"Why, she's in the back," the man behind the counter says, eyeing her with cool interest. He opens the greasy gray curtain, whispering, "Put what you want in a paper bag before you come out," and drops the drape quickly behind her. In the dark room, the pornographic magazines glow with their hot pink, yellow, and flesh tones. "Gotta have it," "Any way you like it," "Do me. Do me," their covers call out.

It is a moment until Lily's eyes are adjusted enough to the light to realize that in the corner a man is paging through a magazine. When he turns to see Lily, he flushes, slams the magazine closed, and shoves it into a paper bag before he goes back through the curtain. Lily feels her own body suffuse with shameful heat, and a few moments pass before she can pick up a magazine. Just as she does, losing herself in the bursting, fleshy pictures and the instantly lurid text, she hears the sound of the curtain. A body presses up behind her. "Read it to me," Will whispers in her ear. The thrill of his body pressed to her—already she can feel his erection—the dank room, which smells of liquor and cheap ink, the nervous thrill of being forced to read aloud, excite her to a point when she can no longer read. "I can't . . . I want to . . ." she whispers hoarsely. Will shoves the magazine into a paper bag, pays in a rush, and they retreat to the backseat of the car, where they indulge in an uncontrollable three minutes of ecstasy under a pile of coats.

"You see," Will says, "the ultimate sex organ is the mind."

"Do you ever— Have you ever done any of this with Sandra?"

He looks at her with astonishment.

"Are you joking? Sandra goes crazy if we don't use the missionary position. Sandra goes crazy if I want to make love to her more than once. Lily, you are such a rare, sweet thing." And he kisses her so passionately, she might imagine he actually loves her.

The letters from Ted have gotten somewhat frantic, for Lily's have slacked off. She still thinks of him, but less longingly now. He writes her that he now has a job making orangeade at a small tobacco store. He walks in the Tuileries after work. He has met a wonderful woman named Yvonne (he says, "don't worry, she is sixty years old at least"), who invites over many young Americans and makes fresh baguettes and reads French poetry.

Not that an engineer like me knows the first thing about poetry, or cares, really. It just sounds so wonderful read in French. I miss studying engineering, though, you know. It's not so romantic as Paris, but the romance of Paris makes me feel funny, lacking. I know intellectually I should be enjoying it more than I really am. Who could not love the beauty, the flavor, of this place? The problem is, I want to be successful in life. I want to know I've really made it. Make a mark. Young enough I can enjoy it. I feel like I'm loafing, wasting time. I end up thinking so often of coming back and finding a job before I forget it all that I find myself missing a lot of what I should be enjoying here. I have enough money to finish out the year here. But I don't know. I don't know . . .

As the end of the term nears, Lily can't help but think that Will will call off his wedding. It is inevitable in her mind. But it is not until then that she would even consider telling Ted her heart's been changed. Still, Will says nothing at all about the wedding, has even excluded Sandra as a topic of conversation, except once, when Lily looks through Will's wallet to find money to pay the pizza delivery man. There she finds a small portrait of a woman dressed in a pale blue sweater set, her blond hair curled around her face, a red bow perched on top of her head, poodlelike, and a countenance as bland and open as a not-yet-used manila envelope.

"Is this . . . ?"

He nods. "Sandra," he says. And she sees he is proud of the picture, of the way that Sandra looks. Her mouth like a Valentine candy. She shudders, knowing he still must love Sandra, after all.

He has been in the print program a full year longer than Lily, so he is scheduled to get his master's degree and leave the university on June 1 to marry on June 15, and she still has a full year to go. By the last week of May, she is frantic, for she knows he has truly meant it: He cannot call off his wedding. They have never spoken of loving each other, though the love is there.

And on May 31, not having spoken of it at all, he rises from the bed where they've just made love all night and says he needs to go home and pack his last things.

"You're really going," she says. She has not allowed herself to be bereft or, in fact, even to expect he would actually go—until now.

"You know I have to," he says.

She wants to say selfish things: "You know what you're doing to me, don't you?" or, "My heart's not going to be able to take this, you know," but she finds herself mute, wounded so deeply she feels nothing but the rush of minutes as he dresses.

Finally, she says, "Well, I wish you the best of luck."

"Don't say it like that," he says. "Like you hardly know me."

"What is it you want me to say? I'm just trying to tell you I hope you'll be happy."

He stares out the window.

"No one's home at the Pulaskis'," he says. His mouth is morose. The backyard lights reflect in his green-blue eyes. "Will you think of me?"

"Will you?"

He turns to her now. "Christ, Lily. I can't get out of this. I'm supposed to marry her. A lot of times you have to do things even if you're not certain. When I make love to her, I feel it's—I don't know—ordained or something. Angelic. Pure. I have to do this. I do."

He turns away again, but she comes up behind him and slips her arms around him. His bones and skin feel loose and pearly beneath her fingers, against her breasts.

"You do what you have to," she says. "Send me a note once in a while if you can." She doesn't know why she is managing to sound so strong, so detached. She knows she can't stop him. She knows there is nothing she can do, and that alone gives her a sense of calm. Like watching an earthquake, feeling it beneath her feet, she feels paralyzed with inevitability.

"I think once we're married, Sandra will learn to like making love," he says.

"I'm sure she will. Because of you."

He puts on his slacks, then straightens. "You think I'll turn into a jerk like that?" he asks, cocking his thumb toward Andres Pulaski's house.

"Do you want to?"

"I guess I already have a taste for cheating," he says, looking into her eyes. He kisses her mouth tenderly, then her eyelids, and turns away. With nervous speed, he buttons his shirt, pulls on his sweater, fastens his watch to his slender wrist, slips on his loafers. When he takes his coat from her chair, he puts it on with his back to her, but she isn't angry. Only sorry for him, missing him already.

"Will," she says as he opens the door. "I'm glad . . ." She hesitates, wants no words that will unnerve or scare him. Only to let him know how intensely she feels. "Will . . . I'm glad I took you home the night of that party," she says at last. She knows he wants to speak. His lips form and reject a number of words, until he just nods, sadly, and leaves her, closing the door gently behind him.

That night, she wakes in a sweat. Her heart is pounding. What is she doing? Letting Will go, letting him think it's okay with her that he's marrying Sandra.

Not quite awake, she rifles through her drawer to find Will's phone number. He gave it to her months ago, but she's never used it. He said the phone was right outside his door, that he was always the one to answer it. Will he answer it now? Two in the morning?

She is shaking as she puts the dime in the chrome slot. How loud the tiny coin chinks into place. The phone at his place rings and rings. Someone surely will wake, will answer it, she thinks. Please. Please. Someone.

"Hello . . ."

"May I speak to Will Sternhagen?"

"Okay." There is a sigh and a shuffling of feet, some knocking, some murmuring.

"Hello." The voice is nearly unrecognizable, anxious.

"Will?" she asks tentatively.

"Sandra?"

The sound of Sandra's name weakens her, adds to her shakiness. "No, it's Lily."

"Oh." He is not pleased to hear from her. It is clear. He has already put her behind him. She can decipher it all from the word "oh." She can't tell him what she feels now. She can't.

"I just called to say good-bye again."

"In the middle of the night?"

"I guess so."

"That's all? Okay . . ."

"Will, don't marry her," she says. "Please . . ." Is that her voice? She can hardly believe she's said it.

"It's too late," he says. "You know that."

"It's a mistake. *You* know that."

"A mistake? How the hell do you know?"

"Because you and I love each other."

"You love me?" he asks softly.

"Yes."

"Oh, God, Lily." His voice gets small. "You never said so." He pauses for a long time.

"Can't you call it off?" Lily says.

"I can't. You know I can't."

"But you and I—"

"Please don't tell me. Just the thought of never touching you again kills me. But this isn't going to change. It can't change. I've made up my mind."

"Please," she begs. She never thought she'd feel this way. She never thought she'd get to this point. She does love him. She's overcome so much to let herself love him. How could she lose him now?

"It's over, Lily. I wish you everything. Really, I do. I can't think of anyone I wish more for, not even Sandra. That's the only consolation prize I can offer."

She cannot say anything. Her tongue feels thick in her mouth. There is no saliva in her throat to swallow.

"Okay," she says.

"I'm sorry," he says. "I never meant for this to happen."

"Neither did I," she says, and then she hangs up.

Chapter Three

All summer, Lily paints and prints. The only time she changes out of her ink-encrusted dungarees and man's shirt is to go to the math or science library to shelve books. Thoughts of Will are with her always, like a cut that just won't heal, that with every movement stings. On June 15th, his wedding day, she awakes feeling weak and uneasy before she realizes what day it is. It gives her a giddy feeling to imagine his slender body draped in a tuxedo, to think of bland-faced Sandra in her beaded gown. That evening, as she works alone in the stacks, Lily imagines their wedding night. Perhaps now that she has her precious gold band, Sandra will indeed learn to appreciate sex. The thought of it makes Lily laugh out loud. And then she thinks of them together, Will caressing Sandra with the same tenderness that he shared with her. And she begins to cry, cry so intensely that she presses her face against the dusty old tomes, presses her fist against her mouth. The smell of the aged, moldering books cuts through her aching senses. She is going to grow old alone, she thinks; she is going to grow as dusty as these books, because she is never going to let anyone else do this to her heart. Men leaving her, men hurting her. Never again. How had she let it happen? Why did she ever let him in? Never again.

Later, as she crosses the pentangle from the library to go home for dinner, she sees Professor Pulaski waving to her. He is a tall, gaunt man, and he stoops slightly as he presses forward in the June wind to meet her.

"Are you here for the summer?" he asks her in his compressed Latin accent.

"I have nowhere else to go," she tells him. Her heart feels so broken, it is hard for her to find the energy to answer him.

"Really? Have you no family? No one?"

She shakes her head, wanting on this day, more than on any other, some sympathy, some sweetness.

He smiles. He was probably once a handsome man, still is in a way, but he is nearly fifty, she guesses. More than twice her age.

"Where are you going now?"

"Home."

"Will you have dinner with me?" he asks. He shifts the books he carries from his right to his left hand, then holds out his right arm gallantly, beckoningly.

She takes it. Feels she must, somehow. She is afraid of him, doesn't know much about him, but at least with him she won't have to think all night of Will.

"Sure," she says. "Thank you."

He brings her to a small Italian restaurant on Clinton Street. She and Will used to call the decor in the place Early Italian Cliché. Red-and-white tablecloths, dripping candles, eggplant parmesan.

"I am happy to see you here this summer," he tells her. "You must know you are considered a fine student."

She looks at him and smiles. He is not entirely capable, she knows, of real warmth, of real compliments. His most giving moments are all couched in the third person.

"You are considered a fine professor," she tells him, ashamed at her own cheekiness, but he takes the compliment sincerely.

"I hope that you think so," he says. "When you were a child, was your hair so dark?"

"Always," she says. "Even though my mother and father both had lighter hair."

"Are they dead?"

She says yes, because though her father is most likely alive, he is dead to her.

"You are an orphan."

She nods.

"I should like to do a print about their deaths. I am doing many prints about death now."

"I know."

"Will you tell me about them, your parents?"

"No," she says. "Maybe later."

"I am pleased there will be a later," he says.

After dinner, he asks to walk her to her apartment when he discovers that they are neighbors. The June night is alive with fireflies and mosquitoes. Near the river, the bats swoop frantically to catch and eat them, and Lily finds herself involuntarily moving closer to Professor Pulaski, who pulls her to him, holds her arm with his long fingers. At her door, she kisses his cheek.

She sees longing in his face.

"Thanks so much," she says.

"I . . ."

"It's late," she says. "It was so nice of you to take me to dinner."

"You've been admired very much," he tells her. And he steps back, and his head bows gallantly. When she closes the door, she longs to laugh but finds herself shaking, and doesn't know why.

On August 12, she is called to the phone after she's already gotten into bed.

"Lily, long distance." She thinks it must be her stepfather, and she considers pretending she is out, but then she wonders if it might be Ted. He's not due until after Christmas, but he might have changed his mind. He might be in New York, or Chicago.

"Lily, did I catch you at a bad time?"

It is Will.

"Oh, hello." In a moment, possible reasons for his call type themselves out in her mind: He's forgotten something at her place. He has a question he knows only she can answer. Sandra hasn't learned to like sex, after all. . . .

"Lily, I'd like to see you," he says. Will's voice almost whispers.

"Are you okay?" she asks. She was going to ask, "How's married life?" but she already knows it's inappropriate.

"I know it's imposing," he says slowly, carefully. "But could I come

up to see you? We're living in Missouri now. I've got a job teaching at a
local high school. Kind of a last-minute thing. I don't start teaching for
a month. It was really lucky to find any job at all. I'll sleep on the floor,
of course."

Lily laughs. "When?"

"This weekend. It's only five hours away."

She pauses.

"Ted isn't back yet, is he? I wouldn't want to mess things up for
you."

"Not yet."

"Please."

"Yes, of course. Okay. Saturday?"

"At one. I'll be there. Thank you."

She feels uneasy when she discovers how much she is still longing
to see him. She will see him, and then he will leave her. Can she stand
his leaving again? But how could she turn down even a short time with
him? Even a few precious moments. She hopes Ted doesn't decide to
just show up and surprise her. She cannot imagine Ted's discovering a
man in her bed. She can only be sure that his exit would be unerringly
polite and that her guilt would be unbearable.

On Saturday, she primps, like a high school girl preparing for the prom,
then undoes it all. The pretty sweater is replaced by her painting shirt;
for the ballet skirt, she substitutes her dungarees. This is how Will
cared for her, she decides. The worst thing she could do would be to
dress like Sandra. When she opens the door to him, she finds that even
in a few months he has changed. His face is pale. He is markedly thinner
and drawn.

"Come in," she tells him.

In her room he stands, not taking off his coat.

"Well," she says.

"I shouldn't be here," he says.

This is going to hurt, she realizes. This is going to hurt both of us.
"Do you want to go home?" she asks him. He shakes his head.

"Well, if you're going to stay, you'd better relax," she says. She feels
she is talking to a five-year-old, scared, hunched deep into his coat.
"Come on, take it off." She prods at the opening of his coat, finally begins
to unbutton it herself.

"I told her I was visiting Erich Melton, you know, he's sort of a friend of mine." He hands her the coat, and she pulls it to her face to smell his scent. Unchanged, it thrills her.

"Yes."

"Want to tell me about everything?" she asks.

He sits in the rocking chair and puts his face in his hands. When he finally lifts his face to her, she knows what is different about him. It's his mouth that's changed. It is strained and pale, all the sensuality pulled tight to his teeth. His beautiful mouth.

"She's very nice," he says.

"Oh, Christ. Please don't start by extolling Sandra's virtues. I just may send you home to her."

He is surprised by her outburst, but not as surprised as she is. It makes them both laugh suddenly, relax.

"She hates sex," he says finally. "I mean, not like she just doesn't really want it. I mean, it repulses her. Like . . . do you *have* to put *that* into me?"

"Well, do you?"

"I've considered life without it. I mean, you and I probably make too big a thing about sex."

"Do we?"

"Well, we hardly put it on the back burner."

"Burner. In our case it's a bonfire," she says, longing even now to touch him, to feel him, to take him into her, the way she's taken no one else.

"Yes. That's what I'm saying."

"Can you make too big a thing about that?"

"Maybe if there's nothing else between you."

"Is that how it is with us? Sex. Nothing else?"

"I think what's always been missing between us is . . . romance."

"Oh . . ."

"You said you loved me that night on the phone," he says. "Did you mean it?"

"Of course. Didn't you know it before I told you?"

"You never said it before. I'd leave her if you'd say you'd marry me now."

"If I'd what?" She looks at him with unconcealed horror.

"If you'd say you'd marry me right now, I'd leave her."

"Seriously?"

"Please." He gets up from the chair and kneels down beside Lily now, all desperation in his shoulders, his hands, the bend of his neck. "I can't think of anything but you," he says. "I'm making love to her, and she's pushing me back with her hands, and I'm only staying with it by thinking of you. Marry me. I'll leave her to marry you. You were right. I made a mistake."

"You haven't even said you love me."

"I'll say I love you if you'll say you'll marry me."

"You've got to be kidding. Does that mean you won't love me if I say no?"

"Why won't you marry me?"

Lily just shakes her head. The concept of marriage frightens her, second only to death. She can't say yes to marriage. Even with this lovely man. Even with this man she clearly loves. She just knows if she marries him it will kill the way she feels about him, defile it forever. And she knows the second she says her vows, it will be like a horror movie where people exchange brains. She will instantly transform into her mother: helpless, uncertain, begging.

"Do you want something to eat?" she asks suddenly, getting up. His face grows crimson with anger. He grabs her wrist and pulls her back down in the chair.

"Jesus," he says. "Don't walk away from this."

She wishes now she'd worn the sweater, the ballet skirt, the chignon. She wishes now she could feel imperious, cold, that he could not tear so accurately at her heart. Nearness to him inflames her, and she feels such need to stay in control.

"When you called me that night, what were you asking me to do? To leave her for what?" he asks.

"Just to be with me, Will."

"Look at me. To be with you? What did that mean? You knew I was going to leave town one way or the other. If you don't want to marry, what is it you want? To drive once in a while to see each other?"

She looks at him. He is just a man. Not the handsomest man. Not the most romantic, smart, brave, different, man she's ever met. But he's captured her. She is squirming. She is frightened. What did she think she was offering him that night? What?

"Just to be in love. Can't we just be in love?"

"No. It's marriage or nothing. Say you'll marry me and I'll leave her."

"Look, if you need to disentangle yourself from Sandra, do it first. Then come to me."

He shakes his head.

"I can't,"

"Can't what?"

"Can't leave her without knowing you'll marry me."

"What is it with you and marriage? Will *anyone* else do? Why don't you call Louise Lewis? You seem desperate enough to marry anyone. I think you're kind of confused."

"You're the one that's confused," he says. "You're not listening to me at all." She sees he looks choked, angry, scared.

"I'm sorry."

He eats his turkey sandwich, drinks his glass of milk. How furiously he eats. She sees the childish mustache the milk makes, watches him lick it away with his tongue. He is swallowing his anger. By the end of his lunch it is neatly tucked away, not visible at all.

After lunch they talk about his job, which sounds less boring than she had supposed. She tells him that at the end of the year Ted will return.

"Do you love him?" Will asks.

She shrugs. "I don't have a clue anymore," she says. "I think he's good for me."

"I think he doesn't know you. Will you marry him?"

"I told you. I don't want to get married. Not you. Not him. Marriage is terrible. Look. You should know."

He nods. The fact is, she knows she'll never feel the same way about Ted again, not after her time with Will. Why can't she tell Will that? But the words won't come out. What's wrong with her? What does she think will happen if he knows how much she cares for him?

Later, they walk around the campus, but he doesn't hold her arm now. As they sip sodas at the local shop, she notices his wedding band. Because he has gotten thinner, it is already too big for him, seems to float on his slender finger. It is Florentine gold, gaudy, not at all what she might have chosen. He is conscious of it, always twisting it around his finger with the thumb of the same hand. Pushing it over his knuckle, then back, then over again, until finally it falls off, bangs to the table, then to the linoleum of the soda shop, with a frightening, tinny bounce.

When he lifts it, he discovers, to his horror, that it is slightly dented along the rim.

"She won't notice," Lily says.

Will gives her an angry look. "Jesus, you're a bitch."

"What did I do?" she says.

"Look what I'm doing. Cheating on her just by being with you. Plotting to leave her. She's a good person. A kind, good person. And it's all because of you. Jesus. If it weren't for you," he says suddenly, "I'd probably be perfectly happy with her. I would."

"What?"

"You've ruined it for me. I was happy with her before. I was perfectly happy with her just the way she is. Even the sex. And then you had to show me otherwise. And you had to go and call me that night. Why? For nothing. Just to own me, knowing I was going off to her. . . . You were just manipulating me. You don't even want me. It's all your fault. I was perfectly happy—"

"Why don't you get your things and go home?" Lily says. "I called because I love you. Because I didn't want you to make a mistake. I don't know why that means we have to marry. You know I'm afraid of marriage. Why does it have to be on your terms?"

"Because my terms are the terms of people who are committed to each other. I'm living in a hell of guilt as it is. I hate myself for being here. I can hardly bear to touch you. I'm not going to leave Sandra and cause her so much pain just to have you run away from me."

"I won't run away. But I won't marry you."

"I'm leaving."

"Fine."

They walk back, shoulders only occasionally bumping in anger. It is nearly five-thirty, still light on the pentangle. Their footsteps rush and beat upon the paths, like two walkers competing. Once, Lily even finds her feet are leaving the ground; she is running. Up the stairs of her rooming house they move. His bag, not even unpacked, sits against the bed, and he grabs it.

"I thought we cared about each other. I thought we'd stumbled onto something bigger than either of us could face," he tells her. "God, I was a fool. You're not even capable of loving me."

In a flash of coat and suitcase, the sound of a beat of wings, he is gone.

For good, she tells herself, and in her mouth is the bitter salt of unshed tears. She swallows them before they come to her eyes.

She thinks of calling Will. All the following week it is her curse: this need to finish the conversation, to pose options. She won't marry him now, but could they be together? Could they make some kind of interim commitment? Maybe he could help her not be so afraid. Just to hold Will again, just to feel safe in his arms . . . But she can't call. She picks up the phone. She thinks of calling the high school. Again and again. But her fingers will not dial. Nearly every morning, the receiver of the phone is lifted, and then panic paralyzes her. He is just desperate to get out of a mistaken marriage, she tells herself. It's not his feeling for me that's speaking but his need to run away from an error. If he cares for me, he won't give up so easily, she thinks, but she has no trust in him.

In the middle of the night, a few weeks later, there is a terrible pounding on her door, and all she can imagine is FIRE! She jumps from bed, puts on her heavy loafers, throws her coat around herself, and opens the door—to Ted. He is standing quietly, a felt hat in his hand, his knapsack, bulging and shapeless, on the floor beside him.

"I drove from Chicago the minute I landed. My parents don't even know I'm here."

"Ted . . . Ted." She just stands and stares at him a long time before she can react. He gives her a lopsided smile.

"My God, you must be exhausted." She draws him in, trying to straighten her sleep-mussed hair, mortified about her loafers, her coat. He must think she's a lunatic! When she imagined him coming back, it was always with the warning of a phone call. It was always with her hair tucked perfectly up, her neck scrubbed, her mouth smelling of Ipana.

"I thought there was an emergency," she says, gesturing to her coat, her loafers.

He reaches to kiss her, but she pushes him back. "No, wait."

She throws off her coat and shoes. In the bathroom she brushes her hair, washes her face, and brushes her teeth. At least she looks and smells clean. She opens her nightgown an extra button. This is not a chignon or a beautiful outfit, but at least it's the way she wants Ted to see her. Now she goes to him and kisses him.

"I can hardly believe— Well, you know, that it's you," he tells her. His kiss is completely unfamiliar to her. So careful, so hygienic. But still, it quietly excites her. He tastes of Certs and smells of airplane disinfectant.

"I didn't expect you until Christmas."

"It was time to come back," he says. "I don't want you to think I intended to stay the night or anything. I don't want you to be offended. It's just that you're all I could think about flying back. I rented a car at O'Hare. This is awful of me coming at four in the morning. Don't think I don't know it." She looks at him. He is a tall man, dark, his eyes coal black, his body graceful, but penurious in a way, ungiving. There is a nervousness in his hands that Lily used to find appealing, a way of speaking that says he doesn't entirely believe in himself.

"You can sleep here, Ted."

"Well, actually, I do have my backpack. You know, I don't think— I'm not sure if I've ever seen you in a nightgown before."

"Yes you have," she says. "When I stayed at your parents."

"Oh, yes." It is the wrong memory. His face darkens. He squeezes her hands, no doubt recalling the ugliness of that time. But Lily doesn't want to remember. She smiles at him, makes him see her smile. He looks exhausted. He has a two-day beard, which, with his dark hair, looks faintly criminal. His tall body seems creased with weariness. Why does she feel so cool toward him? She tries to stir up the memories, the things that made her love him.

"Have you eaten?" she asks.

"Somewhere along the way I did. I guess I'm hungry." She used to marvel how Ted rarely ate. Food never seemed to matter to him.

"What does someone eat at four in the morning?" she asks.

"Eggs?"

She fixes him an omelet on the hot plate, stuffing it with cheese and green peppers. She remembers it's what he used to order for breakfast when he would visit her at her college. He never really ate much of it. He would just pick along the edges until it darkened and grew oily.

He always stayed at the Student Union on those trips and would be embarrassed when she visited his room. If she kissed him there, he would say, "Please, Lily, don't get me going. Not here." She smiles now, thinking she has never gotten him going, doesn't know if he can be "got going." What would have happened if she'd kissed him more in that Student Union room? Found the lobe of his ear, the shadow of his neck? But she cannot picture it. She remembers how neat his suitcase always was, sitting on the luggage rack, how fresh and crisply piled his shirts.

He loves order like nobody she's ever known. It surprises her to see his knapsack. He has tried to broaden himself, to see things in a way he's never seen them. But in the end he's come home early.

Ted sits down at the table and begins to eat in the slow, disinterested manner he always does. He is so polished in some ways—table manners, etiquette—and so uneasy in others, sometimes it breaks her heart. Small talk is painful for him. Romance is anathema.

What does he see in Lily? A release from the buttoned-up quality of his life? An ease in the things with which he is most uneasy? He says he loves her for being artistic, adventurous, but she's often reflected that it's a lie. He would really like to recast her into the movie star he has a crush on: Dolores Hart. Virginal, temperate, making every movie she appears in slide down like melted ice cream. Ted is a perfectionist. What has he ever seen in Lily?

Ted sleeps on the floor in his sleeping bag, still wearing his gray flannel slacks and white undershirt, though she nervously invites him into her bed.

"Not a good idea," he tells her, weakly smiling. Is there really so much passion in him he can't control?

Lily lies in the dark and thinks of confessing. Or of seducing him, introducing him to her sexuality with pure longing. She does find him sexy, always has. The long basketball-player body, his shy coffee-black eyes with their dark, sooty lashes. His presence has always stirred her. And now, lying in her bed, longing for this sleeping man, she suddenly remembers the night she did try to seduce him, long ago.

Just once. It was only six months after they met. Christmastime. Before her mother died. Ted came home from MIT and stayed at his parents; Lily, with her mother and Jack.

Lily's mother had put up a beautiful Christmas tree decked in white paper flowers and golden doves. The fire was burning, and her mother and Jack were out playing bridge in Glencoe. And meeting after months of letters and caring, Ted and Lily still felt like strangers, wanting to be together but at first not remembering why.

"We're all alone," she remembers telling Ted with a twinkle in her eye. He sat by the fire in an isolated chair, his hands nervously flattened against his knees.

"Well," he said.

"Why are we so cautious?" she said. "Come sit by me." She patted the sofa. The golden doves shot light off their wings as they turned in the fire draft. At that time, she was certain that his sexual reticence was respect, his effort to protect her and her reputation. And she thought if she let him know in a polite way that he didn't need to protect her, he might give in, open up.

He handed her a package. A small silver box wrapped in a red satin ribbon. Inside was a pair of earrings, tiny hearts with ruby centers. They weren't expensive. The rubies were too tiny to be of monetary value, but they were pretty, and touching.

She covered his hand with hers, reached over and kissed his mouth. "I love them," she told him. "I couldn't love them more."

"I didn't remember if your ears were— What do you call it?"

"Pierced."

"Pierced." He pronounced the word as though he'd never heard it before. "Honestly. I never bought a gift for a girl before. This one gave me a sleepless night or two."

She took the earrings from the card and put them in her ears. Even without a mirror they made her feel beautiful, throwing light back at the room like a Christmas tree, she thought.

"You are so sweet," she said. "So sweet." She kissed his ear, his neck. "Like a little boy."

"Come on, Lily," he said, steadying her shoulders. She could see by his blush that he was embarrassed.

Then she was flooded with longing, a longing bottled up painfully. Saved just for him. It so overwhelmed the moment, she couldn't control it. She hadn't slept with anyone since she met him last summer, waiting, hoping that this Christmas vacation she would finally come to know his long body, his odd mix of gracefulness and awkwardness.

She had daydreamed about it a hundred times, all fall, and the scenario was different each time. In the end of each fantasy, though, he came face-to-face with his own passion and released it. It was like opening an overpacked suitcase. A spill of feeling, a spill of longing. What a good dream it had made.

But now he was here, and she had to make it happen. He wouldn't be the one to make the first move, she knew.

"I want you," she whispered to him. He looked better to her in the firelight than she had remembered. His face was long and elegant, his fingers endless. And then she showed him she meant it.

She ran her hand along his jaw, letting her mouth follow, down into the salty crook of his neck. Unbuttoning his shirt, she found his nipple and tasted it, felt it hardening against her tongue. And her hands went places they had never tried to go before with him. His chest, his buttocks, his leg were not familiar to her at all. He was breathing so hard, it surprised, even scared, her a little. She took his hand to have him touch her, to feel her breasts through the velvet of her dress, for until that moment he had been passive, soaking up her desire for him.

"Touch me," she crooned. "I need you to touch me."

And that's when he froze in place, stiffened. As though, by participating, he would have to acknowledge what was happening, have to take responsibility.

"Don't, Lily," he said.

"We've waited all this time," she said. "They won't be back for hours. Don't you want me, too?"

"Stop it," he said, standing up. There was a rage in his voice that startled her. She slid down onto the floor, heat flooding her face, her heart thumping. "It's just not right, right now."

"Why?"

"I know you can't possibly really want to . . . to do this. We're not married. . . . We don't want to make this mistake." He helped her up, hugged her. His voice softened. "Okay? I mean I know you like the earrings, but this wasn't the effect I was planning for."

"It's not gratefulness," she said. "It's pure lust."

He laughed nervously. His hands began to work together, the nervousness energizing them.

"I should go," he said, crumpling up the wrapping paper of the present she had bought him: an initialed silver key ring.

"I'm insulted," she said softly.

"You should have been insulted if I'd agreed to make love to you, Lily. Don't you see? Then you'd be just a . . . a . . . nothing to me. A body. Unless that's what I am to you."

"Of course not."

"I hoped not. I don't want you to think I don't want to see you. I don't even want you to think I didn't sort of like what you just did."

Sort of? She shivered.

And she had let him go, into the night, into the snow. The earrings cut into the backs of her ears that night as she lay awake. She thought of calling it off with him. She could not determine if he was cold or cautious or respectful.

In the morning, he called to say he loved her and hoped she wasn't angry. And she told him she was, a little. And he said that someday he would make it up to her, though he didn't elaborate on what that meant.

After that, she stopped even thinking about seducing him; she gave into his time schedule. Until he left for Paris, she didn't so much as kiss anybody else. She hung his picture on her dorm-room bulletin board. She lived for his letters. And why? Because he represented purity to her, normalcy, something she craved even before her mother died. And because, in a way, he was right. He'd said if they slept together, he'd be just a body to her. And looking back, all the men she'd slept with before, in time, in memory, became just bodies to her. Until Will.

In the morning, she doesn't know what to do with Ted. While he sleeps, burrowed deep in his sleeping bag, she walks to the corner and buys him a paper to read. When she comes back, he is taking a long, steamy shower. She can't help feeling that if he were Will, she would have slipped into the shower with him. And they would have laughed together, like two children, soaping each other's backs. Instead, she sits by the window, trying to read the headlines, waiting to see this man she was once so sure she loved.

Later, not addressing the breakfast she's made him, Ted says he doesn't feel too well because of the jet lag, and indeed, his face has a blurry, grayish cast, like a badly tuned TV. He gives her a present: a velvet beret with a jeweled crown. The jewels are red cut glass, beautiful against the black velvet. She feels for a moment that he really knows her. She would have chosen this beret herself.

"I'm sorry," he says. "I was pretty broke by the time I started thinking about presents."

"I love it. I wouldn't have wanted anything more expensive."

She asks him questions about Paris, but his answers are short and dull.

"How was the Left Bank?"

"I don't know. Bohemian. Interesting, I guess."

"Did you taste madeleines? Proust always wrote about madeleines."

"Who?"

"Proust, the writer."

"Oh. I liked the bookstalls."

"You wrote about that. What sort of books were there?"

"All sorts."

"Were they in French?"

"Some."

"Can you read French perfectly now?"

"Not perfectly."

After a while she gives up on the effort, doesn't have the energy anymore to draw him out. Especially when what she really wants to talk about is what happened to her mother and why Ted took off so unexpectedly for Europe when he had planned that June to look for an engineering job in Chicago. To stay closer to her.

Just before her mother died, everything between them had intensified, and she was finally seeing a glimmer of passion in him. There were times he would kiss her so deeply, it was as if he were drinking from her. He would talk about wanting to be in the same town so that there wouldn't be a night they couldn't see each other if they wanted to. Meanwhile, he was going to get settled in Chicago, driving distance, at least, from her. And when she finished graduate school, she would join him. They didn't talk about marriage, just about being together. She was so happy, she felt electrified.

And then her mother died. He stood by her. He was there for the worst of it—identifying the body. He was there for her to tell him what had happened, and his face showed no blame or distaste, the very things she was feeling for herself. He took her home to his parent's house to shelter her. When he brought her back to Jack's to get clothes for the funeral, he punched Jack so hard, Jack wore a black eye for weeks. And then Ted left. He left her living with his parents for two weeks before her graduate school started. He left with only a week's notice. He escaped like a thief. No one could understand or explain it. He had never done anything so unlike himself before.

"He can't live with what happened," Lily cried to his mother, who hugged her.

"This doesn't have anything to do with you," she said. "This has to do with one person: Ted. He'll come back."

At noon, they go out. It is a Saturday and warm for September. The semester won't begin until next week. The campus is nearly empty. Candy wrappers blow in the warm breeze across the pentangle. He's been to her undergraduate school, the University of Illinois, but never here. They walk along the river in a silence that troubles her.

"I'm scared," she tells him.

"What about?"

"About us," she says. "I don't think there's anything between us anymore."

"Don't say that," he says. "Please." He grips her wrist. "Don't give up on me yet."

"What are you going to do?"

"Go back to Chicago tomorrow, look for a job. Start a life. Then there'll be plenty between us."

"What do you mean?"

"I know I'm not very good company. I keep my distance from you, I know. It's just that I— You want more from me than I can give right now," he says. "You always did."

"I don't understand. You drive five hours from Chicago on no sleep at all because you're desperate to see me, and there's this emptiness between us."

"I know this won't come out right. It's just that— Well, I think it's easier for me to love you when we're apart. Can you understand at all what I mean?"

"No. But I have a feeling I should be offended."

He shakes his head, and there is a thick silence. Lily can't think of anything to say, doesn't know how she feels.

"I'm going to go to Chicago and get a job. Prove myself," he says suddenly, as if that were the topic all along. "I came back early because I knew I had to. I have to make it in life, make a place for myself. I always feel like I'm playing catch-up ball. At Harvard, at MIT, I was running when all the other guys were sauntering. But it was you I thought about the whole way back. Give me a chance to get used to us being together again. If I could just prove myself to myself . . ."

Again, they are silent for a long time. The river is dark and turbid for September. Lily lifts a stone from the path and throws it in. "Oh, Lily," he says with a sigh.

There is the nervousness. The nervousness that trills his voice and makes him hesitate.

"You don't believe in yourself," Lily says. "I've never understood it."

"But you believe in me. I've always felt you have. You think I'll succeed in life."

"I just take it for granted," Lily says. She is incredulous that he worries so. She has never met a man more poised for success.

"Then when things are in place, I'll devote myself to you. I'll romance you. We'll get married, and I'll be one of those devoted guys: Jimmy Stewart."

"I don't even know about marriage," she says. "I don't think I ever want to marry."

"You will, someday. Lily, I can't help feeling since I've been here— I mean, you're distant, too, in a way. I've just got to know. While I was gone, there was someone else, wasn't there? I mean, when you slowed down on writing me letters . . . there was another guy . . ."

"Yes," she says softly.

Ted slams his hand down on the railing that separates the walk from the river. "Are you in love with him?"

"It's over," she says.

"Were you in love with him?"

"Yes."

He turns her to him, and she sees furor in his eyes. Underneath his silence, she sometimes sees a flame of violence. She saw it the night he punched Jack. She saw it the night she once harmlessly flirted with one of his college friends.

"How could you?"

"You ran away from me when I needed you," she says.

"What happened with your mother—what you expected from me then—I felt like I was choking."

"I felt like you were the only thing keeping me alive."

"I know," he says. "That's what did me in."

Not a word is exchanged as they walk back to her room. She feels so tired, everything around her is glazed in dizziness.

That night, as Ted lies once again in his sleeping bag, she watches him, rather pretty with his eyes closed, peacefully asleep, and she hates him, wishes he were dead. He saw the most vulnerable underbelly of her life, and now he's confirmed it: He couldn't live with it.

In the morning, Ted leaves.

"I know you don't want to see me anymore. But I'm not going to let this be over. I can't. You're everything to me, Lily. And someday I'll be able to be everything to you. Listen to me," he says. "It's not over."

When he is gone, there is no trace in her room that he was ever there except for a wad of lavender tissue paper clutching the velvet beret. She lifts the glossy tam in the sunshine. Light seems to hiss from the red glass bijoux. The black velvet is iridescent and fine. In front of the mirror she raises it to her head, sets it so it grazes her eyebrows, tilts to one ear. In it she sees she is almost beautiful, but how hollow her eyes are! Eyes depleted by pain, eyes that have found nothing to replace the pain. She yanks the beret from her head, strands of hair catching, stinging, as she flings it across the room.

Chapter Four

Andres Pulaski knows something is wrong. Last week, the first week of class, Lily Beach looked so exhausted, so pale, so shaky, he stopped her twice to ask if she was all right. And this week she hasn't come to class at all. When he asks the other students, no one has seen her. Since their dinner together, he feels responsible for her, is even more sure that she is living through some tragedy or heartbreak so painful that she exudes it. And now that he knows she has no parents, his sense of responsibility is relentless. So where is she? Two nights in a row he has walked by her rooming house and looked up at all the windows, wondering which could be hers. Shadows through voile show him distorted silhouettes. Not every window is lit. He can't help but wondering selfishly, after all his unselfish worry about her health, her emotional state, if she has gone, has escaped, knowing how deeply, how religiously, he cares for her, and not wanting the weight of his concern to be a part of her life.

The week after Ted leaves, Lily finds in herself a surprising, terrifying wealth of exhaustion. Finally, she can barely get out of bed, only to eat bread with jelly, go to the bathroom, or look out at Pulaski's house. In the dark she weeps so loudly, she fears the other people in the house will hear her and crushes a pillow to her mouth to muffle the sound. Now, a week later, she understands what she was mourning. To her, Ted was her only family. He was there when her mother died. He is the only one who knows. He was there to comfort her. And though he ran away, she had deluded herself into believing he would be there for her if she really needed him. Besides Jack and Will, there are no other people in her life. There are no other friends. No other girlfriends. No other acquaintances to turn to. She has sealed herself off. And now she feels truly alone.

On the fourth night, lying on her bed in the dark, "Are You Lonesome Tonight?" playing again and again on the hi-fi, she is told there's a call. Wearily, she puts on a robe and goes to the phone. She is glad no one is in the hall waiting to hand it to her. It dangles black and waiting from the cord.

"Hello."

"Are you ill?" At first, she doesn't recognize the accent, its funny nasal lilt. She thinks it's a prank.

"Your possible illness has worried me. No one has seen you, Miss Beach."

"Professor Pulaski."

"Is everything quite right?"

"Yes. It's really nice you called."

"You're not ill?"

"I was. I was. But I'm fine. I'll be back in class tomorrow." And suddenly she knows she will.

"Miss Beach, I have been worrying about you. For a few weeks."

"You have?"

"I have been worrying about you, orphan. I will see you tomorrow."

He hangs up before she can reply. The sound of "orphan" repeats in her ears. She goes back to bed and sets an alarm for tomorrow morning. But it is a long time before she goes to sleep. A long time before she can expel the elation that someone cares about her.

In the morning, she goes to Professor Pulaski's class. She feels odd, muffled, as she walks into the classroom. The way she once felt when she had such a severe ear infection that she lost some hearing in both ears. Around her are the people she has been seeing for almost two years now, and she doesn't really know any of their faces. The women seem pinched and gossipy. The men seem to take more than their share of the space; their arms stretch out and gesture in conversation more than men's arms usually do. Some of their faces are more feminine than the women's. When Professor Pulaski comes in, he is like a gray shadow that extends from the wall where he stands and covers the room. The women pinch up tighter. The men seem to sit on their hands. Lily feels so bundled in bandages that she does not move or change position for his entrance, though he is looking straight at her. His eyes seem to smile, though his mouth is almost bitter in its firmness.

"I want to see where we are. I want to see if any of you have done work worthy of this class."

As he goes from table to table, clucking, admonishing, scolding so brutally, the class occasionally laughs out of fear. Lily feels his eyes on her, his sharp blue eyes. But when he sees the print she has been working on for two weeks, he is for a long time silent. The class shifts together, waiting, wondering.

"I am moved," he says. "This is a print about pain. I am moved."

"If it isn't hateful or ugly, he doesn't like it," Lily hears a girl whisper to another girl behind her.

"He's a jerk," Lily hears.

But she finds her mouth is filled with tears she's holding back.

The print is about her mother's death. And it is as filled with pain as anything she's ever done. It is a woman at the top of a tall building, arms tensed, pressed backward, trying to fly. But she has no wings, and her face is stricken with fear. When Professor Pulaski dismisses everyone, she takes time gathering her materials. The professor comes over. His gnarled hands lean forward onto her table.

"You are well?" he asks.

She nods.

"No, I think you are still not well." He takes her face in his hand. "Such a lovely face. So full of sorrow. The first time I saw this face, I knew it had seen a hurt too great to be spoken."

She finds herself looking down. This old man embarrasses her. Even his tender touch embarrasses her. She finds herself longing to push his hand away, to rush into the hall, where the air is not so dense with the stench of acid and metal. But before she can, he leaves her, rushing himself into the hall and away, so that she is alone in the print room, shaking.

•   •   •

That night, when she takes her mail from the pigeonholes in the rooming-house entrance, she finds an envelope emblazoned: Senncrest High School, Columbia, Missouri. The handwriting is the purposely spaced, almost architectural printing that Will uses for everything—shopping lists, signing his name. Fearful, she waits until she is upstairs to open the letter. She doesn't know if it will lambaste her or apologize. She removes her coat, almost forcing herself to wait to read it. The letter crackles as she unfolds it.

> Dear Lily,
>
> Let's start over. Why do I feel we spoke right past each other when I was there? I can't believe I came to see you and ended up accusing you for my own stupid problems. But I am a sick man. Sick with guilt. How could I have married this good, kind girl and not really wanted her? I know she is suffering, and it gives me a horrible taste in my mouth. And then I come to you and maybe I asked too much of you. And ended up accusing you. God. You have no reason to see me again, but will you let me come? If nothing else to just apologize. Can I come up and see you and hold you.
> I still feel the same way, though. I still want to marry you. I can't help it.
>
> > Love,
> > Will

He gives a school address to reply to. The letter saves her from the abyss of her feelings for Ted, and she reads it again and again. Except for the last line. The last line freezes her blood. She wants to love him openly, to give him all she can, but she can't stop feeling that if she lets him really own her heart, if they go so far as to marry, she will fold, she will lose herself forever.

Andres Pulaski has not slept well in days. He sits up half the night in the room his wife calls the study, then falls asleep in a chair with the lights on. It is an ugly room, once a maid's room, maybe, with very little light and a smallness that seems squeezed. But he feels squeezed, too, ungiving. He finds it hard to sleep next to his wife, to spend any time with her. Even his children strip his nerves these days, his little wild American children with their dirty T-shirts and scrappy muscles and lack of table manners. They always seem to look at him as though resentful that he must take up any of their mother's time. When he tries to pay attention to them, they talk about guns and baseball. They push and shove and tease each other and end up ignoring him.

The source of his discontent is clear. He cannot free himself from thinking of her. He cannot think of a way to grow closer to her. Seduction cannot be the way. The very nature of seduction is manipulative and false. She deserves courting. She deserves an innocence of the heart. And his heart is too racked with longing for her to find innocence.

The morning Will is to come, Lily is so excited about his arrival, she goes over to the art building to calm herself, to spend an hour or two working on a new print. But she can't concentrate. On the phone he sounded so vulnerable. And his voice cracked when he told her how he'd lied to Sandra that he was going to an art teacher's convention in Chicago. "Don't give me a hard time about Sandra, okay?" he asked somewhat breathlessly. "I'm in real bad shape about her, about me. . . ."

When she returns to her rooming house, Will is already sitting on the porch steps, his duffel bag beside him. He stands as she comes up the porch steps and reaches out for her elbows. There is so much angelic shakiness in him. A chattery feel to his mouth—like a child that's just stepped out of a cold pool.

"Will. Come on. Come on up."

In her room, he unbuttons her coat, visibly trembling, drops his own on the floor, and hugs and kisses her until she feels mussed, overwhelmed.

"Lily, God," he says, alternating the two names like a chant. Lily feels herself tightening. She has longed for his passion, so different from Ted's coolness. But now she feels afraid. His pain is so palpable. "Please, wait, Will."

"What?"

"I need some air, is all."

He sits down as though she's deflated him, collapsing into the chair, doubling forward, his head in his hands.

"GOD!" he yells. "Don't reject me, too. I can't stand it. Not you, too."

Lily stands up against the wall of her room. His anger fills the whole space, presses her back.

"This place smells of him."

"Who?"

"Ted. Unless there's been someone else here."

"Literally?"

"Yes. Like cologne and sweat and—"

"You're imagining it. Ted doesn't smell like anything."

"It just doesn't seem like yours anymore. Did you let him— Did he fuck you, Lily? I've got to know. I know you never did before but—"

"No. Nothing happened. And don't use that word. You never use that word."

"What happened?"

"There was just nothing between us."

"He stayed here and he didn't sleep with you?"

"No."

"What a fool. What an ass. How did you ever think you loved him?"

"How's your marriage, Will?" she asks dryly.

He shakes his head. She can tell he is making an effort not to crumple; it seems so inevitable in his face. The toughness in him is a flimsy shield.

She has never seen him so silent. He slowly gets up and, gently tugging on Lily's shoulder, brings her over to the bed. He is uneasy as they undress. Uneasy in how he touches her. Like a man favoring a broken arm or a bruise, an internal wound. He flinches; he takes deep breaths. And in the end, he can't make love to her.

"It's okay. It's okay," she coos. "I feel nervous, too."

That night, in the dark, he is exhausted. She can feel it in his muscles, his loose hug, his sighs.

"I'm a fiend. Too filthy to live," he says. When Lily touches him, he pushes her hand away.

"Why? What have you done?" She tries to keep her voice steady.

"I've broken a vow. Not just to Sandra but to myself."

"Are you going to tell me about Sandra?" she says. "You're leaving too early in the morning to tell me then."

"I can't," he says. "I can't share it with you. Bad enough that I'm committing adultery with you. Just touching you that way, just trying to make love, that's adultery, too, isn't it? I can't also complain about my wife."

"Oh," Lily says. "I thought adultery and complaining about your spouse went hand in hand." She is shaken by the word adultery. She wonders if she's ever really broken one of the Ten Commandments before. She is shaken, too, by how changed he seems. Last time he was openly ready to commit to her, to love her. Now there is so much standing between them.

"Are you going to leave her?" she asks.

"How could I leave after a few months? I can't believe I even mentioned it to you before. You have no intention of marrying me. I have no intention of leaving Sandra." How pointedly he says it. There's determination in his voice, and a dark shadow of anger.

"She can't be happy the way you've been feeling. Don't you think she's miserable, too? You said in your letter—"

"No. I think she's fine. She's in heaven. She thinks marriage is just delightful. She tells me every day."

"Are you teasing me?"

"Look. I can't talk about this. She's happy. I'm making sure she's happy. I've done a lot of thinking. Ever since I wrote you that letter. I mean, I talk to you about commitment, and this is how I honor the commitment I've already made. I shouldn't have come, Lily. I thought of calling it off, but I'm too damn weak. I wanted to be with you one more time. And I couldn't even do that. You're bad for me now. Like an addiction. This has got to end."

"I wish you hadn't come, either," Lily says, feeling helpless and defeated. How much better it would have been to remember him the way he was before.

Lily doesn't want to lie near Will now, after he is asleep, the time she normally finds him utterly appealing, childish. Last year, when he would fall asleep after lovemaking, he'd be so sprawling, so innocently selfish. She always wanted to wrap herself around him. Now she finds the edge of the bed and stays there. The clock ticks. The lights at Professor Pulaski's house burn all night. In the early dawn she gets up and leans on the windowsill and watches the silent white mansion's lights recede into daylight. She cannot bear to look back at the bed and see Will. She looks forward to his leaving.

As the school year comes to a close, Lily wonders what she will do. Since her relationship with Will, she hasn't slept with another man. No one has even interested her. He taught her what it feels like to be so close to somebody that your needs mesh, that desire is as constant and familiar as the need to eat. Without the hope of having him back, she is lost.

But she finds herself in her art. All year, she's spent twelve- and fourteen-hour days in the print lab. Her prints have a life of their own.

Her fellow students ask to buy them. Professor Pulaski praises her so often that she is embarrassed by his interest. But she doesn't trust it— or herself.

She thinks about teaching college. There are sheets in the art office with lists of colleges hiring instructors. One in North Carolina, another in New Mexico. One even in Alaska. But she can't imagine herself alone in a totally new place, for now she has no real ties at all. Not her mother, not Ted, not Will. And something in her life needs to be familiar.

So she is thinking of Chicago. Though she has never actually lived there, important scenes of her life have been staged along its lakefront. Every Christmas night since she was a child, returning from her aunt's Christmas dinner on the South Side, she found a strange thrill in passing through downtown Chicago, the streets wreathed in Christmas ornaments. And on so many Saturdays she indulged in Marshall Field's, as a child, staying patiently by her mother's side, through dentist appointments and jewelry repair shops, just so that she could be rewarded by a walk through the packed toy aisles of Marshall Field's, to choose a bisque-faced doll with a pink velvet skirt and real leather slippers. As a teenager, trying on twenty outfits and twenty different attitudes. Which would she be?

And one of her few clear memories of her father is set in Chicago. She recalls a boat ride from Monroe Harbor on a polished wooden boat of one of his friends or business acquaintances. The men drank beer and joked until their judgment was barely functioning, and when the sail came about, it met the side of her head with a force that sprawled her onto the deck. Her father pulled her up by the collar, his face just a blur of red through her watering eyes.

"Stop it," he said. "Stand up. On a boat you have to know how to get out of the way."

"Hey, ease up, Howie," one of the other men said. She can't remember now if it was the owner or just another passenger, but later, when her father was cooling his angry lips with more beer, the man who had spoken up for her came over and rubbed her head.

"I'll bet that hurt," he said. His voice was as rich as a radio announcer's, and he was more handsome than her father. Dark hair, blue eyes. "You're a pretty little girl," he said. He took her hand in his. His hand was warm and large and flat and smooth. It seemed to envelop her, ease her.

"See that skyline," he said. "It's a beautiful city, isn't it? I always think it's like the Emerald City. Just when I think things are kind of crummy, I see this skyline and feel like things have possibilities. Know what I mean?"

Always since, she has looked at the Chicago skyline with pleasant, expectant familiarity.

And even though Jack works in Chicago, even though Ted is there and she doesn't want to see him, she thinks Chicago is where she must be.

In her graphics arts class, her instructor stands in front of the students, rubbing his hands together.

"I'm wondering what you're all going to do next year. I've got some news. Teaching pays"—he holds up his forefinger and thumb to make a zero—"Zip," he says. "*Nada*. Don't have expectations." He smiles. With his crew cut, he is an eagle, a predatory bird.

"I've got a word here for any of you 'fine artists' who want to do better. Financially, I mean. Advertising. And I've got a name here of someone who can help you get in it. Any takers?"

"Who is it?" a woman asks. She is one of those women in a twin sweater set that lives in a sorority and wants to be a children's book illustrator. The type of woman who looks at Lily disdainfully.

"It's a guy who shot an International Harvester commercial on my dad's farm. A guy at Faber, Lowe and Barton in Chicago. He says he's about to hire some assistant art directors. If I could do it over, that's what I'd be doing right now. Raise your hand if you want the address."

Lily has never thought of advertising before, but he said it's in Chicago. And the idea of being really settled, of true financial independence, certainly has its appeal. She holds up her hand.

"You?" he says. "I thought you were one of the print geniuses. I didn't think Pulaski would ever let *you* leave."

She shrugs, feels small in her seat, blushes. The others look at her, wondering what he's meant. She herself is unsure.

When the class is gone, she goes up to him.

"Why did you say that?" she asks.

"What?"

"About Professor Pulaski never letting me leave. What did you mean by that?" Her voice has an unexpected edge to it that makes her blush again.

"Pulaski's putting you up for the Breckner chair."

"What's the Breckner chair?" It sounds like the electric chair to her.
"He didn't tell you?"

She shakes her head.

"The Breckner chair. You get fully paid for a four-year doctorate.
And you have a guaranteed two-year instructorship during it all. It even
pays better than most instructors." He glares at her.

"I didn't know."

"Pulaski thinks you have 'the gift.' " He twinkles his fingers in front
of her in a condescending way. She sees that this man is actually jealous.
Jealous of her. She wonders if Pulaski thinks of her as really talented or
if he is merely as lecherous as she's been warned. Still, he has never
been anything but kind to her. Has never done anything but shown his
admiration for her.

"I still want the name you have," she says.

The man shrugs and writes it on a torn piece of paper in perfect
block letters. "It seems a shame to take a good job away from someone
who really needs it," he says as he hands it to her.

She takes the paper, feeling angry. "Other people have parents if
they don't get a job. They've got a backup." She leaves before he can
reply. Of course, she's not being entirely accurate, because, after all,
she's got Jack. But falling back on Jack is like jumping off a building into
a paper safety net.

When Lily Beach enters his cramped office, Professor Pulaski feels her
presence even before he looks up.

"Lily," he says. It's the first time he's ever spoken her first name out
loud. He keeps regular office hours, but students almost never come to
see him. He made sure at the beginning of the semester that there was
nothing inviting in his eyes when he recited his hours. And he knows
what students think of him: that he is frightening, that he is cold.

But now the one person he's been most wanting to see is standing in
his doorway, looking anxious.

"Am I disturbing you?" she asks in that deep chocolate voice that is
always lower and more pure than he expects.

"No, come in," he says.

She is dressed in a black cotton dress, almost innocent in the way it
is fitted in the waist but cut down at the shoulders, revealing the delicacy
of her collarbones.

"Sit down."

"I have to ask you . . ." she begins. He looks into her eyes. In each of them, he sees a miniature of himself. How little he looks. He will never be worthy of her.

"I heard from someone about . . . about the Breckner chair."

"Well, it is news that travels," he says. He always seems to lose his English when he speaks to her.

"Tell me yourself, then," she says.

"It is not only my decision. There are four others who must agree. I recommend students. They say yes. They say maybe no. One every four years . . ."

Her hands lie quiet in her lap, small, elegant fingers as delicate as her collarbone. "I have simply given you my recommend—recommendation."

"But why?"

He feels his heart constricting and takes a deep breath.

"Your work," he says.

"Because my work is the best?" she asks.

"Well . . . yes," he says.

"There are other print students as good or even better than me, aren't there?" He presses his lips together. Then he takes her hand and begins to stroke her wrist, her elbow. Her skin is so soft it barely registers on his acid-roughened fingertips. She begins to draw her hand away, and he grabs it.

"Please," he says, and finds his breathing embarrassingly ragged. "You can't know how this man feels . . . feels about you."

"It's because of that." She stands, backing away in clear revulsion. The black of her pupils crowds out all the soft flecked green. Her cheeks instantly pale.

"Please," he says. "Don't feel this way."

"It isn't because of my work at all."

"Your work is much approved by me!"

"What?"

"I like. Your work is fine, good. Very fine." He is horrified that his poor English won't support him when he most needs it.

"Well, you're hardly objective, are you?"

"Please." He is begging, but the word barely escapes his constricted throat. "I could not offend you. I could die first, but to make you feel— You are like no other woman to me."

She hitches the strap of her bag onto her shoulder and turns to the door.

"I want only happiness for you," he says.

"Then stay out of my life," she says, leaving him alone, feeling as small and as stupid as a child in a grown man's office chair.

Standing in the hall of her rooming house, still in her coat, still shaking with anger, Lily calls the man at Faber, Lowe and Barton.

"Hello," she says, trying to find the alto in her voice, to direct it to sound as confident as she knows it must be. "Is this Joe Forrest?"

"Last I checked," he says.

"My name is Lily Beach. I'm calling from Iowa City. Your name was given to me by Lloyd Sammis. You shot a commercial on his father's farm?"

"Did I?"

"He's a graphics instructor at the University of Iowa. He said you might be looking to hire some assistant art directors."

The man gives a full, throaty laugh on the other end, though Lily can't imagine what she's said that warrants it.

"Well," the man says. "You want to come see me?"

"Yes. When would be convenient?"

"You're the one that has to travel two hundred and fifty miles."

"I'm willing."

"You willing to live twenty-four hours in rubber cement? And put up with our bad tempers? We have very bad tempers."

Lily hesitates. The man seems awfully jolly. She even wonders if he might be drunk.

"I'm used to bad tempers," she says. "If we could make it a Friday . . ."

He names a date two weeks ahead and just two weeks before the end of the semester, two weeks before she must make enough money so that she doesn't have to think about taking it from Jack. Standing in the hall, she shivers.

"May tenth, I'll be there," she says.

For two weeks she plays hide-and-seek with Professor Pulaski. If she sees him coming, she ducks behind an easel, turns the corner. She knows he is looking for her. In class, she will not look up at him. One day, he conducts the class in a surprisingly pleasant manner.

"Well," he says just before the bell, "I want to announce the winner of the Breckner chair." People settle into their chairs. Apparently, they are all familiar with the Breckner chair, though she never was until she heard of it from her instructor.

"The board has just approved Lily Beach." Lily feels her face flush as they turn to her. "And there's never been a student I am more pleased to give of this honor."

"Well, we know how she got it," one of the twin-sweater-set girls whispers.

"She's very talented . . . on her back," she hears another say. When the bell rings, she turns to the two of them, glaring at their pug, snotty faces.

"You can be jealous if you like," she says. "But not on that account. Besides, I'm not accepting it." She draws her sketch pad to her chest and, keeping her back majestically straight, makes as regal an exit as she possibly can.

Before she reaches the stairway, Professor Pulaski calls her back.

"Come to my office, Miss Beach." His voice is both stern and pleading.

In his office, he sits down, gesturing broadly that she, too, must sit.

"I'm not—I can't take the Breckner chair," she says.

"Miss Beach. It is a fine honor. The board does not approve everybody. But they think the work you have is fine, so fine. Miss Dukes says it makes tears in her eyes. The chairman of the department, Mr. Tunney, says you have genius in you. Maybe you don't know why *I* put you up for the honor. But *they* give you this honor truthfully. Do not walk away because I have such bad manners. Do not run from this opportunity because I have made you so angry. I say this not selfishly. If I make you . . . if you find me . . . what is the word . . . repulsive . . . I still . . ."

"I don't find you repulsive," Lily says, seeing the sadness in his usually impenetrable eyes.

"You think I think you are just another coed. I know you know people think me to be Don Juan."

"Aren't you?" she asks.

"I have not been a perfect man. But you are different to me. You think you are just a girl I want to— What is the word? Use? You think I want to use you. Is this the right word? Use?"

Lily shrugs. Not entirely sure what he is trying to say.

"To me, you are not like other girls. Not like any other."

"Why?" Lily asks.

"Because in you I see something. Beauty all covered by sadness."

Lily nods. "I wish it wasn't so visible," she says.

"What is it you have seen, my dear child? What?"

"Please. I can't talk about it. Not with you." She squirms in her seat, feeling like an ant under a microscope. She has the feeling he wants to see into her, to dissect her.

"Why not with me?"

"What do you want from me, anyway, Professor Pulaski?"

"To watch over you."

"Why?"

He leans toward her, smelling spicy, herbal. It is a subtle, sexy scent, like the smell leaves give off as you walk over them. "I have known sadness, too. I want to know you, to help you, to . . . care for you. To know your sadness. To show you happiness." She looks into his eyes, sees in them only sincerity, care. Why should he want to know her, to help her?

"You're married," she says.

"What do you know of marriage?" he asks. "Do you think people marry and forget there are others in the world? Do you think that one person is all to another? No one can be so good. Someday you will know."

"And you are so much older than me," she says.

"When you are my age, age squeezes smaller, so that twenty is not so different than thirty, is not so different than fifty."

Lily looks at him in a new way now. She suddenly knows why women go to bed with him. His arrogance is lined with vulnerability.

"If you do not take this opportunity, the Breckner chair, it is because, I think, you do not believe in the art you make. Or, if you do not take this opportunity, it is because you run from your art, because it is too painful. Do not make this decision in any way because of me."

Lily lowers her head. Something he has said has stabbed her full-heart, but which is it? Or is it both? And yet she can't stay. She can't imagine walking each day into a building filled with people who think she won the chair by sleeping with Professor Pulaski. She cannot believe that her art will speak for itself, will say that she is special enough to deserve such an honor.

"If you do not stay in Iowa City, you must keep the touch with me," he says.

"Stay in touch?" she offers.

"Yes. Stay in touch. I want to know where you are, what you do, everything in your life."

"Why?"

"Because you will be special to me. You will see. I will be the uncle of your soul."

"Is that a Paraguayan expression?"

"It is my expression, the expression of a man who loves a woman he cannot have but loves her still. I will be the angel that guards you."

"Thank you," she says, not knowing what else to say. "I will let you know what I decide to do."

As she leaves him, she feels a soreness, a sadness, for he is perhaps the only person alive in the world who cares about her. And she suddenly finds that she cares for him, too.

It's cold for May, but Lily bundles herself in a coat and crosses town to the Stylegirl Shop to find a new outfit for the interview. Until now, she has measured clothes by their homeliness, she has gleaned chic out of simple, she has been drawn to vegetablelike and dark colors. But now she knows she must remake herself.

"Career woman," she says to herself, hearing its independent sound and its negative cast all at once. Career women are tough, punctual, reliable, and not married. Maybe will never marry. Maybe don't want to marry; that's always been the implication.

As Lily pushes through the hangers of Stylegirl's rack of suits, she feels she is touching with her fingers whole lives. This red suit is the suit of a perky girl who once just missed being chosen for the cheerleading squad. This emerald green one belongs to a secret vixen whose allure is hidden behind a polite, sweet voice. She chooses to try on a pink-and-gray tweed suit and an olive green nubby one with gold buttons. It is hard for her to imagine herself in either, to decide which sort of woman she is or wishes to be.

"May I help you?" the saleslady asks. She is elderly and wears imperfectly applied lipstick, which makes her mouth lopsided and sweet.

"Aren't they pretty suits!" the saleslady says as she carries them into the dressing room, Lily trailing behind her. "You'll look quite the lady in these."

"They're for an interview," Lily confides.

"Well, the job will be yours, I'm sure." The saleslady whooshes the curtains closed, leaving Lily with two mirrors and two new images to try on.

She starts with the olive green suit first. Its slender skirt seems to cling frantically to every curve of her hip and thighs. The jacket's gold buttons are cold on her fingertips, and their shanks clink as she buttons them. In the mirror, she looks truly silly in her broken-down ballet flats, her straight, lanky hair. The suit doesn't suit her at all.

The pink-and-gray suit is better, but not much. The pink brings up the rosiness of her cheeks, and the gray has a soft, subtle sophistication, but she simply looks like a little girl playing dress-up.

"How are you doing in there?" the saleslady calls through the curtain.

"Not well at all," Lily says, drawing the curtain, inviting her in. "Why does it look so wrong?"

The woman smiles. She's elderly, but she has style. And she's an old pro, Lily can see.

"It's very simple," the woman says. "The suit is quite fine. But in order to wear a suit, *you* must change. Your hair, for instance. You need to have your hair cut and put up in rollers, you know, so you can have one of those new pouffy dos."

"Pouffy dos?" Lily asks.

"Here. Stay right here and I'll show you."

The lady returns with a magazine and flips through until she finds the heading "West Point Weekend." The spread shows young, bouncy girls amid uniformed cadets, flirting, smiling, looking remarkably long-legged and lean in tweedy little suits just like the one Lily is trying on. But their hair defies gravity, is full and curvy around their pretty faces.

"See here," the saleslady says. "Pouffed hair . . . chubby rollers . . . ah, yes . . . a widened arc that curves so becomingly around the bright young faces of 1961. You see?"

Lily bunches her hair and pushes it up to get the effect. Already the tweed suit looks better.

"And your shoes, of course," the saleslady says. "You must buy pumps. Ones with stacked leather heels are very popular this spring. And gloves. And maybe a hat."

"Do I need all that?" Lily asks.

"Don't you want it all?"

Lily shrugs. "I've never needed to look this way before."

"If you're starting a new life, it's time to start a new look," the saleslady says cheerfully. Lily glances over at her black sweater draped over the chair, at her droopy clay green skirt.

"I'm game," she says.

The saleslady helps her with gloves, stockings, shoes from Stylegirl's shoe department, and a girdle, something Lily's never had. But Lily stops her at the hat. The three she's brought into the dressing room are shaped like Keystone Cop hats. "Not my style," Lily says.

"But they're the latest style," the saleslady says.

"Not for me," she reiterates.

The saleslady smiles. "Only so much change at a time. I understand."

At the counter, Lily counts out the bills with trepidation, remembering all the afternoons she's spent shelving books to earn it. The saleslady says, "Some of the younger girls here get their hair done at Geraldine's over on Clinton Street. Now, I've never been there, but that seems to be the place. You know it?"

Lily nods.

"And here," the saleslady says, tearing out the page of the magazine with the young stylish women and the solemn cadets. "Show them this."

"Thanks so much," Lily says, truly grateful.

"I wish I were young enough to start a new life," the saleslady calls to her as she steps out onto the sidewalk, the dress bag filled with treasures, clapping against her leg.

At Geraldine's they frown when she announces she has no appointment but brighten up when she presents the picture of the women and the cadets.

"That's the 'do' to do," the woman she is assigned to says. "It's perfect for you."

The woman washes her hair in a porcelain basin, yanking at it, tugging it, rinsing it with water so hot, then so cold, that every root in Lily's scalp tingles.

"You're going to have to set it, of course," the woman says as she cuts off the first hank of hair. Out of the corner of her eye Lily sees the hair spilling onto the linoleum and feels a twinge of loss.

"Every night. Big rollers. You can sleep on them. That's what I do. You get used to it after a while. You know how to handle rollers?"

Lily shakes her head.

"Hold still. I'll show you when I start to set your hair. Easy as pie." She snaps her coral-nailed polished fingers.

The instruction is simple, but Lily knows the implementation will not be so simple. As she bakes under the hair dryers, the rollers so tight they pull her eyebrows into a startled expression, she reads a magazine devoted to young unmarried women.

"SNAPPY DRESSING!" the glossy cover reads. "WILD WITH STYLE!" it proclaims. "LOVE AROUND THE CORNER!" it coos. Life, according to this magazine, is one big exclamation point. Men are devilishly handsome! Women are tremendously romantic! Love is thrilling! or even better, zesty! Lily's feet wriggle in their broken-down flats. She takes a deep breath that tickles with hair spray and setting lotion, and though she knows life can't really be like that, she can't wait to find out if it at least might come close.

Lily cannot stay at Jack's. She thinks about it. She wonders if after what happened to her mother he will be more careful, less threatening to her, but she can't trust that. She wants to go to his house, though, to take the things she wants for good so that she will never have to return. And just the idea of seeing him tightens her throat.

She calls a motel not far from Jack's, built two years ago, an ugly place she passed often while they were building it, purple-glazed brick, small windows. The idea of staying there depresses her and scares her a little. She has never stayed at a motel or hotel by herself before.

"You want to face the parking lot or the highway?" they ask her, and she takes a deep breath before she can make the reservation. Later, she pulls a name from the ride board of a woman who's driving to Chicago on Wednesday, the week Lily needs to be there, on Friday.

And then she calls Jack.

"Well, if it isn't my little step-responsibility," he says. She can tell he's been drinking. "Need some cash?"

"I haven't taken any money from you in almost two years," she says. "Look, I'm coming in on Wednesday."

"I'll get Estelle to make the bed."

"I'm not staying with you."

"You're not staying with me?"

"No."

"Why?"

"How can you ask me that?" she says.

"Listen . . . Lily." She hears his voice grow lachrymose. "I want you to stay here. You're all I have left. Really. All I have."

"No, Jack. I just want to come by to get some things."

She tells him about the job interview and briefly about her plans.

"I can't reconcile this," he says. "You not staying here with me. As if I'm some . . . some—"

"Let's not talk about it," she says.

There is a long silence, and then he says, "So you're going the career route. I always figured you'd just get married. What's going on with your pal Ted?"

"I don't know," she says. "He's in Chicago."

"He was always too straight arrow for you, anyway," Jack says dryly. "A sexy girl like you needs someone different."

"How would you know what's right for me?" she tells him, feeling the fingernails of her left hand biting into her palm with anger.

The thought of seeing him scares her, but somehow she has to. She has to put it behind her, though there are days she thinks that will be impossible. She sees in a flash of memory her mother's face just before the end and then cannot bear to think of her at all.

"I'll see you, Jack," she says.

"I'd much rather you were staying," he says. "You're doing this to spite me."

"That's only half of it," she says.

On the ride to Chicago, Lily thinks of Ted and wonders if she should call him. He's living with his parents temporarily. They get along well, and it's allowing him to save some money as he begins his job with Naughton Shivak. He's written her six letters since he moved to Chicago in September. They are like he is: simple, informational, hesitant. In them he describes the government contracts for NASA he is working on. He talks about what it is like to be sleeping in his childhood room. Humbling, he says. There is no romance in the letters. They are not even signed "Love." And he writes: "So, I've been thinking of you, if you know what I mean. . . ."

If she didn't feel so distant from him, she might stay with his parents, too. They are wonderful people, especially his mother, with whom she's always found great rapport. His mother was there for her in a way no one else was, when her own mother died.

The driver's name is Suzy, and she smokes cigarettes and wears a fraternity pin on her yellow sweater. She's hesitant to leave Lily at the purple motel.

"You're sure you want to stay here?" she asks.

"Yes."

"Don't you have family or friends or anything?"

Lily says no.

"Gee, sorry, kid," she says.

Lily takes her suitcase and nervously goes to the motel desk, a windowed box at the front of the rectangle of purple brick. The sound of Suzy's bright red convertible speeding away makes her feel small and alone.

"I have a reservation for Lily Beach," she says.

"Beach. You asked for parking lot, right? Much quieter." Lily doesn't remember what she asked for, but she takes the key in her hand. Dragging her bag behind her, she walks down a corridor of purple doors. The motel smells of janitor products and a sour vinyl newness and makes her feel so sad, that she has to bite her lip to keep from crying. The room itself is cheerful enough, until she starts to touch things. The curtains are a clean turquoise, but when she holds one in her fingers, it's made of a stiff vinyl. The bedspread is purply blue but must be fiberglass, or something, because it feels like soap. She flings her suitcase on the bed, and the soapy material seems not to dent at all.

Lily sits down next to her suitcase on the bed and stays frozen for a long time before she finds the energy to get up and unpack a few things: her suit, her book, her nightgown. She thinks of Suzy, who drove her here, how tonight she will be sleeping in the room she's grown up in. How her mother will simmer beef stew or chicken à la king or some other loving food as a welcome-home dinner. Lily takes out of her suitcase a smashed tuna sandwich, a Hostess twinkie, and undressing one of the sanitized water glasses, she fills it with tap water and the gumdrop-shaped ice from her ice bucket and eats all she's going to have until tomorrow.

Late that night, Lily calls Ted. She doesn't want to, really. It's weakness that makes her dial. She's relieved when Ted himself answers. As much as she likes his mother, she doesn't want to have to explain why she isn't staying with them.

"I'm in Chicago," she tells Ted.

"Not at Jack's."

"No. At a motel."

"Lily. You didn't have to do that."

"It's creepy here," she says.

"Well, you should come stay here. You know you're always welcome here."

"Not tonight," she says. "I already paid."

"Are you going to see Jack?"

"Tomorrow. I'm going to pick up some of my old things from there."

"Do you want me to come with you?" he asks. "I could take you tomorrow night and bring you back here."

"Maybe," she says.

"My job's going great," he says. "I never thought I'd like it so much. I'm not up to it, of course. Not really. I mean, it takes every ounce of energy just to stay to standard, if you know what I mean."

"I'm glad you like it so much," Lily says.

"But maybe I will succeed here, like you said."

"I'm sure you will, Ted."

"I'll tell my mother you're coming tomorrow night to stay? Okay?"

Lily thinks of the comfy down sofa in their living room, the old quilt Ted's mother used to give her, the pillowcases that smelled of Ivory Snow.

"Okay," she says. "I wonder if you— Would you pick me up at Jack's instead of driving me there?"

"You want to be there alone? With him?"

"Please. I don't know if I want to say anything to him or just be in my room alone. I don't know. I just would rather you pick me up there. You could honk when you arrive. Or just wait. I could check out the window for you."

"Well, at least I won't have to lay eyes on him," Ted says.

The next evening, at six-thirty, as her taxi slides down Jack's street, Lily feels her stomach cramp up as tight as a fist. His house (though she lived there for seven years, it never became her house, or even her mother's) is a shrimp brick Dutch Colonial set on a shallow hill a block from the lake. The shutters are robin's-egg blue and will need to be painted soon. A stone birdbath, which her mother bought at a tag sale a year before she died, stands abandoned on the lawn near the driveway, filling with stagnant water. Lily rummages in her purse for the key she hasn't used in almost two years. It's on a silver key chain, in the shape of an E, that belonged to her mother, whose real name was Helena but was called Elaine by everyone.

The entrance hall of the house smells like the cleaning lady's just been there: Vinegar and Ajax rise astringently to Lily's nose as she steps in.

"Jack?" she calls, setting down her suitcase. He has changed nothing.

The living room is still stuffed with the needlepoint pillows and china figurines her mother loved and collected to a point of annoyance. Pictures of the family still line up in gold frames on the piano.

Jack comes in from behind her. He has aged since her mother's death. His hair has grayed; his eyes have sunken. They glitter cold and green from dark hollows beneath his brows. He is wearing a blue tennis shirt with a pumpkin-colored poodle-knit cardigan. Lily's mother would never have let him put colors together so crassly. His pug, smart-ass look, however, is precisely as she remembered it.

"Well, the prodigal child returned. Your hair certainly is perky. Very Betty Coed," he says. "Have you stopped growing? You don't look taller."

"I'm twenty-two years old," she says. "I stopped growing about six years ago."

She can't tell if he's been drinking, but he has a forcedly lazy look in his eye that makes her nervous.

"What have you been up to?" she asks.

He looks unnerved by the simple question.

"What do you mean 'up to'? If you're implying something, just say it."

"I didn't mean anything by it."

"Sit down, since you've come. The career route. I can't get over it. I always thought you'd marry that stiff Ted."

"So you've said."

"I've never liked him."

"He's never liked you. Especially after what happened with my mother. And me." Venom seems to cling to each word Lily speaks to Jack, and she has no control over it. Temporary insanity. Ever since her mother died, her hatred for Jack has made her understand this concept perfectly.

"If you hadn't opened your mouth, your mother would be sitting over there on that fucking armchair. Can't you imagine it? Right over there. Don't start with me."

"If you hadn't done anything to tell about—"

"Shut up," he says. "I'm getting a drink."

Lily gets up and starts up the stairs. She can hear him muttering below and isn't sure if he's still trying to talk to her, but she doesn't care. It's because of him she made the worst error of her life. It's because of him. She hated him before, and now the very sight of him brings back the guilt, the confusion, the utter hopelessness of two years ago. The fear. Her mother's dead body. The numbness. Being so racked with guilt she couldn't get out of bed. Ted knows. For a moment, it eases her mind to think she's going to see him tonight.

Her bedroom is really a little girl's room. She remembers her mother showing it to her for the first time. The house was Jack's house from a previous failed marriage. And Lily's bedroom was once his son Freddie's room, whom Jack, in some tortured divorce decree, had agreed never to see again. But to entice Lily to accept her new marriage and this new living arrangement, her mother had had the room papered in daisies and had bought a canopy bed frosted in ruffles and tucks, with a multitiered bed skirt, each tier another color, like a Spanish dancer's hem. And her mother had had it all installed before Lily saw the room. At the age of not quite thirteen, Lily had been appalled by the room's overkill; now it just looks old and ugly. Jack hasn't touched a thing. The bulletin board is still layered with clippings of teen idols. The pink vinyl record player sits neatly closed in the corner with a stack of 45s on top. In the rocking chair are a few wretchedly disemboweled stuffed animals and sad-looking dolls; notably, a stuffed dog named Corky, which Lily's real father gave her for her fifth birthday, and a ballerina doll with a twisted leg that can't be turned right. Still, she looks beautiful in her gold-and-pink tulle and satin toe shoes. Lily picks the doll up and lays her face against the golden curls. Why couldn't she have had a life like other girls? With kind, bearlike fathers? Or stepfathers who loved them?

All these years she's lived in fear of Jack. When she was a teenager, he used to touch her surreptitiously, smooth her blouse over her breasts, touch her buttocks when she wore stretch pants. And whisper to her. The things he would whisper to her! At night she would lie in bed and want to die. It was the only way, she felt, she could keep it all from her mother.

And then, the night before her death, her mother was out at a friend's playing bridge, and Jack came into Lily's room reeking of liquor, drunk, pushed her against the wall, and began to not just fondle but grab at her. She remembers the smell of his mouth on her. How she struggled, realizing they were alone. This can't be happening, she kept telling herself.

"You want me," he said. "You do," he whispered to her. His mouth was on her ear, her neck. His hands were on her breasts, his body shoving her, pressing her so painfully against the wall, she kept feeling she might flatten like a cartoon character. To have no third dimension

at all. She kept kicking at him, struggling, and thinking about flattening.
If only she were so flat she could slide down, slip away. He wouldn't
even notice he was molesting an empty wall. He slid his hand into her
panties and began to try to get her excited. "Oh, baby," he kept saying.
With her shoulder blades crushed against the wall, she felt paralyzed,
shaking, unable to move. And in the midst of his brutality—how many
times in her life will she have to relive it?—she felt a sickening, horrifying moment of desire, sharp as an ice pick. Shortly after, he unzipped
his pants. "It's about time, isn't it?" he said.

And then all she remembers after that is kicking him in the head.
She doesn't know how his head could get so low that she could kick him.
She doesn't know how or when he left the room. She just remembers
the clocking, perfect sound of her foot contacting his skull, and then he
was gone. For an hour after, she sat against the wall, trying to find her
third dimension. In the cartoons, Sylvester the cat pops up in seconds,
comes back to life. But she sat there mussed and torn—no, it must
have been more than an hour—wondering if she would ever be three-
dimensional again.

In the morning, she told her mother. All these years, she had kept the
secret. Nothing had ever happened before, nothing but terror and self-
loathing. But after that night, even though she managed to make him
leave, she thought she had to. Because, for a moment, for that sickening,
horrifying moment, she had almost wanted him. And nothing he could
have done to her would have made her feel more ashamed than that.
How could she want the man who had terrified her, brutalized her
mother, even for a second. Her own body had betrayed her. She felt she
would punish it forever.

Telling her mother, though, was the worst error of her life. Her
mother nodded while she spoke and said only, "Oh, God. Oh, God."

Later that day, her mother drove to Chicago and found her way onto
the roof of an eighteen-story building at Fullerton and Lakeview, the
building where she had grown up. And from there she jumped, sailing
down, with a view of Lincoln Park, to the neat pavement, where her
legs accordioned and her femur was driven into her heart.

Lily had killed her mother as surely as if she had driven a knife into
her heart. The blood stained her hands. The guilt broke her. She and
Ted had to go identify the body, and she could not stop looking, staring
at the death mask of her mother's face, for in death, her face, even with

its eyes closed, looked terrified. Even long after some morgue worker might have kindly closed her lips, her mouth was still twisted open like a scream. At the last minute, had she changed her mind? Had she been afraid?

Why hadn't Lily stayed quiet about Jack, taken care of things herself? She could have left home for good. She could have threatened Jack in some way. She could have threatened to tell her mother, for instance, and then never have done it. Why had she ever imagined that her mother was strong enough to accept the news about Jack, to defend her? And now her mother was broken and gone forever.

Being here in this room is the closest Lily's been to anything relating to her mother since just a few weeks after her death. Here in this room, the night her mother died, until Ted insisted she come and stay with his parents the next night, Lily lay here, sorting out why it had happened, how it had happened, and who was to blame. Here in this room, with the bureau shoved against the door to keep Jack out, she had held a bottle of sleeping pills in her hand, turning them in the light of the ruffly bedside lamp. The very ticket to see her mother again. Turning and turning them until the pills in the brown vial blurred, until her fingers fumbled and they spilled on the floor. Maybe there are still one or two under the bed, lodged in the meeting of carpet and wall. She never told anyone, not even Ted, how close she came. And through it all Jack was silent and emotionless. The only way she was sure it had affected him at all was that the liquor bottles emptied at an alarming rate.

She knew she didn't want to take the sleeping pills when she realized what she really wanted was to give the pills to Jack. Her desire to snuff him out, to annihilate him, was so strong, she pushed the bureau aside at two in the morning and went down the stairs, ready to dump the bottle of pills into his scotch. She had no trouble locating the Johnnie Walker Red in the dark. She knew just where he kept it, recognized its heft and shape. The cork gave a warning thunk as she drew it out. She waited a moment to see if he'd heard, but when he didn't come down, she dropped in a single pill. The scotch foamed so noisily, so alarmingly, she knew the whole bottle of pills would look as if she'd dropped a package of Alka-Seltzer into it. Besides, she told herself, her hate for him didn't warrant turning herself into a murderer. So, instead of adding the rest of the bottle, she merely brought its glass opening to her lips and, drawing on all the saliva in her mouth, spit into it.

The next day, when Jack poured himself a drink, he said the scotch was no damn good, tasted funny. He said he couldn't understand it, though he never looked suspiciously at her, and threw it out. So had she spiked the scotch with every last Nembutal, it wouldn't have killed him. Still, it made her feel wickedly good that she'd come close.

Jack walked through the funeral looking shocked and stricken. His friends comforted him. "What a shock, buddy. She wasn't stable. You mustn't blame yourself." Never once did Jack look Lily in the eye.

The night of the funeral, Ted, simmering with anger over why her mother had killed herself, held Jack by the collar and threatened if he ever laid a finger on Lily, if he ever even suggested it, he would kill him, and he punched him so hard, the bruise bloomed, it seemed, in seconds. Lily remembers the pleasure of seeing Jack blanch to paper white, of spotting his impotent fists, clenched, fearful, of Ted letting go so that Jack slumped back and moved away like an animal caught in the threat of a light.

That night and all the rest of the nights until she left for school, Lily slept at Ted's parents' house, with Ted's mother fussing over her like an injured lamb and Ted awaking sometimes in the night to kiss her brow, to watch over her as she slept on the couch. And the whole time, she kept feeling she didn't deserve Ted. Any girl who could even for a second have allowed that filthy man to touch her, to even vaguely want him, deserved only hateful men, punishment. A month later, Ted left for Paris.

Lily gathers the ballerina doll, Corky the dog, and a few old letters wrapped in a ribbon her mother had written her when she was at sleep-away camp. And then she remembers the emerald ring. Her mother left her jewelry to Lily in her will, but there is nothing of value but a few silver bracelets and a ballerina-set emerald ring with diamonds radiating from it. Lily always hated the ring. Maybe because Jack gave it to her mother, maybe because it looked ostentatious on her mother's tiny, slender finger. Because she hated it, she hasn't claimed it, has let it linger in her mother's still-full jewelry box. All the rest that fills the box are cheap costume beads, gaudy clip-on earrings from another era. Lily walks into her mother's room nervously. It's Jack's room now, but it hasn't changed. When she opens the top drawer of the mahogany chest, it's still filled with her mother's things, still smells of her mother's sachets. The jewelry box is blue velvet, the color of ice. It creaks when Lily cracks back the top. When she picks up the ring, she feels a cold tightening in her stomach. Her mother wore it as an engagement ring, though it came a few years after her marriage to Jack. The gold feels cool as Lily slips the ring on her left-hand ring finger. It is not so overwhelming on Lily's broad hand as it had been on her mother's. She can see her mother now, wearing it, sitting in front of the mirror, putting on concealer over a bruise Jack had inflicted.

"Let's leave him," Lily told her. What was she? Fourteen? Fifteen years old? Why did she know how evil Jack was, and her mother didn't? "He's bad to you, Mom."

"He's bad to me for a reason," her mother answered, dabbing her injury so carefully. "He just expects a lot from me, and obviously I haven't been living up to his expectations. But you live up to my expectations, Lily," she said, turning and taking Lily's chin in her hand. "You always do, darling." God. Lily can hardly bear the way loving her mother hurts. What would have happened if her mother had left him? She knew her mother was weak, that she needed someone to tell her what to do. Why couldn't it have been Lily? She could have taken care of her mother. Even waited on her. She would have been willing to do that. She puts the ring to her lips and kisses it, can even imagine she smells her mother's spicy cigarette scent. She is too worn out to cry, but the feeling is there— the aching throat, the emptiness in her stomach.

Leaving the ring on her finger, putting two thin silver bracelets into her pocket, she closes her mother's drawer, turns off the light, and comes back to her own bedroom to take one last look. This is her childhood she is escaping, she tells herself. She will not be safe until she is free of it. She looks out the window and sees the welcome sight of Ted's car parked in the driveway, then goes down to face Jack.

He is deep into his scotch now. His eyes seem even more green, glaring out from their bloodshot frames.

"I'm never going to see you again," she says to him. She feels so young and small clutching her old toys, like a child running away from home.

He shakes his head at her.

"Give me a chance," he says. "Let's put this all behind us. You can't not see me again." She looks into Jack's eyes. He looks truly upset, lost. What does he feel? Can he even imagine what his actions have done to her? How could he? He can't even accept what his actions did to her mother.

"Why?"

"Because I'm your father. Legally your father. Because I love you. Please, Lily . . ."

She laughs, but the sound of her own laugh haunts her as she goes out the door.

Ted opens the car door for her, and she puts in her suitcase, her pitiful, old toys. He is silent as she sits down next to him.

"You okay?" he asks. She nods.

"He didn't . . ."

"No."

Ted pats her hand. As he drives her to the safe harbor of his parents, she feels that same sense of crying without tears, but the silence and his presence are a comfort, like a great arm that gathers her up, and holds her, and soothes her.

Chapter Five

The next morning, she awakens on the sofa in Ted's parents' living room. It is still dark. She's gotten up early to dress for the interview. The house is silent as she tiptoes to the bathroom. By Ted's partly opened door, she listens to hear his safe, even breathing. The rollers have left her scalp feeling sore. She takes them out one by one, and they look like little animals, their brushes coupling in the sink. In the mirror, she appears different from before, but she can't define what has changed. Last night, when Ted kissed her good night, she felt his concern, and she let it warm her.

The pink-and-gray suit buttons up crisp and good across her breasts. She rubs perfume on her wrists and puts some behind each ear. In the pretty pearl gray pumps, she already feels older, more reliable, like a perfect job candidate, like the girls in the twin sweater sets, only more interesting, like an ordinary, perfectly nice girl on her way to the big city.

At the door, she checks her purse for Faber, Lowe and Barton's address, for her lipstick and powder. When she takes her art portfolio and closes the door to the house, she feels as though she's left behind another younger and sadder Lily Beach.

•   •   •

The office building that Faber, Lowe and Barton occupies sits dark and grand on the northern edge of the Loop. The polished brass revolving doors glide in total silence, propelling Lily into a lobby dressed in gilt and marble. The elevator man looks her over as she steps in.

"Seventh floor," he says.

"Fourth," she says.

"Okay. Let me guess. You're here for a job interview."

"How did you know?"

"It's that worried look on your face. You should only look worried if they hire you. Secretary, right?"

"Art department."

"No kidding. They're hiring ladies now? You don't need a suit, honey. You need a smock. And a gorgeous gal like you's gonna need a very tolerant disposition." Lily feels color seeping into her cheeks.

She steps into a hallway that reeks of rubber cement. On the walls are pinned maybe a hundred ads for cake mix, dishwashers, soap, tractors.

"Leave your hot temper outside your door. Air/Cool's going to cool you down!" one ad reads, showing a man standing inside a house, his eyes closed with pleasure, his back against the door, holding the world outside.

"You looking for someone?" a man asks. He's maybe thirty years old and handsome.

"I'm supposed to see Joe Forrest."

"Come on," the man says. "I'll take you there." Lily follows the man through a hallway of offices, each containing a drawing board and filing cabinets. People are cutting, pasting, painting, talking on the phone. In all the offices, Lily sees only one woman. She's dressed in a coral-colored smock, she's painting, and she doesn't look very happy. If Lily can read a look on her face at all, what she reads is boredom.

Joe Forrest is sitting at his drawing table with his back to the door, smoking a cigarette. When he turns to her, she is surprised. He looks a lot less businesslike than she expected. His sleeves are rolled up, his tie is loosened, and his feet wear only socks. He is a small, balding man with crystal, pale eyes, and—Lily can already see—an outsize personality.

"You've got an appointment with this pretty lady, Joe," the man says, handing her off.

"So I do." Joe Forrest gestures to a chair, then reaches over and clears off some layouts so she can sit down. The office isn't large, but there are two drawing boards in it, fully equipped with pens, inks, watercolors. Lily wonders who sits at the other table. She settles into the chair Joe Forrest has offered her, balancing her portfolio on her lap.

"So you want to be an art director?"

"I think it would be interesting," she says, having weighed "exciting," "challenging," and "something I'd be good at."

"Why interesting?"

Lily swallows. "I like the idea of illustrating words."

"Well, we're not illustrators. We *hire* illustrators. We just do layouts."

"I know. I mean, I like the idea of deciding what *should* illustrate words," she says.

"You like the idea of deciding. I hate deciding, personally. You're a cute kid. How old are you?"

"Twenty-two."

"At twenty-two, I couldn't decide a damn thing except that I didn't want to end up like my father, driving a tractor. So look at me." He gestures to the layouts pinned around the room: "International Tractor Roundup." "Wow! Now I love to plow!" She smiles.

"See the irony?" he says. "Want a cigarette?"

"No, thanks." He lights another.

"There's only one woman in the art department right now," he says. "Joy. Takes everything too seriously, so every man in the department teases her. The only other women are secretaries and art buyers."

"I don't see why that is," Lily says. "It seems like women could do as good a job."

"Well, during the war, they did, I guess. A bunch of them then. Their work was a little precious, it seems to me. But they did okay. Come on. Show me your portfolio."

"Do you want to see my résumé first?"

"Naah. Let's break some rules. Show me your portfolio. It matters a lot more to me."

Before Lily left Iowa, she put together what she thought would make an appropriate portfolio for the interview: a few ads she'd done for her graphics class, a few logotypes they'd assigned the class to do, even a mock book jacket. Also, at the end, she included a few of her best prints.

After the second ad, Joe Forrest looks up at her, surprised. "You've got quite an eye," he says. "You must have been teacher's pet."

Lily shrugs. She isn't about to tell him that her graphic arts teacher resents her.

"You know, you've got to spend at least a year in the mount room. Everybody does. Then you become an assistant art director. You sort of serve an apprenticeship to an art director, share an office, you know. You only get to do resizings, some trade ads, maybe. Everyone has to pay their dues. So you wouldn't get involved in ideas and decisions for a long time. You're whipping-boy material. It's messy. It's boring."

"I'm willing."

"But why? Why not be a secretary in a law firm. Don't have to worry about messing up your pretty clothes. Meet some hotshot. Have babies?"

Lily feels her ears grow hot. "I don't know how to type," she says.

"Jesus. Did you do these prints?"

"Yes."

"Jesus! They're fabulous. You ever sold any of your work?"

"No, I've never tried."

"I'd buy this one." It is a somewhat abstract print that appears to be a woman standing by a gate or a break in a wall. The wind is blowing madly, and she's hanging on to the post to keep from being forced through the gate. Or it could be just a landscape. It's all how you perceive it, Lily figures. Some people have said that she's heavily influenced by Matisse. Certainly this one was.

"You can have it," she says.

"Uh-uh. I want it fair and square. It's too terrific. What do you want for it?"

Lily shrugs. Her heart is pounding. "Ten dollars," she offers.

"I'll give you twenty."

"I couldn't . . ."

Joe Forrest pulls a twenty-dollar bill from his wallet. It is as crisp as a potato chip and crackles prettily as she stuffs it into her purse.

"Thank you," she says.

"We only pay forty-one hundred a year, starting salary for kids in the mount room," Joe Forrest says.

"That's all right."

"When can you start?"

"You want to hire me?"

"What else could 'When can you start' mean?"

"Just like that?"

"Would you rather have an uphill battle?"

"June. June seventeenth? I mean, that would give me time to find a place and move."

While Lily is gathering her things, Joe Forrest is fondling the print.

"I'm going to frame this," he says. "Oh, by the way, don't tell everyone around here you're a fine artist. People resent the heck out of people who can do things they can't. But don't stop doing it, either. Because if you come here and become an art director and stop doing your prints, you'll resent the hell out of yourself. Take it from me."

Lily is afraid to ask what he means.

"Okay, thanks," she says. She shakes his hand. He smiles. She can hardly believe her luck.

Putting her portfolio under her arm, Lily walks down Michigan Avenue, feeling as if she could burst. No one will believe she's found a job so quickly. She can hardly believe it herself. She can't wait to go back to Iowa and tell Lloyd Sammis, her graphic arts teacher. She smiles just thinking of it. She longs desperately to tell somebody. But she doesn't know how to reach Ted during the day, and besides, she'll see him tonight. She hardly could call Jack. For a moment she thinks of calling Will. She doesn't even know why she thinks of him. She just imagines his sweet mouth smiling as she tells him. He would be happy to hear, she knows. She is sad thinking of him. Somewhere out there he is unhappy, and she can't do a thing for him.

She crosses the Michigan Avenue bridge and walks up toward the Gold Coast. She notes the energy of the other people walking, the smell of the air, and picks up a sense of thrill. This is where I must be, it tells her. This is what I've always wanted.

As she passes Saks Fifth Avenue, she sees lots of suits in the window similar to the one she's wearing. She will need more of them. And more pretty heels and stockings and girdles and a bottle of candy pink nail polish. And hell! a bed, a sofa, a chair. She wonders how she will do it all. She thinks of the twenty-dollar windfall in her pocket. Maybe she will sell her prints, she thinks. Even a few would help. She can buy used furniture. Or rent a furnished place, as she's doing in Iowa. But she hopes she doesn't have to. She wants desperately to make a home for herself. A real home. A furnished place will never feel like a home.

Past the old water tower, near the Palmolive Building, she begins to look at streets that are suddenly residential. It is here she would like to live. She remembers seeing a real estate agency on Walton Street the last time she walked around this neighborhood. At least, she thinks, she will stop in and see how much apartments rent for.

There is a woman at the front desk of the real estate office applying lipstick as Lily walks in.

"Yes, ma'am," the woman says. Lily can't help but smile. No one has called her ma'am before.

"I'm looking for a rental apartment," she says.

"How big?" the woman asks.

"A one-bedroom. Somewhere near here. Maybe on the lake? I mean if there is anything I can afford."

"How much can you afford?"

"No more than fifty dollars a month."

"Well, there's not much," the woman says.

"I'd rather have something not so new," Lily says.

"Not new? You're kidding. Well, Millicent will help you." She points behind her, as if she is no longer interested in Lily's case.

Millicent turns out to be about seventy years old, with wispy yellow-white hair and a purple wool dress that is too heavy for the season.

"Sit down, dear," she says. "I take care of most of the apartment rentals. Tell me what you want." By the end of their talk, Millicent has drawn out six cards of what she calls "suitable apartments for young ladies."

"Are you sure you want to live alone? We could help you with roommates."

"No. Absolutely sure," Lily says.

"These are truly suitable in any case," Millicent says. Lily wonders what she means: that they have matrons at the desk that log you in and out, like at the college dorm she was once so anxious to escape.

"Shall we go look?" Millicent asks.

"Now?"

"Of course. Didn't you come to look?" Everything is going so fast, it takes Lily's breath away. No one gets a job the first time out, in a single day, let alone an apartment.

"Well, I might go look," Lily says, suddenly aware that finding an apartment on this trip means she can move right away from Iowa to Chicago and not worry about staying at a motel or with Ted's parents. She is thrilled at the thought. She leaves her portfolio at the real estate office, and together, she and Millicent go out to discover Chicago.

After four apartments that are either too coldly modern or too dingy to consider, Lily is giving up hope of riding her good luck. Then Millicent says coyly, "The last one I've been rather saving."

And Lily's good luck holds like a Las Vegas winner.

For the building is one of Chicago's finest, a Lake Shore Drive building from the twenties, the lobby a faded gem, the elevators lined in cherry wood and brass. And when the door opens to the apartment, Lily walks into opulence: a ceiling encrusted with floral plasterwork, tall, grand windows. A room that must have been decorated in the twenties and never changed.

There is a celadon green brocade sofa by the fireplace and two comfortable chintz-covered chairs, a semicircular commode made of burled wood with a marble top, and an oxblood red lamp with an enormous tasseled shade. A double bed with a white-and-gilt headboard. On the floor lies a faded but still rather pretty Oriental rug with all the colors in it: the celadon, the oxblood, the shadowed lavender from the flowered chairs. The room is dowdy but still somewhat beautiful. There isn't a piece in it that Lily would have bought. All the upholstered pieces have skirts: There isn't a leg showing, nothing the least bit modern, and yet every piece seems mellow and at home in the sun-washed room. Millicent says the apartment was once the bedroom of a much grander place, maybe a fifteen-room apartment, and that Lily must buy the furniture; that is the drawback. But Lily is already imagining her things here among the old and gracious furniture. She knows it must be hers. And she is even more certain when she goes to the window. The lake is throwing off sparks of sunlight, the boats are gliding by each other with shameless grace, and the light is more beautiful than any light an artist could long for. The kitchen, which once, according to Millicent, was the most ridiculously large closet, is built in with mahogany cupboards that must have been designed for clothes. In fact, as she opens one, she sees an old label that reads: "Woolens."

"How much?" Lily asks.

"You love it, don't you. I just knew you would."

"Can I afford it?"

"Absolutely. Forty-five a month. The only problem is the furniture."

"I don't mind it."

"Really? Well, it's been the sticking point with most everyone. But she only wants five hundred for it all. I mean, it does seem like a lot, but you're getting a lot."

Lily nods. She doesn't have five hundred dollars. It's more than she's ever had. But she knows somehow she can find it. She has to.

"I want the place," Lily says. "I'll have to find the five hundred, of course."

"What kind of job do you have, by the way?"

Lily smiles and, as though she's said it a hundred times, reports squarely, "I'm in advertising."

"Really, well. Maybe you ought to just tell the building you're a secretary. Advertising might be a bit . . . fast for them."

"But I'm not a secretary. I'm an art director."

"Well, you know that, and now I do. But they don't need to," Millicent says. "Tell them you're a secretary."

That night, Lily cannot wait to tell Ted. She has done the impossible: settled her whole life in a single day. The job, the apartment, are almost too good to be true. When Lily was a little girl and her mother had an astonishing bout of luck, she would perform a strange ritual Lily's never forgotten: She would give something away. Usually, it was something she really liked, jewelry or a pretty dress. And she would give it to the most unlikely person—the cleaning lady or the milkman.

"Here," she would say. "I don't need this anymore. I wonder if your wife might want it."

Once, it was a beautiful red dress with white polka dots that Lily had helped her choose just the week before.

"Why did you give it away, Mama?" Lily asked, pained by the loss of the dress she'd fondled and wished had come in a little-girl size. "I thought you loved it." That was a time after Lily's father had left, before Lily's mother had married Jack, and there was little enough money as it was.

"Good luck doesn't just come along," her mother said. "You have to pay for it."

Now Lily looks back and sees that her mother never felt entitled to anything. Not even the pleasure of good luck. Who had made her feel so small and unworthy?

That night, Ted's mother cooks a dinner to celebrate Lily's success: a big ham glazed with brown sugar, spears of broccoli big as fists, potatoes sliced thin into wine cream sauce. They toast Lily and call her lucky. How generous the Nicholsons are. And relaxed. It reflects in everything. The liveliness of the apartment, for instance. Unlike the house where

Lily's mother lived with Jack, a place that always felt perfect and em-balmed, here the chairs are colorful and worn. Books spill from bookcases onto piles on the floor. The rugs are bare in spots and Oriental. And the paintings are avant-garde. Despite the worn feel of the place, Lily knows that the paintings are good: abstract expressionists by names that sound vaguely familiar to her. Her favorite is a Jack Tworkov painting in colors that seem to punch into the room. What a wonderful childhood Ted must have had with parents like these. And yet the only thing that isn't generous and relaxed at the Nicholson house is Ted. Maybe he is what balances them. Their only child, so different from them in every way. Once, Lily, watching the Nicholsons, so happily in love with each other, thought that maybe as a child Ted felt excluded or unable to glean from them the intensity of love that they felt for each other. Maybe that's why he's always such an overachiever, never satisfied he can perform well enough at anything.

And she remembers one more thing. Once, before her mother died, Ted was late getting home, and Edith, Ted's mother, was out grocery shopping, and Ted's father, Hal, insisted she sit down and have a drink with him. Lily felt so grown up, with the ugly-tasting whiskey in her hand, as Hal leaned toward her to share confidences.

"Ted's always been a standoffish kid from the day he was born," Hal said, sipping thoughtfully. "He never tried a new game until he'd watched it played ten times. It's reluctance to make an error. He's terribly hard on himself, a perfectionist. Have you ever witnessed his temper? It's all part of that perfectionism."

And then Ted's father said, with his teasing, understanding, tell-him-anything face, "Edith and I used to joke that Ted was a result of one of those hospital mix-ups. You know, not really ours. We wanted a beatnik for a kid, and we get a Harvard, MIT whiz. Is this irony or what? You, you're the kid we thought we'd get." He laughed and let the ice cubes clatter in his glass. "Don't get me wrong. We love him like you wouldn't believe, but he's interested in things that make us scratch our heads. You know, I never knew Ted had good taste until the day he brought you home. We think the world of you, Lily." The compliment warmed her like a shot of brandy. She's never forgotten it or her longing to be the child they always expected they'd have.

"I'm glad you decided to come stay with us," Edith says now as Lily follows her into the kitchen with a stack of dirty dishes. Ted and his father are back at the table talking, Hal nursing a cigar. "You're always welcome here, and you know you're safe here, kiddo," she says. Lily has always liked her, her crisp red-brown hair, her teenage confidence.

"But I was wondering. You scared to live alone?" Edith asks. "This new apartment you're so excited about?"

"No. I'm sort of living alone now," Lily says.

"But in a rooming house, right?"

"Yes."

"It will be different in an apartment. Lonelier, maybe. Soon enough, I hope, Ted will come to his senses about you, stop trying to make you wait until he's 'made it,' as he calls it, and you won't have to be alone."

She efficiently begins to scrub the dishes with her small-boned red hands.

"I like being alone," Lily says. She scrapes the leftovers into garbage, loving anything she can do to help Ted's mother. "Have you been lobbying to have Ted marry me?"

"Well, and why not? I'd love it if Ted would marry you. You're the best thing he's ever had going. He never had a girlfriend before you. You know he's painfully shy. And listen, he wouldn't be half bad for you, if you ask me. But what do I know? I'm his mother." She takes oranges out of the refrigerator and begins to peel and section them, stirring them into a bowl of chilled litchi nuts. The fruit scents the kitchen, and Lily breathes it in with pleasure.

"I can't help thinking, though," Ted's mother says, looking up from her slicing. "I suppose you'll think this cruel . . . I can't help thinking that this thing with your stepfather's frightened you off men, if you don't mind my saying so. It would frighten any girl. Ted says you don't seem too interested in him right now, not that he's given you much reason, much encouragement, the brat."

"I don't know," Lily says. "It's Ted that doesn't seem too interested in me. The whole thing with my mother. He did run away to Paris, Edith; he told me so. He couldn't deal with it."

Edith shakes her head. "Men can be real cowards," she says.

The phone rings.

"Lily, it's for you," Ted's father calls.

"For me?" Lily says to Edith, "I don't know who knows I'm here." She goes out to the hallway, expectant, trying to guess who might be trying to reach her, but before she even says hello, she knows.

"I want you to come right back here," Jack says in a slurred voice. Oh, God, she thinks. Oh, God.

"Jack . . ."

"You come to Chicago and you waltz in here and—"

"I'm not coming back there, Jack. Not ever." She looks over at the dining room. She's whispering more than talking. Her voice is more hiss than speaking, but she wonders if they can hear her, Ted, at the table, Ted's father and that endless, carefully smoked cigar.

"We have to talk . . ." Again, the childish voice, the plea.

"What do you want, Jack?" Lily sighs, prepared for almost anything.

"Look, I want to see you," he says. "To apologize to you. Look, I didn't have the courage when you were here."

"To apologize?"

"Sometimes, when I drink too much, I know I can get a little out of hand."

"That's a polite way of putting it," Lily says, thinking he is certainly drunk now. She shivers.

"Don't be fresh with me. I'm trying to make amends."

"Can you bring my mother back? That would be making amends."

"I loved Elaine. I loved her, and I took care of her for ten years. You think it was easy? She wasn't easy. Clinging to me, whining, begging all the time. Nothing I did satisfied her. I couldn't love her enough. I couldn't give her enough. Look, I adopted you. I paid for you. I took care of you."

"You call that 'taking care of'?"

"It only happened a few times."

"No. It never happened. I never *let* anything happen." She is whispering so violently, her mouth is vibrating.

"Oh . . . I was never sure—"

"What?"

"I don't remember much. I was never sure if we did it."

"Oh, God," Lily says.

"I was sure that once—I dreamed it, maybe—that I was inside of you. You were so sweet, panting like a little dog."

"Don't ever call me again. Not ever."

"I called to apologize."

"Don't ever call again, Jack."

"You still have my name."

"I'll change it. I've always wanted to change it. I hate your name."

"I'm still legally your father."

"To me you're dead."

"I'll never be dead to you," he says.

Lily hangs up. Her heart is thumping, and the room seems out of focus, Dutch angled. Lily turns her face to the wall, making every effort not to cry.

"Now I've paid for my good luck," she tells herself bitterly. "Wouldn't my mother be happy? It's all paid off."

Ted's mother comes out to the hall, wiping her hands on a kitchen towel.

"What's going on?" she asks. "You okay?"

"It was him. It was Jack."

"The bastard, why doesn't he leave you alone?" Edith puts a hand on Lily's shoulder. Such a patient hand, such an understanding hand.

"He says the most horrible things. As though he knows just how to get to me."

"Obviously he does. Come here," Edith says. "Come on." And she draws Lily down the hall into the Nicholsons' bedroom and closes the door.

"You're still letting it eat you up, aren't you? What that bastard did to you."

"Nothing really happened," Lily is almost too quick to say. "I didn't let anything happen." The whole thing sickens her.

"Just the fact that he approached you . . . Now, stop looking so pale. Good Lord. Do you think anyone blames you for that?"

Lily nods, finds tears in her eyes. "I blame myself. Maybe even Ted blames me," she says suddenly.

"There, sweetie, my God." Ted's mother comes over and hugs her. Lily feels the knot of the dishcloth against her back and Edith's thin arms, and she finds herself sobbing. She cannot imagine why she would do this in front of Ted's mother. But it feels so good. So needed. Edith pats her back, helps her sit down.

"There, there," she says. "You're in good hands here." Lily looks around the bedroom. The colors are dark and warm and almost Christmasy. A cranberry-colored bedspread, evergreen curtains splashed with dark red berries. A rug the color of wine. There is such peace and fidelity here. Nothing for show. All for comfort and warmth. Why couldn't she have been born into this family, sitting here with her mother, talking, the way mothers and daughters are supposed to?

"Do you miss your mother?" Edith says.

"Yes," Lily says hesitantly.

"Look. I want you to know something. I never told another living soul, and I'll never tell another after you, and if those guys out there try to come in here, I'll stop right in the middle of my story . . . but I want to tell you this. I think it will help." Lily looks up at her and sees her face distort with a story she doesn't want to tell. "Men are pretty slimy characters, believe me. I ought to know."

"Why?" Lily asks.

"I couldn't tell you this when you came to stay with us . . . when your mother died. I didn't think sharing this would help you then. You were so confused, and it was so painful. You didn't need to hear about anybody else's pain. But, Lily, I had an uncle who acted just like your stepfather. Only I was just twelve years old. And my mother washed my mouth out with soap when I told her."

"Did he—"

Ted's mother grips her arm. "Many more times than once," she says. "And it took me a long time to realize it wasn't my fault. Now don't you ever tell anyone this. Especially Ted. I'm telling you this to help you."

"I never would," Lily says, out of breath, shocked.

"You can't let him make you feel you're to blame. You can't make yourself feel that way. You'll sink like a stone if you do. I nearly did. Until I met Hal, I spent half my life drowning because of something that wasn't my fault at all."

"It's not my fault . . . ?" Lily says, tasting these new words.

"You can put it behind you," Edith says. "You're going to. A lot of women couldn't. But I think you can. I know you can. I believe in you." Lily rests her face against Edith's breast and closes her eyes, and wishes she could stay there forever.

Late that night, when Lily thinks everyone in the house is asleep, as she packs in the living room, Ted comes quietly in and sits in the armchair by the fireplace.

"I'm glad you agreed to come stay here," he says.

"Thank you. It made it so much better for me. I would give everything to have parents like yours."

"Yeah, they're okay," Ted says. He comes over to her and, gently touching her elbows, says, "Don't give up on me, Lily."

"I don't even know what to think about us," Lily says, turning to him. "Every time I think about you and me, I feel hopeless, somehow."

"I know," Ted says. "Right before your mother died, I felt closer to you then, you know?"

"Yes."

"I was able to let you in somehow. It could be like that again."

"I want to get settled in Chicago," Lily says. "I don't want to be committed to anyone but myself for a while."

"I know. Me, too. But will you see me sometimes?"

"Sure," she says. "You're the only person in the world who knows all about me. Even if it's something you can't live with."

"I can live with it now."

"I'd better get to bed," Lily says.

Ted draws her forward and kisses her. Lily wishes she had the courage to seduce him. She has never felt so much need to be close to someone, especially now, to Ted, to be drawn together as they have never been.

When he's gone to bed, she lies on the sofa and thinks about the apartment she saw today. There she can create a life for herself that will shelter her, that will perhaps feel a little the way this apartment feels, even if nothing happens between Ted and her. And then she thinks of the $500 she must raise. How will she do it? The sofa is so deep, it's hard to toss, to turn on it, and yet she feels restless. She wants her life to be settled.

And then she pictures her solution like a line drawing in a dictionary: the emerald ring. The ring her mother loved but she always hated. She will sell it. In the end, it will be like a gift from her mother: the apartment she wants, the life she will soon lead.

In the dark, she thinks triumphantly of her solution and wishes she had thought of it at the dinner table, where she could have shared it with Ted's family. They would have toasted her and laughed at the irony of the solution. How she wishes she could love Ted again and make this family her own.

And just as she is thinking this, closing her eyes, she feels a presence by the sofa, and she sits up with a start.

"Shh," Ted says, gently settling her back. "It's okay. It's me." He kneels down beside the sofa and kisses her tenderly, longingly, then rests his head on the sofa beside her.

"Ted . . ."

"Don't give up on me, Lily," he says. She takes him into her arms, takes the weight of his long, fine body on top of her. His kisses are sweet and deep. In a moment, through his thin robe, she can feel his erection. Just as she is about to ask for more, to touch him in all the places she has never touched him, he gets up. Even in the silhouette of the hall light, he looks sheepish, embarrassed.

"Good night," he says, drawing his robe about himself, and starts toward his room. His shadow flickers across the couch where she lays. A shiver of longing grips her.

"Don't go to bed yet," she says.

"Yes," he says. "I think I'd better." He takes his hand and, drawing it to his lips, he blows her a kiss.

Chapter Six

Andres Pulaski, knowing that this is the first morning of the last week of school, can hardly get out of bed. He hears his wife and children dressing in their rooms, talking. He hears the beat of their feet on the stairs, the clink of their cereal spoons, and their shared laughter. Each day, he feels more distant from all of them. Sometimes, his sons do not seem to have come from him at all. They are sturdy blond giants who resemble only their mother. Even as small babies, they were not the tiny, vulnerable infants he craved. They were huge, slobbering, and demanding and totally attached to their mother's breasts.

"Andres, you'd better get going," his wife calls to him. Her voice is young and chimelike, though with the babies and time, she has grown soft and slow and broad-hipped, and age has strung a net of lines around her dark eyes.

As he dresses, he focuses on what has been tormenting him these last few weeks: Lily Beach is leaving. She has grown warmer to him, and sometimes after class, she will join him for coffee. And once she even let him hold her hand a minute while he talked to her. The touch

of her hand scalded him, stays with him. If that alone seemed thrilling
. . . But he won't allow himself to think further.

Lily is excited about her future in Chicago, talks, it seems, of nothing
else. His longing for her has transformed into a desire to be whatever
she needs him to be, and now it is a friend, a sounding board, even a
father. Each night, he goes to bed, full of thoughts of her. At least now
that she acknowledges him, he's sleeping. But she has bewitched him,
left him feeling as though some terrible itch will never be scratched, and
he doesn't even mind. It is a feeling of helplessness he has not experi-
enced since his last days in Paraguay.

His wife has noticed, said she wondered if he even knew she was
alive anymore, cried in his arms more than one night over his lack of
attention to her. He has even begun to think he will leave his wife. He
feels that in his life with his family he is only going through the motions,
has for years, really. But there is nothing to leave for; Lily would never
in any way take him in, will never, he knows, love him. Still, her
incandescence has spoiled him, and no one can take away or quench his
need for that life-eating quality that is hers alone.

The first business Lily must accomplish back in Iowa City is to sell the
emerald ring. She has looked through the yellow pages, asked lots of people,
including local jewelers, professors, acquaintances, and has decided to take
it to a well-respected jeweler in West Branch, a town of farms, grain
elevators, and silos. The man's jewelry store is an extension of his house:
a little box of a place. Chickens peck at the gravel out front. A tinny radio
is playing old songs as the taxi drives up: the McGuire Sisters, maybe. The
taxi driver has reluctantly agreed to wait for her. He pulls out a textbook
about Nietzsche and puts his feet up on the seat beside him.

A bell tingles as Lily enters the shop, and in a moment, a man pulls
aside some old bark-cloth curtains with palm fronds on them and joins
her, a sandwich in his hand.

"Yes?"

"I have a ring to sell you," she says. "For the right price."

"Everyone wants the right price," the jeweler says.

Lily pulls the black jewel box from her jacket pocket. As the jeweler
opens it, it creaks.

"Well," he says without emotion. "What do you want for it?"

"You tell me." Please make it five hundred, she says to herself.

He pulls a jeweler's loupe from his vest pocket and squints his eye around it, then retires behind the curtain, to see it, Lily imagines, in a better light.

"I don't deal with jewelry like this much," he says. "Not much call for it."

"I'll take it to someone else," Lily says.

"Now hold on. I didn't say that."

"So what will you give me for it?"

"I can't give you more than five thousand dollars. I don't have it."

Lily tries not to show the shock of his amount. She swallows. "Oh," she says, stalling, wondering how to respond.

"Okay. Sixty-five hundred. It's a fine piece. Tiffany. But no more. I don't have it."

Lily looks at him. She never looked inside. Never guessed it was from Tiffany's. Her face must look blank. She feels staggered by her good fortune. She presses her lips together and reaches for the ring, really to see if she can read inside the band, but the man grabs for it.

"Eighty-five hundred dollars," the man says. "That's it. Absolutely my last offer."

"Okay," Lily says. She is truly rich. She cannot believe it. Eighty-five hundred dollars is two years' salary compared to what she will make in her new job. She can bank it, invest it, know it is there when she most needs it. She feels safe, finally cushioned. Air streams into her lungs as the man snaps the box and closes his hand around it, looking as though he's just got himself a bargain.

"Thank you," she says as he hands her a check.

"The check's good," he says. "I stand by my word."

"I believe you," Lily says.

Directly from West Branch, she asks the driver to take her to the bank. She'll be transferring her account to Chicago soon, but at least in the bank this piece of paper will be safe. Her freedom is assured.

"Thank you, Mother," she says in the dark that night. "Thank you."

That night, Lily finds a letter from Will. Again, she is reluctant to open it. Why do her feelings for him always have to be tainted with doubt?

The note says in a rushed hand:

I'm thinking of leaving Sandra. Please let me know where you'll be after graduation. If I find the courage to leave her, I will cross the globe to find you.

Lily thinks she will not send him her address. After the safety of Ted and his family, the wildness of her feeling for Will discomfits her. She cannot think of Will without wanting to close her eyes, for the thought of him still breaks her heart.

Having passed up graduation ceremonies—there is no one she wants to invite—Lily's last night in Iowa City will fall on a Thursday. Andres Pulaski leaves an ink-smeared note in her graduate mailbox saying that she must spend this last evening having dinner with him at a restaurant Lily knows is the most beautiful, expensive place in town.

"Won't your wife mind?" she asks him after class on Wednesday.

"She won't mind if she won't know," he says.

"You're not worried she'll find out?"

"If I'm not worried, why should Lily Beach be?" he asks with rhetorical grace.

When he picks her up in his white Ford, Lily feels embarrassed by his courtliness, his sense of expectation. He is wearing his nicest suit, a gray flannel that's far too heavy for the weather or the season. His shirt is crisply starched, and Lily can see that the collar is already darkening with perspiration.

"Take your jacket off," she tells him.

"No, no," he says. The car is not new, smells of his children—an unmistakable aura of peanut butter and jelly. Just this afternoon, maybe one of his sons ate his lunch here. Along the ledge by the back window are a pair of child-size black high-top sneakers, a red toy truck, and what looks like a rolled-up kite.

When Lily turns back to him, after observation, she sees he is looking at her, glancing only occasionally at the road. "My Christ! You are beautiful," he finally says. She smooths the folds of her candy-pink taffeta dress, happy that it pleases him.

The restaurant is nearly empty, for it is a Thursday night, and the place is really too expensive for Iowa City. The waitresses lean against the walls, nearly one per table. Lily is mortified that their waitress turns out to be a girl in the art department, though Lily doesn't know her name.

"Professor Pulaski," she says, handing them each a menu, sounding truly thrilled to have drawn a patron she knows. She nods at Lily suspiciously.

"Oh, no," Lily says as soon as she is gone. "Maybe we should go."

"And why should we?" he asks. "I am a professor taking my prized student out for dinner of cele—"

"Celebration?" Lily offers.

"Yes, that. Please, now. Let us order drinks. Let us celebrate."

When the student/waitress comes back, Andres orders champagne, and the waitress's eyes glaze. Lily thinks she is formulating her story to the other art students. It isn't until the second glass of champagne that Lily realizes it no longer matters. She will probably never see any of these people again. If they label her fast, if they find another word for her that satisfies their need to scorn people who do more publicly what they themselves do in fearful silence, then it won't matter at all. This insight gives her a rousing taste of freedom. Another glass of champagne and the roast beef tastes astonishingly delicious. Andres Pulaski is more charming and funny than she would have imagined. His tortured English begins to sound normal to her, even pleasant. When the dessert is cleared, she finds herself disappointed and allows Andres to pour her a fourth glass of champagne.

"Lovely companion," he says to her. "Your face will be found in every print I do."

"Thank you," she says, blushing, warming to him.

He pays the bill, and he takes her hand. In the car, before he drives, he smooths her hair under his large, kind fingers, and for a moment those fingers just brush her neck, sending a sensation down her spine.

They do not speak all the way back to her rooming house, but the car seems thick with feeling, almost as though, she thinks, there is no room for air. He parks, and without asking her, he walks her up to her room, lets her open the door, and comes in behind her. When she turns to him, she expects him to kiss her—and why shouldn't she let him? She has slept with no one in over a year. There is no certainty that Ted will ever open up and let her be a part of his life. And this man has finally managed to tap in her a liquid, willing desire she never knew she could have for him. Maybe it's the champagne. But maybe it is just him. Instead, he smiles, shakes his head, and kisses her on the forehead.

"You want me, do you?" he asks.

She does not speak, her eyes burn, and she feels the heat of her drunkenness.

"Well, I surprise myself," he says. "For I care too much to be—what is this word?—casual with you."

She is too astonished and too drunk to realize his English is perfect.

"Moreover," he says, "I respect you too much to make you hate me later." He pulls her to him and kisses her with a passion that will later wake her in the night. And then he leaves.

Andres Pulaski parks the car a half block from his house on Summit Street. It is going to rain soon, and branches whip in front of the streetlight, throwing shadows on the big Gothic houses. He is shaking so, his hands can find no stillness, and his stomach feels just as it did when, as a refugee from Paraguay, having spent months in the gay safety of Buenos Aires, he left in 1954 to sail up through a roiling October Atlantic to an unknown America.

He has just turned down what he has most longed for. And for what? Because he is too cautious? Or perhaps from utter terror? But no. Tonight he saw in Lily's eyes what he always sensed about her, something so raw and painful, something so accustomed to hurt, it seemed ineffably cruel to have gone further. Despite her longing, despite her encouragement.

He can hardly believe he found the character in himself to turn her down. For he knows, clearly, that it would have taken no extra effort to bed Lily Beach tonight. How easy it would have been to kiss and undress her, to slide into her wet desire with all the longing of this past year, to breathe in the crisp perfume of her once-reluctant longing, in the tuck of her neck, in the curve of her breasts. And then, how clearly he can see it, turning her over, entering her from behind, rubbing the growing nub of her clitoris, feeling her buck, then lose certainty, and then be overwhelmed by her own excitement. Instead, he sits, masturbating in the mildewed dark, throwing his head back as semen splashes on the dashboard of the family Ford.

PART TWO

Chicago

Chapter Seven

This is what Lily has been waiting for. It seems that within a few weeks of moving to Chicago, each day unfolds so exhilaratingly, Lily feels as though light has flooded her life, and she reflects back to see the last two years as dark and airless. Each night, the apartment makes her feel like a palace guest. Its faded grandeur has so much personality, she can't help but consider that the room is only grudgingly allowing her to disrupt it, only impatiently letting her assert her own personality. She has hung some of her prints on the wall and bought a bedspread that matches the old drapes. She loves sleeping in the double bed. How decadent it is to be able to stretch out in all directions and touch no edges. She wonders what people will think when they see it. Single women aren't supposed to have double beds. Not if they don't want to give the wrong impression. If only she'd had it all those uncomfortable nights, trying to share the bed with Will. She thinks of Will but still doesn't send her address. She is too happy to bring the sad complication of him into her life.

Lily is enthralled with Chicago—the traffic, the lights, the stores, the smell of Lake Michigan, and the feel of the lake in the air, cool fogs that burn off by noon.

But the job tops it all. It feels so perfectly right, so exciting. And it is the job that gives her the independence she's craved. Working in the mount room is hardly prestigious. But there she can see and learn everything that goes on in the office. With staples, a huge can of rubber cement, and an oilcan of Bestine, she mounts the watercolored layouts and any other thing they give her. Her day combines the sharp smells of the rubber cement and Bestine with the innocence of baby powder, which all the art directors sprinkle on their wet layouts to dry them before they hand them to her.

The men's faces begin to attach themselves to names and personalities. Joe Forrest ushers new people in to be introduced to her two or three times a day, as though she is the dignitary that must be courted. She hears over the mount-room wall (where there is a two-foot opening up to the ceiling) the men congratulating Joe Forrest for having hired her.

"Adding a little beauty to this place, Joe. Good idea"

"Thank God Sammy got promoted. This one's a peach."

She learns that the only other woman in the art department (besides secretaries and art buyers) is named Joy Grey, the sour-faced woman in the coral smock she remembers Joe Forrest talking about. "Killjoy," the men call her behind her back. When Joy comes in one day with a layout to be mounted, Lily tries to talk to her.

"Lots of wolves around here, huh?" Lily asks, hoping for a sense of camaraderie.

"Yeah. If you're always putting out bait like you do, they come around."

After that, not a word passes between them. Not even a thank-you when Joy picks up her mounted layouts. But Joy is just about the only sour thing about Faber, Lowe and Barton. Well, that and one other thing: Joe Forrest is drunk every afternoon. Everyone knows it. Everyone avoids him or tolerates him. And he is sloppy, loud, embarrassing.

"Hey there, Lily," he calls in to the mount room. "Mount some for me, will you, darlin'?"

She feels sad for him, and confused. How do you help someone who is perfectly happy being a fool? In the morning, no matter what he was like the afternoon before, he is pleasant, efficient, special. Lily notices that he has framed her print. It looks beautiful in the mat and frame he chose. He has beautiful taste in everything—his clothes, the things in his office—and his layouts, even if they are for tractors, are terrific. Everyone knows. But everyone also knows he is a hopeless drunk.

The other men, who once seemed like a pack of wolves, seem less so once Lily gets to know them. They show her pictures of their children and shirtwaisted wives in Highland Park and Hinsdale. They call her "Hi-Lily-Hi-Lo." They bring her sugary doughnuts from the canteen, like love notes.

Each Saturday night at eight o'clock, she sees Ted. She is disappointed. She had thought that now there might be passion, now there might be a new feeling between them, but her proximity has made him suddenly nervous and standoffish again. They go to dinner, and there are long silences. At the door, he always kisses her efficiently.

"I'm putting every ounce of energy I have to make a place for myself at my job," he tells her.

"I can see that," she says angrily. But he doesn't hear the anger, must not want to.

One night, she asks him in for a drink, and he says no, he's going to work in the morning, even though it's a Saturday. And she says to him, "You know the night I slept at your house, the night you came in and kissed me? I liked that. I've thought a lot about that night."

He visibly blushes. "Yeah," he says, "I know." And the subject is closed.

She would think he can barely tolerate her, except that once in a while there is an odd flair of passion, or a peek at the feelings he has for her. Once, a car runs a red light as they are crossing the street, Lily lagging behind as she fools with a slipping sandal strap, and when the convertible almost hits her, Ted drags her aside just in time. At the curb, Ted holds her, rocking her with his feelings of her preciousness, murmuring her name. But an hour later, he is, once more, detached, talking only of his job, kissing her neatly, coolly, at the door. Lily is thinking she must meet someone else. Her longing for sex haunts her. It has been so long, and her taste for it just won't go away. But she feels cheated. She still wants to be a part of Ted's family. She still remembers Edith's admission, her kindness; Hal's saying she was the child they always wanted; and again and again, the night Ted lay on top of her in the dark and wanted her.

Each Sunday morning, Lily shops at the A & P and afterward sits with her groceries a few minutes in the play park at Astor and Goethe. All around her is the city: the art deco buildings, with their sleek lines, the Gold Coast children in their too pretty clothes: bonnets and bow ties and patent leather shoes, acting as wild and out of control as any children. Lily sits there, her brown paper bags overstuffed with lettuce and pork chops and Sugar Smacks and coffee, and she feels swellingly proud, for somehow she is able to afford to be here in the big city, buy her groceries, pay her rent and electricity. All by herself.

Lily has thought a lot about Professor Pulaski since the night she last saw him. She remembers how much she had actually come to want him by the end of the evening. And how his denying her only spurred on her desire, so that the next morning, before the movers (two college guys with a rickety yellow van) came, she considered calling him to come over. She didn't, of course. She could never have risked speaking to his wife. Couldn't even have risked the rejection if he'd said no again. She is touched, though, by his saying no because he "respected her too much." She never imagined the formidable Pulaski capable of such concern or care. There are few men in the world she considers capable of that.

She writes him a letter, telling him all about Chicago and the excitement she feels, about how hard it is to buckle down to her art. Her detachment from what has sustained her in the past year—her prints, her drawings—is frightening to her. She asks, was he ever so enamored with a new situation that his art took second place in his life?

In less than a week, he writes back a letter equally open, and kind, telling her of the time he first fell in love and how guilty he felt for not working on what he knew must matter to him most. He tells Lily that without her in Iowa City there is a painful emptiness that makes him more creative and much less happy. Why, he asks, must there be this trade-off? Happiness or art. What man in his right mind wouldn't choose happiness? he asks.

An art director at work asks Lily out, and she is excited. He is handsome and slick and funny. She wears her prettiest dress, a ribbon in her hair. They see *West Side Story* and afterward have dinner at a restaurant named La Coquette, where a dark man in a red vest plays violent love songs on the accordion. The art director, Greg, leans over the table to her.

"You and I have to get to know each other. I haven't been the same since I met you." She is flattered and embarrassed by his overzealousness. In a few minutes, she finds him working his hand up her knee and slaps it away. He shuts up like a Venus flytrap, takes her home, acting so bored, she realizes that he has no interest in her—he only wanted to sleep with her. Once, she would have done it. She would have been wild with him, spilling her anger with every flash of movement, every gesture. It makes her realize how much she's changed. And besides, she knows if she sleeps with him, the news will be all over the halls of Faber, Lowe and Barton come Monday morning. So she does what "nice" girls are supposed to do. Later, in bed, she thinks of Will and misses him for the first time in a month.

Jack calls. He's been drinking, she can tell. There is that dark scotch scratch to his voice and a looseness of pronunciation that makes her heart thump with unspoken fear.

"Just calling to see if you're all settled," he says.

"How did you find me?" she asks.

"The nice Bell Telephone operator. I think I should see where you live. You're still my responsibility."

"I stopped being your responsibility when I turned twenty-one."

"I want to see where you live."

"If you step foot in this building, I'll have you thrown out," Lily says. "I don't owe you anything. I don't need to ever see you again."

She thinks of what Edith said: She can put it all behind her. She can. Edith believes in her.

"I'm just so lonely, Lily," he says, his voice suddenly totally different, so childlike, it chills her. "You're the only family I have left. When I turn over in bed, I still think Elaine will be there."

"I'm sorry for you, Jack," Lily says, and feels the helplessness she's felt so many times overtake her, socking the breath out of her lungs. "But I can't do anything for you."

"We did her in, Lily. You and I did her in," Jack says. Unable to say anything, Lily hangs up and cries all night, only soothed finally by the sound of the waves.

Lily paints her room the color of the inside of a conch shell, not beige, not rose, but somewhere between the two, and all the moldings ivory. The paint seems to scoop up the lake light, enhance the "beachiness" of the room, make her feel as though she is sleeping in some sandy place.

One month after arriving in Chicago, Lily makes her first girlfriend in years. It is an unbearably hot day, hotter than it usually gets in August, people say. And the mount room, where there are no windows and little air circulation (despite the space between the top of the walls and the ceiling), gets so thick with the smell of chemicals, baby powder, and humidity that Lily has to take a break in the ladies' room, where, curiously enough, there is a window. She opens it and leans out into the not-much-cooler June air. But whatever air does stir cools off her soaked blouse and the waistband of her skirt, where the perspiration has run.

"Don't do it," a voice says. "Don't jump."

Lily shivers at the words, then turns to see a young woman, not much older than herself, standing bemused, in a blue-red Gypsy dress, just the color of the lipstick the woman is applying in front of the mirror. The woman is enormously tall. Maybe even six feet, and her dark, glossy hair is pulled back severely from her face into a high ponytail that hangs to her waist in a perfect braid.

"Don't you think they'd put air-conditioning in this place or something? I hear NW Ayre's got air-conditioning. I see people going to work there wearing sweaters."

"I guess it's too expensive to install," Lily says, not sure how to join what seems to be a monologue.

"Oh, come on! If this place isn't rolling in dough these days, I don't know what is."

The woman takes out a cigarette and lights it expertly, as though she's been smoking since she was ten. Lily notes that her fingernails are slickly polished a dull red and that even her toes, peeking through the toe guard of her stocking as she rubs her foot, are polished the same red.

"How long have you been working here?" the woman asks, blowing out a plume of smoke. "I don't think I've seen you before."

"Since the end of May."

"Who do you work for?"

"Everybody. I'm in the mount room."

"No kidding! Wow! You going to be an art director?"

"I hope so."

"Good for you."

"What about you?"

"I'm a secretary in the copy department. Though, frankly, half the time I make suggestions on the copy. Lately, my boss has been giving me assignments. Last week I wrote copy for a bourbon ad. That was easy. But, I mean, really. I have a B.A. I don't see why they won't let me write more."

"Have you asked to be promoted?"

"Oh, listen. They say, 'Why's a gal like you interested in doing this stuff, anyway? You'll probably just leave and have babies, anyway. Why should we bother to train you?' My name is Claire Guthrie, by the way, in case you keep a Rolodex. You think I'm dressed too wild?"

Lily introduces herself and tells Claire she likes the dress, though she knows she'd never even consider wearing a dress like that to work.

Later in the day, Claire pokes her head into the mount room while one of the wolves is hanging out, waiting for his layout to be mounted.

"That skirt really shows off your curves," the wolf is saying to Lily as Claire comes in.

"Why, thank you," Claire says in a mincing voice, as though the comment were made to her. The wolf puts his arm around Claire's shoulder, which is perfectly equal in height to his shoulder, and pulls her to him in a very familiar way.

"Quit flirting with the employees," she says to him.

"I'll pick up that layout later," he says to Lily. On his way out, Claire jumps, and Lily can tell he's pinched her.

"You know him?" Lily asks.

"Rich Hardy? Yes. Biblically."

Lily swivels around to look at her. Claire's face is as smooth and straight and untroubled as a child's.

"Did you mean what I think you did?"

"Yes. We went out for a while. He's too silly for me, though. Nice guy and all. About as serious as a banana peel."

"You slept with him?" Lily asks in a hushed voice.

"Yes. You're not like a nun or anything, are you? Tell me now and save me the lecture."

"No. There's nothing nunlike about me," Lily says with intense relief. To be even bragging about her sexuality to another woman! She can hardly believe it. Someone else who likes sex, too, and isn't afraid to be open.

"I'll tell you a secret," Claire says. "I don't even know why I should tell you. I don't know the first thing about you, but I think it's okay. Listen. Wait, come closer," and then, sotto voce: "I'm seeing Wally Payson."

"Really?" Wally Payson is the creative director. Lily has never met him, only heard people in the mount room telling her to hurry up and mount their ads because Wally Payson's asked to see them. "Isn't he . . . I mean . . ."

"Yes. He's married. You're not the type to gasp or anything, are you?" Claire asks.

"No. I once was close to someone married," Lily whispers. She thinks of Will, realizes she's never really considered him married. It's Professor Pulaski who really fits the description. If he hadn't put her off that night, surely she would have slept with him.

"Are you in love with Mr. Payson?" Lily asks, realizing the absurdity of referring to him so formally.

Claire shrugs. "Power is an aphrodisiac," she says coolly.

"What?"

"Aphrodisiac," she says. "You know, like a love potion. Something that makes you want to make love."

"I guess I never needed one." Lily smiles.

"I think I'm going to like you," Claire says.

The next day, Claire comes into the mount room with a brown paper bag. "Look what I bought Wally," she says, pulling out a pair of white boxer shorts with dogs and fire hydrants printed on them.

"Will he like it?" Lily asks, horrified.

"Are you kidding? He's about as 'stiff upper lip' as they come. I'm just trying to loosen him up. "You know how I said Rich Hardy isn't serious enough? Wally is half-dead. I consider it a challenge, though. I guarantee in a week he'll be wearing them. Maybe he'll just put them on before I see him, or something, but he'll be wearing them, with a hard-on like a fire hydrant."

Lily is amused by Claire and relieved by her friendship. She has felt lonely and isolated so long. But what attracts her most to Claire, whom, with a clear eye, she might consider crass or a lunatic, is that Claire is no victim. Not in any way. For so long Lily has shied away from women who, like her mother, cannot distinguish between what they want and what someone wants them to want.

It is nearly midnight on a Saturday night. Ted dropped her off at eleven, and she is just into her sleep, into the sliding-down moment where cogent thoughts lose their form, when the phone rings.

Lily can hardly believe it: It is Will.

"How did you find my number?" she asks him, groggy, lazy with the relaxation she's just lost.

"There's only one L. Beach in Chicago. It wasn't much of a risk. Lily, I'm here. I'm in Chicago."

"What are you doing here?"

"I'm here to see you."

She is silent for a moment. "I don't understand," she says finally.

"I just thought if I came here, you'd have to see me. I left Sandra. Two weeks ago. I thought to call first, but I was afraid you'd say you didn't want to see me."

"You really left her?"

"Trial separation. So can I come? I have the address here."

"It's late. I'm in bed."

"Even better. I have nowhere to stay."

"My doorman will wonder."

"I'll say I'm your cousin Will."

"I don't have food for breakfast. I shop on Saturdays."

"I just want to see you."

She is silent again. She thinks back to how much she's felt for him over time and how much pain he's caused her by being wishy-washy, guilty, hateful.

"Okay," she says, not convinced, worried, but anxious to touch the pearliness of his skin, see his sweet, pouty mouth again, hold him close in her big, decadent bed. To feel him inside her. "Where are you?"

"On the corner."

"Didn't you even consider that I might have someone else, might be with someone else?"

"Are you?"

"No."

"Well, no, I didn't. And I guess I was right."

It isn't two minutes before the bell rings. In that time, she has managed to brush her teeth, smooth her hair into a headband, and put on rouge, lipstick, and her diaphragm.

When she sees him, it is a shock. In her mind, she has seen him many times in these past few months. But she's never had a picture of him, has only imagined him hazily. She remembers better how he felt than how he looked. He seems suddenly to have grown up. He is less like a boy now and more like a man; his curly blond hair cropped, his milky green sweater stretched over bigger, more developed muscles.

"What did my doorman say?" she asks.

"Do you care?" He is only halfway into the room before he kisses her. She draws him in from the hall, worried about her neighbors, that they might see her in her nightgown, that any infraction might make her lose her glorious place. He looks around the room and whistles.

"They must be paying you big bucks," he says.

"Hardly anything. I got a good deal."

"I'll say. Do you think two can live here?"

She says nothing. Getting no response, he shrugs, goes to the window. There is a cluster of lights on the lake, boats bobbing. Music, waves, and traffic come up from below. It is the middle of July. The breeze blows in like air-conditioning to cool what's been a sticky, hot day.

"You don't want me here," Will says.

"I didn't say that. I let you come up even though it's after midnight."

"You don't want me living here."

She says nothing.

"I thought you'd let me come live with you."

"Why? Why did you think that? Live together without being married . . ."

She feels angry at his assumption but sweet toward him. He sits down next to her on the bed, shrugging his shoulders in plain defeat. The sheets are still rumpled, the one thing she wasn't able to fix before he came up. He runs his hands through them.

"This bed smells of you. I've missed that smell." He grabs a fistful of sheet and pulls it to his face as though he is smelling a bouquet. "I've been through hell," he says.

"Have you?"

"I can't tell you now. But could I tell you in the morning? You will let me spend the night, won't you. Just tonight, at least tonight?"

She reaches for him and feels these new, baffling muscles in his arms. His kiss is direct and needy, so different from what it has been the last few times. He unbuttons, pulls her nightgown down and off her, and stares at her body for a long time, not even touching, as though he is drinking in each shape and color, and then he touches tentatively, not to give her pleasure yet but to explore, to know again. There is such tenderness in his touch it breaks her heart, melts her.

She begins to cry.

"Now, now," he says. "I'm here. I'm here." The relief is palpable, having him here with her, finally wanting her without regret. "I've been gone, but I'm here."

She makes him take off his sweater, his shirt, his slacks. His body is new to her, so different.

"What is it?" he asks.

"You never looked like this."

"I've been lifting weights," he says. His muscles are thick and smooth. When they kiss, she sees his eyes close. He seems so vulnerable, so young.

His desire for her is the old desire. His penis is so hard, so delicious in her fingers. When it slides into her, it brings her so much pleasure, she winces, knowing it can't last. The rhythm comes back to them, the breathing, the neediness. All their acrobatics, experimentation, variations, are nothing compared to this time. As she feels herself tightening right before climax, she feels him growing. Simultaneously, their voices rise. Later, deep in the night, when even Lake Shore Drive is silent, he says, "Oh, Lily, God, I need to tell you. I love you."

And so she takes Will in. She calls Ted at work to tell him she just can't see him for a while. She needs time alone. He is silent, incurious, but his voice is sad.

"Are you sure?" he asks.

"I'm sure," she says.

"I know I haven't been very good company."

"It's not just that," she says.

But he seems not to hear. "When I'm more settled, more able to give myself to you . . . you know . . . I'll call you," he says. She is blue for a long time after she hangs up. She doesn't know why she still feels tied to him, why she still cares.

Will says he can just stay until August, when he has to return to Missouri to teach the fall semester at the high school. But at least they have the rest of the summer together: the boats on the lake outside her window, picnics on Oak Street Beach, tickets to the Chicago Symphony, to movies, to plays. Will has nothing to do all day while Lily works, so he reads the paper; he knows everything that's going on in the city. He takes her to a folk club called the SeeHear, where they drink sixty-cent coffee and hear a woman named Jean Ritchie sing such sad, old folk tunes, Lily says they need to add extra sugar to their coffee to keep them from crying. They sip bourbon at jazz clubs on Rush Street and eat three-inch steaks at the London House. And they spend evenings at home with books and talk and the lake view and the increasingly good quiet between them which means, as they read or dress or touch, that there is an understanding that needs no words.

To her doorman, he is her cousin. She complains about him.

"Sometimes I think he'll never leave," she says. "But he's like a brother to me."

In the elevator, she says, "Oh, Mrs. Ritterhoff, this is my cousin Will."

When he makes love to her, he says, "Just two cousins getting to know each other." Or, "Here comes your lecherous cousin Will, watch out."

It's almost two weeks before he will tell her about Sandra.

"It's like I've been disemboweled or something," he finally says one night as they lie in bed. All his mood of joyfulness is suddenly drained from him. Yellow traffic ghosts transverse the ceiling, and he is lying far away from her in bed, hugging the edge like a little boy. "I'm almost numb from everything."

"How could it happen? You loved her."

"There was no feeling between us from the start."

"You said you loved her. You always said you loved her."

"No." Will shakes his head. "I loved what I thought she was. She was the person I thought I should marry. Do you know what I'm saying?"

"No."

"She was cute, popular, blond, white, Anglo-Saxon nice. Do you remember—I think of this often—do you remember when we first met, I said something about how 'nice' was a boring word? How it meant boring. And I said, 'My fiancée is nice,' and you said, 'Your fiancée is boring'?"

"Yes. Sort of."

Will moves closer, puts his arm around Lily. "I'm doing pretty well, don't you think? You have no idea what a mess I was before I came out here to see you. She still loves me, or at least says she does. So when I told her I was leaving, she cried every night. She threatened to kill herself. She threatened to kill me."

"But what I don't get," Lily says, "is why there wasn't any feeling between you."

"She hated sex. She hated me touching her. That was it partly. Don't you see why I was angry with you?"

"No. Why should you have been angry with me?"

"Because until you came along, I wasn't so clear on what I was missing. I thought all women were like that: reticent, shy, uninterested, queasy."

"Have you been doing any art?"

"Art?"

"Prints, drawing?"

"No. Not for a long time. Have you?"

"Not since I moved to Chicago."

"Do you think we'll just let that part of us disappear, not get used?"

"I teach art."

"It's not the same. You think life just eats you up in the end?" Lily asks in the dark, feeling suddenly afraid and very alone. "I mean, you think you're going to lead this lovely life. Love, art, fun, happiness. In the end, your dreams are all shifted around. All you really want to do is make it through the next day."

"But you like life here, don't you?"

"Yes," Lily says. "I just see people older than me, and that's the way they seem." And she thinks of her mother and Joe Forrest.

"We won't be like that," Will says. "We'll never be like that."

Lily's told Claire that Will is staying with her, and Claire is thrilled.

"Are you going to marry him?" she asks as they eat lunch one day outside the office—a steam-table place on Wabash Avenue that costs $1.65 no matter what you eat.

"I don't think so," Lily says. "I mean, we haven't even discussed it."

"But you love him," Claire says, slapping her fork into the watery mashed potatoes.

"That doesn't mean I have to marry him. Would you marry Wally Payson if he said he'd leave his wife for you?"

"Depends on the size of the ring."

"You don't mean that," Lily says. "I mean, you just can't mean that."

"I don't know," Claire says. "The fact is, it's so far from reality, I haven't considered it. I get excited when I just get him to wear those hideous boxer shorts to please me. You know, lately, I don't even like him much. But he's my ticket to copywritership."

Lily shakes her head at Claire. "God, I hate it when you say things like that. You don't mean that, either, do you?"

"I'm just teasing you. I am getting bored with Wally, though."

"You know what worries me most about Will?" Lily asks. "That the people in my building will realize he's not my cousin and have me kicked out. I mean, I'm sure my doorman suspects."

"Doormen have seen everything. Don't worry. Do you think you're the only one who fools around? Relax. Give your doorman a big tip for Christmas. Or a pair of fancy boxer shorts . . ."

One night, Will and Lily double-date with Claire and a man named Jeff Berris. Claire's still sleeping with Wally Payson but dating whoever asks. Jeff is an account executive, about thirty-five years old and divorced. He smokes Camels and drinks too much. Lily learns this within the first few minutes of the date. They are having dinner at the Berghoff, which is crowded and smoky tonight. The German music can hardly compete with the din, despite the oompahpahs.

Lily remembers the Berghoff from when she was a little girl. Her father took her mother and her there once and drank too much. It was only a few months before he left them. She remembers the almost medicinal taste of her Shirley Temples while he indulged in drink after drink and her mother commented, growing more indignant and bitter with each order. She remembers the cheerful, plodding German music and the dark wood bar where the waiter kept picking up drinks for her unquenchable father. Her mother had to take the wallet from his jacket pocket to pay the waiter, for by the last drink, he was slumped down in his chair with a carefree, boozy smile on his face. Then, somehow, they got him outside.

Their car was parked about two blocks away. When her father got behind the wheel, he rested his head against the seat and immediately started snoring. Lily remembers her mother crying. She remembers sitting in the dark, afraid, the smell of her father's liquor filling the car, as he snored with his mouth open. Her mother whispered over and over, "I wish I knew how to drive." And then they left her father in the car, tried for what seemed like hours to hail a taxi, and ended up walking to the Northwestern Station, Lily's dress shoes biting at her ankles. When they finally reached that towering, echoing waiting room, there was blood seeping through her anklets, right at the buckle of each foot.

When Will read in the paper about the Berghoff, a famous German eatery, Lily had no idea that it would be the very place, though she recognized it the minute they walked in.

Jeff Berris is already on his third drink before Lily or Will or even

Claire are halfway through with their first. Lily glances over at Claire, who seems fully into the party spirit. She's telling stories about work, about how she's written an ad her boss pawned off as his own.

"Why the hell you want to be a copywriter, anyway, Claire?" Jeff says, his speech already slurred by the liquor.

"Because I'm as good at it as any of the copy trainees. And they make twice what I do."

"You're a good secretary, too. Why the hell do you have to be a copywriter?"

"Well, why do you have to be an account executive? Why don't you work in the mail room?"

Lily can see Jeff's eyes narrow. There is such tension at the table, the air seems to buzz. Will looks over at Lily nervously.

"Because I have a B.A. in business."

"Well, I have a B.A. in English. What's the difference?"

"You're real pretty, Claire," he says, and the threat, the tension, is gone from his eyes as suddenly as it came. Now he's going to conquer her another way. He reaches for her, his face suddenly moony. Lily takes a sip of her vodka and lime just so she doesn't have to watch them kiss. Lily can't imagine why Claire would even go out with a jerk like this.

"I just don't know why you'd want to be anything but what you are. You're perfect just the way you are."

Later, fifteen minutes into dinner, Jeff has managed to fondle Claire's shoulders, neck, and knee all in plain view, and clean his plate, scraping the sauce with the bottom of his fork so it squeaks.

"Let's get out of here," he says to Claire in a voice perfectly audible to Lily and Will.

"Yeah," Claire says, setting down her fork. "Sure."

"Sorry," she says to Lily as she gets up, looking pleased, excited. Jeff is already halfway to the door as Claire finishes putting on her sweater. "Hot-blooded," she says, poking her thumb in his direction, smiling.

"There goes Jack and my mother," Lily says.

"What?" Will asks.

"Never mind."

Lily can't remember ever being so happy. She dotes on Will's every move, can hardly believe how devoted he is to her. He brings her small surprises—an art book he bought at a tag sale, a handmade vase he bought at a thrift store. He makes love to her with total devotion. Two, three times every night, as though he can't get enough of her. And he is desperately concerned with her pleasure. "Does it feel good, sweetheart? Does it feel good?" he will chant to her. And he is never afraid to say he loves her.

"You and I were made for each other," he tells her one night. "I never thought I would find someone I could love like this or who loves me so well."

Sometimes, Lily wishes her mother were alive just to meet him, to see the sweet way he treats her, to know that men can be loving, kind, giving. Sometimes she thinks her mother *is* watching.

The phone rings in the middle of the night. Lily moves her hand across the surface of the night table, trying to find the source of the intrusion. The receiver is cold in her warm, sleepy hand. Foreign.

"Hello."

"I'm looking for Will Sternhagen," a woman's voice says in a practiced, controlled way.

"Will," Lily says. "It's for you."

Will sits up. His face, in the streetlight, looks stricken. "Hello? How did you get this number? No. No. I can't go through this again. Sandra, don't make me. Please. Don't say that. It isn't fair."

Lily notices that Will's voice rises with each sentence; his throat seems to shut down around the words. She takes his wrist in her hand. It feels damp, electric. He is shaking his head and breathing like a runner.

"Don't say that. I can't stand it when you say that."

Lily gets up, feels he deserves the privacy, but he grabs at her arm, grips it like a drowning man grips a life preserver.

"Why must you say this? Can't you call your mother or something? Why don't you go back to California. I'll arrange for the tickets. Sandra . . ."

He looks at Lily. "Oh, God," he says to her, his hand over the receiver. "Oh, God . . ."

"Yes," he says now, into the phone. "Yes. Tomorrow. You won't do anything until tomorrow? It could be late. It's a long drive. Yes. I said I would. She's a friend. I'll tell you tomorrow. I'm not going to tell you now. No. She's a friend, Sandra. An old friend. Nice enough to take me in when I needed it. I'll be there. I said I would. I said I would, didn't I? Don't you understand English? Okay, I'm sorry. Of course I'm upset, what do you think? I'll be there, Sandra." His voice is so flat, it hardly seems like his. It frightens Lily. He hangs up the phone with a bang and sits there blank-faced for a moment, sucking in air as though it's the most difficult thing in the world to do.

Lily says nothing, knows she mustn't.

He looks up. "I've got to go back," he says.

"I figured. Why?"

"She says she's going to kill herself. She says she told a doctor she couldn't sleep at night; he gave her pills. She says she's sitting there with a glass of water and the pills."

"Then you have to go," Lily says, finding her voice now is as flat as his. "You should leave tonight, even."

"No. I'm staying with you until morning."

"I don't think she's serious or she wouldn't have called you in the middle of the night."

"Why do you say that?"

"When my mother did it, she didn't tell anyone. She just did it. I've read that people who call for help usually just want help. But maybe not always, though. I wouldn't want her blood on my hands."

Will looks at her. "Your mother committed suicide?" he asks softly.

Lily nods and swallows.

"You never told me that."

"I couldn't."

"I thought I knew all about you."

Lily shakes her head. "No one knows all about me," she says. "Least of all me."

"I thought I knew you. I thought I knew Sandra. I thought it was going to be all right." Then Will is crying, bowing his head so low, all she can see is his hair, his tender neck, and the tears splashing on his bare, crossed legs.

"Sweetie," she says.

"I don't believe this," he says. "She was doing well enough for me to leave. She was doing okay. I left my number with the high school—your number—because I had to. She got it from them. I wish to God I hadn't." He is wiping tears with the back of his hand, angrily, bitterly.

"Don't. You did what you had to do."

"Do you think she's laughing now, do you?" he asks.

"No."

They lay down again in bed, but what was dark and warm before seems exploded, filled with violent street light and traffic noises.

"It seems like . . ." he whispers. "It seems like every time we're really happy with each other, you and I, every time we really love each other, I have to go."

"Maybe someone is telling us something," Lily says.

"No," Will says. "Fate isn't that telegraphic."

"Don't you think so?" Lily says. "I do. I think fate is always telegraphic. I'm just never smart enough to read the signs. Can you sleep?"

"I'm going to try," he says. He turns away from her. Even with his usually soothing presence, she now feels lonely, really alone; and every rush of traffic, every siren, is like a punctuation of her disappointment. For it seems she will never own Will as he has owned her.

In the morning she wakes to find his bags are packed, that he is sitting at the table with a cup of tea, looking almost cheerful in the sea-green sweater he wore when he arrived.

"You finally got some sleep," he says.

"Did you?"

"Not much, but I'm okay."

"Let me know what's going on," she says.

"Sure. Of course I will."

"We had a few good weeks at least," she says, knowing suddenly he's not coming back. She can't explain how she knows. It's in the way he's sitting, the way he's looking at her. He is closed and polished, formal, and different.

"I need to leave now," he says. "Before there's morning traffic." He gets up stiffly. The cool morning air is blowing the curtains into the room. There is a thin fog over the lake.

Lily says nothing at all, just hugs him. And Will only says, "Good-bye," and hugs her back.

Just like in Iowa, Will has changed her life and now is gone. Just getting dressed for work seems painful. The mount room that she was so happy in just a few weeks ago feels claustrophobic, and even the smell of baby powder sickens her in the afternoon heat.

And one afternoon, feeling sticky and angry and clumsy, Joe Forrest calls into her. "Lily's wearing red. Could you be my tomato, Lily? I could take a bite right out of your cute little red skirt. Then maybe I could see your cute little thighs. . . . And then I could take a bite right out of your—"

"Shut up," Lily says, shaking. "Just leave me alone."

"Wuzz wrong," he says, coming into the mount room. "Don't you have cute thighs?"

"What's wrong?" she says, letting her tongue speak without thinking. "What's wrong? You're disgustingly drunk. Get out of here." He reeks of liquor and garlic as he approaches her, but she turns her back on him, doesn't know what else to do, for she is close to crying and wants to swallow the tears down.

And when she turns back, there is a small crowd outside her door. A few of the wolves, one of the secretaries, and Joy Grey. Joe Forrest turns to see them just when she does, looks blearily at them, and pushes past to leave the room.

For a horrible moment, she knows they are staring at her, and she can't determine by their faces what they are thinking: whether they are feeling sorry for her or whether they are angry that she hasn't tolerated Joe Forrest, as they all do, or whether they think she will be fired for what she has just said. In a moment, they all go except Joy. She is standing in her coral smock, her hands folded across her chest. "Bravo," she says in a cool alto. "Couldn't have said it better myself." And then she, too, is gone.

Will calls and says Sandra's much worse than he imagined and he's going to have to stick it out awhile.

"I knew you would," Lily tells him.

"I knew it, too," he says softly. "I'll write you, and you can write me at the high school. They collect mail even in the summer."

"Okay," Lily says, but she has no heart to do so.

"You are the love of my life," he tells her earnestly.

"I wish I was," she says.

"Everyone's talking about what happened with you and Joe Forrest yesterday," Claire tells her over lunch.

"Oh, God, what are they saying?"

"It depends who's talking," Claire says coolly, taking a bite of her ham sandwich. "Don't look so stricken. Jesus H. Christ. Who cares what people say?"

"Tell me."

"Well, a few of the men are calling you a prick tease. A few of the women are calling you a saint. A few people in management are saying it's time to send Joe Forrest away to dry out. Have you seen him since?"

Lily shakes her head and finds her heart feels squeezed. She is close to tears.

"What's up?" Claire says. "It's not like you to yell at him, anyway, is it? I mean I hardly know you, but flirting is flirting."

"Will's wife called. She said she'd commit suicide if he didn't come back."

"Oh, Jesus!" Claire says. "The tyranny of the weak. So what's going to happen?"

"Well, he went back. What else could happen?"

"He could have said, 'Good riddance,' and called his lawyer."

Lily shakes her head.

"Well, that's too bad. You going to be okay?"

"Okay as a person can be who's lost all hope. No, sorry. That sounds so self-pitying. Tell me something about your love life. Lighten things up, will you?"

"Well, listen, I just might be in love," Claire says. "This Jeff is hot stuff, let me tell you."

"What do you see in him?" Lily asks. She realizes that sour self-pity has made her feel mean inside. Angry. She smashes her tuna sandwich with her thumb, watching the tuna frill along the edge.

"What do you mean?"

"Well, he treats you like trash."

"He does not. Why do you even say that?" Claire sets down her sandwich and leans toward Lily, eyes like darts. "He does not. He treats me just fine."

"I mean, the way he made you leave the restaurant in the middle of the meal, and you weren't even done. And you know he never paid."

"Well, if that's it, here's your damn money," Claire says, rummaging in her purse. "He was so excited about being with me, he forgot. If that's it, here's your damn money."

"That's not it. That's not half it. Claire, he's crude."

"Yeah, and what am I? I'm not as refined as you, Lily. I'm not some coddled Winnetka beauty like you. I got to get back to my desk."

"I didn't mean to offend you," Lily says.

"So what did you mean to do?"

"I won't say anything else about him," Lily says.

"You know what I think? I think, now you don't have Will, you're just jealous that I do have someone." Claire gets up from the table, slapping down a ten-dollar bill. "That's for dinner, too. I only had a salad that night, so don't say it's not enough."

"C'mon," Lily says, getting up after her.

"Just pay the damn bill," Claire says.

Coming back into the building, Lily sees Joe Forrest on his way out to lunch. He's with two other men. He looks as cool and sober as ever, as he always does in the mornings. A khaki suit, a smooth-shaven jaw.

"Hi there, Lily," he says. "The mount room's never been as functional as it is with Lily," he tells the other men. "She's our peach."

The other men, neither of whom she's ever met, smile at her condescendingly as they go through the revolving door. As the glass comes around, Joe Forrest waves to her before he steps out into the street. He must remember nothing, or if he does, he's not admitting it. Lily feels infinitely relieved but still uneasy.

Later that day, Lily takes a break and goes by Claire's desk. Claire is hunched over her typewriter, mouthing words to herself.

"I'm sorry," Lily says. "I didn't mean to hurt your feelings or make you angry."

Claire puts her hand through the air as if she were shooing away a fly. "I'm trying to write. What's another word for delicious?"

"Tasty. Yummy. Mouth tingling. Good?"

"No. None of the above. How about ambrosial?"

"A little highfalutin."

"It's champagne. Champagne is highfalutin."

"Okay. Ambrosial. Did you hear me, though? I said, I'm sorry. I didn't mean to hurt your feelings."

"It doesn't matter," she says. "Even if you're right about Jeff, it doesn't matter. I didn't really want to hear it."

"I know," Lily says.

Claire looks up at her. "You're not too practiced at being a friend, are you?"

"What do you mean?" Lily asks.

"Friends, real friends, are supposed to say, 'He's great,' even if he isn't. Friends support each other no matter what the other one does."

"Do they?" Lily asks. "I would hope if you thought I was seeing someone inappropriate, you'd tell me."

Claire shrugs. "I won't. I'm not that kind of friend. If I want honesty, I call my sister. If you want honesty, call my sister."

"You'll have to give me her number," Lily says.

"What's another word for bubbly?"

"Sparkling?"

"Hey, if you get tired of the art department, come on over."

"Do you forgive me?" Lily asks.

"What's to forgive?" Claire says. "Listen, I'm sorry about Will. I know that hurts."

Lily nods.

"I got to write this by four-thirty," Claire says.

"Okay," Lily says, and leaves.

Two weeks later, and only one short letter from Will, Lily feels deflated, exhausted. She doesn't even want to write him back. If she can't share each day with him, what's the point? There's no reason to swap details, describing what she's done or seen, if it's not likely he'll be back for a long time.

Since Will left, her life, which seemed perfectly full before he arrived, seems quiet and empty. No more movies, plays, dinners, folk music. The only thing new since his departure is that she's contacted the school at the Art Institute to see if she can use their etching press. They have agreed, for a small studio fee, to let her, and she has spent a few nights this week in the half-light of the Art Institute's printing room, remembering the joy of creating. But the weekends are especially lonely now. She writes Professor Pulaski and tells him how lonely she is. She describes the prints she's working on. In less than a week, again, she has a kind, warming letter from him that makes her feel much less alone. She thinks of asking him to come visit her but is still a little afraid of him, can't bring herself to impose on his feelings of kindness toward her.

At work on Monday, David Barber, one of the associate creative directors that Lily once included in the pack of wolves, comes in and leans against the wall of shelves that is stacked with Bestine, extra boxes of staples, watercolor boxes, and pencils, and says, "How would you like to do a bus card?"

"Me. Really! For what?"

"For Carter's cough drops. The copy department sent it down." He hands her a yellow work order.

HEAD: CARTER'S COUGH DROPS. THE MEDICINE'S FOR MY COUGH.
THE CHERRY FLAVOR'S FOR ME.
MEDIUM: ONE BUS CARD. 11 × 28. TWO-COLOR

Lily is so excited she holds the yellow slip of paper close to her as though it might disappear from her hands.

"Thank you. I'll get on it right away."

"We need a layout by tomorrow. I figured you could eke it into your schedule."

"Sure. Sure I could," Lily says.

Now, all day, between stapling and pulling up old rubber-cemented layouts, she sits at the little cast-iron drawing table in the corner of the mount room. Until now it's just been a place for people to make changes on their layouts when the spirit hit them. Now it's hers. Her first layouts look so bad to her, she covers them with her arm while she works. But after a little while she gets an idea: a bunch of cherries shown three times. The first time, they are on a stem like a regular bunch of cherries, but instead of cherries, on each stem hangs a cough drop. The next time, they are transforming, getting spherical, redder. The third time, they are real juicy, ripe cherries. She watercolors the cherries red, the stems black. She pencils in the copy, tracing the type from a type book. By four, she's relatively pleased with her efforts and looks for David Barber to show it to him. His is a corner office. Light pours in on his modern fiberglass furniture. The base of his drawing table is sculptural and reminds Lily of the shape of Dixie Cups and their silver holders at soda fountains, two cones point to point. David looks up from his reading.

"Done already?"

"I wanted to see if it's any good."

"Well," David says, spreading the layout before him, focusing his lamp on it. "Very nice. Nice concept. I like the cough drops on the stems. It's backward, though."

"Backward?"

"Well, yeah. The cherries should be first; then they turn into cough drops. You know, that implies that the cough drops are made of cherries."

"Oh, should we imply that? Are they?"

"No, of course not. But the taste . . . Well, very nice. Just change the order and we'll show it to the client tomorrow."

"But the copy talks about the medicine for the cough first and the cherry flavor last. That's why I did it in this order."

"No. It should go the other way around. Thank you, Lily." Having been dismissed, Lily leaves the room, but for her the argument's not over.

The bus card is approved for production. The client likes it (with David's change). And David says that they might even use the image of the cherries if they do a print ad.

"If we do that, you can be the art director," David tells her.

"Thanks for the chance," she says.

"And, of course, I'll supervise it, but you can be the one in charge of finding a photographer and choosing a retoucher."

"I guess I thought it would be illustrated," she tells him.

"Oh, no. We sold it to the client as photography. It wouldn't be nearly as magical illustrated."

"I don't know," Lily says.

"Trust me."

Lily goes to the art buyer on the account, and together they look through the photography books and choose one—and the retoucher's book, too—David approves her choices, and Lily, for the first time, knows the feeling of succeeding in the business world.

One night, missing Will so badly, it is a physical pain, like a stone in her throat; she goes to a bar and meets a man, much older than she, with gray temples. An airline pilot. She takes him back to her apartment, and after a few drinks, they undress and get into bed. She tries to pretend that he's Will. She shocks him and excites him, asking him to do things to her that only Will has done before. Doing things to him that make him call out and moan. When he leaves, he kisses her, but he never calls her again. She doesn't want him to. She doesn't even know his last name.

The experience sobers her. But the next week, she does it again. And the next week, again. The anonymity of her encounters is demoralizing, sometimes frightening to her. In college, there was a certain safety in the men she met. They were friends of people she knew or in her classes. She was out of the norm in going to bed with them and uncomfortable about that. But now this is different. She is taking strangers into her bed, strangers who don't know or respect her, don't want to. What am I doing? she is asking herself. And yet the loneliness tastes so bad, the moments of pleasure so good, so delicious.

But she cannot deny she is wounding herself. Her nights are often sleepless. And the next day, she always feels the ache of last night's lovemaking. She reminds herself of it in the stall of the ladies' room, touching her swollen vagina tenderly, like a six-year-old touching a tongue to the socket of a just-lost tooth. It all seems painful and inevitable.

Will calls.

"You're not writing me any letters," he says.

"I just haven't felt like it," she says.

"But you and I . . . I thought we . . ."

She is sitting in her nightgown by the window, eating cookies. It is almost midnight, and she's felt empty, worried, not sure why. She is not glad to hear from Will. It even hurts to hear his voice.

"How's Sandra?" she asks.

"Better. I've got her taking some courses this fall, to make her life more interesting. She's enjoying them. I figure if I could build her up a little, you know, make her feel better about herself . . . She's a sweet kid, Lily. I don't hate her. I can't bear to hurt her."

"Why don't you have her get a job? That might make her feel good about herself."

"Oh, no. Sandra wouldn't be good at getting a job."

"She's a teacher, isn't she?"

"But she never got her certificate. Sandra likes keeping house. She likes cooking, taking care of . . . well, me."

Lily wonders if maybe that's why he's still with her. Lily will never take care of him quite that way. Never. They've always been equals, partners. Except that she can never thoroughly have him to herself.

"But why aren't you writing me any letters?" he asks. "I write you, and you don't even answer my questions."

"I just don't really think you're coming back."

"Or maybe you don't love me."

Lily says nothing. When she thinks of Will, there's always the pain of disappointment. There always has been, except for those few glorious weeks. If she does love him, she doesn't want to.

"You don't," he says.

"I didn't say that." And she hears in her voice the smallest whimper. "Oh, Will . . . I do love you. You broke my heart . . ."

"I never wanted to. You know I never wanted to," he says. And then, taking a deep breath, he asks, "Have you been going out?"

"Yes."

"With men, I mean."

"Am I not supposed to?"

"I can't stop you. No, I didn't say that right. I would never stop you. What right do I have to stop you—how's that? I know this is hard. Here I am with Sandra. There you are with— You're not seeing Ted again?"

"Not right now."

"But there is someone."

She says nothing.

"Who? Tell me."

"I'm seeing a lot of people, Will."

There is a moment of such pressure and silence, Lily feels it like a hand squeezing on her heart.

"You've been sleeping with any of them, these people?"

All of these people, she thinks, hating herself.

"No, I don't want to know," he says. "I don't want to know."

She wonders if she should reassure him. Or torture him with details. But she does neither.

"I'm miserable without you," she tells him suddenly.

"I'm sorry, baby. I'm so sorry."

"If you're so sorry, why can't you do anything about it?"

"Sandra," he says simply.

"I hate her: Sandra. And her fucking weakness. I want to kill her."

"She isn't so bad. She's suffering, too."

"I've got to go," Lily says.

"Don't hang up angry."

"I don't know how to feel anymore."

"I'll see you, Lily," he says, and she isn't sure how he means it: pointedly, as though he'll see her soon? Or in a breezy, offhand way you say good-bye to someone you may never see again.

"I'll see you," Lily says.

• • •

The cherry-cough-drop bus poster becomes a cherry-cough-drop outdoor poster and a print ad, and David asks her to do all the resizing and designing. A few people stop by to tell Lily they like it. One day, Joe Forrest comes into the mount room. It's still morning, and he's wearing that fresh-starched pleasantness that lasts until noon.

"Hey," he says. "I liked what you did—that cough-drop campaign. Nice graphics. Good type."

"Thank you."

"Only one thing bothered me. Keeps bothering me. I just thought I'd mention it. Shouldn't the cough drops turn into cherries instead of the other way around?"

Chapter Eight

Andres Pulaski's new apartment is like a cell. The walls meet at right angles with no moldings. The doors are gray metal with levers. The heat drones all through the night. It is only a few blocks from the house where, amid noise and chaos, his family still resides. His wife now merely nods when he comes through the door, but he can tell that she is relieved to have him gone. On exploring the house, he has discovered that she has already filled his closet with her shapeless dresses and his dresser drawers with her handkerchiefs, garters, cigarette cases, and earrings. When he told her that he wanted to move out, that there no longer was any feeling between them, that there hadn't been for a long time, she said, "So what? What sort of feeling do you expect after eleven years? Did you want me not to age? Do you think I didn't know about your girlfriends?"

He is shocked by her offhandedness, her face, which shows no upset, as though she has expected this for a long time.

He misses his sons, but not so much as most fathers would, he knows. He was never the sort of father to play ball with them in the yard or teach them craftsman secrets in the wood shop. He was never much of a father at all, he knows.

He is ashamed of himself in general. His recent life has been cream-puff easy, and he's grown equally soft inside. Since he left his wife, he has slept with four female students, all perfectly willing, all angry at him now for only seeing them once each. And though he still compulsively seeks them out, those girls with that look in their eyes, he seems to have lost his taste for meaningless couplings, for his meaningless life.

But he never stops thinking of Lily Beach. Not sleeping with her was the one good act of his last five years, seems almost heroic to him now.

He has written her letters, and she has written back each time. And toward her he feels a fatherliness that he never felt for his own children.

Now he is writing that he would like to see her, to come up to Chicago and meet for dinner. "I feel about you as kind and fatherly as a priest," he writes, changing the English six times until it makes sense.

Your good and bad life I would like to share, if you can feel good to tell me. And you must know that I have left Alice and my boys with not all sadness. My life is not good or bad, but new. And is not "new" the best kind of good? I think this. I know my prints are more interesting now. They tell me so, my New York dealer and my patrons. I wish you could see them. Maybe I will bring some with me. Maybe I will bring one to you. A present. Would you hang a Pulaski on your wall or put it in with mothballs, under your sweaters? Tell me.

The night he writes the letter, he finds himself alone in the dark, which loneliness has made cloying. For so many years his nights have been filled with companionable breathing. There was warmth in it even after he no longer loved his wives. And he grew addicted to the magic, rich smells women give off in sleep. But he thinks now that he has never in his life matched real, giving love and longevity. As soon as he felt giving to his wives and they responded in kind, it was as though he gave away his love and had no more to give.

Lily waits in the dark restaurant, glancing every so often at her watch. She and Professor Pulaski have agreed to meet here, in this roast-beef palace with its walls of books, its false fireplace with its chunky brass fenders and its waiters who do a song and dance before they allow you to eat the quite ordinary salad they concoct in a spinning salad bowl. She waits at a table by the bar, where there is a television turned down low and businessmen sipping something to make them forget their day.

There are few women in the restaurant. It is still early—cocktail hour, really—and even at the tables it's mostly men that sit smoking and leaning in toward each other with what looks to Lily like a special rapport. Her father had always had that with other men. She remembers poker games and cigars and heavy, chesty laughter waking her in the night. She remembers wandering in her nightgown to see them play, all of them stubbly-faced, noisily drinking beer, totally absorbed. Even her mother was hiding somewhere else in the house, no part of this party. Sandwiches on rye bread, covered with plastic, were left for them on the sideboard. Big ruby glass ashtrays her mother never used otherwise were placed at each position at the table, as though her mother imagined that no one wanted to share.

"What's she doing here?" one of the men asked in a surprisingly annoyed voice.

"She's like a little ghost," another said. "A little pink ghost."

"Go back to bed, Lily," her father said. "We're very busy here."

"I want to stay and watch."

"I don't need to tell you more than once."

But Lily stood firm in her long pink nightgown. Why should she have to leave? It was her house.

"I'm warning you . . ." Lily looked around at the faces, almost criminal with their full day's growth and beer-thirsty mouths, the nervousness of their game. And then she saw the cruelty in her father's face. He'd warned her in front of them, and he had to act. He dragged her off her mark and across his lap and began a spanking she never would forget. More venomous than usual. Done to prove a point: that he was in control, that he put up with no guff.

As Lily turned her head, bitterly holding on to the tears, she saw in each man's eye a need not to see, to turn away, as though they knew they were responsible for creating this cruelty.

"Tough little thing, doesn't even cry," one man said. And the next thing she knew, her father was taking off his belt.

"I can make her cry," he said. "Just watch how I can make her cry." The first swat of the belt was so stinging, it snatched the very breath from her lungs. But the next didn't come. More than one man was holding her father back, the belt poised in the air like a charioteer's whip.

"Hey, Howie, you made your point," one said.

Now Lily's mother entered. Her hair was pulled back; she wore the chenille bathrobe Lily owns now: sea green.

"What's going on?" she asked sweetly, almost too meekly. The men let go of her father, and he sank red-faced into his chair as Lily scrambled off his lap.

Then Lily's mother turned to her. "What did you do to your father?" she asked.

But the tears were really flowing now. Her mother hadn't come to defend her but to accuse her. If the men had not been here, she would have stood by while her father whipped her. If her mother was acting this way, surely she had done something wrong. Something really wrong. Or there was something wrong about her that made them side with each other, always accusing, always punishing her.

Her mother grabbed her wrist, far too roughly, and dragged her down the hall to her room.

"Get in bed," she said. "I don't know what you did, but don't do it again. It's hard enough living with your father, you want to kill me, too?" And then she shut the door with a slam that the men must surely have heard.

They were quieter now and left not long after. For days there were leftover sandwiches in the house her mother made her eat, though she hated rye bread. And for days her father's eyes blamed her with their dark, sunken anger.

Thinking of this, as Lily watches the men around the green tableclothed tables, she feels hollow and tired. Her work is still good. She is spending more time in the Art Institute's print lab. She is exploring abstraction, color, in ways she never has before. But her nights are still sometimes dark with bars and liquor and strangers. Blots of obsession she cares not to remember. Will has not written in months now. It is the end of October, and autumn in Chicago is brittle and punishing. The wind wheezes off the lake with hostility. And her art is as hollow as she feels. Angry but empty.

She sees Professor Pulaski come in, giving up his muffler and coat and hat to the checkroom girl, setting a large brown paper-wrapped package against his leg while he combs his hair briefly, not knowing, she thinks, that she is watching him. As he stuffs the comb into his breast pocket, he spots her, seems to glide across the wooden floor, the package crackling at his side, and comes to the table to kiss her cheek. His cheeks are inflamed with the cold. His hair is grayer than she remembered. And he smells so good: fresh and woolly.

"Lily," he says, smiling, sitting down next to her. "My lovely girl. I am terribly sorry, of this I assure you. You are much respected by me, you know, so do not think that I am late of purpose."

"I'm sure you had a good reason," she tells him. She is pleased to see his face, its familiar arrogance, to hear his voice no matter how tortured his language construction.

"I am making an agreement with a gallery, and the man who is the owner says, 'no, this discussion is not *half*-done. Not *half*-done.' So I stayed as long as I had to stay."

"That's all right." Seeing Pulaski lifts her sadness, eases her somehow. She knows in his eyes, again, the sweet caring he'd shown to her at Iowa.

"Life is good for a young girl in the city?" he asks.

"Good enough," she says.

"I don't hear that you believe it," he says.

She shrugs. "Did I write you about the Art Institute printmaking room? It's very nice, and they've been very nice about letting me use the equipment."

"Yes. This is good. And speaking about prints . . . here," he says, lifting the package. It is heavy, maybe thirty by forty, and large. As she pulls aside the paper, she gasps. For clearly it is one of his masterworks, already matted and framed. It is of a woman, nearly naked, sitting up in what might be a bed, giving off a light, being the source of light in the whole picture, and a man, in a corner, reflecting back that light, bathed in it. It is very abstract, of course. Distorted, even. And as she looks at it, she knows the woman might be her.

"It's the most beautiful I've ever seen of yours," she says. "It's wonderful." She finds tears are welling, and she brushes them away before they can fall.

"You really want me to have this?" she asks.

"If you think you would like to live with it, yes. If you say you will not give it away or grow tired of it."

"Never," she says. "Not ever."

"It is my sincerest gift to my sincerest pupil," he says.

"Thank you." She reaches over and kisses his craggy cheek. Again, she feels desire for him, as she did that night at dinner. It confuses her.

The waiter comes over, takes their drink orders, and hands them menus. Embarrassed by her feelings toward him, she looks at the slick page for a long time, its antiquated type and voluptuous descriptions. And suddenly there is a noise in the restaurant: The TV has been turned up quite loudly, and the men, who moments ago were leaning into male gossip, are hushed. President Kennedy is on the screen. His face looks small and tense.

He is talking about Cuba, but it is hard for Lily to understand. Something about a quarantine, about ships.

Professor Pulaski looks up lazily from his menu for a moment and then hears something that rivets him to the screen. The waiters, with their spinning salad bowls and silver trays, stop as if frozen by the childhood game Lily used to play: statue maker. The room fills with the president's Boston accent, the TV having been turned up even louder now.

Lily had heard this morning that the president was going to give an important speech this evening, but somehow she didn't think much of it. By the look on everyone's face she sees that there is a seriousness here she never dreamed of.

"What is it," she whispers to Pulaski. "Is it war?"

He places his hand on her wrist to say he's heard her but to hush her, too. When the speech is over, the room seems to suddenly roar to life. But the noise is different now than the camaraderie from before. The sound is high-pitched, worried, almost wailing.

"What is it? I didn't understand," Lily says.

"The Russians have built missile sites in Cuba. Your president does not like threat—"

"And?"

"And he says Khrushchev must take them away. There are ships to stop more to be deliveried."

"Delivered."

"And he says Russia must unassemble the others."

"Disassemble."

"Lily, I cannot speak English in crisis. Will you learn Spanish? Or even Polish?"

"There will be a nuclear war," Lily says, her voice rising, squeezed by the thought. She has not lived. Not lived at all. "You can't joke now, Andres," she says, using his Christian name for the first time, though he has often asked her to.

"The world will always joke when disaster comes. Who can live with a war that kills all? Joking makes us think we are— What is the word?"

"I don't know," she says, sighing.

"Invincible?"

She nods.

"I learned in Paraguay. My life was close to the end there."

Lily's held-back tears come now, slicking her face, and she is ashamed. For Andres Pulaski has known terror. He told her once that both his mother and father were killed by General Stroessner's regime. His brother was tortured. And yet he makes art, awakes each day, teaches others. But she remembers her childish horror at the pictures of Hiroshima. A weapon that can make New York disappear, turn Chicago to a steaming crater.

"You must pull together," Andres says, trying to stanch her tears with a damask napkin. "There is no war yet."

"But I don't want to die, Andres. I've never been to Europe. I've never had a baby. I've hardly even *held* a baby. And I always wanted to take piano lessons," she says. "My mother and I used to look at the pianos at Marshall Field's and she'd say, 'Someday this one will be ours.' But it never was ours."

"May I take your order?" the waiter asks.

Pulaski orders for them both while Lily wipes her tears. The waiter occasionally glances over at her with a nervous smile. And before he leaves, with his wallet of order checks filled out for table 6, he says to her, "Kennedy's a good guy. He'll see us through."

Lily remembers nothing about the dinner. Whatever Pulaski ordered for her, she did not eat, and his kind ministrations and soothing, inverted chatter have not registered at all.

"I will take you home," he says, though she can see he hasn't finished his plate of roast beef. "You are not well."

"I'm sorry," she says. "Finish. I'm all right."

But, ignoring her politeness, he calls the waiter and pays quickly with large, crackly bills, newly received from his gallery, Lily thinks. And retrieving both their coats, he ushers her out into the frozen night.

After a few hours of tender, relaxed talk at Lily's apartment, he insists she get ready for bed, and she wonders if he will finally break whatever code has kept him from intimacy with her. She is calmer now. Hysteria has left her weak and remorseful, and she is anxious to make up for the scene she caused at the restaurant. She picks a negligee and robe the color of dried roses, edged in lace that looks as though it's been dipped in tea. It was, she thinks bitterly, a present from her mother and Jack. In the bathroom mirror, she sees a pale girl who looks no more than twelve.

Pulaski is making himself tea in the kitchen.

"Would you like some?" he asks.

She nods.

"Everyone feels much the better after a cup of tea. Sit here by the fireplace. I will bring it to you."

"I should be making it for *you*."

"No." He sets his own tea on the table by hers, and gathering a few logs from the basket, he sets a fire.

"This place makes me think of the house where I was a child."

"Was it this grand?" she asks.

"Yes."

"I didn't know you were wealthy."

"Yes. Each child had a servant and a horse. There were seven children. My own room, my sleeping room, was like this. I have been very rich. And very poor."

"And rich again," Lily says. "When you think of this threat, Andres, are you afraid to die?"

"When I was your age, I was much afraid to die. And then my parents were shot with a thousand bullets. I had to leave the country I loved. And now I am more afraid of not making art or to be lonely."

"But for whole cities to die . . ."

"I think, my Lily, that we must accept what is given. Do you believe in God?"

Lily shrugs. "Yes, I guess."

"It is easier to believe in God. Or even fate. The Chinese say if you flow to the river, you will be safe."

"Flow with the river?"

"Yes, that." The fire paints Andres's face with a rosy glow. Lily has only lit one fire before tonight. She lay in bed long after the embers were all that remained, listening to their spit and crackle. Would a city spit and hiss and crackle if it were burned?

"The fallout shelter is two blocks from here," she says. "If it were a near miss, we could survive there. Two weeks, they say."

"I think it would not matter. Would not help. I would not like to die in a dark basement with strangers," he says. "But I don't think there will be a war."

"Why not?"

"Because your president is brave. And Russia is a noisy—how you say?—coward. And because you have not taken piano lessons yet."

Lily smiles and sips the sweet tea. "You don't think there will be a war?" she asks, yawning. The fire and Pulaski's voice have made her sleepy.

"I don't think so," he says. "Go to bed. I will stay a while by the fire."

"But is it because you want to? Wouldn't you rather share my bed with me?"

A softness crosses his face. He looks handsome, almost noble. He takes her chin in his hand, as one might touch a child. "I would rather sit up with you, like my father did when I was crying from the dark. Is it not good comfort? To have someone watch over you?"

"Yes."

"Once, I told you I will be the uncle of your soul? Here is my chance. I can think of nothing that would please this man more than watching over you. Go. Go wash your face and go to sleep. I will let myself out later. After the fire is gone."

Under the covers in the flickering semidark, Andres across the room by the fire, Lily marvels at how she has never felt safer, though, she reflects in half sleep, she may never have slept through a more dangerous night.

In the morning, Lily awakes, expecting to find him asleep on the couch or in the bathroom, but he is gone. She's slept so well, has felt so safe through this frightening night, she can't imagine he's not there somewhere. And she feels strangely abandoned.

When she calls his hotel room, the phone rings twenty times, and the operator never gets back on the line. She dresses and goes to work, and the office is abuzz with nothing but Cuba.

"I went down there once," David Barber says. "The rum, the music, it was some intoxicating place. You wouldn't believe how close it is to Miami. A spit away," he says. "But I don't know." His voice becomes suddenly lower, macabre. "It seems like a good year to die. I just turned forty. I'm not so young anymore."

"Wanna get bombed?" Claire says, sidling into the mount room after lunch, though she's on a mission to carry memos elsewhere. "I figure they'll bomb us, so why not get bombed?"

"Aren't you afraid?" Lily asks.

"I have a funny way of showing fear," Claire says. "I always act like I want to jump right into the flame."

"Funny choice of words," Lily says.

"Yeah," says Claire, "I see your point."

When Lily returns to the apartment that night after a drink with Claire, her doorman seems agitated.

"Miss Beach, it's up there. No one quite knew where it should go."

"What's up there, Frank?"

"Come on. Didn't you know it was coming today?"

"What?"

"Someone had to go up with them, and I couldn't leave the door. So Tim—the temporary engineer while Lew is on vacation?—he went up there. They sort of guessed where you might put it."

"Thanks," Lily says with a sigh, deciding she'll get no more out of him and wanting to see for herself what could cause such consternation.

In the elevator, she breathes deeply, feeling exhausted. The state of the world is still hanging, like this elevator, on a single cord.

In her apartment, there is no missing the surprise. They haven't put it where she might, but it hardly matters. It stands on the wall by the kitchen, a glossy black Steinway piano. The cover is pushed back to expose the ivory keys, as though the movers have played it. The foot pedals gleam. She sits down on the slick bench, pulls it tight to the piano, and straightening her skirt, like a virtuoso straightens his tails, she plays the only thing she knows: chopsticks.

Can she really keep so generous a gift? What does he want from her? No gift this astonishing, this touching, could be given without expectations. And she wonders, as she randomly runs her fingers over the white keys, if she will have time for piano lessons, the state of the world being what it is.

As she plays, she sees that on the piano's face, in the corner, away from the grand, golden Steinway decal, there's another smaller decal that reads, "Marshall Field and Co." She finds herself so touched, it's difficult for a moment to swallow. Well, she tells herself, this is just the sort of extravagant gift you give when the world is soon going to end.

"It is the most beautiful gift, Andres," she says, finally reaching him at his hotel. "I was so surprised. I almost cried. But I don't know if I can keep it," Lily says. "It cost so much."

"And why does this matter?" he says. "It makes me happy. And money. What is money to me?"

"It's beautiful. Would you like to come over and see it?"

"To see your face when you show it to me will give me great pleasure."

He comes only minutes later. Tired, and appealing in his slouchy gray suit, smelling of after-shave and hairdressing, he wears his age like a cosmetic. It makes him both worldly and vulnerable.

"I go back tomorrow," Andres says. His fingers stroke the slick ebony with a tender caress.

"No word yet about Cuba," Lily says. "I can hardly stand it. Last night it meant so much to me that you stayed."

"Did it? I hoped it would." He is beaming. His thin mouth, which Lily once read as morose, turns up into a subtle smile. She touches his face with a sense of fear, his craggy cheek, the sweep of his brow. Despite his obvious caring for her, he has made sure to keep his distance, and Lily finds rejection frightening.

"I love your face," she says, knowing for the first time it is true.

He gently takes her hand and kisses it. "Lily . . ."

"You're not living with your wife anymore . . ." she says.

And then she reaches up and kisses him softly, quickly, on the lips.

And for a moment he responds hungrily, but then pulls away. "No, Lily, please don't."

She hears that he is nearly breathless, that his foreign voice breaks with feeling.

"Andres, it's okay. I don't even know if I should say this. Maybe you won't care for me if you know, but you don't have to be careful with me. I've been with a man before. I'm not a virgin."

"Somehow I know you are not a virgin. It is not that. But listen. I want to be careful with you. We mustn't."

"You aren't attracted to me?"

His laugh is soft and scratchy. "It isn't that, Christ knows."

"You buy me a beautiful piano. You give me your most beautiful print. Doesn't this mean you care for me?"

"I more than care," Andres says gravely. "You are all I care about. I am truly in love with you."

"Then why?"

He just shakes his head and presses his lips together until they are pale. "I know no English to explain it, my dear one. Just know that I love you. Just know that I will be here when you need me. That I watch over you. I think maybe—I don't know how to say this—maybe we are the same? When we love with our bodies, we stop loving with our hearts. I should not speak for you. I don't know for you if it is so."

"It doesn't make sense."

"Just tell yourself: Andres is a complicated man."

"But what do you want from me? There must be something . . ."

"What I want," Andres says, almost impatient now, "is to love you unselfishly. As I have never loved in my life. The way a father loves a child. And what I want is for you to take this love with no questions, the way a child takes love. With hunger."

And then he hugs her tenderly and is gone.

Chapter Nine

In his cell of an apartment, Andres Pulaski is sitting with a highball glass, getting thoroughly drunk. Though what he did, or did not do, in Chicago with Lily Beach may seem incomprehensible to anyone else, to Pulaski, it was a brilliant and noble choice. He is not getting drunk from remorse but because for the first time in more than a decade, he is totally, unsparingly, in love.

And it is denial that keeps this love in place; rather, he reflects, like the miracle of a souvenir he saw in the airport magazine store on the way back from Chicago: a fresh-cut flower preserved in a cube of Plexiglas. It will never wither, will never lose its precious color, will always hold its form, like the day God made it.

His feeling of satisfaction is especially keen when he thinks of Lily's desire for him, her longing kiss, and then the glowing sweetness of her smile, the intensifying of the gleam in her eyes, when she discovered she owed him nothing.

Her longing for him will never die, like his second wife's desire, and his desire for her did, draining life juice each day, withering, until it seemed to simply blow away in the first prolonged draft.

• • •

The warmth of her few days with Andres leaves Lily more panicked
than ever. The night he leaves, she finds herself at a bar again. Two
businessmen from out of town begin to chat with her. One has a gray
business suit, eyes precisely the same color, and cropped hair the color
of straw. He is the sort of man she would be attracted to as a friend, as
someone she would really want to know. He is intelligent, an importer,
traveling often to Japan, where he says amazing things are beginning to
happen since the war is over. The labor is cheap, he says, and there is
such beauty in the culture. From his briefcase he produces a silk fan
abloom with irises. "Take it," he says. "It suits you."

His friend is dark and silent, reminds her of Ted; there is something
circumspect about him, and censorious at first, as though he wishes his
friend wouldn't talk to her. After a few drinks, though, he becomes
flirtatious. His friend, too, after a few drinks, joins the flirtatiousness
until all three are becoming suggestive, their laughter throaty, their eyes
luminous.

And then the dark-haired one suggests she take them both to her
house, where they can relax, he says. And she knows: They both want
to go to bed with her. She feels the heat rising to her face. Is it curiosity,
or is it because she is truly attracted to the one man, who, even with his
drunken glaze, strikes her as worthy? She is blushing, uncertain.

"You don't have to," the light-haired man says. She knows they don't
respect her. She is something to be used and thrown away. But she is
curious about making love to two men at once. It is a fantasy she's often
had, and she's drunk enough, worried enough about Cuba, and sad
enough about Andres leaving to feel careless. Together they stand on the
street outside the bar and wave down a taxi. The cold night air slaps her
awake, and she wonders what she is doing. But she tastes the same
compulsion, to follow her desire without feeling or limits.

At her apartment, they ask her to put on something more comfortable,
that creaky euphemism that begins seduction. And she does: a nightgown
the color of coffee ice cream. The light-haired man keeps reminding her
that she can ask them to leave, but she doesn't want to. When they begin
to caress her, giddy with something neither of them have ever tried
before, embarrassed themselves, she feels queenly in the focus of their
attention. It doesn't matter to her that the only reason they want her is
because she is willing. It doesn't matter that she will never see them
again. The danger of the moment is a drug. One's lips are at her neck,

another's fingers on her breasts. The first is undressing her; the other is undressing himself. And she loves it, is thrilled by the variety, the sensationalism of pleasing them both, of both pleasing her. And mostly, she is high with breaking every rule she's ever known. They share her all night in combinations that seem mathematical. And then, while the light-haired man is passed out on her bed, the dark-haired man wants her to get down on the floor with him and suck him until he is hard again. "I've just begun," he says. Lily would like to lie near the other one, to rest, but she tries to excite the dark-haired man, knows by the ugly violence in his face she shouldn't tangle with him now.

"You fucking bitch, you're not trying hard enough," he says.

"I'm trying," she says. "I guess maybe we should rest," she says after a while. "Maybe later." She starts to get up, but the man grabs her hair in his hand and yanks her back down.

"Get down there and make me ready," he says. Lily's heart is pounding. She feels the blood rush to her face. She tries again to rouse the flaccid penis. She is scared now. And she watches from the outside, hating herself, thinking what Andres would think if he could see her. How horrified he would be.

"You fucking, fucking bitch," the man says, and somehow, suddenly, he is pushing her back, and her head hits the rug hard. Before she can fill her lungs with air again, he is leaning over her, slapping her face. "You whore," he says.

"No," she calls out. "Stop."

The other man rises from the bed, confused at first. It seems so long until he does something, and then he is grabbing his friend's hand just as he is about to punch Lily's face with a closed fist.

"What the fuck's gotten into you, Frank? Jesus. You okay?" he asks Lily. The few slaps have left her cheeks hot, sore, but the man has hurt much more than her face.

"Let's get out of here," the light-haired man says to the dark-haired one. "Look," he says to Lily when he is dressed and his coat is on. "Let me give you something . . ." He takes out his wallet, but Lily, chilled, slaps it away.

"I don't want your money!" she says.

"Hey, sorry," he says. "I didn't mean anything by it."

When they are gone, Lily goes into the bathroom and, on her knees in front of the toilet, throws up again and again until she is dry retching. In the morning, when she wakes, the blood vessels broken around her eyes from the slapping, or the throwing up, her hands shaking, her mouth bone-dry, she drinks a cup of coffee to steady herself. And just as she is feeling better, good enough to straighten up the apartment, she finds, by the entrance-hall door, the iris fan the light-haired man gave her. She takes it to the kitchen sink and, weeping, burns it, watching the black flaky ashes rise and fall onto the old, scoured porcelain.

The rest of the week is agony. Her life feels so dirty, so empty. Hardly worth saving. When President Kennedy made the announcement on Monday, who could have imagined that now, Thursday, there would still be no resolution of the Cuban crisis? Each night, she looks around her room, thinking that in the morning, it and she might not be here.

She decides that if the crisis is favorably resolved, if the Russians remove the missiles from Cuba, she will start her life over; she will cleanse herself and live as though nothing since the day Will left really happened. And then she thinks of Ted. To be exact, she thinks of Ted's mother. She considers calling her and talking to her, the only other person who lived through something similar to what she's endured. But when she thinks of calling Edith, she remembers Ted's long white fingers, his clean, innocent face, his respectfulness, and she misses him. Once she hated him for not wanting her sexually—or not displaying it, in any case. But now she craves that very thing. His sexual innocence seems like his greatest asset.

When she dials his number, her hand is shaking. Her mouth is dry. Edith answers, and her voice is so sweetly familiar, Lily almost cries.

"How are you, kiddo?" she asks. "I think of you all the time."

"Not so good," Lily says.

"No? I was afraid you'd say that. I could hear it in your voice. Are you letting ghosts haunt you?"

"I'm doing everything wrong," Lily says.

"No. I'm sure that's not true. Did you call to talk to Ted?"

"Yes. But could I come talk to you sometime?"

"Anytime, Lily. You should know that. I'm always here for you, understand? I mean it. I'll get Ted."

"Lily . . ." Ted's voice sounds pleased and surprised.

"Ted, I know this is awfully forward, but . . . can I see you?"

"Of course. Is something wrong?"

And then she says, knowing it is painfully true, "Ted, I miss you so much."

"Oh, honey," he says. "Oh, sweetheart." His voice is so wistful, it tugs at a place just below her ribs, makes her giddy.

"Will you come over? Is it too forward of me to ask?"

"I'll be there as soon as I find a taxi. Sit tight. I have a lot to say to you, too. I'm so glad you called. I'm really glad you called."

Tingling with the excitement of his response, Lily spills some crackers into a basket, slices some cheese on a plate. She brushes her hair in the mirror and looks carefully at herself. In the months since she's seen Ted, has she changed? She feels utterly changed. Hardened. Ugly. But her face doesn't show it. How she wishes to obliterate every titillating memory, every fleeting pleasure that now haunts her.

When she opens the door to Ted, her heart seems to tickle her throat. He looks so handsome to her in the hallway, his long, open face, his eyes, with their dark, glossy lashes. He steps forward and kisses her, lovingly, holds her for a long time in the doorway, like the time she was almost hit by a car, as though her preciousness overwhelms him.

"I'm so glad you called. I'm so glad," he says.

"How have you been?"

"I've been doing great at work," he says. "I got a promotion in September. I'm going to get an apartment next month, I think. I'm crazy about my parents, but I'm ready to do things my way. I guess you know what I mean. Have my own place. Make my own life. What about you? Are you okay, Lily?"

She shrugs. The last few months weigh on her. "I've been rotten for a while," she says. "My job's great. I'm even doing some art, for a change . . . not as much as in school, but . . . this Cuba thing's made me think."

"Me, too. How does it make you feel?"

"Scared to death. What about you?"

"Yes. Like I'm holding my breath. Like nothing I've done's made my life worthwhile."

"Me, too," Lily says. "Exactly."

Ted sits down on the sofa and takes a cracker, then looks up at her with his clear eyes. "You once asked me if I had anything to do with guided missiles. Well, I do. I'm ashamed to say I do. It's my specialty. I wonder if you could even give a guy a chance who's involved in stuff like that."

"I could give you a chance."

"Someone's got to defend the country. I keep telling myself that. Someone does, right?"

"Yes. I wish there weren't bombs, but there are."

"Well, if Khrushchev would throw his out, I'd hope we'd chuck ours in a day. But this Cuba thing is so damn sobering." Ted munches his cracker thoughtfully. "I've been thinking about my grandfather when I was a kid. . . . I was maybe ten or twelve, and he was dying of cancer. He said, 'Ted, I can die in peace. My life's been just what I wanted it to be.' But I feel like my life's nothing like I wanted it to be. It's uncanny you called me. Because the way things ended with us, I can't even decipher what happened. I want to see you again. If you'll give me another chance."

"I want to."

"I know you and I are like a car with a bad battery," he says. "But not anymore. Things are going to be different between us now," he tells her. "I'm doing really well at work. I'm feeling more . . . you know, secure. I've been dating other girls since we stopped seeing each other."

"Oh . . ." she says. The thought has never crossed her mind, and she feels remarkably jealous.

"But it made me see . . . you're what I've been wanting. I've been trying to get the courage to call you. I'm going to devote myself to you," he says.

"Let's not go too fast," Lily says. "Let's just get to know each other again first."

"I feel so comfortable here," Ted says. "I always feel lucky in your presence. Let's put everything that's happened in the past behind us. Do you think we can?"

"Yes, I know we can," she says, feeling it, believing it.

And then, for the rest of the night, they talk about everything. She has never felt so relaxed with him. He seems remarkably changed, at ease. And he loves her. He makes it clear in everything he does. He loves her.

At two in the morning, he gets up and goes to the window.

"Look," he says. "It's snowing!"

Lily starts with pleasure at the enfolding of his large hand around hers.

"Come on," he says. "Come out in the snow with me."

"Really. Now?"

"C'mon." She puts on her coat and her boots, and they go down the elevator, smiling like children.

The air is alive with light, fat flakes that make the ground astonishingly slippery. Ted grabs her hand and begins to run, and then he stops, and they skid on the slick sidewalk, laughing as their feet skate across the cement.

Lake Shore Drive is almost silent. They can hear the waves crashing on the beach on the other side.

"C'mon," he says. "Let's take the underpass. Let's go across." In the dark tunnel, she feels the warmth of him near her. He seems so large and solid in his navy pea coat. She has never seen him so exuberant or so happy.

When they come up the steps, the beach, in the pier lights, seems festive, though entirely empty. The sand is frosted with snow. The waves are crashing up in glossy, spectacular crests.

"It's beautiful," she says. "I've never been here at night."

He puts his arm around her.

"Let's come here a lot. Let's come out here every Saturday night and see how it's changed. Everything's going to be different now," he says. "Everything."

The wind off the water stings her eyes, makes her nostrils brittle. She buries her face in Ted's coat, which smells of wool and snow and him, and she feels safe and calm for the first time in a while.

And so, she falls in love with Ted all over again. It's not the sort of falling in love that she had with Will, where body love comes first. Or even of Pulaski, whose sweet denial has been followed by long, romantic letters about art and life that she reads over and over again.

This time, she has simply willed herself to fall in love. For Ted has all the safety, the solidity, the innocence she knows she needs. And he is so entirely self-contained, that there is ease in knowing he needs very little from her but her presence. Often at night, he stays over late, discussing John Kennedy and his brilliant stand against the Russians, who finally agree to remove all weapons from Cuba. Or they play Scrabble or watch "Saturday Night at the Movies" on TV. Or "Bonanza." Some weekend nights, they have dinner with Ted's parents. She enjoys seeing Ted newly relaxed in front of them. Lily feels proud that she is Ted's ticket to gaining their full respect. How happy he is when they are all together!

At Christmas, for the first time in years, she is part of a family. Edith has decorated the tree so originally, so beautifully, by hanging thin, dried horizontal slices of apples, with their natural stars in the centers left by the seeds, and dried roses, and small, creamy candles, and mounds of tinsel. The sparkling tree, the mountains of gifts, so well chosen for each other, warm her, thrill her. These are people who feel for each other the way families should feel. And they make it clear they want Lily to be a part of their family.

Christmas Eve, Ted takes Lily to Holy Name Cathedral. When he was at Harvard, he fell in with a group of Catholic friends and converted. He is very serious about his Catholicism. His parents are uncomfortable about it when he talks about it—it seems like his one clear rebellion against them—but they respect the way Ted feels about it. Ted tells Lily he wishes she'd convert.

"It's the ritual," he says, "that holds me."

"Why?" she asks.

"Because no matter how bad things are," he says, "there's always something to do about it."

But Lily feels all religions are a sham. She cannot believe that the kind Catholic God he sees would have given her two such hateful fathers, would have allowed either of them absolution, or would have made her mother suffer so. When she tells Ted this, he holds her in his arms and says he understands. Someday, he says, she will find her faith again. She wants to believe it's true. She does not mind going to church with Ted sometimes to see the pageantry. But she cannot imagine that she will ever see life as good enough to believe again.

Ted calls nearly every day, usually from the office, where he works until ten or eleven o'clock. He asks her not to go out with other men and says, of course, he won't go out, either.

One night at dinner he tells her, "Last summer, I saw you walking with another guy. It was a weekday night."

"You did?"

"A blond guy. Skinny."

Will. He saw her with Will.

"And I thought you must have been in love with him, because you were holding hands and laughing and walking so close. And after I saw you, I got so angry I couldn't eat or sleep for a good week. It was like puppy love. My mother said, 'What right do you have to be angry with her?' but I was. I wanted to knock your teeth out. Or his. I always have wanted you to selfishly wait for me. . . . I'm not saying it's fair. Who was he?" She shakes her head.

"Just someone," she says sadly.

"What happened to him?"

"He's gone. He left town."

Ted smiles.

"Did you love him?"

"It's over. It hurts to talk about it," she says.

"I'm sorry," he says. "I'm sorry, honey. I won't bring it up again."
But she sees an odd jealousy in his eyes. Something in the way he looks
that makes her uncomfortable. And he does bring it up again, when he
is feeling insecure.

"It's over, right . . . with that guy?" he asks.

"It's over," she reassures him, and then he's happy again.

When six months pass, Claire, Pulaski, Dave and Joe at work, and even
Will know that she is going "steady."

"I càn't deny you," Will says in a letter that seems pained and has
so many scratch-outs, it was clearly hard to write.

> But make sure it's right for you, whatever you do. Things are quite
> bad right now with Sandra. I won't get into it, but I feel so trapped.
> Don't do what I did. Don't marry who you *think* you should instead
> of who you need. I can't seem to get out of this thing. Every move
> I make to extricate myself makes me feel guilty. Do you ever think
> of me the way I still think of you? God, if you knew how I think of
> you. . . . For God sakes, don't marry without letting me know,
> without making sure I'm not free or ready to get free. We belong
> together. You must know that.

At work, Joe Forrest calls her into his office.

"It's very unusual for us to promote someone in less than a year," he
tells her, leaning back against his drawing table, crossing his arms. "But
you're the best mount-room trainee we've ever had. All the layouts and
resizings and things people have given you have been superb. I don't
know if you've heard, but Kevin is being promoted to a full art director.
I want you to take his place, to be my assistant art director." He smiles,
showing his straight teeth, and pats his knees with pleasure. "I'll teach
you all I know. I mean, really, we're talking apprenticeship here, and
it's going to be great."

Lily hardly knows what to say. It is an honor to be Joe Forrest's assistant. And yet she knows it means extra work in the afternoons when he is drunk, covering for him. It might even mean being harassed. Still, she can hardly turn it down. If she does, she'll be scorned, cast out, lose her only chance to advance.

"I can't wait."

"Kevin will have his things out of here by Friday, and you can move in. Oh, and there's a raise. A nice one," he tells her, and she blushes. A raise, she discovers, feels even better than a lover's compliment, though not dissimilar.

"Thank you."

"Thank yourself. You're the one doing the great work."

Lily is on her way out the door to go to the Art Institute one night when she gets a call from the police. She can't imagine what's going on at the police station. The background noise is roaring. The officer has a small, annoyed voice as he introduces himself.

"We've got your father here," he says.

For a moment, Lily doesn't know. Could it be her real father, lost to her for so many years, found again? She sees his face as clearly as the last day she saw him, when he was packing up his car. When she stood by the trunk watching, he'd said, "What are you looking at?" and turned away from her.

"Who is it?" she asks.

"Your father. He's been drinking and driving. We'll release him if you're willing to come and take him home."

"You sure it's my father? What's his name?"

"John J. Beach. He made us look up your number. Gave us your address and everything. Isn't he your father?"

Lily takes a deep breath. Jack.

"No," she says. "You must have the wrong Beach."

"Look. He said you might not say okay to taking him, but, miss, if he's your father, get him out of here. You don't want him spending the night in the Cook County jail drunk tank. Believe me, I'm doing you a favor calling you. He's not our classic drunk, if you get my drift."

"I'm sorry," Lily says, her voice frighteningly sugary. "Believe me, Officer, I don't know him." When she hangs up, she feels such a pressure in her face and ears that she has to sit down. This lie doesn't go down easy, and there is none of the pleasure she expected to feel in telling it.

• • •

During the night she awakes in a cold sweat. She's dreamed that Jack's been bludgeoned to death by men in wet suits, hitting him unmercifully with the cords to their oxygen tanks. She turns on all the lights, but even the dark window unnerves her.

"Why can't you just go away, Jack, you pig!" she says aloud. She ends up sleeping on the kitchen floor. She spreads out a blanket there, in the narrow room, drags over her pillow. For some reason, she feels safe among the cupboards labeled "Woolens," the faint, ghostly smell of lavender and mothballs, and her dishes, neatly stacked and washed and waiting to feed someone.

A year passes, and sometimes Lily realizes that she feels somewhat numb, that she doesn't think of her mother as much as she used to, or even Will, and when she does think of him, there is just a quiet hopelessness that overcomes her, not despair. She tells herself she loves Ted again and again, reminds herself. Sometimes she is impatient with him. But when that feeling comes on, she remembers the night she took home the two men, and shuddering, she looks over at his solidity and feels pleased, calm. Mostly, she just feels safe. There is none of the discomforting passion she feels for Will. None of the worry that comes from knowing how intensely Andres feels about her.

One night, on the first anniversary of getting back together, Ted says he has something important to ask her. He sips a full glass of wine, leading up to the question, and keeps refilling hers until she has to put her hand over the glass to stop him.

"I was thinking," he says finally, "of getting more serious."

"More serious?"

"Getting married."

Lily sets down her wineglass. "You know I'm scared of marriage," she tells him. So many times they've talked of marriage abstractly, as though it had nothing to do with them.

"I know," he says. "It's understandable with what happened in your life. But you're not afraid of me, are you?"

"No."

"I want to be with you," he says. "*Be* with you," he says pointedly, and she knows he means sexually. Lovemaking between them has consisted of tentative, careful caresses, but she has begun to realize he does want her, that mostly he is being correct, waiting.

"I want that, too," she says. "It's marriage that scares me. It always seems to go sour in time, like milk."

"Just think about it," he says. "Just mull it around," he says. His voice is hypnotic. He takes her hand. She feels so small and safe when he holds her hand. Like a child again.

"I will," she says, but she wonders how to stall him, hopes he won't bring up the question again.

Happier with her life in general, Lily allows herself to become more and more absorbed in her job. Joe Forrest is letting her do real ads now. And she is surprised to find that he gives her total credit in front of everyone.

"Lily did this all by herself," he often says. He is proud of her, in an unselfish, fatherly way she couldn't have guessed was possible.

But in the afternoons he is another man entirely. The first thing he does when he comes back from Riccardo's, where everyone knows he orders the "Mike Ruddi" salad and three double martinis, is to smoke three cigarettes in a row and hold court. There are four people who tend to show up for the festivities: Ben Graebel, the print director, who also is somewhat sloshed after lunch. Eleanor, the fiftyish secretary from down the hall who wears Cleopatra eye makeup and smokes cigarettes in a long red holder that is nearly bitten through at the tip, who clearly has been, is, or wants to be Joe Forrest's lover. Sam Klaff, the art director in the next office, who says "No!" to every punch line of every sick joke Joe tells, and Andrew Brucci, who is a young art director, used to be Joe's assistant, and worships him enough to laugh at him and stick with him even when he's embarrassing. Each day, when they come in, Lily tries to sneak out. Sometimes she's able. At other times, they needle her.

"Can't stand the heat, huh, Lily?"

"Are we too vulgar for you? Let's clean up this language right now. We've got a blushing virgin in our midst," Joe Forrest says.

"Just going to the ladies' room," Lily feigns. Or, "I've got an errand before lunch hour's over." Or, "I'm just going to another office to make a call."

"Ted!!!" they say in harmony, in an embarrassing swoon.

"What's wrong with that limp dick?" Joe once says. "Doesn't he want to marry you? Rocket scientists don't have the stuff? Excuse my French, of course!"

Usually, Lily hides in the ladies' room, reading a book on the fainting couch. Sometimes she escapes to Claire's desk. By two o'clock, the gang is gone, and Lily tiptoes quietly back into the office; for from two to three, Joe Forrest sleeps, tilted back in his chair, his head back, his mouth open, feet up on his drawing table. He looks precarious, uncomfortable, and childlike in sleep. These are the best moments of the afternoon, the only time Lily can get work done uninterrupted.

Sometime after three-thirty, Joe wakes up mean. He goes from office to office, shouting loud, negative comments. He tries to rework his layouts and usually ruins them. And then he starts his tirade about advertising. About how "we're all telling lies, screwing the people, making them consume when they simply don't need the crap we've got to sell." And Lily is the sole recipient of this. Every day, she tries to work, sitting at her drawing table, not looking up, except occasionally, as he goes on and on. And then he gets sentimental, telling her how beautiful she is, wondering why she puts up with a nasty old drunk like himself.

Between four and five he sits quietly, uselessly, shuffling papers on his drawing table, until it is time to take his briefcase and catch the Northwestern train to Aurora and his wife, whom he calls a "saint if there ever was one."

One afternoon, between two and three, while Joe Forrest is sleeping, a pretty young woman knocks at the door.

"He's very busy," Lily says, blocking her view of Joe's upturned face and slack mouth.

"No, it's you I want to see," the woman says. "I'm Wally Payson's secretary. He'd like to see you at four. Is that possible?"

"Me? Lily Beach?"

The woman looks down at a three-by-five card. "Lily Beach. That's you."

"Where's his office?" Lily asks. She's never met Wally Payson and is afraid on two counts: He has the power to sack her in a second if he doesn't like her. And also, she knows too much about him. She knows he cheats on his wife, that he's willing to wear boxer shorts with dogs and fire hydrants on them, that he is breast obsessed, and likes bright-colored lingerie. This is far more than Lily would like to know, considering.

"I'll come get you," the secretary says sweetly.

"You don't have to," Lily says.

"I don't mind," she says. "Just part of my job." Lily watches the woman walk away, down the hall, and feels a rush of excitement she hasn't felt for a long while. After all, Claire said power is an aphrodisiac. She never said how sexy it would feel to sense your own power, even with no man around at all.

Wally Payson's office is as big as four regular offices put together in a square. Banks of windows on two sides spill light across the loud, splash-patterned rug, across the Scandinavian furniture, with its honey-teak smoothness. A crystal chandelier hangs down as a vulgar little note of attempted gentility.

Wally Payson is sitting behind his desk when Lily comes in. With the grand, sleek desk and his chair, which is much higher than the one he directs her to, Lily feels meek and small, as though she is in the principal's office. Payson is a slightly overweight man. His dark hair is slicked to one side with Brylcreem. A short, filterless cigarette trapezes on his mouth, moving with every word.

"Come in! Come in!" he says. His shirt collar looks so tight, his ruddy neck appears to be the result of squeezing. "So you're Lily."

"Yes."

"I've heard some remarkable things about you, young lady."

"You have?"

She thinks of Claire and wonders if she has not only spoken to him about her but actually has told him Lily knows about the two of them. But no, Claire always said if he knew she'd told anybody, he would have cut off the relationship and fired her without a glance backward.

"The scuttlebutt on the eighth floor is that you've got the stuff—you hardly need any guidance. Pretty impressive for someone so wet behind the ears. And for a woman."

Lily swallows, wonders if the gulp is as audible as she imagines. "Thank you," she says.

"The first thing I want to say is, I think you can be anything here you want to be. You can move up the ladder like the best of us. I know some people think women should marry and stay home, period. But my mother worked all her life and did just fine. I mean, it was a factory job, but she became a union leader. I was busting proud of her.

"And during the war they hired lots of women here. I was mad at first. Here I was, twenty-six years old and flat-footed, with asthma. I wasn't going to the front, let's face it. And here come these women, with no real training, to join us. There were women writers, art directors, media types. Even a woman account executive. Josephine Glasser. Oooh!

She was tough. Wined and dined the Harvester folks until they didn't know which way their tractors were facing. I got impressed real fast.

"I was the first to speak up for the ladies after the war. I said, 'Why should they have to quit if they don't want to? They know the business as well as anyone coming back from the Pacific.' But you know, everyone said, those boys fought for our safety. They deserve jobs. Josephine Glasser stayed three more years, until she was squeezed out. I admired that broad like you wouldn't believe.

"So, do you see what I'm saying? I figure, a woman is good at what she does, she deserves a berth. You got my vote."

"Thank you," Lily says.

"Do you say anything else besides thank you?" Wally says, smirking.

"Please and excuse me," Lily says.

"Good. Not too easily intimidated. That's refreshing in a woman."

Lily thinks: Well, I'm not too easily intimidated by someone who wears boxer shorts with dogs and fire hydrants on them.

"Now there's something else I've got to get off my chest," Wally says, smashing out his cigarette. "It's Joe Forrest."

"What about him?"

"What about him? He's a lush. Even if you're a Pollyanna, you can't deny it. Rumor has it he's laid a few thumbscrews on you."

"I don't mind him," Lily says.

"You *are* a Pollyanna."

"He's a great art director. His layouts are beautiful."

"Yeah, sure, in the morning. What about the afternoon?"

"He does twice the work in the morning as most people do all day."

"Yeah, well, that's not a bad argument. I'd like to see it verified, though."

Wally Payson leans forward across his desk, his bulldog face making her sit back in her chair.

"I want you to keep an eye on how much he does. Keep a record. I want to review it in two weeks."

"I can't," Lily says.

"You can if you're told to."

"But it feels so traitorous. Can't someone else do it? He hired me."

"Actually, it's a very simple choice, Lily. I'll fire *you* if you don't."

Lily feels her stomach clamp down, her heart clatter. She can't think of a thing to say.

"So, that's settled," Wally says. "Good." He gets up and shows her the door. "It's been delightful getting to know you," he says.

"Your boyfriend is a monster," she tells Claire, leaning over her desk, whispering.

"Jeff?"

"Payson."

"Oh, yeah. He's a real manipulator. Makes a lot of people nervous. What did he do to you?"

"It's so awful, I can't even talk about it."

"Great. So don't tell me."

"He wants me to spy on Joe Forrest."

"Spy? Like read his diary? Like empty his pockets while he's sleeping? Like listen in on his phone calls?"

"No, like keep a record of the work he does so Wally can evaluate if he's earning his money."

"Oh, because he's soaked all the time?"

"Just in the afternoons."

"Since when are you Joe Forrest's big fan?"

"Since I became his assistant. He's really good, Claire. No one else in the department could have taught me as much as he has. And he never claims the credit for the things he helps me with. Besides, I owe him. He saved me from taking money from my stepfather by offering me a job on the spot."

"And he used to call insulting things into the mount room, all based on the idea of being mounted, and he breaks your eardrum every afternoon with his tirades."

"If I'm willing to put up with it, what does it matter?"

"So, what are you going to do?"

Lily shrugs. "Look for a job at J. Walter Thompson?"

"No. Just lie. List everything *you* do on Joe Forrest's lists of accomplishments. You said he helps you, right?"

"Yeah."

"So fudge a little. Don't be so literal. Wally's a bonehead. He'll never know."

"Why do you sleep with this man?" Lily asks.

"Power," Claire says, blinking. "Raw 'I can do anything I want to anybody' power."

• • •

Lily writes "Work Log"—the most benign heading she can think of—at the top of the page and writes in what Joe Forrest accomplished today:

"Layout for International Harvester Trucks Jamboree."

There is nothing else to put down. Is one layout a day too little? she wonders. Maybe. She writes beneath it:

"Exploratory work on IH Spring Sellout. Discussion with International Harvester client about new ways to reach consumers."

Actually, this is what Joe Forrest did yesterday, but who's going to call her on it? And now she starts to make things up. She writes down things they talked about, but never did, a week ago for Carter's cough drops. She writes down work done on a pro bono account that Andrew Brucci is actually working on. After all, Joe talked to Andrew about it and gave him the idea.

Then Lily folds the slip of paper in half and puts it in a file marked "Ideas" and goes home, feeling weary and lost.

In two weeks she is called to Wally Payson's office. This time, she finds herself shuddering, quietly gathering up the work logs she's written for Joe Forrest.

Wally doesn't even look up at her when she comes in. He's writing something but says, looking only at his page, "Well, did you keep a record?"

"Yes."

"Well." He holds out his hand, still not looking, and she hands him the papers. He glances at them, then looks up with a sourness that makes Lily step back.

"What the fuck is this?" he asks.

"The work logs you asked me to keep for Joe Forrest."

"Yeah. For Joe Forrest. Not for the entire art department."

"He was involved in *all* the work there," she says, her voice growing high with fear.

"Right. Starting in 1902. You are a loyal bitch. My God. Aren't you ashamed to bring this to me, knowing it's completely false?"

"It's not," she insists. Merely heightened, she thinks.

"You can go now," he says.

"You want to fire me, Mr. Payson? Go ahead." All of a sudden, she is using the voice she uses with Jack. Defiant. Terrified. All at once.

"And have you tell the entire agency that I'm playing house with your little friend Claire? Please. I'm not a fool."

Lily gasps.

"Like Claire thinks I don't know she tells you everything. Just get out of here," he says.

Two days later, Joe Forrest is called to Wally Payson's office, in the afternoon, during his nap.

"He can't come," Lily says. "He's very busy. He's getting ready for a meeting," Lily says, blocking the door, trying to talk over his snoring.

"I'm sorry," Wally Payson's secretary says. "Mr. Payson said he had to come no matter what he's doing."

"He's on the phone. I'll send him up when he's off."

"Joe!" Lily says, shaking him. He murmurs in his sleep, nothing more. "Joe, Wally Payson wants to see you. You've got to get up." Once he's awake, she helps him with a cup of coffee and breath mints.

"I'm a mess, aren't I?" Joe says softly as he sips the last of the coffee. It breaks Lily's heart.

When he comes back down from Wally's office, his face is very nearly gray, and his normally good posture is slumped, defeated. He says nothing at all to Lily. Just takes his briefcase and coat and leaves. Lily sits at her table, her heart thumping, her throat swelling. She knows what's happened.

The next day, when she arrives, all of Joe Forrest's things are packed in boxes outside the office, even the framed print she's sold him, and her things are on Joe Forrest's drawing table. Her watercolor tray, her brushes, even her picture of Ted. And on the drawing board is pinned a note:

"You lied for him. Now you can have his place." It is signed: "Wally."

Chapter Ten

Ted begins a campaign a politician would be proud of. Each night, when she comes home, there are a dozen roses waiting at the doorman's desk for her to claim. The first day they are pink; the day after, white. The next, yellow. Her apartment begins to look funereal. Every shipment of flowers arrives with a note that says, "I love you. Will you marry me?"

When he calls each night, she says, "Thank you for the flowers."

And he says, "So?"

"They're very pretty," she says. "I'm going through hell with this Joe Forrest thing. I'm just feeling so guilty—"

"Is that all you can say?"

"For now," she says. And she struggles. For she truly loves him, even his innocence. But the thought of marrying him actually presses on her chest, makes it hard for her to breathe. Her vision of marriage can't be revised. It stars a pale version of herself doing whatever Ted dictates— begging for attention, begging him not to leave, lying alone in a green chenille robe in the dark, waiting for him.

Saturday night he takes her to dinner at the Gay Parisian. He orders Dom Perignon. He insists she have steak glazed in butter. Then, after he's made sure to refill her glass three times, he pulls out a little blue velvet box and sets it in front of her.

"It's not my birthday," she says.

"Every day will be your birthday if you say yes," he says. She sighs. She can't believe the panic she feels. Each day, she senses he is getting closer, stealing her air and her judgment, making her say yes.

"I won't open it," she says.

"You can't be that cruel," he says, smiling.

She imagines that the spring-snap box is a device that will ensnare her as a jawed trap in a forest catches wild animals who are attracted to its contents.

"You wouldn't believe how cruel I can be. You don't know how I can be at all."

"Come on, Lily. You're being so silly about all this. You love me. Just relax."

"I can't," she says. "I can't." And surely he must hear that her voice is mournful.

And then it happens: President Kennedy is shot. She is sitting in her office with her new assistant, Fred Fotis, when the news comes through. Andrew Brucci hears it on his radio. No one knows for sure what's going on, but it's clear that the president's been severely wounded in Dallas by an unknown gunman.

"It can't be true," she says, looking up from her drawing board at Fred, who's gone as pale as the paper he's working on.

"Bad things are always true," he says.

There is a television on the sixth floor, and by the time Lily and Fred rush down there, the room is already overflowing. The announcer is a slight, nervous, softspoken man named Dan Something, and he is trying to explain that no one really knows anything except that the president seemed to suddenly sink into his seat in the official car and that the motorcade veered off course suddenly to Parkland Memorial Hospital, where there have been no announcements and no eyewitness reports. Dan Something seems both perfectly poised and perfectly choked up at intervals, and the crowd in the room shifts and murmurs, waiting for real news.

The mournful electricity makes Lily wonder if everybody secretly, even subconsciously, hopes that the president is truly dead, longing for the tragedies that define life, make us feel lucky and awestruck to be alive. Her own mother's death was too crushing, too guilt ridden, to have that life-affirming quality, but a distant death, like the death of a president, can be achingly close and yet distant enough to feel. Lily thinks all of this as she sits next to Fred and Jeff, Claire's friend, and Eleanor, the secretary who had the crush on Joe Forrest and is the only one who's managed to stay in touch with him, keeping them all informed of his job hunting, her red cigarette holder bobbing with the power of her knowledge. Her red cigarette holder bobs now as she chews on it, listening for news of the president.

In the end, most everybody returns to their offices, waiting out the news, but there is a miserable silence in the halls. Andrew Brucci, taking a cue from Joe Forrest, pulls a fifth of whiskey out of his taboret and pours some into everyone's coffee cups.

Lily holds out her cup and swallows it down, though it burns like turpentine. When the announcement finally comes, the cacophony of different radio stations becomes one as all the stations feed into the same press conference.

"President John F. Kennedy died at approximately one P.M. today, central standard time, here in Dallas. He died of a gunshot wound to the brain. I have no other details of the assassination." The voice of the press aide is flat and weary, and echoes in the silent hall.

Lily, despite her cool appraisal of everyone's intense emotions, bursts into tears, is truly inconsolable. Since almost all the people in the surrounding offices are men, her sobbing rises above their low murmuring and draws a parade of men to her door.

"Poor Lily. You're taking this harder than I am, on the outside, but I feel just the same on the inside," they each say in their own way, coming by to pat her back or simply nod at her with sad agreement. Even a few of the assistant art directors come by, though they have been cool to her, and suspicious, at her having been promoted before them. "You really like the guy, huh?" one of them says. "He was a prince, wasn't he?" another offers.

A memo quickly circulates that the office will be closed this afternoon, tomorrow, and will not resume until Monday, in memory of "our president." And if the funeral is planned for Monday, the office will not open until Tuesday.

As Lily packs her things, straightening her drawing board and taboret, as she does before each weekend, Ted calls. Her hands are shaking, and her heart beats hurtfully in her throat.

"I'll come pick you up," he says. "I'll walk you home."

Most of the people in the office are gone when Ted is announced. The minute he walks into her office and sees her red eyes, he puts his arms around her.

"Our hero's dead," he says softly.

"Yes," she says.

"I guess he was just too good to be true."

"No," she corrects. "Just too good to last."

All weekend, they watch the endless news, the morbid diagrams of the impact of the bullets on the poor president's head, the photos of Jacqueline Kennedy in her pink suit, the skirt and stockings splashed in blood. And the murder of Lee Harvey Oswald right before their eyes.

Each night, Ted has trouble leaving, stays until it is late. Sunday night, he stays until dawn, holding her, kissing her. On Monday night, after a long day of watching the funeral and all the talk and all the mourning, he says, "I want us to be together so badly. I want to make love to you, know you. I can't stand it anymore. Please say you'll marry me." And because it is the first time his longing for her seems based on passion, she responds.

"I can't wait, either," she says, kissing him.

"Do you mean you will?" he asks, barely getting the words out.

She can't say yes. The word won't come. But she nods and hugs him tightly so he'll stop talking about it. Later, alone in bed, she wonders why she's said yes. It is a decision somehow independent of her. Like something previously fated she cannot change.

Everyone seems ridiculously overjoyed that Ted and Lily are getting married. Claire starts dragging out *Bride's* magazine and tearing out pictures of pouffy, ridiculous wedding dresses, nunlike veils, long satin gloves.

"Don't forget," Lily says. "I'm paying for this."

She finally lets Ted give her the blue velvet box, and she is thrilled that it is an antique ring of three stones: two diamonds and a sapphire. Each day, she discovers that Ted has taste, good sense. He asks only one uncomfortable thing of Lily: to attend a few weeks of classes with a priest. It is a class specifically designed for spouses of Catholics who are not Catholics themselves.

"Must I?" she asks.

"If you love me," he says.

The priest is a short, nervous little man with a lisp. She distrusts him before he even opens his mouth. And as though he knows it, he never once looks her in the eyes, yet she sees him making eye contact with everyone else. He must see me as a lost soul, she thinks wearily. But she completes the course out of duty to Ted, hearing hardly anything the priest says. A good portion of the last few classes is about not using birth control. Lily wonders if she can insert a diaphragm without Ted's being aware of it. The day she finishes instruction, Ted says, "I'm really glad you did that for me. It meant a lot."

"Good," Lily says, just glad that it's over.

Then Ted shrugs and clears his throat, and her hearing sharpens. There is something he wants to tell her.

"About birth control," he says.

"Father McNally mentioned birth control."

"Well, we don't want to have children right away. I don't see why we can't use rubbers, at first, anyway. Okay?" He winks at her and squeezes her hand.

Lily is relieved and surprised. Maybe he isn't such a stick-in-the-mud, after all. "Okay," she says.

They agree to marry in May. June is such a cliché month for weddings, and besides, every place they would choose for the reception is booked already in June. They choose the Drake Hotel Gold Coast Room. They go on a tasting tour of caterers and decide on one that someone later tells them is really *the* society caterer.

"I don't want *the* society caterer," Lily tells Ted.

"Oh, can't you enjoy this, Lily? This will be a dream wedding."

"I don't want a dream wedding," Lily says. "I'm a Bohemian."

This makes Ted laugh, sit down, and fold his arms and shake his head at her.

"You're a successful young woman in advertising," Ted says. "And I'm a successful young aerospace engineer. And we deserve the wedding of anyone's dreams."

"You make us sound like Barbie and Ken," Lily says.

"Well," says Ted. "Aren't we?"

Chapter Eleven

Andres Pulaski's rented tuxedo chafes when he dons it in front of the mirror. He is thinner now than the last time he wore a tuxedo, for his own first wedding, many years ago in Paraguay. Then, he was still fat from his mother's cooking: the hot charcoaled meats of his childhood, the garlic herb sauces that you sweated out the next day in a purifying kind of way. Now he is thin from living alone for the first time in his life. His freezer is stuffed with waxed boxes of TV dinners. Though he eats these meals nearly every night, his appetite never holds out to finish them. The taste of the freezer intrudes, makes him set down the drumstick or his forkful of wet meat loaf and sigh. His last wife was an excellent cook, and though he grieves for her cooking, he is still happy to be alone.

The bow tie feels loose and confusing in his fingers. Once, he wore bow ties often, with white dinner jackets, to the nightclubs in Buenos Aires, where they often went for entertainment after his escape from Paraguay. How slick and fast his life had seemed then. Still, after all these years, he manages to make an acceptable knot.

He is both flattered and wounded by what he is going to do today. It is thrilling that she called him, that he is the one person she wishes to annex as a member of her family. But the fact that she has chosen another man burns in a way he hasn't expected. Lily. He says her name out loud to the mirror. Lilla. He was certain, by loving her unconditionally, he would own her forever. Instead, he must now publicly give her away. It is a painful lesson in humility. He might have had her all to himself had he reached out more, made himself clearer. But in the end, he would have lost her. He knows this. And vows not to stop loving her.

In Lily's memory, later in life, there will be no space at all between her decision to marry Ted and its actuality. As though six months of her life were entirely lost or never happened. All she will remember is one day saying yes, the next day walking down the aisle in a floor-length satin dress on Andres Pulaski's steady arm.

It was the truest of loves that Andres showed when he sweetly agreed to give Lily away. She was afraid he'd be hurt. But thinking she was an orphan, with no one at all to give her away, he sounded so truly touched, so choked up, when she asked.

So here she is, a bride. Here she is in the Gold Coast Room, dressed in ivory satin, slips, and veils and a garter belt trimmed in pale blue ribbon, and she feels like someone's lost Christmas package or a Halloween merrymaker or a refugee from a high school play. The sense of unreality brings on an icy fear as she comes down the long aisle. Behind the flowers are faces of the people she works with: Claire, Andrew Brucci, and Sam Klaff. Even Joe Forrest and his wife, who does look saintlike. And there are the more vague faces of her aunt Kate, her mother's older sister, and some of Ted's friends from his company. And Edith, her red hair set like a teenager's, tears in her eyes, and Ted's father, looking very pleased and sober at the same time.

And despite all the sense of hopefulness, the good people wishing them well, it is as though Lily is watching the wedding on TV and fearing for the heroine. It is as though she can hear the steady, worrisome thrum of "something terrifying is about to happen" music.

As she stands next to Ted before the minister, she refuses to look at him, though she senses he's trying to catch her eyes with his. The more excited he's become about the wedding, the more she's longed to step back from him, to wrap herself in some protective covering that keeps a pocket of air between herself and his love, which she fears will smother her. Her feelings for him, which grow each day, make her certain she will disappear beneath her duty to him like a house beneath a mud slide.

All week, Lily has remembered how Will would not call off his own wedding, though she was certain he'd grown to love her. Now she understands. Weddings are events with their own momentum. People are temporarily insane when they agree to marry, and then the wedding simply pulls them along to the altar.

She wrote Will a letter last week saying she was marrying, but she didn't mail it until yesterday. Almost as though she didn't want him to try to stop her. She wonders if he would stop her.

The problem is, whenever she thinks of him, something still stirs in her. Part of it is the pain of losing him. Part of it is still wanting him, still wanting the equality she felt with him, the wild desire that only with him felt pure and safe. She still dreams of him, still wants him in her dreams, awakes filled with desire for him nearly once a week.

After the steak dinner and the passion punch, the wedding cake and the toasts, Lily and Ted leave the remaining guests and take the elevator up to their suite. It isn't the bridal suite. The bridal suite costs too much, and after the wedding, there isn't much to spend. But it is a nice room nevertheless, with a view of the lake.

Ted opens the door for her and lifts her over the threshold.

"It's not like we're going to live here," she tells him.

"What?"

"Aren't you supposed to do this over the doorway of our first house?"

"Let's pretend," he says. In fact, he's already moved his things into Lily's apartment. His much better hi-fi and all his records, most of which she doesn't like: Andy Williams, Steve Lawrence and Eydie Gorme. He scorns her Elvis records and her Beach Boys and her Jan and Deans. "Kid stuff," he calls them. His clothes crowd her drawers. His pillows, underneath the pillow slips, are yellow with use and age. And his towels fill her towel racks, too skinny, folded wrong.

Tonight her sexuality feels sluggish, denied, clotted. She wonders if she will even want to make love.

Ted sits on the bed. He is handsome in his tuxedo. There is no denying his appeal. So tall and strong looking. His hair so full of light. His chocolate-black eyes, looking at her warmly, lovingly.

"Come here," he says.

She unpins her veil by the mirror. In the last hour, it's begun to tug at her hair, made her scalp burn, and given her the slightest blush of a headache.

"Come here," he says.

"I will."

"Are you afraid?" he asks.

She is afraid. But not as he's imagining it. She's afraid she feels angry at him for making her wait so long. She's afraid there's so much he doesn't know about making love. She's afraid he'll realize she's not a virgin.

She comes over to the bed and sits down, has the strongest desire to turn her back to him, but moving at all in the wedding dress is something of a maneuver.

"I'm tired," she says.

"Are you?"

"It must be the punch."

"Pretty room, huh?" he says, looking around at the damask chairs, the French provincial desk.

"I kind of wish I was at home," she says.

"Why?"

"I miss my bed." And then she begins to weep. The lace handkerchief she's worn all day, tucked into her sleeve, doesn't do much to catch her tears.

"What's wrong?" he asks gently, putting his arms around her. "What's wrong?" he says. "We've got each other now. Isn't this what we've really wanted? To be together." He kisses her wet cheeks, wraps her in his arms, and then, astonishingly, he becomes passionate. It is thrilling, strange, wonderful. He kisses her ears, her throat, undoes the wedding dress, button by painful button, gasps when he sees her lace brassiere, her decorated garter belt. His breathing is so loud, she can barely think, barely keep her own breath from tugging, from longing.

He kisses her breasts, undoes the bra and kisses them more. And then, when he touches her between the legs, she is ecstatic, moaning, thrilled. But before he's barely given her that pleasure, he's unzipping his pants and taking out his swollen penis. She gasps, because she's never seen one so large, so thick. She wonders if it will hurt her, if she can receive all of it. Then, immediately, it seems, he is pressing it against her and pushing.

"I hope it doesn't hurt," he says. "I've been dreaming of this."

But it does; it makes her brace herself, push against his chest with the heel of her hands. She is crying, feeling it opening her, tearing at her. And just when the pain becomes wild pleasure, just as she feels the heat begin to stir, rise, as he fills her with its enormity, his whole body shakes, and then he is saying, "Oh, my God," and pulls out of her, semen ribboning across her stomach.

"Why did you do that?" she asks him, panting, lost.

"I forgot to put on a rubber," he says. "God, I'm sorry. But we agreed. Too early for a baby, don't you think?" He rushes to the bathroom, his wedding shoes still on, his pants around his knees, and comes back with a wad of Kleenex he uses to sponge up the thick ropes of semen on her stomach.

Her vagina is aching, and when she touches a Kleenex to it, it comes back with a splotch of blood.

"See," she says, tasting the irony. "Just a little bit of blood." Virgin blood.

"Are you okay? I'm sorry. Did it hurt?"

She wants to tell him that he is endowed with a member other men, and some women, would kill for, but she just takes a deep breath and tells him it was really fine.

"I guess I'm not very good at this. You didn't get a chance to climax, did you? Do you think you'd know it if you did?" he asks.

"I think I'd know it," she says, trying not to smile. She hopes that he will touch her again, make her come, maybe with his fingers, but shortly he is asleep, snoring lightly. She gets up and goes into the bathroom, locks the door, and taking off the garter belt and stockings, she sits on the toilet top, feeling worried, lost. He's just learning, she tells herself. I can teach him. When she comes out, she is wearing her silky nightgown, her teeth are brushed, her face is washed, and she is once again the virginal bride.

In the morning she wants to make love again.

"Maybe we shouldn't go too fast," he says. "I hear you can get sore."

"Please," she says. "But touch me here first. Touch me so I can come, too."

He stares at her quietly. As his fingers begin to draw circles across her swollen sex, she closes her eyes and feels it to her soul. When she comes, she pulls up her knees, folds up like a baby and moans.

"Did I do it?" he asks.

"I think it's safe to say you did," she tells him.

There is no honeymoon. Once again, after the wedding, there isn't enough money. So instead, they plan a week together, going to the Art

Institute and the Field Museum, the Museum of Science and Industry, the Shedd Aquarium, and the Adler Planetarium. Like an eighth-grade field-trip kind of honeymoon, she tells Claire over the phone.

But the phone is mostly used by Ted, calling into the office. He calls three, four times a day. From the aquarium, from a restaurant, from home. "We're on our honeymoon," she tells him. "Can't they do without you?" But really, she suspects, he can't do without *them*.

The lovemaking gets better but seems infrequent to her. Usually once a week is all Ted wants, even if she suggests more. "I'm really trying to finish this paper," he'll tell her. "Maybe tomorrow." But rainchecks aren't often honored. The next night, he's always trying to finish a new paper. After waiting so long, Lily feels vaguely cheated. Gypped. And the lovemaking still hurts sometimes. She never knew a penis could be too large to enjoy, but she worries it will always feel this way. "Always open the box before you buy," Claire once said. Now she wonders if she should have. The other thing is, when she gets really passionate, when the passion really controls her and she begins to talk out loud, and breathe loud, and moan, Ted grows cool, withdraws. She is afraid to ask him why. She thinks he must be repulsed by her intensity, her need, and she starts trying not to show it, so the pleasure begins to drain out of lovemaking for her. In a way, she begins to dread it.

At night, while he sits at the dining-room table poring over papers from work, she stares at the gold band, the diamond-and-sapphire ring, which makes her hands look as if they belong to someone else. Sometimes at night she plays the piano. She is taking piano lessons and is thrilled to actually be able to make music on the beautiful instrument Andres gave her. But the piano annoys Ted's work. And once, in a flush of warmth toward Andres, she tells Ted how he had given her the beautiful instrument, and ever since, Ted's seemed to hate it, saying it's too big, in the way, and can't she practice when he's not around?

"Mrs. Nicholson," the doorman begins to call her. The people in the co-op congratulate her. "Your husband is a lovely fellow," the old ladies say. "Quite a nice guy you married," the old men say. Lily can't help thinking that she's fooled everybody, that she is the rose with the canker inside, that the secret of her dark, lusty past will now show itself to the world.

Will calls her at the office. "I got your letter," he says. "How could you marry?" he asks. His voice is hot, loving, frightening. "You didn't let me know ahead of time. And I'm so close to getting out of this thing with Sandra."

"Will, I don't think so. I don't think you'll ever leave her."

"I thought we loved each other. You gave me no warning at all."

"I've been waiting a long time," she says.

"I can't believe you married him. You. You who's so afraid of marriage you wouldn't marry me even when we were really in love. Why would you marry him now when you wouldn't marry me then? I was willing to leave Sandra then for you. I might have been able to, back then."

"I don't know. A lot of time has passed. I didn't want to be alone anymore, waiting for you."

"You love him, this rocket scientist? You love him more than you love me? I never thought you'd go back to him."

Lily sits in her chair at her drawing board. It is spring now. The lake is rocking with boats. The early-evening air is flushing the office with the first cooling breeze. Her assistant has left for the night. Hearing Will's voice has thrilled and unnerved her. But now her allegiance has to be with Ted.

"You don't, do you?" he asks softly. "You don't even love him as much as you love me."

"Will, I love him. I wouldn't have married him if I didn't love him."

"But you don't love him the way you love me."

"I have to go now. It's late."

"I've been longing for you. If you knew how many nights I think of you. Remember that one night in Iowa? Remember the night before I left for Christmas vacation? When I came that night, I saw stars. You did, too. I know you did."

"I can't talk about this," she says. "You don't understand. I can't."

She hangs up. Her heart is aching, twisting. If she had never known those nights with Will, her life would have been empty, meaningless. And even her nights with the clarinetist and all the others had made her what she was, were made out of what she was. But to have to obliterate that truth of her life, *to have to go forward as though that part of her never existed,* reduces *her.* Makes her into that twin-setted cardboard cutout of a girl she's never wanted to be.

If you could chart a marriage and see before you all its dips and valleys, you would discern the painful push and pull of people, even with the best intentions, struggling to share.

From the moment Ted moved in, Lily's felt the keen struggle of wanting to scream out, "That's my closet, that's my drawing board, that's my bed." Even an undershirt thrown across Lily's drawing board in a tired midnight discarding of clothes angers her in the morning, makes her sit down on the bed in the middle of the room, draw her knees up to her chest, and freeze there. When he has left for his office, nearly an hour before she does, she feels herself unwind, get up, take over the room again. The pristine simplicity of her palatial room seems violated by Ted's constant presence, his things that don't begin to fit.

And Lily finds when Ted is there she can't draw or work on her prints, not even a little. She sits at the drawing table with pencil or stylus in hand, feeling watched, even when he isn't watching, feeling crowded, even when he's sitting in the most remote chair in the room. And if she is brave enough to put down a line, it never feels like her line. Her attempts are self-conscious, sketchy, like the lines she drew when she was a freshman in art school. They lack authority. They lack feeling.

Ted's hours are still intense. He often doesn't get home until ten. But even with a whole evening alone, she reacts to the intrusion of him when he finally arrives: the smell of the outdoors on his clothes, the clatter of his things. She blames herself. She's been spoiled. She's gotten too used to solitary pleasures. Sometimes, when he isn't there, she still feels that frozenness, that inability to move. She'll sit in a chair or on the bed, pulling herself in like a turtle with no shell.

"I knew I never should have married," she tells Claire.

"You'll get through this," Claire says. "I should think everyone feels that way in the beginning. Especially since it was your apartment in the first place. Why don't you look for another one. Something bigger. It might help."

One night while Ted is out, Jack calls. "I'm coming to see you," he says.

"Why are you calling me?" she demands. It is one of her frozen nights, when part of her feels dead and unmovable. But his voice makes her blood course, forces her to stand up in the middle of the apartment, alarmed, fists clenched in self-protection.

"I think there's lots we can say," Jack says.

"I'm married now," Lily tells him, holding Ted up as a shield. She is frightened. She wants the part of her life that contains Jack to be behind her.

"Yeah. I heard you married that wimp. And I know where your apartment is," Jack says.

"If you come here, I'll have my doorman call the police."

"I have things to give you from your mother. I'm thinking of selling the house. There are things I've finally cleaned from her room. Things you might want to have."

Lily is silent for a long time. She is suspicious, scared.

"I'm sure there's nothing I'd want," she says finally.

"Why are you afraid of me?" he asks almost sweetly. "Do you think I'd hurt you?"

"Yes."

"I haven't been drinking," he says.

"I don't care."

"I want to give you these things. I want to see you. You're the only family I have left."

"I'm not your family, Jack. I've never been your family."

There is a squeezed sigh on the other end, a deep breath that ends in the smallest whimper. Lily hears pain, and for a moment she softens.

"I don't know," she says. "If you want to meet somewhere public—"

"I want to see you alone."

"Forget it. Just forget it."

"Think about it."

"No."

"I'll call again soon," he says. He hangs up before she can tell him never to call again. When Ted comes home, he sees that she's been crying, but when he asks why, she doesn't even want to bring up Jack's name.

Two weeks later, Ted says, "I spoke to Jack today."

"What do you mean?"

"He called. He wants to see you, Lily."

"Oh, my God." She sets her purse down on the table by the door. She is already shaking.

"He sounded really contrite. Nervous to be talking to me."

"He ought to be."

"No. Sincere."

"I can't believe you spoke to him. Why didn't you just hang up? Why didn't you tell him I can't speak to him. Don't you understand? He's poison to me! Poison."

"I guess I know that better than anyone," Ted says. "I think there's something he was trying to tell me. I think he may be sick or something."

"Serves him right," Lily says.

"Maybe it's time you faced this, confronted Jack."

"How can you say that, Ted?" Lily asks weakly. "I can't face him. I don't ever want to see him. He's not done hurting me."

The very thought of Jack makes the back of her ears hot, makes her stomach queasy.

For days, she's been working late on a new campaign for cake mixes, and she's already exhausted and nervous. Everything Ted does seems to set her off. Her patience level for him has dropped radically in the last few weeks, and she feels guilty and confused about it.

But it is more than overwork and cake mix, for it has been nearly two months since he's asked to make love. The few times she's tried to be the initiator, he's readily complied, but she never feels his heart is in it. He sits in one of the chairs by the fireplace afterward, writing incomprehensible formulas on a yellow pad. He says he's preoccupied just as she is: He is close to some breakthrough, some revolutionary guidance system, he says. But the difference is, she can focus on him no matter what her preoccupation. He cannot focus on her. There is a haze between them, a fogginess she can't quite clear. She thinks it must be her fault, that there is something she's doing that deserves such coolness. Is it the way she looks? She checks the mirror each day with worry. Or is she not loving enough? Maybe she needs to ask him more questions about his job, or less? Or is it her sexuality that frightens him? For days she has been experimenting, wondering what will recapture him, make him love her again. The closer she tries to feel toward him, the more he seems to back away.

Later that night, in bed, Ted lifts himself on one elbow and says softly but insistently, "I think you should see Jack, Lily. You don't have to remind me what happened between you. But he tells me he's not drinking anymore, and he just wants to speak to you and give you some things of your mother's. Surely you want those things."

"I don't care about anything I left behind."

"Maybe there are things you don't know about. Or things she kept in a vault. It's possible, isn't it?"

"Why are you suddenly Jack's champion? What makes you even care if I see him?"

"I just wonder if it's possible that maybe you can learn to forgive him. Go on with your life. Clear it all up."

"I am going on with my life."

"You're still angry at him."

"He killed my mother, Ted."

"That's what you say. He says you both did." And then Lily does something she never thought she could. In one smooth and irrevocable minute, she sits up and slaps Ted across the face. The feel of the flesh of his cheek searing her palm terrifies her. The room bloats with silence. Ted shrinks away from her, and already she can see the perfect outline of her hand on his smooth, dark cheek. The culprit hand moves to her mouth, aghast, feigning innocence.

"Don't ever mention Jack again," she says. "Not ever. How could you have repeated that to me?"

"Don't ever hit me again," Ted says, and he shoves her against the headboard so hard that the sound of her back hitting it is tremendously loud. She knew he was capable of violence, but he's never before directed it toward her. Still, it is not the violence itself but the look on his face that terrifies her. Three decades of pent-up anger. He gets out of bed and pulls on some jeans and shoes and stalks out, though it is a wet spring night, too cold to go out without a coat.

When she awakes in the morning, after a night of tossing in an empty bed, wondering about him, he is there beside her. She doesn't know when he returned. It must have been late. He is sleeping with his mouth open. The mark is still on his cheek, bluing now in the cool dawn light. She begins to sob uncontrollably, as loudly as she can, hoping he'll wake and comfort her, but even after she gets out of bed, slamming cabinets and drawers, he doesn't stir. He sleeps smoothly as an angel. When she leaves, he's still asleep.

But when she calls him from work, he's gone. She tries his office and finds he's in a meeting. And even by late afternoon, he hasn't returned any of her calls. She hates him for making her feel so guilty. Didn't he provoke it? she asks herself. Didn't he know she could not bear the accusation that she had anything to do with her mother's death? Now, thinking about it, she realizes that he *did* attribute it to Jack. Maybe he was about to denounce Jack for it or defend Lily. She never gave him a chance.

That night, she gets home before he does and cooks fondue, something he likes more than she does. She pours two glasses of wine. She hates herself, her life, him. He comes into the apartment right on time, not really looking at her, but he says, "Hello."

"Forgive me," she says.

He looks over at her, says nothing.

"Let's never talk about Jack again. Not ever."

"I just want you to know something, Lily. I'm not Jack. Get it? I'm not Jack. I've never tried to do anything to you that you didn't want."

"I know."

"I've been kind to you. Fair to you. I treat you like a damn queen. So don't ever get me confused with him."

"Okay."

They stare at each other silently. There is no warmth here. No kissing and making up.

"I'm sorry I hit you. I can't forgive myself for it."

He nods. But she knows he's still angry.

"He did this," she says, starting to cry again. "It's Jack's fault. All of this. It's my mother's fault for marrying him."

"Uh-uh," Ted says. "You're the one that hit me."

That night, when they lie in bed next to each other, she is wound tight with anger. He has withdrawn from her even more. She feels that no matter how she's treated him, he withdraws further each day. And this has been a death blow. The distance between them is palpable, unbearable. She feels nearly as angry as the night she wanted to kill Jack, and she doesn't even know why. She hates herself for it. And in a while, exhausted from her sleepless night the night before, she swallows it down and sleeps with a cementlike taste in her mouth and a burning in her throat.

In time, her anger lightens, but she feels changed and wary. In a few months, she gains nearly twenty pounds. She doesn't feel as though she's eating more. She's never had a weight problem before. But she feels paralyzed by what's going on between the two of them. His withdrawal from her is so painful sometimes she finds herself unable to do the simplest things, to even get up from the couch to pour herself a Tab, or to turn off the TV, or to get a new book when she's finished one.

From her paralysis, she notices things about Ted she never did before.

For instance, he's not just neat; he's obsessive. The books are arranged on the bookshelf by topic. The medicines in the medicine chest are divided between prescription and nonprescription and are alphabetized. Anacin, Bactine, Dristan. And she finds herself shuffling them sometimes with hateful glee, then, later, going back and realphabetizing, feeling ashamed of herself, guilty.

He keeps a calendar of activities on the wall that they might or might not choose to do and then circles in red the ones they actually pursue. "So that we can keep a record," he says. And this is how he fills the little time they have at home together.

"Can't we just spend Saturday not doing anything this week?" Lily asks during a particularly grueling week at work.

"Like take a walk to Lincoln Park, check out the zoo, see a movie, stuff like that?"

"Like doing *nothing*."

"Like reading books?" Ted asks.

"No," Lily says. "Like hanging out with our feet up, talking. And taking naps together."

When Saturday comes, Ted spends the entire day at his office.

"I didn't think you'd mind," he says, "since we didn't have anything planned."

And then there is his anger. She never really saw it before the night she slapped him, but now it peeks out unexpectedly. He swears at inanimate objects, not apologetically, as he once did, but explosively, hatefully. The house can echo with his anger. He slams his hand down on tables when he stubs his toe on them. Once, he broke a bottle in the refrigerator when he couldn't find what he was looking for.

"I think we need to move," Lily says finally. There is so much unsaid between them now. She can't help thinking it has to do with not having enough space to live, enough space to even want to share.

It breaks her heart to leave her beautiful apartment. From the very beginning, this apartment has felt like the visual embodiment of her soul. Its orderly elegance has pleased her every day. But clearly, there isn't enough room for its elegance and Ted at the same time.

And she is now severely depressed about her art, her inability to produce anything at all. She feels so watched, so fallow. Besides, she wants desperately to be somewhere Jack can't find them.

Ted takes little part in the apartment search, though he says he approves of it. But Lily loves the process, the glimpses into other people's lives: unmade beds, love letters on desks, furniture choices that shock and amuse her.

Finally, she finds an apartment that speaks to her. It is the top two floors of a Victorian building. The building has a pointed roof, like a child's drawing of a house, and two windows set into the middle of the point, replete with shutters. And even more like a child's drawing, the building has been painted a sky blue, trimmed in white. But it never was a house. In the beginning, the ground floor was a corner store. The plate-glass windows are still there, as is the merchant's door, set into the corner. But now they are draped in white, and a sign is tucked neatly in the corner of the big window that reads: "Private Residence."

The house is on a quiet street and seems more at home now that the store is gone. The ground floor is the owner's apartment. He greets her at the door. A tall, rawboned man with a long face and nice hands. He asks her in and gives her a glass of wine. It is only three on a Saturday afternoon, but she takes it. The wine makes everything seem more sophisticated, easier to enjoy. He shows her his apartment. His name is Chris Codman, he says. He's an architect. The apartment is high ceilinged, as the store must once have been, and except for the tin ceiling, which is now painted white, there is a cold starkness to the place. An unrelenting modernness that makes Lily want more wine.

"Come on, Mrs. Nicholson," Chris says, pouring her another glass. "I'll take you upstairs." He touches her arm to guide her, and she finds her response to his touch surprising. Is she so body hungry from Ted's withdrawal?

The steps are steep and smell mysteriously of cinnamon. She feels she is changing eras. And indeed, the apartment upstairs, what probably had once been the store owner's apartment, is a comfort, a respite from downstairs. All the original features are gracefully restored. The floors have pretty ribbons of dark wood spun along the edges of pale oak. Pocket doors glide between the rooms, dark as chocolate. The original counterweight windows distort with their subtly bubbled glass. And on the top floor, what once surely was an attic is now two bedrooms. The room with the two shuttered windows is the smallest. But there is a skylight there. Through it Lily can see trees, sky, and an airplane, totally silent in the distance. This will be the room for her drawing board. This is where she'll draw again. Her veins thrill at the thought.

Another glass of wine and she is signing the contract. They are laughing together. She feels lighter and younger than she has in days.

Later, outside, Lily stands looking at the house again, not wanting to leave. It is kissed on all sides by trees: an elm that shelters the street; a maple already darkening in the last days of August. A child plays on the grass of the house next door—a little girl with pink socks and no shoes and a nearly bald doll.

Taking one last look, Lily feels certain that this is the house where she and Ted can begin a whole new life.

Chapter Twelve

"This is where I'll put my drawing table," she tells Ted.

"Fine," he says.

"I haven't been able to work in our place. It's just too crowded, but here I'll be able to close the door. I know I'm going to get a lot of work done."

"Are you saying it's my fault you haven't been doing any drawing?"

"I'm not saying that. I said because it's crowded."

"I think you're implying it's me. It's my fault. I've been perfectly encouraging to you."

"Yes," she says, but inside she doesn't feel it. He has no interest in her drawings and prints, really. She's tried to interest him in art, taken him to the Art Institute three or four times. Even the paintings that excite most people, the Monets or Seurat's masterpiece, A *Sunday After-noon on the Island of the Grande Jatte*, make him shrug. "It's very nice," he says, which reminds Lily of Will's comment on the word nice. "Stulti-fying, boring," he once said. "Your fiancée is stultifying? Boring?" she remembers asking.

Lily has tried not to think of Will much since her marriage, but he lives in her dreams, is constantly with her somehow. It is distressing how often she remembers small details of him. There is a man who rides the bus she takes when the weather is bad. She's seen him a number of times, and each time, she finds herself staring, for his mouth is nearly identical to Will's. She's even thought of talking to him, she is so drawn to this small similarity. Now she will never see this stranger again, for with the new apartment, she takes a different bus. Funny, even this makes her sad.

She has just sent out an announcement of their new address, printed forms that say, "Ted and Lily Nicholson have moved! We now live at . . ." She thinks Will will be hurt by the coldness of the form, by seeing her name changed. And she is not sorry for that. For he has let her down. His inertia has maddened her. And though her sweetness toward him hasn't really changed, she thinks it's all because of him that there is no hope their lives will ever cross again.

Even in the new apartment, Lily doesn't draw. She wants to. She thinks of ideas for drawings and writes pages about them, to remind herself, to keep herself from losing the ideas. But in the end, her drawing board is quietly catching dust. Until Ted begins to use it. The war in Vietnam is escalating, and Ted is suddenly assigned to a secret project that he won't even discuss with Lily. He stays late so often, she begins to wonder if he is having an affair, though she knows it would be unlike him. She searches his pockets for clues, his briefcase. She smells his shirts for perfume. Their sex life is nonexistent now, so even that seems like a clue, though it is hardly something new.

Finally, Ted says he's going to start bringing some of the work home. Now that summer's come, it's unpleasant at the office late at night—the air-conditioning stops at 6:00 P.M. So the next night, he arrives home at six-thirty and puts his briefcase by her drawing board. And that is how the drawing board becomes his. Soon it is fitted out with a pencil holder, a blotter, and a slide rule. Her easel, which she had also set up in the spare room, first sits closed against the wall, then is moved to a closet, and finally ends in the basement of the house, where they share storage space with Chris.

"You don't use it. You haven't used that easel once, and we need the space in the closet." Ted says. Lily doesn't know how to tell him that her spirit is broken. If she is not using her drawing board, which she paid for with her own money when she was a struggling undergraduate, surely he should. If she is not using the space in the closet, shouldn't he? It is all very logical. There is nothing to argue about. Then why does it feel so wrong?

And then there's Chris Codman. In the beginning, he would often come up to talk to her in the evenings, when she was home alone eating dinner. He would join her at the table, and soon she'd be dishing out whatever she was eating, which he always reassured her was wonderful. He was a much better audience for cooking than Ted. Ted rarely noticed what she cooked at all. But even her simplest dishes seem to thrill Chris Codman. Soon she found herself cooking extra to make sure there was enough for him, experimenting with dishes she would never have cooked for herself. And she caught herself looking forward to their dinners as she might have looked forward to a date. But with Ted coming home early, things have changed. If Chris comes up and finds that Ted is there, he says, "Oh, sorry. I didn't mean to disturb your supper."

"No, stay," Lily begs, but Chris always demurs. Once, when she runs into him on the steps, before Ted comes home, she asks him, "Why won't you eat with us? I miss your company."

"I miss yours," he says.

"Then why?"

"Because I'd much rather have dinner with you than with you and Ted."

Lily finds herself blushing.

"Sorry. That's just a fact. Ted is a drag, you know?"

Lily nods solemnly. Her mind is percolating. Is he saying he's attracted to her or that he just doesn't like Ted? What she can't tell Chris is that she's begun to have sexual dreams about him, though she has never consciously found him attractive. In her dreams she does things to and with Chris Codman that Ted won't even try. Here, on the stairs, Chris Codman stands so close to her she can smell the laundry soap on his shirt, see perfectly the smoothness of his pink nails, the grain of his leather watchband, and she remembers fondly her dream, the taste of his penis in her mouth. She knows she is blushing furiously and turns to leave, but before she does, she turns back and kisses him. His fingers are gentle on her arms. His breath is sweet, like clover.

Now he is blushing as he draws back.

"Wait," he says. "I don't think you want to do that."

"But I do," she says.

He stares at her. And she suddenly feels hot, panicked.

"Excuse me," she says, and starts up the stairs, but her ankles have become unreliable. One twists, and she has to grab onto the railing, making a clatter with her shoes.

"Are you all right?" he calls to her.

"I love my husband," she says.

"Are you sure?" he asks.

She nods. It seems to be all she can do. There are no words she can find to defend Ted. She does think she still loves him, but there is a defeated quality to her love now. A sadness that doesn't leave her. If all this is *her* fault, she has yet to figure out what she's done or how to change it.

"I wish I could help you," he says.

She nods and puts her key in the lock.

"If your husband loves you so much, why doesn't he pay any attention to you?"

"It's cruel of you to say that."

"He's never there."

"He's around more now. Isn't that why you won't come and have dinner with me?"

Chris just shakes his head at her sorrowfully and turns to go down the stairs, but he looks back with each step, as though he cannot stop looking at her. She is watching him, unable to move until he is gone.

When she finally enters her apartment, she finds herself drawn to the refrigerator. There, in the beating silence of the kitchen, she eats everything she finds. She has never felt so shaky, so hungry. Strawberries, chocolate pudding, leftover tuna casserole. No food will fill her. Nothing will satisfy her, but her desire to eat it all is uncanny. When Ted comes home, she says she's got a stomach ache and quickly goes to bed.

The war in Vietnam is becoming an issue in all the newspapers. There are critics who say Lyndon Johnson is escalating the war as quickly as Barry Goldwater would have. Lily is uncomfortable with politics or taking sides, but she does not like to hear that people are dying, even women and children, that bombs are being dropped somewhat indiscriminately.

Her old fears of nuclear war haunt her. When she talks to Ted about it, he is not as reflective as he used to be. "We die . . . so we die," he says.

"Don't you worry about making rockets that bomb innocent people?"

"You have no understanding of what I do. Or of the Vietnam War. What are you saying? That you want to have a Communist government? You think John Kennedy died so we could have Nikita Khrushchev in the White House?"

"Is it a matter of that?" Lily asks.

"As far as the U.S. government is concerned, it is quite clearly a matter of that."

At Lily's office, people speak of the Vietnam War in different terms. They say the U.S. aggression is uncalled for, that Lyndon Johnson is feeding the war machine to boost the economy.

Lily lies in bed at night and looks at her husband, who even after all this time, seems like a stranger to her. She sleeps close to him in bed; she knows his scent, his touch, what generally annoys him, and even what not to expect from him. But she feels she hardly knows him. This man is making a war work, she tells herself uneasily. And for the first time, she begins to question him morally.

She avoids Chris Codman as much as possible. She is mortified that she kissed him and even more mortified that she isn't sure about his response. Was he rejecting her or just being polite? All they ever say to each other anymore is hello. Eventually, she sees that he has a girlfriend, a pretty girl with coffee-colored hair. Lily sees her leaving Chris's apartment in the morning and feels a twinge of jealousy, but nothing more. Mostly, she eats. She eats without knowing it. She craves butter and desserts, sugar and chocolate. And she craves it all in quantities she never has needed before, but she doesn't even realize she is eating more.

She is now fat. It isn't something she can ignore any longer. While it's not the sort of fat that people point and stare at, it does mean her dress size is now fourteen. It means that the baby-doll dresses and baby patent-leather shoes that have come into style look ridiculous on her. Dresses are worn so short now, with her large size, the very shape of them is a perfect square. Her body seems to ache and complain in ways it never did. She is embarrassed to be seen. Even at work, she is shyer, less likely to speak up.

Ted doesn't say anything. He doesn't look at her or treat her any differently. They still almost never make love and only do when she initiates it.

Lily tries to diet. There are lots of diets to try now. Grapefruit diets, cottage-cheese diet. Each woman's magazine presents its own cure. And after each, she loses some, feels better, and gains it back.

Claire says starvation is the only real cure. She says when she gets overweight, she stops eating altogether. She just drinks water and takes vitamins, and in no time flat she's back to normal. Lily tries that for three days, but by the third day, she's almost hallucinating, she can't concentrate at work, and finally she begins to eat again, feeling completely defeated. She tries Metrecal for a while, a diet supplement that comes in cans and tastes like the cans, and she loses so much, she really starts to feel pretty again, sexy. People are looking at her; men are smiling at her again.

"You're looking well," Chris Codman says on the stairs one day, and she feels ashamed that he should have seen her when she was fat. "You know, I don't know how to say this, but I feel for you, Lily." Lily feels her heart ache, finds it hard to sleep that night. She thinks about going downstairs and knocking on Chris Codman's door, spilling it all to him— her loneliness, her longing for more. Ted would never know it. He sleeps through anything. But Chris has that girlfriend now, or at least she thinks he does. She hasn't seen the woman in a while. She's wondered. . . . Now, she tosses, she kicks Ted in his sleep, but he is stone. Senseless. She nearly hates him, hates that he is not there for her. Not when he's awake, not when he's asleep. He takes her space. He steals her drawing board.

She goes out to the kitchen. Its acidy fluorescent light paints green the tremendous quantity of food she eats, nearly without breathing between bites.

Jack finds them. Lily doesn't know how. She specifically asked the telephone company not to leave a forwarding message on the phone. They are not listed in the phone book. But one day, Lily comes home from work, and Jack is sitting on the house's corner step, near Chris's door.

He looks older than she's remembered him, stooped over. For a moment, she realizes he hasn't seen her yet and that she can escape, turn around, save herself. But just as she is turning, he calls out.

"Why are you here?" she asks as she approaches him. Her tone is so hateful, she feels ashamed.

"I found you," he says superfluously, standing with the sort of rote politeness, the only politeness she's ever expected of him.

"What do you want?"

His face is childlike, conspiratorial. "To speak to you. There are things of your mother's— I sold the house."

"Is there really anything I could want?"

"It depends how much you want to remember your mother."

"Do you want to remember my mother?"

"My God, you've really gained weight," he says. "Too much cooking for the hubby?"

"Shut up," she says softly.

"How are things for you?" he asks.

"Things were better before I saw you sitting here."

"Nice house," he says, turning to look at it, his hands clasped behind his back. His face is judgmental, but not the face she's feared.

"You have the whole house?"

"No."

"Okay. So it's not the whole house, but is it big enough to ask me in?" When she nods, he picks up a cardboard box she hasn't noticed before.

Though she is unnerved at seeing him, she feels none of the things she feared she would: overpowered, remorseful, anxious. In his benign, sober presence, he is just a sixty-year-old man with a drawn face, a red nose, nervous hands. As he follows her up the stairs, she can hear his raspy breath, the difficulty he has in the short climb.

"You okay?" she actually hears herself say.

"Too many cigarettes over too many years," he says, but even this simple sentence is interrupted by his fight for breath. She feels a surprising amount of sympathy toward him, though there are lurching moments of anger. She hates that she cares for him in any way at all. How she once loved him, loved that her mother was marrying him. She thinks once again of the moment in the restaurant when her mother announced they were getting married and Jack reached over and squeezed her arm lovingly, crushing her taffeta sleeves. "My new daughter . . . my new daughter."

She directs him to sit in one of the living-room chairs and offers him a soda, though she is certain he would prefer a scotch. She lays out a plate of cheese and crackers, feeling lost, listless, wishing surprisingly that Ted were here.

"Well," he says, sipping the soda ceremoniously, "and how goes the advertising career?"

"Fine. I've been promoted twice."

"In so little time. You always were very creative. And competitive. I'm proud of you."

She can't find the energy to say thank you.

"I'm retiring next year. They've asked me to. New management. No room for people who represent the old regime—as though we don't know more about the company than they do."

"You might like retirement."

Jack shakes his head. "I have nothing, Lily. Work is when I see people. Almost no other time."

"All the friends you and mother used to have . . ." Lily remembers the upscale suburban crowd, the crystal dishes of caviar, the catered dinner parties, the talk of country clubs and "our kind of people."

"Yes. Our Winnetka friends. I seemed to drop out of all that when your mother died. I don't know if it was me . . . or them. I just didn't seem to keep in touch with all of them. Probably the husbands thought I'd be 'big bad wolfing' after all the wives."

"You probably were."

Jack shakes his head. "No. You can think that, but I wasn't."

"Oh, come on, Jack. You think I don't know about your philandering? You think I don't know what you put Mother through?"

"Why can't you understand? Sometimes a man needs someone on the side. To make him feel better. It had nothing to do with your mother."

"Maybe it wouldn't have if she hadn't known."

"I was as discreet as I could be."

Lily turns away from him and looks out the window. She is fighting back the tears.

"Look," he says, snapping down the sides of the cardboard box. "There are just a few things here, but I thought you might want them."

She turns to look. Out of the box he pulls a beaded nightgown Elaine had always told Lily came from Paris, a handmade lace handkerchief, a gold-framed picture of Lily's grandmother, her mother's mother, a gold chain in a leather case that Lily's real father gave her mother as an engagement gift. Lily's mother never wore it after her father left. And a diary covered in Moroccan leather. Lily has never seen it before. It looks very old, from the forties maybe, and smells the sweet way only old leather can smell.

"There's no key," Jack says. "I thought I'd leave it to you to pry open."

Suddenly, tears are rolling down Lily's cheeks.

"Why did you have to do it to me?" Lily is begging, weeping. "Why did this all have to happen?"

"Bringing these things?"

"No. You know what I mean. Why did you have to jump me like that?"

Jack is shaking his head. "I've got emphysema," Jack says wearily. "My liver's shot. I got my punishment."

Lily doesn't know what kind of answer that is. She doesn't know if it will suffice. Obviously, Jack doesn't, either. He's still struggling for words.

"Sometimes people make mistakes," he says.

"Jack, you tried to rape me."

"Rape! I never would rape you. I wanted to love you. You can't know how much I wanted you. I dreamed of you every night. I had to be drunk to tell you."

"No. You're a liar."

"I was never meant to be with Elaine. I was with Elaine because I was meant to find you. At night, when you were a teenager, I used to come into your room and fondle you, and you would moan in your sleep."

"Get out, Jack"

"I'm an old man, Lily. I'm dying now. I can't hurt you anymore. Can't you say you care for me?" He gets up and comes toward her, and the touch of his hand on her bare arm cuts through her like lightning. He bends his head forward as if to kiss her.

"Get out!" Lily is screaming. A scream she can hardly believe is her own. Soon there is pounding up the stairs, a knock on the door. It is Chris Codman.

"Lily?" he is calling through the door.

"Chris!" She tugs open the door, and Jack steps aside, all cool politeness in his gray suit.

"Are you all right?"

"Just stay here for a moment. Come in." She tugs on his arm and draws him into the room. He looks from her to Jack and back again.

"Now get out," she tells Jack. "If you ever try to see me again, I'll . . . I'll get a court order to keep you away from me."

"I'm going," he says in a drawn-out, tired voice. Someone not knowing what he is capable of might find him pathetic. "Good-bye, Lily," he says. She slams the door before he is barely past the doorstep.

"Who was that?" Chris Codman asks when Jack's footsteps are finally gone from the stairs.

"That," Lily says weakly, "was my stepfather."

"Jesus. Now I know why you're such a mess."

"Am I such a mess?" Lily asks.

"Oh, poor Lily," he says, looking at her. She looks down at herself; her overweight body doesn't look or feel as though it belongs to her.

"I am, aren't I?" She begins to cry. Chris puts his arms around her, but her body stays rigid, is afraid to melt into his. It might arouse her, make her desire him the way she used to, and that wouldn't do now. For surely Chris will reject her, as overweight as she is. In his body stance he is telling her that he thinks of her only platonically.

But she does begin to melt, to flow into him. No one has held her this way for a very long time, and he is so warm and so focused on her.

Suddenly, there is a key in the lock. Ted. They pull apart like sticky tape. Parts of them still remain attached, clothing, hair, desire.

"Hello," Ted says, looking at Chris with little interest.

"See you," Chris says. "I've got dinner on the burner. If I ever see your stepfather around here again, I'll kick his ass out of here before he knows what hit him," he says. "I did see him on the stoop. I just didn't have any idea you didn't want to see him."

"Thanks."

"What was that about?" Ted asks.

"Jack."

"Was he here?"

Lily nods, and the tears come again.

"What? What happened."

Chris quietly leaves while Lily tells him.

"That fucking bastard," Ted says. Lily looks at him with shock. She is surprised he even cares. "I'll rip his lungs out."

It is as though there is blood in his eyes. "You wanted me to see him," Lily sobs, and his worried eyes darken with anger. She climbs the stairs to her studio and lies down on the extra bed, feeling wrung out, confused, and sick at herself for ever having trusted Jack, no matter how minimally. But Ted doesn't come in, doesn't join her. He sits in the living room until he realizes Lily isn't going to cook dinner, then makes himself a sandwich and spends the rest of the night at Lily's drawing board.

In the morning, Lily decides that as long as Jack knows where they live, they must move. And with this thought in mind, she finds a hairpin to snap the lock on the old diary. Her heart is pounding. What will it say about Lily's real father, or Jack, or will it contain her mother's own feelings, the feelings she could share with no one? But as the brass lock snaps and she carefully turns each of the soft gold-edge pages, she finds nothing. Not even her mother's name in the fly leaf.

Lily hasn't been using her diaphragm for a while, but there's been so little sex with Ted, it never seems to fall on a key day when the diaphragm's needed. And now she is standing in front of the bathroom mirror, trying to remember when her last period was. Her periods are normally so regular, she thinks nothing of them. But now she is certain it's been well over a month. Her breasts *are* tender. She *did* feel a little queasy yesterday morning before she ate her toast. The thought that she might be pregnant elates her. She and Ted haven't talked much about having a baby. When they married, they agreed they'd wait a while. But they've been married two years now. It is only Ted's distance, her own desire for other men, that have kept her from the commitment of a child. Lily smooths her T-shirt taut and shoves out her belly to see how she might look. She imagines that the softness, the maternal roundness of pregnancy, will flatter her. Pregnancy is a chance to be fat with consent, to billow with approval. Lily calls her doctor and can't get an appointment until the following week, but with each hour she feels more certain that the test she receives there will only verify what she already knows.

The doctor is an older man, maybe fifty, with just a fringe of hair along the back of his head between his ears.

"Your cervix is already ripening," he says.

"My what?"

"I'm quite certain you are pregnant." Ripening seems an apt word.

Lily feels fragrant and full, like a peach. That night, she waits until she and Ted have finished dinner, until they have talked about finding a new place.

"I can't understand why you want to move again. I thought you loved this place."

"It's very nice. I just think we could use more space. Like two real bedrooms and a study. And I wish we were on a more convenient bus line." For two weeks she's been trying to tell Ted they must move.

"Actually," she says, "there's a reason for moving I haven't told you. It's not absolutely certain, but I went to the doctor today."

"Why? I didn't know you weren't feeling well."

"I'm fine. More than fine."

"What? Are you . . . no!"

"Yes. Well, it's not absolutely certain, but the doctor sees some signs. The results aren't available until tomorrow. I thought I'd wait to tell you, but I can't."

"Oh, Lily." He looks at her more warmly than he has in months. He puts his large hands on her arms and draws her to him. "What do you think? A boy or a girl?"

"I don't know. It doesn't matter much. What about you?"

"A boy. I really want a boy," Ted says with a childishness she rarely sees in him.

"Do you?"

"A boy, then a girl. Definitely more than one child, though. Neither of us are better off for being only children."

"Yes. At least two. But a girl, then a boy, would be okay, too."

"I've been too busy to pay much attention to you lately, haven't I?" Ted asks tenderly.

"Yes."

"I'll do better. The project's at an intermediary stage. Maybe we can take a vacation. A real one. To Wisconsin or something."

"And find a new place to live, okay?" Lily asks.

"Okay. You're the expert at finding places to live. You should start looking."

"Maybe we can rent a house."

"Or buy one. I'm due for a raise."

"Do you think so? Really?"

"Okay, then. We'll start looking to buy a house."

"Maybe the suburbs?" Lily asks. "I mean with a child . . ."

"Of course. If we can afford it."

"We'll share the looking?" Lily asks.

"If you want, honey. Anything you want," Ted says, hugging her.

Chapter Thirteen

Lily finds a little house in Evanston, not far from the train station. It's cottage-small and smells squeezed and musty, the way a house smells when it's been sitting with shades drawn and windows closed for forty years. The old woman who owned it has recently died. Her niece and nephew are hoping to sell it without having to put any work into it, though it is desperately in need of paint and cleaning, weeding and mowing, so Lily and Ted bargain it down to maybe half the price it would have sold for in better shape. Lily feels ridiculously happy. The little brick house has all the touches of the early teens: a porch with built-in, face-to-face benches painted white, window seats in the living room, built-in bookcases, bedrooms with bed alcoves. The baby's room is the sunniest room in the house; at nearly every time of day, it seems to be stippled in light. Lily sits on the newly mown little handkerchief of a backyard, petting the grass as though it's velvet. It may not be velvet, but it is hers.

Together, Lily and Ted paint the rooms. Edith and Hal put on blue jeans and help, too, and later they eat chinese food on the floor like a picnic. Edith touches Lily's stomach fondly.

"I can't believe I'm going to be a grandmother," she says. "You never have to give me a gift again if you two pull this one off."

Ted seems more caring, more involved, than at any other time in their marriage. He makes sure that Lily rests often, that the rooms are well ventilated when they paint so as not to harm the baby. The old smell leaves with the new paint's arrival. The house seems to stretch and yawn. Each room takes in more light than Lily would have imagined.

Finally, the moving van comes to gather all of Ted and Lily's possessions from Chris Codman's house. Just before the van leaves, when Ted is upstairs going over the rooms for forgotten pieces of their lives, Chris comes out of his apartment, and leaning on the stair rail, he confronts her.

"Did you find a nice place?" he asks.

Even when she slipped him a note that they planned to be out by the fifteenth of October, Chris hadn't come by to find out the details.

"A nice little house," she tells him.

"I hope you'll be happy," he says, touching her hand.

"I'm going to have a baby," she says.

He presses his lips together, and the light dulls from his pupils. "Are you?"

"In June."

"I'm happy for you," he says, but he is frowning.

"You don't sound it."

"It's just Ted," he says.

"You really hate him, don't you?" she asks.

"No. I just like you so much better. I wish you could be happier."

"I hope you find a nice tenant," she says fatuously.

"I hope you find a nice life," he says sadly as Ted comes down the stairs.

Lily's pregnancy is a pleasure to her but a clear embarrassment to the men at her office.

"When are you going to quit?" they ask her almost daily.

"I'm not sure yet," she says, though she is wearing the baby higher, rounder, and more obvious each day.

Finally, Wally Payson summons her to his office.

"Any day now?" he says.

"Two more weeks," she answers wearily.

"Well, I think, and a lot of us think here, that you would be more comfortable spending those weeks at home."

"I'm feeling fine," Lily says.

"Wonderful to hear it. It's been a pleasure having you work with us. I hope you enjoy your new life as a mother, and good luck to you. I think we might help you take those last few weeks off. With pay, if you like."

"Oh . . ." Lily is sure she is expected to thank him, but she doesn't feel any desire to. She has relished her last few weeks at Faber, Lowe and Barton. She is feeling pain that what has been a remarkably successful career for anyone, let alone a woman, should come to an end so abruptly, so purposelessly.

"If I wanted to come back someday . . ." she says.

"I'm sure you won't. A woman has a kid and forgets all about this rat race. Believe me."

"But if I wanted to."

"Well, I told you all about my mother. I respect working women. We can certainly discuss it when the time comes. Meanwhile, surely there are hotter topics on your mind?"

Lily nods. She realizes, as she gazes into his face, that he is glad to see her go, that she has a blackmailer's hold over him and he is relieved to be free of her. He holds out his clammy hand, and she shakes it. The memory of his hand stays with her a long time after she forgets he has not entirely closed the door to her coming back to Faber, Lowe and Barton.

Baby-boy Nicholson is born that very Sunday, two weeks early and squalling and big. Eight pounds. The pain of the first labor stays with Lily long after the drugs and confusion of the birth have worn off.

"It still hurts," she keeps telling the doctor, finding that especially at night the cramps are excruciating.

"Nonsense. Just the uterus shrinking back to size," he says. "Enjoy the baby."

Ted and Lily name their son Peter. He has a sweet, rosy face and delicate hands, and he takes a bottle with delight, so that he is easy to quiet and please.

In her arms, he seems a miracle. The fact that making love could produce another human being . . . Lily feels humbled and in awe. She worries, as she holds him, that there are too many opportunities to make mistakes, and she thinks of her mother, whose own miserable life reflected on hers. At least this little boy will not see his mother beaten or shamed; at least he will not witness his father's drunkenness. Ted's aloofness has caused her pain, but she remembers, at the birth of this precious being, why she married him.

And he seems changed by the baby. He is as thrilled with Peter as she is. And especially happy that it's a boy. He even cried when he heard the news. In Ted's long arms the little baby looks even tinier and more helpless, and the sight of her big, respectable husband, cooing at the tiny boy, makes her heart bubble with new feeling for both of them.

But there is the pain. The doctor insists she go home from the hospital. He tells Ted that sometimes women fantasize pain after labor and eventually forget about it. He tells Ted it is sometimes a cry for attention if the mother selfishly feels the child is stealing the show. But even Ted is shocked at the doctor's cavalier attitude and tells Lily all he's been told word for word.

Two days after she's home with the baby, a starchy baby nurse in attendance, she is sitting on the sofa, feeding Peter his bottle, when she feels a growing wetness beneath where she's sitting. When she stands up, she sees a pool of blood a good twelve inches across.

"Mrs. Carris!" she cries out, seeing green before her eyes, afraid that she'll drop the baby in her faintness.

The baby nurse comes, her face wearing the cool annoyance of a woman who often hears new mothers cry for virtually no reason at all.

"I'm bleeding," Lily says, and then Mrs. Carris must see, for she grabs the baby from Lily's arms and settles the shaking Mrs. Nicholson back down on the bloody couch.

"I'm calling an ambulance," she says.

"Call Ted," Lily begs, and realizes with pleasure and wonder, in all her crystalline faintness, that she really feels closer to Ted since the baby and has come to trust he cares.

Mrs. Carris calls both, and soon an ambulance is wailing up to the little brick house with heat and urgency, and Lily is laid on a stretcher, her pulse and heartbeat carefully recorded.

"Hemorrhaging," she hears the medic say.

In the chilly ambulance, which smells of alcohol and bandages, much like the doctor's office, Lily closes her eyes. For no reason that she can discern, her mother is suddenly sitting by her side, cool fingers on Lily's wrist.

"Mother," Lily says.

"Yes. It's me." Her mother looks younger than she has in years, though she still is wearing that out-of-date Betty Crocker permanent she wore when she died and the pretty polka-dot dress she gave away to the milkman's wife.

"I hear you had a baby," her mother says matter-of-factly.

"A little boy," Lily says.

"Boys," her mother shrugs. "Not my favorite. Thank God I had a girl. And your husband, Will? I hear you're very happy together."

"Oh, yes," Lily says, happy, but confused to realize that indeed she's been married to Will Sternhagen all along.

Her mother sighs. "If only Jack and I had been happy."

"He's a bad man, Mom. He's dirt."

"Yes. But we take what we can get."

"You could have had better."

"I didn't deserve better."

"You did. I did, too."

"Yes. Jack never had a real moral sense, did he? That *did* disturb me." Her mother folds her hands and blinks at her. The cold pleasantness of her mother's face upsets Lily. Could she care so little what Jack had attempted to do to her own daughter?

Now her mother reaches behind her and takes the bottle of rubbing alcohol, whose smell has been the keynote of the ambulance, uncaps it, and begins to drink.

"What are you doing?" Lily asks.

Lily's mother shrugs. "I can't stay here," she says. "Too much pain."

"Don't do that," Lily calls out. "You don't have to do it this time."

"Too much pain," Lily's mother says.

"Too much pain," Lily hears herself call out. She knows she is no longer in the ambulance. She is in a room with a strong central light. Then someone blocks that light and is looking in her eyes with a penlight. He is wearing a blue gown, a blue mask. Another pair of hands is taping her wrists down, and that's all she remembers for a while.

When she awakes, she feels exhausted and peaceful. Night air is coming through the hospital-room window, blowing the heavy woven curtains. The other bed of the semiprivate room is empty. She is alone. No nurse waits by her side. She is feeling no pain, and if it weren't for the tug of the IV, which runs from her wrist to a gleaming metal pole, she might be anywhere at all.

She presses the call button, and a crisp little nurse comes in on crepe-soled shoes.

"Mrs. Nicholson. Welcome to our floor. I'm Nancy Rizzo. How are we feeling?"

In the next three minutes, Mrs. Rizzo informs her that a piece of her placenta was accidentally left attached to her uterus and that in the past twelve hours she nearly bled to death, had to have two transfusions and what Mrs. Rizzo calls a "D and C, don't you know?"

"You were talking like a banshee through it all. Upset your husband a bit, I might add, because you never said a word about him."

"What did I say?"

"Perfect nonsense, I'm sure. He hung around here a good long while. But I sent him home a few hours ago. He was worried about your baby, anyway."

Lily starts to cry. She is so exhausted, she hardly has the strength to regulate her tears or even wipe them.

"Well, why are you crying? You've lived through the worst of it. You're lucky, I'd say." But Lily is crying for something so totally remote and untellable, she turns her face to the pillow. She is crying because in her dream she had been so happy to have discovered she was married to Will Sternhagen.

"I love my husband," she says out loud.

"Well, isn't that dear of you? Affection is rare enough in this world, I'll tell you," Mrs. Rizzo says. "I'll be sure to tell him that if he calls in."

Chapter Fourteen

Andres Pulaski receives two personal letters in one day. This is a rarity. Usually his mail consists of a bill or two, some sort of art-supply catalog, and an occasional flier from the hardware store. The first letter is from Lily. He recognizes her thin penned hand. The loops of her letters are full and irregular and give the impression they wish to fly off the page. He brings the letter to his nose before he opens it, hoping to draw in her scent, but the envelope smells only of mucilage. Tearing it open, he sees that it is not merely a letter but a letter tucked into a formal printed card. The baby. He knows before he reads it. He has been waiting to hear of the birth, worrying about Lily giving birth more than he ever worried about his wife. But for some reason, he's been afraid to call. He has met Ted only once—at the wedding. Since then, he has wanted to drive to Chicago to see Lily but puts his feelings into letters only. And he has the odd sense that she doesn't want to see him, or even that she doesn't want him to see *her*. As though something has changed about her, something she can't bear Andres to witness.

Peter Ryland Nicholson
8 lbs. 2 oz.
January 31, 1966

He reads the card three times, then carefully unfolds the letter. He is shocked to find out about Lily's operation and decides he will come see her, that he must see her. To think she almost died. . . . He cannot imagine living without Lily in the world. He loves her more than ever, thinks of her more than once each day, sometimes all day. What would he have done if she had died? Would Ted have even thought to let him know? He imagines his discovery of her death months after the fact, the cold, singular mourning he would be plunged into, alone. The realization that he has allowed himself to be such an outsider to the woman he most truly loves upsets him, and he vows to change the situation.

Now he opens the other letter. He doesn't recognize the handwriting at all, or the postmark, Columbia, Missouri. He doesn't think he knows a single person in the state of Missouri.

> Dear Professor Pulaski,
>
> I don't know if you remember me, because it's been quite a few years since I was your student. My name is Will Sternhagen. I left Iowa City in spring 1961. The reason I'm writing you is I'm trying to reach Lily Beach. I know that you've stayed in touch with her and thought you might know where she is now. Her address has changed, and the post office doesn't forward her mail. She no longer works at the advertising agency where she did, and they won't tell me where to reach her. And if she is still in Chicago, her husband's name doesn't seem to be in the phone book. Please, I'll pay for a collect phone call for the information. Or maybe you would rather write, in which case my address is . . .

Andres folds the letter, feeling deflated. He remembers Will Sternhagen. He remembers hearing rumors about Will and Lily, but he discounted them at the time. Will was a good-enough artist, but ineffectual, passive. And he was engaged to be married, the other students said. He couldn't imagine that Lily, in all her incandescence, would be attracted to him. But even now, so many years later and with Lily married, Andres feels jealousy. He has bedded twenty students since her day. He has enjoyed their tight muscles and elastic embraces and blank, clear faces. But he has loved Lily with each indiscretion, as though he is sliding into her sweetness and not Sonia Crossman or Mary Jane Grolnick. At night, alone, he calls her name. His feeling for her, forever unfulfilled, is still that preserved flower he hoped it would be. And there is not a fiber of him sexually or emotionally that does not belong to her. He wonders if he should give Will her address. He reads a desperation in the letter, wonders why Will must reach her. For a few minutes, he considers ripping up the letter, pretending he did not receive it, but after a while he decides to merely send it on to her, in a letter of his own, and let her decide what to do with it, then to block the incident entirely out of his mind.

It takes weeks for Lily to get her strength back, and they have to keep the baby nurse long after Lily would have liked to see her go. Lily wants to be alone with the baby, to feel she can care for him herself. There is a tremendous self-awareness that comes with loving her new baby. It is unexpected and thrilling. Not unlike being in love. When she draws his skin to her skin, when she cradles him to her breast with affection, there is a remarkable sensuousness. She is sorry now that she didn't nurse the baby, as some mothers are doing, though the operation would surely have dried up her milk. Sometimes the baby tries to suck on her breast nevertheless, and Lily is shocked by the pleasure it gives her.

Every one of her senses is alive to the new baby. She revels in his smells, his cooing sounds, his suede-sweet skin, even the taste of his fingers, which she draws to her mouth. Just to feel those little bones in her mouth, the nails nearly too tiny to see. Her tongue finds them, their smooth, polished pearliness. She loves to pet his pale, spiky hair and is respectful, and curious, about his tiny bluish penis. Sometimes while he sleeps, she stares at him for twenty or thirty minutes at a time and finds a depth of love inside herself she would not have guessed possible. Surely no one ever loved *her* this much.

But her own sexuality feels muted. Being a mother entirely absorbs her, even that side of her. And Ted, with his own muted sexuality, doesn't seem interested in lovemaking, anyway.

When she receives Andres's letter with Will's letter inside she is upset by the excitement that wells up in her, like a sharp light invading a calm, dark room. But she is able, in her love for the baby, to shroud it and not answer, not for weeks, not for months. The baby feeds, grows, smiles, learns to roll over, lift his head, and crawl. And in Lily's absorption, time is meaningless. If she'd been asked, Has time gone quickly or slowly since the baby was born?, she would not have been able to answer.

And only sometimes does she think of Will. She thinks of parts of him, glimpses of him—his tapered fingers, or the particular peal of his laughter, or his bruised mouth—and treats these rushes of feeling and remembrance as her private jewels, wonderful, incalculably valuable gems she does not often take out to examine.

Though the baby's needs rule her day, Lily's able to do things for herself she couldn't do when she was working, like read magazines, like take afternoon naps when the baby is napping, but she misses the praise of work, the pride that others think she's doing well. She misses the camaraderie. Claire calls, but seems uncomfortable when she talks about the baby. "So, did he burp a lot today?" she asks dryly. "I mean, what is it that babies do that makes their mothers so fascinated?"

"Come over and see," Lily says, but Claire never does. Evanston, though just a few miles away, is not part of Claire's world.

As the baby gets old enough for the park, Lily meets other mothers. Some, like her, have given up jobs. Most, like her, have been lonely and isolated in new motherhood and are hungry to share the small worries and pleasures their babies bring to them. For the first time in years, Lily feels a part of a community of friends.

"Where's Jeannie today?" they ask each other. "Does little Michael still have an earache?" "I spoke to Lois about my teething remedy, and she's trying it." "I can't believe Peter's not even teething yet and he's almost seven months. I never got a wink of sleep during Stephanie's sixth month." The mothers sit on the benches in their above-the-knee skirts and boots. They are all young but feel subtly left out of the younger generation behind them, the "baby boom generation" that seems to be getting all the press, whose music seems harsh to Johnnie Mathis—trained ears. They reminisce about college and the years when men found them irresistible or when romance was their chief concern.

"I wouldn't give motherhood up for anything," Polly says. Polly is the one young mother Lily likes best, with her long red braid and her redheaded baby boy that Polly even breast-feeds in the park, under a plaid poncho. "I'd rather wear Kevin's spit-up than go out with handsome David Coverwell, whom I almost married until I realized he just thought of me as a bauble. Really. It's infinitely more fulfilling."

"I'd much rather do this than become senior vice president of the bank I used to work for," Barbara says, blowing out a prize smoke ring. She's a serious-looking woman with glasses and plain brown hair, and she smokes when she talks, holding the ashes away from her baby's tender head. "I mean, there I was day after day behind those fucking security bars. I was a bank teller for five years. Even if I were sitting at a desk, what would I look forward to?"

Swearing is a new and contagious thing among the mothers. It makes them feel tough and irreverent. It makes them feel more a part of the generation beneath them that they outwardly disdain but silently wish to join. Lily finds herself swearing, too, and it empowers her. There is anger in her swearing, and letting it out makes her feel as though she is gulping a lungful of fresh air. But she never swears in front of Ted. She knows he would notice it and hate it. He calls women who talk like that "sewermouths." And he especially seems to think Lily above all that since the baby was born. And when he swears in front of her, when a hammer slips and smashes his thumb and the swear word steals out before he can stop it, he apologizes as though she is the Madonna herself.

One day at the park, the mothers start to talk about sex. It comes out that all the mothers have pretty much relegated sex and marital love to the second tier of importance. "When we were first married, Leonard wanted to jump my bones every night," Lois says so loudly the rest of the park can hear. "I thought, okay, but I didn't really *like* it. I mean he came so fast I barely got going and he'd be grunting ooh! ooh! that's it, baby! But now I do like it, maybe because Leonard takes his time and it's kind of delicious, but who has time? Who feels like screwing, really, after a day of diapers and sour milk?"

"You know," Polly says. "It's totally unfair. Colleges are bursting their seams with sex these days. I mean, open sex. I mean, sleep-with-whomever-you-like sex. Not like our day."

"Oh, the newspaper just says that," Barbara says, soothing her whimpering baby.

"No. My sister's at UC Irvine. I'm not exactly talking Roman orgies. But sex is everywhere. Sex is out in the open."

"Well, everybody's crazy in California. I think they've put LSD in the water out there. But are you talking about 'nice girls' or 'fast girls'?" Lois asks.

"Girls. Any girls."

"Well, it seems to me," Lois says, "that's just the road to illegitimate children and heartbreak. I mean, Leonard's no Nobel Prize in the husband category, but I'm glad I slept with only him."

"I slept with more than one man before I married Rob," Polly says. "But I couldn't exactly talk to people about it."

"Were you sleeping with them simultaneously?" Barbara asks coolly, lighting a fresh cigarette.

"Not in the same bed at the same time."

Lily hears herself swallowing audibly.

"Ooh, now *there's* a delicious thought," Naomi says. She's been smiling quietly through the whole discussion but now leans forward to Polly with confidentiality. "Was Rob one of them?"

"Yes."

"Does he realize you were sleeping with someone else, too?"

"No. And if you are all polite about it, he'll never know." Polly smiles her cat's smile directly at Lily.

"You haven't said a word, Lily. Where do you come out on all this?"

Lily shrugs and feels her face growing crimson.

"I bet Lily was a virgin when she married, just like me," Lois says. "Weren't you?"

"I can't tell if she's blushing because she was or because she wasn't," Barbara says.

Lily looks at all of them. For years she has hoarded her secret and wonders if it is safe to bring it out in the open. The women all regard her at once.

"My husband thinks I was a virgin, but I wasn't." A chorus of surprise and approval rises above the park.

"How many?" Polly says. "Come on, Lily."

"I used to be thin and kind of pretty," Lily says apologetically.

"Oh, we all were," Barbara says, but Lily knows she is the only one with a real weight problem. It is the one thing that makes her feel separate from the rest of the women. They still look young and attractive. She has never felt less attractive.

"So tell us."

"Yeah, come on. We won't kick you out of the sorority."

"I had a few lovers, over time, um . . . eleven."

"Eleven?" Lois says. "You had eleven lovers?"

"Not at the same time. One at a time."

"Eleven?" Barbara says. "What a showboat. I was going to admit that my sister had three. But eleven?"

"Did you love them all?" Naomi asks.

Lily shrugs, thinking of the men she took home from bars.

"Why did you tell Ted you're a virgin, anyway?"

"Because I felt"—Lily pauses and looks at them all, at the sisterly sympathy in their eyes—"that no one could ever love me if they knew."

"Eleven lovers!" Lois says.

"Shut up, Lois," Barbara says.

Lily is crying. She is holding Peter to her breast and crying because she has revealed what has been so long withheld.

Suddenly, the women are all crowding her, putting their arms around her, around each other.

"I just wish I'd had eleven," Barbara says.

"Me, too," Naomi says. "I never had the guts. I always had this fantasy about two at once."

"Six," Polly says.

"You always were greedy, Polly," Barbara says, sighing.

Lily bites her lip.

"Well, I'm glad I've just had Leonard," Lois insists.

"Shut up, Lois," they all say simultaneously.

In his last three calls to Lily, Andres Pulaski has asked to see her, but she keeps making thin excuses, and he waits with nervous doubt.

"Do you have no more feeling for me?" he wonders.

"You know that's not it," she says.

"Then why won't you see me?"

Lily sighs. The depth of the sigh plumbs Andres's heart. "I just don't want you to see me this way," she says softly.

"What way?"

"I . . . look changed, is all."

"A woman changes when she has a baby."

"You used to say your wife got very fat with children. Slovenly, messy, I think you said."

"Messy. You could never be messy, my Lily."

"I've gained a lot of weight. So much, you can't imagine. I don't want to go out of the house some days."

"So bad as that?"

"I don't want you to see me this way, to stop caring for me. Your feeling for me saves me sometimes."

Andres basks in her admission. "I will never stop caring for you," he says. "I am the uncle of your soul, remember? Troubled souls need special care."

"Please don't come."

"I must see you and the baby. I must see you to make your mind rest. So you know this man will never stop feeling you are admired."

"All right," she says. "But don't hurt me. If you think I'm disgusting, don't tell me."

"I could never hurt you," he says. "You are not capable to disgust me, that you must believe."

They agree upon the date, when Ted will be out of town, so they can talk and really spend time together. Maybe, Andres thinks, if Ted isn't there, it will be as though Ted doesn't exist. But he worries not that her changed looks will put him off but that she sounds so lost, so self-doubting. And he worries he won't be able to help her.

He arrives on a Thursday night and checks into the Palmer House. The grand old hotel reminds him of Europe. The lights. The bustle. The smell of the city rouses him. It is still early, and he crosses the street to Grant Park, where summer has brought out hundreds of people in their lightest summer clothes. Buckingham Fountain's gush gives off a refreshing sound. He sighs and sits on the edge of the fountain cautiously, staring out at the skyline.

When he retires, maybe he will come here to Chicago to live. Then he will be close enough to visit Lily whenever he likes, to be a real part of her life. He imagines himself in a two-story studio in the Cliffdwellers Club, overlooking the park and fountain, a strip of blazing blue lake, a brace of boats.

He is growing tired of being a Svengali to hundreds of faceless students. He is growing tired of his empty indiscretions and the needless and foolish risks he takes by sleeping with current students. Soon his hair will be gray down to the last strand. Even his pubic hair has turned gray, a fact that amused his last dallying interest to no end. "I never knew," she said breathlessly, "that *that* turned gray, too!"

Here in Chicago he is free from his own past, anonymous. And here he is near the only person he cares about anymore.

In the morning, Friday morning, Andres takes the Northwestern train to Evanston. It is a pretty enough place, leafy and quiet, not unlike Iowa City. He walks per instruction to Lily's house, just a few blocks from the station. The lonely little bungalow fills him with unexpected dread. It has been so long now since he's seen Lily. And never has he viewed her surrounded by so much domesticity, a domesticity that excludes Andres entirely. When he knocks on the door, he hears in the ensuing wait a baby's faint, disturbed cry, some maternal cooing, and then the latch being undone.

"Andres."

She has changed drastically. But the greatest change has nothing to do with her weight. She *has* gained a lot of weight, but she wears it in a remarkably graceful and womanly way—a Rubens come to life. Her breasts are melon round, her hips are full beneath her gathered skirt, but her waist is still small, and she doesn't wear the weight in her face or neck, as his wife did. Her face is still small, her features delicate. The greatest change is in her eyes: All the incandescence is gone. Her eyes—her enormous green eyes—are dull and tired. She no longer flashes with life. In her eyes alone, she is an old, despairing woman. The change startles him so that he is silent for a moment after he kisses her smooth cheek and chucks the little boy under his dimpled chin.

"You can't stand me anymore, can you?" she says, looking down at herself with naked self-loathing. "You're shocked, after all."

"You are still the most beautiful woman I've ever seen, Lily. You always will be."

"Oh, tell the truth," she begs. "I've always counted on you to tell the truth."

"I always tell you the truth. It's your sadness that breaks my heart."

Lily sets the boy down. Obviously new on his legs, he toddles around her, holding on to her hem, which, fashionably short, reveals full, bare legs.

"Does it show?"

"Vividly. Is that the word? Come on. You will let me in your house?"

"Oh," she says, gathering the baby's sticky fist in hers. "I'm sorry. Come in."

The living room isn't large but reveals an artistic hand. The stroke of color in the pillows, the way the books are stacked, a silver bowl with a single green apple. The Steinway sits by a window, and a stream of light comes down from the window and splashes on the ivory keys.

"Have you played?" he asks. "Did you ever take your lessons?"

"Yes. I told you. And I still play. Even since Peter was born. Listen." She sets the baby on the floor and goes over to the piano. With a ceremonial flourish, she spreads out her skirt, finds the pedals, and then she is playing a charming rendition of a Chopin etude, one of Andres's favorites.

The baby gurgles and chews on his wrist as Lily plays. He is a beautiful boy, joyful and funny. The music, and the shaft of light, and the baby calm Andres's worry. Lily's happiness can't be irredeemable with all this.

"What is it that makes you so sad?" he asks her a few minutes later as she is fixing him a cup of tea. She shrugs.

"Is it Ted?"

"Ted is always so self-absorbed. But he does pay attention to the baby."

"But not to you?"

"No."

Andres sees a deepening, a further shrouding of Lily's eyes. She is a woman who feels unloved, who crumples under lack of care. Poor Lily, an orphan. She has no one but him.

"I would marry you in just a moment, truly," he tells her, "if you would love me."

"Would you, Andres?" she asks distractedly. He can tell she doesn't believe him or isn't even listening. She is as far away as she accuses her husband of being.

"I truly would, Lily. I love you the way no one else can." He is shocked to hear himself begging to commit himself to her when he has grown to love her simply by not owning her. But maybe now, could he be ready to risk everything?

"I wish I could accept." She sounds dazed, singed.

"But why can't you?"

"Oh, come on," she says, setting her teacup down and getting up from the sofa. "Why would you want to strap yourself down with me or little Peter? A little baby at your age. And I would want more babies. Two more, maybe. Or even three more."

"You wouldn't!"

"I would. Peter's the only thing that makes me feel alive."

"Oh, my dear, I would make you feel to life!"

"I wish I could accept, Andres, but I'm already married."

Andres sips his tea for a long while.

"I made a will," he tells her. "I made a trust fund for my boys, but I am leaving all else to you."

"Andres."

"All the paintings, everything."

"You are so kind to me. . . . I don't know what to say."

"Perhaps you can . . . someday say you love me."

"I do love you. Really. Terribly."

"But you won't have me."

"I wouldn't do that to you. How can we ignore our age difference?" she says.

He finishes the cup of tea, hoping it will dampen the ache in his throat. He has come to comfort her and has allowed her to break his heart. The irony doesn't escape him. Love is ironic, he thinks. Maybe that is why he has failed at it time and again.

"Well," he says, "how is your art?"

"My art?" She falters.

"Aren't you doing some prints or paintings?"

She shakes her head.

"Drawings?"

Again she shakes her head.

"Why?" Andres can hear the disapproval in his voice and wishes he could take the words back before she notices them.

"Oh," she says, "don't make me feel worse than I already do."

"I don't mean to. You know I don't. Is it since the baby that you are no longer an artist?"

"I am an artist," she retorts.

"I didn't mean . . . my English."

"Not just since the baby. Since Ted."

"He does this to you?"

"I did this to me," she says. "I try to work. I try to draw, but I have no confidence. There is a critic in each line I draw, mocking me." She sighs a sigh that shakes him. "I knew you would not want to see me," she says. "I shouldn't have let you come."

"Lily, you mustn't say that. Nothing could keep this man from you. I am not to judge you. I am the one that loves you no matter what you do."

She examines him. He feels the depth of her probing, dull eyes and knows he can't do a thing for her he isn't already doing.

"I'm glad I got to see you," he says, rising and shaking out his pants legs. He feels weak and slow.

"Are you going so soon?" she asks.

He nods and kisses her and the baby. Out in the hot Evanston street, he feels as broken and hopeless and orphaned as she must feel.

One day, Lily is grocery shopping when she becomes aware that a man is watching her from the other side of the store. Each aisle she goes down, he is there, arms crossed, watching her. When she finally looks up, it takes only a moment to see it's Jack. Letting out an involuntary, fearful sound, she darts down the laundry-detergent aisle, wondering how she can avoid him. Peter is in the cart, chewing on a rubber toy, and he watches her growing panic with worried eyes as she tries to pass other carts and get around the stock boys who have staked out the aisle. When he starts to wail, a cry that rises above the loud buzz of the freezer cases, the clattering checkout girls, she knows he is only reflecting her fears. She picks him up, and clutching him, her heart beating in her ears, a cartful of groceries left behind, she shoots down an empty checkout lane, and as though she is pushing through a corridor of smoke, she cannot breathe until she is outside the supermarket's doors.

Later at home, she wonders if she only imagined it was Jack. Did she really get a look at him? It was a big store, and he was on the far end of the aisle. Surely there were other gray-haired men with golf sweaters, slouchy faces. And why would he be following her, anyway, she wonders? He can't possibly know where she lives now. She's made sure of that. She even refused to give the post office her Evanston address to forward her mail for fear he would trace her. For some reason, thinking of the post office's not forwarding mail reminds her of the letter Andres sent her from Will. She finds it now, in a desk drawer where she keeps things she has no intention of using but can't bear to throw out, and is surprised how much better she feels to write a short card that just says:

> Will,
> My address is . . .
> You can write me here if you are looking for me.
>   Lily

Whenever Lily speaks to Polly, she feels keenly how her own marriage is lacking. Polly's husband is a documentary filmmaker. He likes his work, but he doesn't let it consume him the way Ted does. In everything he does or says, Lily can see he is thinking of Polly. There is still romance between them. They laugh in a way that says they understand things together no one else can know.

Sometimes when Ted works late, Lily has dinner at Polly and Rob's house. Polly says they like her company, and it is peaceful and sweet the way Peter plays side by side on the floor with Kevin while the adults sip screwdrivers and talk.

It is with Polly and Rob that Lily begins to hear about the antiwar effort. Up till now, she has read that some students are protesting, that there have been Senate hearings, with William Fulbright begging the rest of Congress to slow things down and eventually remove the troops from Southeast Asia. But she has felt no understanding of the situation. Polly and Rob have a personal point of view, and it affects her: "We have no right to be fighting in this war-scarred country." "We're killing women and children." "We are not contributing to the future good of any country." Their voices stay with her as she goes home to Ted.

"Do you think we should be in Vietnam?" she asks him.

"Of course."

"But Polly and Rob say . . ." She tries to repeat the rhetoric she's heard, the simple logic that struck her with such emotion, but with Ted as an audience the words seem hollow, and she can't sort them out to make sense.

"What do you know about politics?" he says.

"It just made sense to me."

"That's probably because you don't know the first thing about it," Ted says. "The fact is, and you should know, the Vietnam War is paying for this house and the food in our mouths. Without the war, I'd be out of a job."

In the last year, Ted has had two promotions. The secret project he's been working on is apparently a great success, though he still won't talk about it. He works long hours, sometimes even longer than he did before, and though he seems to find time and love enough for the baby, he still pays little attention to Lily. They only make love when she initiates it, and her libido is angry and quiet. She feels like it rarely. That is why she is surprised to find she is pregnant again.

She wants another baby. Peter is walking now, starting to say words. She remembers the satisfaction of a small, helpless baby in her arms. But she fantasizes that Ted isn't the father. She tries to dream that Rob, Polly's husband, is her husband and how he would respond to knowing a new baby's on the way. And sometimes she thinks of Will and wonders what it would be like to be married to him. A month after she sends her small note to Will, he writes back:

Dear Lily,

I've been trying to reach you for months. I'm glad you finally wrote. I even sent a letter to Professor Pulaski, looking for you, though he never wrote back. I hope you don't mind. So you're in Evanston. Does that mean you have children now?

I just wanted you to know that I've finally filed for divorce, or rather, I've encouraged Sandra to, and she's agreed. It takes a while for these things to go through, so I can't say just when I'll be free.

I've also taken a new job in Wisconsin at the University of Wisconsin. I'll be just a lowly instructor, but I've started doing prints again, and painting, too, and they seemed impressed, much to my surprise. I'll be going there August 31st. I found a little house outside of town on a lake. It's just a little two-room job, but I felt something there I haven't felt in a long time: freedom, peace. There are stairs right down to the lake from the house and an old rowboat that comes with the place.

The last few years have been hell for me. Sandra and I have grown farther and farther apart, and I became what you accused me of probably becoming: another Professor Pulaski, sleeping with lots of women just because they were willing. Women are simply more willing now, did you know? I don't tell you this to make you jealous but maybe just to show you how meaningless it is to me.

It's you that I can't reconcile to myself. How could I have let you get away? How could I have let you marry? I think of you so often, it's as though we've been in touch all along. Does it feel that way because you also think of me?

Have you been pursuing any artistic endeavors? I forgot how wonderful it felt to have a sable brush in my hand or to work for hours and forget the time. I think in Wisconsin I'll do nothing for a year but paint and teach. I'm so hungry to be alone, to be indebted to nothing and no one, to make my own schedule and do just what I want to do. I know it sounds disgustingly selfish, but it's what I haven't had for so long. Will you at least write me? I've been a dog to you, but like a dog, my loyalties run deep. I just can't forget you.

> Love,
> Will

Lily reads the note every day for a week, sometimes a few times a day. Will is free. But she is not. She touches her belly where her baby is growing and wishes the baby inside were Will's. The sex they might have had conceiving this one! The thought of it gives her a rush below her ribs.

She doesn't write at first. She is often sick to her stomach because of the baby, and tired, and with Peter running around now, she must chase him whenever he is awake and keep him from disturbing the order of the house, which Ted requires. Ted seems pleased about the baby. He pats her stomach. They talk about names. But with the baby inside her, her loneliness seems sealed once and for all. She will have to stay with Ted. Where can a woman go with two babies and no money? And who would want her, puffed up with pregnancy and overweight to begin with.

One day, Polly says, "Are you and Ted happy?"

"Why do you ask?" Lily answers.

"Nothing. It's just the way you speak about him."

"What way?"

"Like he's your father. Like you're afraid of him."

Lily feels too sick to answer or defend.

One day, five months pregnant, Lily takes Peter on the el to see Edith. She loves Edith more and more like a mother and never grows tired of spending time with her or of watching how comfortable she is with Peter, gaining his attention immediately, making him laugh. Edith has fixed them both lunch, a salad with shrimp, lettuce, and tomatoes as dark red as cranberries. She worries about Lily's weight but never pushes her to talk about it or tries to bring it up unless Lily does.

That day, after Peter is mercifully taking a nap on Edith's big bed, Lily leans forward over the lunch dishes and not knowing she will say it, not having planned to reveal anything at all, says, "I've lost him, Edith. Ted doesn't care about me anymore. I'm sure of it."

"Sure of it, honey? I know something's been not right between you for a while. I didn't want to say anything . . . but is it bad as all that?"

"I don't know what I've done. He cares more about work than me, but still he finds time for Peter. I don't know how to win him back."

"Ted's always been distant. He was such a cool child. Never any affection for either of us. He always seemed uncomfortable with the world, as though it were invading his little bubble. . . . Maybe it isn't you, Lily. Maybe it's just Ted."

"I think—" Lily says, "I can't help thinking he's horrified by Jack, my mother, all that."

Edith shakes her head. "I think the person horrified by 'all that' is still you, kiddo."

Lily nods.

"I mean, the thing is, sweetie, you married a cool man. Now, why did you do that? Has he really changed so much from the way he used to be?"

Lily pauses and thinks for a moment. She remembers the night in Iowa he came back from months away and still slept in a sleeping bag on the floor.

"You could be right," Lily says.

"Maybe it's you who's changed," Edith ventures. "Maybe you have to tell Ted more what you need."

"Like love?" Lily asks.

"If that's what he's not giving you."

That night, she says, "Ted, I'm not getting enough love from you. I'm so lonely."

He looks up from her drawing table with glazed eyes. He's been concentrating, and he's quietly annoyed that she's disturbed him, she knows.

"What?" he asks.

She stares at him for a moment, wondering if he really didn't hear her.

"Never mind," she says, leaving him quickly but feeling inside like a dog limping away on a broken paw.

One day when Lily goes to the park despite the hot weather and none of her friends are there, she sets Peter in the swing nonetheless and begins to push him. He loves the swing and gives off long, joyful chortles that make Lily feel foolish and wonderful. Then, out of the corner of her eye, she sees a man watching them. She can just see the silver hair, the golf sweater, too heavy for the heat. She is too afraid to turn and really look at him, but she knows it's Jack. It is in the way he holds his head, the way he puts his hands into his pocket. She is certain this time.

"Come on, darling. Mommy wants to go home," she says to Peter, and lifting him from the swing with a wail of protest, she sets him in his stroller, and without even buckling him in, she begins to run. Her French twist falls loose, Peter is now screaming, and the sidewalk, taken at five miles an hour, thumps and sputters under the stroller wheels. When she runs into Naomi, who is bringing her baby girl to the park, she tries to pretend she doesn't see her.

"Lily, what is it?" she asks. "Is everything okay?" But Lily can't stop running. The fear is a propellant that won't shut off.

"I'm late for an appointment," she calls. Another block and her breath is burning her lungs. Her swollen breasts ache from the run, and a sour feeling creeps up on her. Before she can stop herself, by yawning or reaching into her purse for the soothing saltines she always carries, she is vomiting along the gutter, great, horrifying, painful retching, which weakens her, makes her feel as though she will pass out. Peter silences in his stroller, watching his mother bending over into the curb. She has to hold on to his stroller when it's over, wiping her mouth with a tissue, trying to find her balance and strength again, just so she can get home.

Lily tells Ted she's seen Jack.

"Why would he be following you?" Ted asks.

"He was. I'm certain it was him. And it's not the first time. I thought I saw him a few months ago at the market."

"So why didn't you speak to him, confront him, tell him to leave you alone?"

"I can't," she says, and tears come now, the same hot fear she felt as she ran from him. "He'll never leave me be."

Ted shrugs. "He's just a man," he says. "Just an old man. What could he possibly do to you?"

"He can tear me apart," Lily says.

Ted comes over to her and pats her clumsily. He has never known how to comfort her even when he most wants to. Edith was right. She married a cool man.

"If you want me to call him and tell him to leave you alone, I will." Lily sees real concern in his eyes but finds herself shutting down against his possible intervention. She cannot bear the thought of an all-out war with Jack.

"No."

"Then is there anything you want me to do about this?" His voice is impatient.

"No," Lily says weakly. She can't think of anything at all.

Lily writes to Will and tells him about Peter, about her pregnancy, and about her loneliness with Ted. Then, for a page, she writes him about Jack. For the first time, she explains her mother's death and her lingering hatred for the man who caused it all. It is wrenching just to commit the words to paper—her feelings about Jack, the things he has said to her, and the way he makes her feel now, so afraid, so helpless. She shudders as she writes them but feels safe when they are on paper, ready to be shared with Will. "I don't know why I think you'll understand, I just know you will," she says. She thinks of his cabin by the lake, the solitude he has finally found. "I wish you a sweet time of peace and self-possession. I think of you always," she writes.

• • •

Lily attends an antiwar rally with Polly and Rob at Northwestern University. It is a Saturday. Ted is working. So she brings Peter in a stroller. Her belly is undeniable now; it's bloomed so much faster than in her first pregnancy. There is excitement in the crowd. All her friends are there: Naomi, Lois, Barbara, mostly with husbands, some with just babies. Lily looks around at the young men with shaggy hair, their mod clothes, and finds their self-expression sexy; at the young women with the loose hair, skirts even shorter than her own, Carnaby caps and lace-up boots. The world has been changing around her while she's been shut in the house. It rankles her. She remembers how proud she once was that she was an art major, a Bohemian. Now she feels old and out of it—and fat.

A few people lecture. A shaggy dark-haired man that Lily thinks looks like George Harrison leads some chants. "One, two, three, four. What are we fighting for?" Lily chants, too. And Peter stands in his stroller, arms waving, babbling with abandon. Lily feels a sudden thrill, like a bubble in her heart. After the rally, her friends hug and kiss, and feeling self-righteous and full of camaraderie, they go in pursuit of hot chocolate, ending up in the dark, warm underground of the Huddle, where Lily knows each of them, men and women, hope they will be mistaken for college students.

Lily doesn't tell Ted about the rally. Or the subsequent rallies she attends, sometimes driving hours with her friends to reach remote campuses. When she tells Peter they're going to a rally, his eyes light up, and he claps his hands. "This is our secret life," she tells Peter, and his acknowledging look is uncanny, as though he knows.

Lily's daughter, Anna, is born on a Saturday, which Ted says is wonderful, so he doesn't have to miss a day of work, since his project is at some crucial stage. She is larger than Peter was, and sturdier. Her eyes already seem to focus on Lily's face as Lily nurses her, a decision she made long ago when she watched the beatific look on Polly's face as she nursed Kevin in the park.

Lily loves the grip of Anna's little mouth on her tender nipples, her tough little fists. Maybe she will grow to be tougher than me, Lily thinks. Maybe, Lily hopes, Anna will not let men flatten her like a bug beneath a shoe. This is the very image she has thought of lately when she thinks of herself, unable to run, legs frantically taking her nowhere. A bug beneath a shoe, in the process of being squashed. And she can't help feeling she has placed herself beneath the shoe, a willing victim.

Ted is more tender with Anna than he was with Peter. He is almost afraid of her smallness, which is accentuated because now their standard of child size is Peter, nearly thirty-six inches and sturdy and strong. The new baby's head lolls on Lily's arm in sleep, and Lily says aloud in the empty hospital room, "I won't let you down. I don't want you to remember me under a shoe." If someone had come in and heard her, Lily thinks to herself, they would pronounce her mad.

Life with two children leaves little room for anything else. Peter is at the stage he needs to be watched all the time. He opens cabinets, drawers. Safety latches no longer defeat him, and all the chemicals have to go up on the high shelf—too high for him to reach with a chair, for he is capable and even likely to use one. The house is in constant disarray, it seems, for whenever Lily looks away, no matter how briefly, he has emptied a drawer or dumped a bowl of potpourri or pulled a mirror off a dresser and shattered it. And though Anna is a good, sleepy baby, Lily feels overwhelmed—sometimes too overwhelmed to even go to the park or the grocery store. At the park, she sits listlessly while the other mothers provide the same lively talk, but all Lily can think about is that she is now stuck, that she will never free herself.

"Postpartum blues," Naomi pronounces. "I had that. I mean, you had to keep me away from knives and bridges. I was inconsolable."

"How did it go away? How long did it take?"

"A few months. A record in the annals of misery. The doctor was about to give me happy pills."

"Mother's little helpers," Polly says, smiling.

"It didn't go on forever?" Lily asks, knowing her voice sounds childish.

"Not forever, sweetie," Naomi says. "Don't worry. I worried about that, too."

The only things that cheer Lily up are the letters she shares with Will. He tells her that what she has written to him about Jack makes him love her even more. He writes her about his new quiet, celibate life, the frogs on the pond at night—peepers, he calls them—about the Indian reservation across the lake and how sometimes he hears the Indians pass his cabin at night in their canoes and wonders if they are fishing in the velvet dark, completely by instinct. "How far we are from our instincts!" he writes her.

At night, Lily lies in bed and thinks of Will's peaceful new world and the satisfaction he must now wear, wrapped around him like the warmest coat. She can almost imagine how he feels. He says he is doing a series of unabashedly romantic prints of the lake at dusk, of his house, of an Indian canoeing in the near dark. "Almost like illustrations," he writes. "I don't know why, but somehow I associate all this with you. I can imagine you are here with me. On the sofa with a pencil in your hand. Oh, my God, I do miss you!" The admission saves her, lifts her above her loneliness—the endless baby cries and nap-time silences, the tubes of Desitin, and the toddler lunches of Vienna sausages and smashed bananas.

As for her sexuality, it is entirely gone now, as though it passed out and away from her as she gave birth to Anna. There is a solidness in its place, not a nothingness. No longing passes through her, no sensation of emptiness; she doesn't miss it. During her pregnancy there had been the heightened hormonal desire. But now she is glad to be touched only by the baby, clinging to her breast, or by Peter—in the rare moments he isn't exploring, climbing, or destroying—burrowing into her, longing to be as close as the baby, tasting drops of milk the baby has abandoned. Her body is a giving body, no longer one that knows or cares for the pleasure of taking.

Driving home from Peter's toddler group one Friday, Lily is sure the car behind her is Jack's. She has never seen it before—a recent-model burgundy Cadillac—but she is certain the man behind the wheel, his face alternately obscured and revealed by the reflection of the leaves and sky, is the gray, craggy face that haunts her. Her fingers grip the wheel, and terror scratches a jagged path along her spine. Anna sits in a baby seat next to her, gnawing on her foot through her bootie, Peter is chattering in his seat in the back. She attempts to lose the car, turning suddenly into an alley here, a side street there, but the car doggedly follows. She realizes she is driving erratically, even dangerously, but escape is all she can think of. When she decides to veer suddenly into a cul-de-sac, she sees, in a horrifying, splintering moment, another car swinging around the cul-de-sac toward her. It is only because the other driver is quick to get out of her way that an accident is averted. The other car's horn screams for a full minute in belated protest before he finally leaves the street. She stops the car in the cul-de-sac and, head down, searching for breath, presses her hands to her heart, willing it to continue beating. Adrenaline inflates her with pain. She finds a moan leaving her lips that makes Peter say, "Mommy?" When, after a while, she looks in the rearview mirror, the Cadillac is finally gone. Maybe all she ever had to do was stop and feign confrontation to make it go away.

But Lily doesn't mention the episode to Ted this time. He will tell her that her terror, her sense of being followed, calls for some action, some storm of real confrontation with Jack. And to Lily that is even more terrifying.

So Lily goes on, day after day, looking over her shoulder for Jack. She has searched for his name in the phone book, in Chicago and all the northern suburbs, but sees him listed nowhere. The number given by the phone company when she dials the old Winnetka number says it's out of service. She never intended to speak to Jack when she dialed, just to place him. But he is nowhere and everywhere. She thinks she sees him at the library, at the dry cleaners. He haunts her dreams with terrifying regularity. "Die," she says out loud one night, alone in the house because Ted has gone to Washington. "Die and leave me be."

Chapter Fifteen

This is the summer that Andres Pulaski is a changed man. This is the summer he addresses his art with an aesthete's sense of importance. He's had no lover for months now. He hasn't pursued a single young student or called up his few old lovers that live in Iowa City and have always seemed available to him when times were fallow. He feels, instead, the need to purify himself, to work and think and be alone. The only sexuality he grants himself, his only guilty pleasure, is in the dark, parked far from a streetlight, in the used Volkswagen beetle he bought when he left his family. Each time, listening for footsteps on the sidewalk, he unzips himself, and instantly the exposure to the outside air blowing in from the open car window arouses him. He always thinks of the night Lily wanted him, begged him to make love with her—this is how he imagines it now—and in his fantasies, her desire is unquenchable, her erotic creativity endless. His mind dwells on every detail as he strokes himself, whispering her name until he experiences the one perfect moment before orgasm, when he is completely out of control and swaddled in ecstasy and he lets himself hang there, five minutes sometimes, barely stroking, until finally he explodes into his linen handkerchief.

Sometimes he thinks he will drive to Chicago and see if she is willing not to marry him, as he once unsuccessfully proposed, but to sleep with him, to consummate a love that's haunted him, and maybe even her, for ten years. But whenever he becomes obsessed with the thought, he finds a weariness overtaking him, and in the end, he merely calls or writes her and tells her about his work, about the campus, about the pure affection he still has for her.

Everywhere Lily looks, the American society has become sexual. As though the whole world is experiencing some lush communal adolescence. She reads about "love-ins" and "happenings" and group sex and orgies. "The summer of love," people are declaring it, and though she knows this means love beads and flowers in your hair, it also means shared mattresses and a sort of freestyle, out-in-the-open sexuality Lily has never dreamed of. Polly says it's exhilarating. She says that she and Rob have discussed going to bed with another couple and are close to the point of actually doing it.

"Won't it change things between you?" Lily asks.

"Not if the things between us are strong as they are. It's just an experience we can share. Rob even mentioned asking you if you'd be interested. Not Ted, of course. No one could imagine the 'air force general' watching another guy going down on his wife."

"He's not an air force general," Lily says.

Polly shrugs. "Might as well be," she says.

"Why would Rob want to go to bed with me? The way I look?" Lily asks.

"You're still pretty sexy. Don't you realize it?"

"I'm fat," Lily says.

"So you're a little round. I'm too skinny. Rob always teases that he'll bark his shins on me. You've got breasts most men only see in *Playboy*."

"But wouldn't you be jealous?" Lily asks. "I mean, to see him making love to someone else."

Polly shrugs. "Not if I could join in."

This last comment scares Lily, for she has never thought of Polly in the least sexual way. And despite Lily's sweetness toward Polly and her vague longing for Rob, she can't imagine exposing her body to either of them at the present time. Yet she starts another diet, hoping to feel better about herself, and wonders if she is doing it because she secretly longs to take them up on their offer. Her sexuality, however, despite this hot summer of ubiquitous desire, is as dormant as ever.

Will writes that he is completely celibate, that the Wisconsin air has cleared his head, that now that he is free to sleep with whomever he pleases, he longs to sleep with no one. "My life is a paradox, don't you see?" he asks. "Although, just so you know, I would gladly sleep with you."

He writes again that the story of her mother's death makes him long to cherish her, to make her feel safe. He says it makes him respect her even more to know that she has come through so much and survived.

Lily writes to thank him for his acceptance, tears in her eyes as she does, and then she tells him about her near car accident, about Polly's suggested offer, and at the end of the letter, she writes, "I would like to sleep with you, too."

Claire is a copy supervisor now, writing TV commercials more than print ads. And as Lily's only contact with advertising, she reports in regularly, enthusiastically, about a world she now feels she owns.

"The whole business has changed," Claire says. "There isn't a broadcast department and a print department anymore. There isn't even an art department and a copy department. Just a creative department. And art directors and writers work together. It's much more fun. Wally's gone, of course. They fired him. He was such a dinosaur, really!"

Lucy has noticed in the time since she's left that advertising has changed radically. Everything is more sophisticated—sexier or more humorous—and the layouts are simpler, and no one seems to use illustration at all anymore. TV commercials are much better now, too, more interesting half the time than the TV shows. Everyone waits for a new Alka-Seltzer or a new Volkswagen commercial, and in the park her friends talk about them as if they wrote them themselves, jealously arguing which are better. In fact, Lily can't help feeling that all the changes mean she can never go back to advertising, that she is too far out of it, that she will be too old to return when both children are in school or too afraid that she isn't creative enough. Again, she feels there is no escape from the life she's chosen.

One afternoon, as she is preparing dinner, Anna on her hip, Peter settled down in front of "The Flintstones," the phone rings. She answers casually, her voice too clearly bored, thinking it is Ted.

"Lily," the voice says. "Can you talk to me?" Lily holds her breath. "Will?" she asks finally.

"Your voice hasn't changed at all," he says. His own voice is unchanged, still young. She's forgotten how soft it is.

"Where are you? Are you in Chicago?"

"Wisconsin."

"You're calling long distance. . . . Is something wrong?"

"No." There is a moment of silence that makes Lily set Anna into her swing and pull out a chair from the kitchen table.

"It's . . . it's so nice to hear from you," she says. She has to suppress the disabling jubilation she's feeling.

"Can I see you?" he asks.

"You want to see me?"

"Yes."

"No. I've changed," she says. "I don't want you to see me. I'm fat and maternal. . . . I've had two babies, Will."

"I don't expect you to be the same." She hears him taking a breath. "Can't I see you? When Ted won't be there so we can talk? Is he ever not there?"

"Ted's going out of town in a month. To Washington for two weeks." As Lily says it, she shudders. She is afraid for Will to see her. And she is afraid to see Will, for he is her only hope. If she discovers there is really nothing between them anymore, she will be crushed.

"I can't stop thinking about you. I can't stop wanting you," he says. "I wouldn't be even calling you if I didn't know you weren't happy with your marriage. I don't want to presume—"

"I want you to come. If you won't hate the way I look."

"I don't see how I could. You don't know what that would mean— just to see you, just to talk. What weekend is it?"

Lily looks at the NASA calendar on the wall. Above the weeks, a rocket is cutting through space, leaving a yellow-red flare behind it. Ted must have turned the pages as the months turned. She hasn't looked at the calendar since he hung it. So long since the days mattered. It seems hardly possible that it's September again.

"The fifteenth?" she says. "The weekend between the two weeks he's gone. But hasn't school started? Can you really get away?"

"I can't that Friday. I teach a class Friday night. But I'll drive down on Saturday. I'll come Saturday night. Maybe it's better if I come after dark, anyway. I need to drive back on Sunday. It's not much time."

"Will . . ."

"Don't chicken out on me," he says.

"No. I just wanted to say . . . I'll be glad to see you. I hope you won't be too frightened by how I've changed."

"God, Lily," he says, and she is bathing in that soft, even voice. "I'd give up everything just to see you right now. No matter what, you could not have changed out of being you."

Now Lily is panicked. How can she alter herself sufficiently by the time Will arrives? How can she pare inches off her hips and thighs, remove the lines from her face, be the girl he found so irresistible? It doesn't occur to her she can never be that girl again. It doesn't occur to her that even with a year of dieting, exercise, facials, and pampering, she could not change who she has become. The sadness in her eyes can't be erased by painted-on Twiggy lashes; no moisturizer can give her back the dewy hopefulness of a young girl. No diet can obliterate the stretch marks, the weakened stomach muscles. In the end, starving herself and only losing four pounds, hopeless and deflated, she does buy herself a pretty tweed jumper, a pair of bell-bottom slacks made out of fine wool, a silk blouse much more expensive than any she owns. And underwear: a bra— the first she's had in ages that isn't a nursing bra. It's beautiful: thick with lace, panties medallioned with the same rich stuff. In them, she can at least tell herself she looks better.

The night he is scheduled to arrive, she puts the children to bed early, but they resist. Anna wants to nurse longer than usual. She is nearly a year old now, and Lily would wean her except for the pleasure it gives her to feel her littlest one so close, to smell her baby-shampoo scent, to give her such bodily comfort. Peter wants an extra book read. She can't help watching the clock. The hands seem to run interminably slow and then sprint ahead without warning. Will is scheduled to come at eight, and both children are showing no signs of sleepiness at seven-thirty. And then, as if by a miracle, they both are asleep, and Lily still has ten minutes to brush her teeth yet again, to smooth her hair, to wash the milk from her breasts. As she looks at herself in the mirror, feeling acute disappointment in not being who she wishes to be, she wonders if Will will want to go to bed with her tonight. She has been married now for four years, and with each passing month she has felt more remote from her husband, more abandoned by him. Except for occasional flashes of affection, when she was pregnant, for instance, he has taken her entirely for granted, given no more than he thinks necessary, and kept himself to himself. Lily has felt herself shivering so long in his lonely wake, never once thinking she would, or even should, take another lover. Now she knows, as she brushes her long, dark hair, she has no need to be loyal to him anymore. He only sleeps with her if she asks, and now that she has stopped asking, he hasn't noticed, hasn't cared. If Will is foolish enough to still desire her in her poor ugly state, if he wants to take back the closeness, the intimacy they shared so long ago, she will let him, she will encourage him. She will draw him to her as she never has been able to embrace Ted.

When the doorbell rings, Lily rises quickly, then waits for a moment before she can answer it. In the shadow of the door, he smiles at her. He has changed as much as she. He is bonier and balder, his blond hair receded to reveal a mature and taller forehead. His cheekbones are more hollow, his pretty lips more set and masculine. When he draws her to him, the hug suffuses her with a blush, a warmth, she'd forgotten possible. How well their bodies fit! With Ted, nearly a foot taller, she has to reach for a hug. But Will, only inches taller than she is, molds to her despite his thinness.

Yet the moment of pleasure passes, for she is instantly wondering if he is unpleasantly shocked by the changes in her. When she looks into his eyes, though, all she sees there is sweetness, pleasure.

"Why did I ever leave you?" he whispers in her ear.

She takes him into the living room. She has been straightening it all day, dragging Peter's toys back to his room when he drops them on the sofa, on the ottoman, on the floor. She has put away all the nursing cloths, the bibs, the crawling toys, the things that surround her every day, that add to her sense of isolation.

"I haven't seen a house of yours since your Lake Shore Drive apartment," he says.

"No."

"This is certainly different than that house." He smiles his cynical smile.

"I haven't had anything so elegant since. I probably never will."

Will shrugs. "None of us will," he says. "You're still beautiful," he tells her.

"You haven't seen me naked," she says dryly.

"I'd like to," he tells her. She feels herself blushing. "Lily, I'm actually divorced now. Last month."

"I'm glad," she says. "I'm glad you're free. For you, I mean."

"I've never been with you before when I was really free, have I?" His pale eyes are sparkling.

"That's true, isn't it?" she says. "Does it make you want to run away?"

He shakes his head solemnly. He has never been a truly handsome man, surely not as handsome as Ted. But he has always looked angelic and vulnerable to her, and no good looks could match the power of that effect.

"Do you want to see my children?" she asks him.

"If you want me to." She takes his hand, which is warm and dry and slightly sandpapery, just as she's remembered it.

First she takes him to Anna's room. Anna is flopped on her back, catty-corner to the square of the crib. One foot hangs lazily through the rails. Her dark, thick hair has fallen back to reveal the sweetness of her face. Her eyes, closed, are heavy with lashes. Her mouth is perfectly triangular, the point at the top. Rosebud, people say, but rosebud is an insipid image, and Anna is a tiger, a certain, stubborn little girl with the devil in her eye and a bent toward perfectionism. Lily can only see that tiny mouth as geometric.

She hears Will gasp, and she turns to him. There is tenderness and astonishment in his face she could not have guessed he'd reveal.

"My God, she's beautiful," he says. "She's yours. When you told me you had children— Well, the reality. She's yours. I can't quite believe it."

"I have trouble believing it every day," she says. "Come on. I want to show you Peter, too."

Peter, even in his "big boy" bed, seems so much larger than Anna. His pale, curly hair is fuzzy against the pillow.

"They can't possibly have the same father, can they?" Will says.

"What do you mean . . . ?" For a moment she wonders vaguely if he is actually implying something.

"They are so completely different," he says, finishing the thought.

"In personality, too," she says, relaxing. "They're born with personalities. You can't know until you have children of your own." The moment she says it, she wishes she hadn't. It excludes him, and it hurts her to exclude him, now, when she feels so close to him. Beside her in Peter's room, she has been drunkenly breathing in the pearlike smell she has always associated with him, glorying in the warmth of his body beside hers. She feels uncomfortably excited by him, can't calm herself, so that every word she says is steeped in nervousness, the desire to please him.

He follows her into the living room again.

"Can I get you a drink?" she asks.

"I don't know about you," he says, "but I need one. The last time I felt this way, I was out on my first date."

She smiles. "Wine?" she asks.

"Yes." She fumbles with the corkscrew, and he takes it from her. "Not that I feel any more steady than you," he says.

She can't express to him how warm she feels that he is acknowledging their nervousness, so instead, she touches him tenderly on the shoulder. How firm and slender he is. How exquisite. He turns to her touch, setting the corkscrew down on the counter.

"God, Lily," he says, and then reaches for her. Their bodies come together with a sweetness that dizzies her. His fingers trace her forehead. His hands cup her ears, her neck, as though he is drinking her in. When he kisses her, she feels breathless and gauzy, and everything around her pales but him. In the heat of their kisses he pulls back.

"Let's drink wine first. Let's prolong this like a bride dressing for her bridal night," he says. She nods, mute, weak. The thought of her own bridal night intrudes and unsettles her.

She does not know how he finds the concentration to use the corkscrew. She does not remember searching for the rarely used wineglasses or rinsing the dust from them, but she does. When they are sitting on the sofa in the living room again, the wine cuts through her senses like vinegar, though it is good wine. But she is so overloaded with feeling, her senses are railing at the least new intrusion. She sets the glass down. There is nothing she can say to him. Time has come between them like a wedge, and yet she has never felt closer to him.

Still, he talks to her. He tells her about his house by the lake, the glass porch that overlooks the water, where the light comes in so full-spectrumed each morning, he can't help but paint or draw. He is excited by colors that once seemed vulgar to him, he says. He is tempted by ideas that once seemed unexecutable, and he manages to execute them. When he speaks of his work, his eyes are as shiny as hers must be when she speaks of her children. But his own rich fulfillment makes her relationship to her art paltry and depressing. She has not thought once in years of ideas to etch, colors she wishes to use together. And when she does wish, on those rare occasions, craves, to put on paper Anna's determined little face or Peter's gentle eyes, she feels incapable, fallow, and afraid. The sketch could be nothing like them; her pencil could no longer accompany the whim of her eye. Once, when Peter was just a few months old, she bought a sketchbook, hoping to fill it with the richness of her new feelings, a sketch of his small, wrinkled fist, the slender stalk of his neck, but it was put away somewhere now, still empty. And her drawing board still functions as Ted's desk.

He lifts her chin to examine her face. "You're sad," he says.

She nods.

"Why?"

"I've forgotten how to be an artist," she says. "Maybe I never was."

"You were far better than me," he says. "I never could tell you before. I was too uncertain of myself then."

"I've forgotten it all," she says.

"It's all up there somewhere." He touches her head gently. He kisses it then. "When you're ready, it will come back to you."

"Don't tell me it's like riding a bike," she says. "I'll burst into tears."

"No," he says. "It's nothing like riding a bike. More like a roller coaster." He smiles at her. There is such a vulnerability, almost a shyness, in his smile. It seeks her smile and won't rest until it's found it.

When they've drunk one glass of wine, she pours them more.

"Did you eat dinner?" she asks. He nods. She knows that he is staying at the Sheraton in Chicago. She can just picture the impersonalness of the rooms, then realizes the room she is picturing is the room she stayed in the night she came to look for a job, long ago at the purple motel.

"Do you want anything to eat?" she asks.

He shakes his head. "No," he says. "I just want you."

"You want me?" she asks. "Even the way I am?"

"If you're willing to go to bed with me," he says, "the way I am."

"In the dark," she says.

"I know. You can't stand to look at my balding head."

"No, that's not it!" He laughs at her, and she laughs, too.

She takes his hand—how light and thin it seems to her—and they climb the stairs. She had not thought until this moment where they might make love. She had not thought that it might not be right to make love in the very bed Ted sleeps in every night, curled away from her, his body cool and compact. But now she wants to make love there. Making love there is a rite, an attempt to extricate herself, to free herself from all the years she tried to seduce Ted, to please him, to make him want her.

In the bedroom she lights a candle, a lilac-scented one she bought years ago as a hint to Ted. She wipes the dust from it with a tissue and strikes the match. With the flame, the sweet scent rises, makes her ordinary bedroom as exotic as she always wished it would be.

"I'm scared," she whispers.

"So am I," Will says. He unbuttons her shirt, his fingers slow and cautious with each button. Like a little girl, she holds out her arms to allow him to undo the cuffs. As he strips off her shirt, she is excited by the sight of her own new lacy bra.

"Pretty," he says. He traces the fullness of her breasts. "You were never this big."

"Too big?" she asks.

"No!"

"I'm still nursing," she tells him reluctantly.

"Are you? Can I taste it?"

"Do you . . . do you really want to?" Ted never asked to taste her milk, found the whole idea of breast-feeding somewhat distasteful.

Will undoes her bra, then kneels down and takes her nipple into his mouth.

"It will be sweet," she tells him. "You won't like it." But he sucks with pleasure, much longer than she expects. She feels the familiar tingle of her milk flowing down. And a new urgent heat between her legs that is tremendously unfamiliar, an ache, a longing where there has been no longing for so long. It hurts her, this desire. Still kneeling, he unfastens her slacks. The bell-bottoms, their heavy wool, fall to her feet in a puddle. Now his face is nuzzling the pretty new panties. She worries that he can see how full her legs have become. That he will hate them, but he is drawing the panties down now, settling her back on the bed, and his tongue is exploring her with hunger she cannot remember in him, with expertise that only vaguely worries her.

"Sweet! sweet . . ." he mutters. And in a moment, impaled on his fingers, blessed with the accuracy of his tongue, she comes in a burst of pain and pleasure. The moan must wake the neighborhood, it seems to her. The feeling, so long forgotten, sweeps her again and again. Before it has stopped, he is unzipping his pants, sliding into her deliciously, starting the heat, the intensity all over again.

They make love all night. She learns again the tough, cool knots of his nipples, the taste of his hard penis, the surrendering, bumpy sacks beneath it. And his mouth savors every part of her. And his moans are now as loud as hers. When he comes, it warms her so deep inside, she feels lost to him. She will never again know anything so sweet, so long denied. She will never again be able to live without this lovemaking.

"I'd better go before it's light," he says, getting up after a long silence.

"No."

"It's *your* neighbors I'm worried about."

"You're driving back tomorrow? So soon?"

"After I sleep."

"I'm afraid to let you go."

He seems impatient now and utterly tired. She worries. Has he had enough of her? Has he had too much of her? With his tweed jacket and scarf wrapped around his neck, he looks so young, so innocent. His face is like a little boy's.

"Good-bye, Lily," he says.

"Will." They are standing at the door, and she is grabbing his arm. She hardly has the strength to let it go. And she hasn't the courage to ask if she'll see him again.

"Be careful when you drive. You're so tired."

He kisses her quickly, lightly. She can't shake the feeling that he's acting annoyed.

When he is gone, she drags herself to bed. An hour or two and Anna will be calling from her crib. Peter will be wanting to see if Tom and Jerry are on television. Her nightgown hurts her sensitized skin. She is raw, burned, every part of her aches—but mostly her heart.

The next day is endless. Every silent moment, she falls asleep—on the couch while Anna naps and Peter builds with blocks, in the kitchen chair while Anna picks at her supper. He won't call again; she's sure of it. She gave too much, felt too much. He got what he came for. Why should he call? When the children are finally in bed for the night and Lily is getting ready for bed, the phone rings.

"Lily . . ."

"Will. Are you back in Wisconsin?" she asks. She feels no more surprised to hear from him than if he came back from the dead.

"Just. I slept nearly all day and had to pay for an extra day at the hotel. The desk said they called me and told me I needed to check out and that I said, 'No way,' although I can't remember anything about it . . . Lily."

"I didn't expect you to call me," she tells him.

"Why not? After the night we had? You must think I'm a real dog. Sweetheart, listen to me . . ."

He has never called her sweetheart before, or any affectionate name, and it cuts through her with a delicious twinge.

"The whole way back I was shaking, thinking of you, of us," he says.

"Will I see you again?" she asks.

"After all these years? After the way we felt last night? I won't even grace you with an answer."

"Does that mean yes?"

He laughs. "Do you want my blood? Because I'd give it to you. Every last crimson drop."

"I don't want your blood," she tells him. "I want your heart."

"It's yours," he says. When she hangs up, she feels utterly changed, and for the first time in a long time, not alone.

Chapter Sixteen

The next few weeks, Lily is suffused with such radiance, such high hopes, she imagines sparks must be flying from her fingertips. Will calls her every day, during the day, when Ted isn't home. He talks to her as his lover. He tells her all that he is feeling, worrying about, longing for, and then he never fails to tell her how much he wants her. His words are so seductive, even with her children noisily playing at her feet, that she is so aroused she aches. He tells her all he longs to do for her and with her. He tells her how happy she is making him.

It's been so long since anyone wanted her, so long since she's wanted anyone, she feels as though she's been dead for years and miraculously brought back to life. Sleeping Beauty. She had thought that her time of passion was over, that she could never feel it again, never again feel so young and alive.

It astonishes her that Ted doesn't see it, doesn't sense the change in her. She is so aroused by Will, she even solicits lovemaking with Ted more often now, and he lazily accommodates her. Doesn't he realize how quickly she is excited? All she has to do is close her eyes and think of Will. And doesn't he realize she has suddenly become more beautiful? Even she sees it in the mirror. A flush of color, a glow, a clear-eyed look that, despite her weight, makes her look much more like the woman Will once loved.

A month after being together, Will drives down to see her again. Ted is gone for just the night to Washington, D.C., and they've vowed to each other that the next time they meet, they will spend a few days together at least, but they've been waiting so long for any opportunity, even a single, vibrant night is acceptable.

Lily is afraid that after the intensity of their last time together, this one will seem tepid. But she is wrong. The intensity is higher, for unlike last time, when there was shyness to slow them down, now their longing is unchecked. They revel in each other's voices, in each other's glances. They are equally as loving, as motivated, as cherishing. And even when she tests her good luck, even when she asks him questions designed to make him uncomfortable—for she can't help it, she has trouble believing he could feel so much for her—he is right there with her, willing to answer anything, willing to be whatever she needs him to be.

She has never felt higher, closer to the world. She feels love and patience for everything, everyone. Even Ted. After the trip to Washington, he seems even more withdrawn. He takes to going to the Catholic church on Sundays and is prone to longer, moodier silences. And he is obsessive and more secretive about work. The only thing she knows is that he is working on some sort of missile. And one night, he brings home a trophy, an award he's won for "aerospace design." The trophy is a brass missile mounted on walnut. But it isn't an ordinary missile; it is dazzlingly futuristic: a nose cone so sharp, it resembles an ice pick, seems almost lethal, and the fins are lower than she'd expect, like an afterthought. When she asks what it is, he calls it "a Skink," and when Lily asks if this is the actual project he's working on, he won't tell her. "I can't tell anyone," he says, and he sets the model on his dresser in the bedroom.

She hates the model because it represents to her the time they never spend together, the energy he doesn't have for her. More and more, she loses hope that her marriage can improve. He is angrier now. Angrier at everything. He slams doors. A felt hat that she'd recently bought—an old-fashioned shape, a cloche, like the hats her mother wore as a teenager—disappears, then shows up about a week later, in the trash, mutilated, torn. It hangs in her hands like a dead animal, and Lily asks Ted, "How did this happen?"

"Peter did it," Ted says. "I wasn't watching him for just a few minutes, and when I found him, he was in the kitchen, cutting it with those little pink scissors." But something in the waver of his voice tells her it's not true. And besides, the hat was stored on a shelf far too high for Peter to reach.

And one other thing she's noticed since Ted's trip to Washington is that he's become suddenly ritualistic. Before bed he walks to the window and fiddles with the venetian blinds, even if they're down. Then he walks to his dresser and straightens his comb and brush and the model of the Skink, then he sits on the bed with his eyes closed for exactly ten seconds—each night she counts, amazed—before he drops his slippers and puts his feet under the covers. She has tried to interrupt his routine, but he won't let her. He will gently push her aside if she is in the path of his ritual, and all the while his face is emotionless, concentrating.

She has wondered why he always appears so mild, so passive, when there is clearly anger under his skin, an anger that could be more malignant than she knows. Does he suspect she's seeing someone? She has begun to wonder. Maybe he just sees that she's detached herself from him, that she's no longer under his exact influence. Something's happening with his anger, she thinks. And something is happening to her.

Lily walks through her life as though she has new value. She is no longer the beleaguered housewife. She has secrets, she is deliciously mysterious. She is once again, after so many years, unique. At the supermarket she stands in line, her children in the cart—Anna in the baby seat, Peter in the cart itself, mock shooting at everything in sight—and she thinks, I am the only woman in this line who has a lover. I am the only woman in this line who is truly loved.

She has felt so emotionally abandoned for so long that she feels no guilt at all about her elation. It is her birthright. It is her fate.

One night, Ted turns to her in bed and says, "We have beautiful children, don't we?"

"Yes." She thinks about how kind he is with them, has always been. If only he could be so kind to her.

"You've been a good mother to them."

"I try."

"But I'm their father," Ted says.

"I know you are."

"Do you?"

"What do you mean?"

"You keep them from me, you know. You hoard them."

"You're not around," Lily says. "And when you are, you're not really here. You're formulating some war weapon in your head."

"Don't. I'm talking about Peter and Anna."

"What are you saying about Peter and Anna?"

"I'm saying, give me some room with them."

"I don't see—"

"I'll always be their father. No one else could be."

"Of course not," Lily says, her hands suddenly so cold, she lies on them to warm them. "Of course not."

"No one else could be. You couldn't take them from me even if you wanted," he says.

What does he mean? She is afraid to ask. That same night, she wakes shivering and realizes that the bed is empty. It takes her eyes a moment to see that he is standing by the dresser in the dark, caressing the brass "Skink."

"Ted, what's wrong?" she asks. But he says nothing, just quietly comes to bed, so she wonders if he wasn't sleepwalking.

Will comes two more times, for a night only. The thrill of their time together is so potent, it can last for weeks. Nothing can hurt her anymore or displease her. Below-zero weather is romantic. A night when the electricity goes out because of an ice storm is romantic. Even her loneliness is romantic, when she can spend it thinking of him. On his fourth visit, at three in the morning, after hours of talking, hours of lovemaking, he falls asleep in her arms. She smooths his pale hair and looks at his sleeping face. She leans against the headboard, cradling his head just as she does her children's. How lined his face is. She can even see it in the streetlight. How high and grown-up his brow has become. But his mouth, in sleep, is as sweet and bruised as ever. After all their lovemaking, the bed smells oceanlike. A late, sharp winter wind is splashing the thin white curtains out into the room. She contemplates not waking him up at the first sign of daylight, having him stay as long as he needs to sleep. But at six he opens his eyes. His movement makes her stir. She's been sleeping sitting up, unable to surrender the pleasure of holding him.

As he is leaving, he picks a framed picture up from a table in the bedroom. It has been there all along, but he has never been in the bedroom when it was this light.

"Is this Ted?" he asks quietly.

Lily nods. It is a picture of Ted this summer, in the backyard blowup pool. In his arms he is holding both Peter and Anna, Anna in diapers, Peter long-legged and happy to be in his father's arms. Will looks at the picture a long time. His face clouds. When he sets the picture down, he looks at Lily just as searchingly.

"What?" she asks him.

"I never saw a picture of him before," he says. "He never seemed real to me before."

She presses her lips together. "Does it make a difference?" she asks.

"I don't know," he says. He kisses her good-bye. His face is road mapped from sleeping in her arms.

Once again, in his departure, she can't help feeling she will never see him again.

For two days Will doesn't call, and finally, Lily, hands shaking, her own heartbeat in her ears, calls him collect.

"Will?" she says when, after a pause, he accepts the charges.

"Oh, hi." There is resignation in his voice.

"I was afraid something happened to you," she says, though the lie is so bald-faced it seems to make Will pause.

"Oh . . ." he says.

"So . . . you're all right, then?"

"Yes."

There is a moment of silence, gluey, endless.

"Help me," she says, and the feeling behind the words could not be stronger if she were drowning.

"Oh, Lily, it's wrong."

"What's wrong?"

"We're wrong."

"Do you mean . . ." The words make no sense to Lily. She cannot imagine their source. She cannot believe Will means them. "How could you say that? How could you feel that?" Her heart is begging, but she says nothing. Her throat is shut.

"Oh, God," Will says. "I wish I'd never come down there."

Lily starts to cry, loudly, painfully. She thinks of hanging up, if only she had the courage. With his one sentence, he has stretched out before her the emptiness of her life. Once again, she is the bug beneath a shoe. In a moment, she will be crushed, gone. Her whole life inconsequential. She will be the woman in the supermarket line with the whining children, looking forward only to being checked out.

"It's because of Ted," Will says. "When I saw that picture of him—I never thought that I might break up your family. I never thought before of the impact it might have on your kids . . . The guilt I've been feeling the last few days, you can't imagine."

Now Lily feels indignant. "What makes you think I'd let you?"

"Let me what?"

"Let you break up my family. What makes you think I'd leave Ted for you? Besides, it would be my choice. My decision. It would have nothing to do with you. I would never leave Ted for you. I would leave Ted because I wanted to leave Ted."

The fact is, Lily, in all her infatuation with Will, hasn't exactly thought of leaving Ted. Not physically leaving him. Emotionally, she's been gone since long before she took Will back into her bed. But the act of really leaving Ted still terrifies her. Her feelings, her relationship with Will, are too new, not sturdy enough for her to count on. Especially since it's Will. She cannot fool herself into thinking she trusts his stability, his steadiness. He has left her so many times. When she thinks of Will, she thinks of his leaving, his emotional confusion. She is a mother now, with children. She can't make rash decisions, alter her life without affecting them. Besides, her children are Ted's children. He is right. No one else could really be their father, as angry and distant as she feels from him. Will would never care about them the way Ted does.

"The way we feel . . ." Will says haltingly. "I just thought . . ."

"You assume too much," Lily says, but the tears take the edge off the harshness she intends.

"Maybe it's just the way I feel about you. I haven't felt this way about anyone for so long . . . I just thought you felt . . ."

"Of course, I feel everything for you. Everything. I'd jump in front of a train for you. But I won't necessarily give up my family for you. How would I know you'd be there when I was out of all this?"

"You don't trust me."

"Should I?" she asks.

"I'm not even sure," he says softly. "I don't have the greatest record with you, do I?"

"No. Can't we just go on the way we are?" she asks.

"I don't know."

"Can't we pretend we never had this conversation?"

"You assume too much," he says coolly.

"Don't."

"You think it doesn't hurt to hear that you're never going to leave Ted?" he says, his voice now venomous.

"I didn't say never. And I didn't say it to hurt you."

"It's too late now." For a moment she hates him, hates him for being so cool, so cynical.

"So what do you want to do?" she asks softly.

He sighs so loudly, it presses her heart.

"I don't know," he says. "I'll get back to you."

If there is a living hell, Lily now knows it. She has to go on with the life she was barely able to stomach before, and now she knows how different it can be. Now she knows how alive she can feel. Like any part of the body waking up from being asleep, numb, the pain is unbearable. For the first time in her life, she knows what the expression "a broken heart" comes from. There is a prickly, never-ending ache in her chest, just beneath the base of her throat, that reminds her every second that her life is an agony.

But Ted says nothing. Until, one day at dinner, a week after her angry conversation with Will, she bursts into tears, and he looks up with semiconcern.

"It's the time of the month," she tells him, burying her face in her paper napkin.

"What does Mommy mean?" Peter asks. "What's wrong with Mommy?" He has just joined the real world in the last few weeks. Until now, little that was said around him penetrated his turtle shell. Now he is curious verbally as well as physically. And this is the one time in her years as a mother she doesn't have the concentration to answer him, to direct him, to praise him for his new awareness.

"It means Mommy's had a hard day," Ted says. "Did something happen?"

"No. I said, it's just my time of the month." She leaves the table for a while, lies on her bed in the dark, sobbing, never so utterly alone in her life. Later, she returns to the kitchen to do the dishes, to make life, as meaningless as it is, go on. For her children, if nothing else.

As they get ready for bed that night, Ted stops to hug her, making her aware how long it's been since he was spontaneously affectionate.

"Is it something you want to share with me?" he says hopefully.

"What?" she asks.

"Whatever is making you so low."

She shakes her head. "Hormones," she says.

"I don't think so," Ted says. Why does he look so bright-eyed? So pleased?

"It's you," she tells him suddenly.

"Me?"

"We have no life together," she says. "We never make love. We never talk anymore. Did you really go to Harvard? You seem to have nothing to share with another adult."

Lily realizes that she sounds shrewish, that he has finally wanted to be closer to her and she has pushed him away. And yet the pain, the anger are so fresh, so overwhelming. It is not his fault, and yet it is because of him she can't have Will.

"I have nothing from you," she says. "Except our children."

Ted sits down on the bed and stares at her as though she is a stranger in his wife's skin.

"What more do you want?" he asks.

"Don't you know?"

"Would I ask if I knew?"

"You don't share with me. Anything."

"I haven't changed," Ted says.

Now she is the one staring. Trying to see beneath the calm exterior of the husband that she's grown too used to, the man she agreed to marry. He is saying just what Edith said. Perhaps he hasn't changed at all. Maybe it's Lily that's changed. Maybe she really did marry this cool, detached man. Maybe back then she didn't think she deserved any better.

The next night, they go to Edith and Hal's for dinner. At the table, she feels numb, eating Edith's delicious feast without tasting anything. Ted is even more silent than usual. Even through the diversion of the children, Lily knows Edith sees it.

In the kitchen later, Edith says, "My God, what's going on between the two of you?"

"Nothing," Lily says.

"I see that," Edith says. "That's the problem. Tell me, Lily. We've never kept secrets from each other, have we?"

Lily looks into Edith's eyes, wishes with her heart and soul she could tell her everything. She wants so deeply for Edith's understanding. But how can she? Ted is her son. And Lily is breaking all the rules about marriage. In another woman, Edith would surely understand. But how can she not feel angry when it is her own son who is being betrayed?

"I don't know what to do anymore," Lily says instead. "He's more distant than ever."

"He seems angry," Edith says.

"Ask him. Maybe he'll tell you why he's angry. He won't say anything to me."

"I will. But carefully. He's never been one to tell anybody anything. Don't worry, kiddo. We'll straighten everything out. Don't look so scared."

Later, she sees that Edith draws Ted into her bedroom, leaving Hal and Lily to talk. Through the conversation, Lily tries to listen to what they are saying, but she can hear only low, murmuring voices.

When they leave, Edith tells her by shrugging and holding up empty palms that she's learned nothing. As she kisses Lily good-bye, she says, "Don't worry. There has to be a way to get through to him."

Will calls. Lily is trying to put Anna down for a nap, but she is wailing, a horrible new vocal power that she's discovered, as though she is picking up Lily's own desire to scream. Peter is watching "Sesame Street." The buzzer on the dryer is calling her. And the phone rings.

"Bad time?" he asks.

"Will."

"I'll call you back."

"No, just wait." Lily is ashamed of the panic in her voice. She heads for Anna's room, wanting to put her in her crib, to shut the door and let her scream, to answer the call, but she stops, frozen in the hallway, and knows she can't.

"I guess you should just call back," she says, "in ten minutes."

"Okay." How tentative he sounds, how hurt.

When she hangs up, she wonders if he will call. She doesn't trust him anymore, doesn't know what he's thinking, has almost come to think of him as the enemy. No one has ever made her suffer so much.

About an hour later, desperate, having given up any hope that he'll call back, she calls him. She is limp with exhaustion. Anna is finally, mercifully, asleep. Peter is now headlong into "Mr. Rogers." And she is almost too nervous to dial.

"I thought I ought to call you back," she says.

"Lily. I hear how angry you sound. Please hear me out. I had to sit on my hands all week not to call you. I never went through so much hell. I can't draw. I can't sleep. I can't eat. So please—"

"You, either?"

"You, too?"

They laugh, and their laughter is like rain after a drought. It seems to wash so profusely, nearly drowning them, so that it is a minute before either of them can find their composure.

"Why couldn't you call me?" she asks.

"Because it's wrong. I still think it's wrong."

"Oh, God." She is angry now. Really angry. Even if he is suffering, too. "Was it wrong the first time you slept with me? How about the second time?"

"I told you that I wish I'd never come down there. It was a mistake."

"How can you say that? After what we felt . . ."

"I know. But why do you think this is so hard? I could accuse you, too, you know. How could you feel so much and still sleep next to your husband every night as though nothing's changed?"

"But everything's changed . . . inside me. Don't you know that? Besides, I thought you didn't want to break up my marriage."

"Yes, I know. I didn't say what I'm feeling is consistent." She can imagine his face, its blond sweetness, his soft, bruised mouth.

"Don't stop seeing me, Will. Please." There it is. What she's really feeling. Under it all. He is her lifeline. Her very blood. He has raised her from the dead, and she is afraid to be alone.

"I don't know what to do," he says. How lost he sounds, how child-like.

"I just don't understand something," she says slowly, evenly, as though she *is* speaking to a child. "Why didn't the morality issue bother you when you were married? Didn't you say you slept around . . . with just about everybody?"

"You know," he says just as evenly, "the only time it ever bothered me was with you."

"This I *don't* understand."

"Because you were the only one who ever meant anything to me. Besides, it's not just because you're married. It's because you have children."

"So I have children, and that makes me off limits? What a specialized religion you follow. Let me see if I understand this. Adultery is okay if you don't care about somebody and/or don't have children?"

He is silent a long time.

"I hate it when you're angry at me."

Lily hears Anna calling from the other room. The nap is over. Anna's naps grow shorter every day.

"I have to go," she says. "If you say you don't want to call me or see me anymore, I will personally cut your heart out." But even to joke about his not wanting her hurts.

"You're such a romantic," he says dryly.

"I can't live without you," she barely whispers.

"I know," he says. "That's the living hell of all of this."

Lily feels better now. At least she knows he is feeling pain, too. At least she knows he wishes he could be with her. But she is angry and impatient. Why must he become so morally grounded now? She can't help wondering if he isn't simply afraid of the intimacy between them.

"You seem not so depressed," Ted says.

"Yes, maybe," she says.

"Well, good." That night, she seduces Ted at his desk as he works. She eases herself between his legs and unzips him, takes him into her mouth. Though they have been lovers now for four years, his sexuality is less familiar to her than Will's. There's never been a rhythm between them, never an established flow of desire. Ted is excited by her behavior but befuddled, too. As she straddles his lap, facing him, her desire for Will fueling her, she notices that even as he pumps, even as his breathing becomes ragged, he takes a moment to straighten the papers on the desk behind her.

Lily decides she's going to back Bobby Kennedy in the primary. Polly and Rob are for McCarthy, and Lily is drawn to him, too. But in the end, her affection for John Kennedy decides her. This is his brother. The same political savvy and starchiness are there. The same concerns. And even more experience in Washington.

But Ted says he's for Nixon. He is staunchly for Nixon, and it throws Lily, surprises her. "How can you have changed so much?" she asks. "Nixon is the opposite of JFK. We hated Nixon in the old days."

"These aren't the old days," he says with that touch of annoyance that seems to tinge everything he says to her these days. "And Bobby Kennedy, Eugene McCarthy, all they want is to get out of Vietnam right now. Without honor. Think of what it will be: a blight on the face of America. They're both trying to appeal to liberals, to college students. They're much more concerned with being popular than with making good decisions."

So she does some canvassing alone, goes to rallies, puts a Kennedy bumper sticker on her car. She and Ted talk less and less, it seems, about anything that doesn't concern the children.

Lily tells Ted she wants to go to a Kennedy rally in Madison, where he is scheduled to speak, and Ted shakes his head at her.

"You're getting obsessed with this Kennedy thing," he says.

"I'll just be gone overnight. I'll leave Saturday morning, come back Sunday. It's my only chance to see Bobby."

She tells Ted that she's going to sleep on some fellow Kennedyite's floor, a friend of Naomi's she met last year. "They'll probably be ten extra people there," she tells him. "It will be like college."

"I can't imagine why you would do this," he says. "You have two young children who need you." In the last few weeks, she has weaned Anna, who is so long-legged, she's actually become difficult to nurse, and who is now more interested in the world she is newly exploring than the comfort of Lily's breasts, anyway. Lily's sore, heated breasts, in the transition, have made her long achingly for Will's sweet loving. But now she feels liberated, and that is the thing that makes her want Will most.

She has decided to surprise him, to come to Madison unannounced, to see his cabin, to see his world. She is afraid. He still says he is uncertain about their relationship, but he has done nothing to slow it down. On the phone he is romantic, loving, and once again so deliciously sexual, she feels the power again of being wanted.

Her biggest fear is that while she is away, something will happen to her children, that even though she has left Will's number—it will be easy to say it's just one of the other guests answering the phone—being out of direct contact with her children will spell disaster.

Early Saturday morning, she leaves in the platinum shadows, in the cool air, where every sound, the thunk of the trunk closing, her footsteps, seem magnified. The silence, the winter wind, score her excitement. The drive is not particularly long. Three hours to Madison, a little more to find Will's cabin in McFarland. All the way there, she has worried that he'll be out—shopping, going to the rally himself—but she stops herself from calling him. Although he clearly wants her, if she says she's coming, he's not unlikely to turn her away.

The radio is playing "Lady Madonna" on almost every station. Will always sings it over the phone when Peter and Anna are screaming or getting into trouble during their conversations. "Lady Madonna, children at your feet. Wonder how you manage to make ends meet."

It is almost ten in the morning when, after talking to three different gas-station attendants, she finds the road in the woods that leads to Lake Waubesa. She switches off the radio. Winter jays are fighting. The cold air rings with their angry voices. The naked trees are like masses of snarled black hair against the winter sky. In the summer, the woods must be jelly green, the sun totally obscured by the denseness of the trees. But now, suffused with weak light, the woods are pristine and exude the calm Lily's felt in Will when he speaks of them.

The cabin is a tiny white house at the end of a long, steep driveway. Just beyond it, the lake is frozen, as dark gray as chinchilla. Lily scuffs through leaves to find the front entrance. On the mailbox, a punched tape reads: Sternhagen. Just seeing his name thrills her. She touches the raised letters one by one. Before she can ring the bell, he's standing before her with the door open.

"My God," he says. "I heard someone. I . . . ." He is crimson to the ears. He pulls her in and, kicking the door closed with his foot, draws her to him. "Oh, Lily. How . . . ?"

"Would you rather I left?" she asks.

He touches her lips as if to shut her up.

He unzips her jacket and unties her fur bonnet. His cool fingers thrill her skin. She reaches up to kiss him, and if, at first, there is an imperceptible reluctance, even that is soon gone.

"I hate you for coming," he says, kissing her ears.

"I can tell," she answers.

"Is everything all right? Did you just run away?"

"I told Ted I was coming for the Kennedy rally."

"Bobby will never know what he brought about."

Now he is kissing her neck, unbuttoning her boy's oxford shirt. In moments, they are lying on his clean kitchen floor, amid her winter jacket, her snow boots, and he is giving her the pleasure she's only been giving herself for days and days.

•   •   •

"You assume too much," he tells her teasingly when they have finally gotten up from the floor and found their way to his bed. "What if I hadn't been here? What if I didn't want you to stay?"

"Aren't you glad?" she asks him. "A whole night together."

"I'm just scared I'm not going to want you to leave," he whispers.

Lying among Will's white sheets—they must have been from his marriage, for they are embroidered and scalloped—Lily looks around his bedroom. It is painted white, unremarkable and small, but it smells of him. Fruit and Dial soap and musk. There are no curtains. The woods itself curtains the house all around. The walls are empty except for a single framed print that hangs between the two windows. It is of a woman sitting among Matisse-like fabrics. She is far from slender, full-breasted, full-hipped. Her hair is long and dark; her mouth, soft and rosy.

"Is that me?" she asks.

"Yes." She wants to cry, she is so flattered.

"Is it recent?"

"About a month ago. After the week we didn't speak."

She kisses him on the cheek. He is very thin now, maybe ten pounds less than the last time she saw him, and his cheekbones press through his fair skin, making his face almost Indian-like. She has noticed that his spine ends with a ledge. He seems to have no buttocks at all.

"You haven't been eating much," she says.

"Not much appetite these days."

"Not because of me?" she asks. She has lost ten pounds, too, since the start of their reacquaintance, but it has been entirely intentional, and no bones are showing themselves because of it.

"I just haven't been thinking about food."

"I've lost weight, too," she tells him.

"You worry too much about that," he says. "I like you precisely as you are."

"I'm tremendous," she says.

"No, you're not."

"You don't find it disgusting?"

"The way I think of it," he says, "is you look just like you, with just a little more upholstery."

"I love you," she says just as an exclamation, an answer to his kindness, but he pulls himself up on an elbow and touches her face.

"I love you, too," he says. And then, in the moment, he lies back with a sigh. "It's just fucking humbling to go through this."

"Through what?"

"Oh, Jesus. Not having you. Not ever really having you."

"Why do you think I came?"

"No. You have no idea what I mean. One night of screwing isn't going to make this better." Lily recoils at his language. What they do together has never ever seemed to her like "screwing."

Will gets up and goes to the kitchen, just steps away in this one-story cottage. Naked, he puts on the teakettle. She watches through the bedroom door. After a moment, with sudden furor, he slams his fist into the kitchen-cabinet door. BOOM! The noise thunders through the house.

This is how men cry, she thinks. She lies back among the sheets, feeling for him, worrying about him. She thinks of her children far away. She seems to be doing no good for anyone.

"Maybe I should leave," she tells him when he comes back in the room with two cups of tea on a tray. He shakes his head but says nothing, just sets the tray among the sheets. "I didn't know my coming here would hurt you so much," she says.

"You don't know anything," he says. And indeed, she is completely confused. What is she doing wrong? Why can't he be happy for the time they do have together? They drink their tea silently except for the clink of spoons as they stir in their sugar.

Later, they dress and go down to the lake. It is inches thick with ice, beautiful and bubbled and filled with light and shadow. Lily thinks she would like to paint a picture of it. Across the lake, Lily sees a deer peeking at them through the trees.

"Poor hungry thing," she says.

"They're nuisances all summer," he says. "They attack my garden, even my flowers." She takes his gloved hand, and they step out onto the ice. It is as though, in their contact, tenderness flows between them again. Her heart eases. How squeezed she has felt, witnessing his anger.

"What if we both fall through?" she asks.

He laughs. "You could drive a car across this lake." He kicks his heel into the ice and shavings fly, but the ice is stable as ever.

"Will you come to the Kennedy rally with me?" she asks him. "I should go so I can tell Ted about it. Besides, I want to."

"Sure. I'm going to vote for him, too."

"Are you?" She could not have been happier if he had given her a present. She throws her arms around him, kisses his face, his neck, but he seems to shrink from her. He reaches up and picks a sharp icicle from the low branch of a tree that stretches over the lake, and he pantomimes that he is stabbing himself in the heart.

The rally is scheduled for six o'clock in the University of Wisconsin field house, and they arrive about fifteen minutes ahead of time and find a seat. There aren't as many people as Lily wishes there were. Most college students are for McCarthy. And Lily would be if she didn't feel so strongly about Bobby's being a Kennedy.

When Bobby comes onstage, he is more vibrant, more handsome, than she could have imagined. She squeezes Will's arm in the excitement, and he smiles at her. Bobby's voice is like honey to her ears. She remembers back to the Cuban Missile Crisis, to the bar filled with Jack Kennedy's voice, and later to his announcement that war had been averted. This man could make the Vietnam War go away. She is certain.

Walking back from the rally to Will's car, they hold hands. Will is silent. Snow is falling in big, airy flakes.

"When do you have to go back?" he asks her finally.

"Not until late morning tomorrow."

He shakes his head but says nothing.

"Ted will be out of town in two weeks, for four days. Will you come?"

He nods, and all the way back in the little white Taunus, with its hard seats and a woolly smell, they are silent and sad, touching hands occasionally, like children alone together in the dark.

Just before they reach his road, they stop at a small grocery store, and Lily buys food for dinner. "When was the last time you ate more than Campbell's soup?" she asks him.

"The day I left Sandra. I like soup," he says. "Andy Warhol thinks Campbell's soup is just fine."

"Yeah, to paint." In Will's kitchen, she makes do with the few spices and old equipment, and soon the little cottage is filling with the rich perfume of coq au vin. While it's cooking, they sit across from each other, reading. She has brought a novel; he has a book about Van Gogh's life. Every now and then they look up simultaneously. In all her years of marriage with Ted, she never felt the camaraderie she feels with Will now. Just a glance is a blessing. Suddenly, he sets down his book and comes over to her, unbuttons her blouse, and fastens his mouth to her breasts. When he sucks, he looks up disappointed.

"No milk," he says.

"I weaned Anna," she tells him. He looks sad.

"I wish I could just have tasted it one more time," he says.

"I should have saved it for you." Nevertheless, he sucks her breasts more, and pulling up her short, full skirt, he slides his hand into her panties and rubs her swollen clitoris until she comes twice, throwing her head back against the chair, stretching her legs apart with excitement. She reaches to unzip him, but he pulls back.

"No," he says. "I'm going to please you so much, I'm going to own you. You can't have me until later." Now he draws down her soaking panties and buries his mouth in her sex, sucking, licking, thrilling her. When she comes this time, she nearly screams with the intensity.

"I have to check the coq au vin," she says weakly, trying to pull up her panties.

"No," he says. "You can't put them on." He takes them from her. "Go ahead," he says. "Go check the coq au vin."

Standing by the hot stove, basting the chicken, she is unnerved and excited by her pantyless state. As she cooks, he comes up behind her and rubs her buttocks, her thighs.

"I'm going to own you," he says.

"Just try it," she says. He smiles and takes a fat raw carrot from the counter and holds it teasingly in front of her. She finds it difficult to breathe. With a "mmm," he lifts her skirt and slides it into her unprotected vagina, drawing it in and out until she is panting. When he removes it, it is dripping with her juices. He then directs it softly, carefully, into the vulnerable opening between her buttocks. She drops the basting spoon. The oven pumps out tremendous gusts of heat. The deeper he sinks the carrot, the wider it is, opening her, frightening her. Still holding the carrot, he turns her around and slides his penis into her aching sex, so skillfully, so cunningly, manipulating the carrot, sliding it deeper and deeper, at the same time filling her vagina with his swollen penis. She is moaning, nearly falling to her knees.

"Tell me I own you," he says.

She merely moans.

"Tell me I own you," he says.

"You own me," she whispers.

"Louder."

"You own me," she says.

"Louder."

"You own me," she shouts, and comes. When he comes, he cries out in a thrilling, lost way. She can feel the tremendous shuddering of his penis. "And I own you," she says finally as he slumps against her. "I own you, too."

They eat the coq au vin, talking quietly. With the woods dark, the house bathed in lamplight, Lily feels cozy. But not entirely safe. The wildness of their sex has frightened her. Will has a way of pushing her to the edge and drawing her back just in time. And then withdrawing emotionally. She feels that he could make her do almost anything. There is a subtle violence in his hold over her.

At eight o'clock, she calls home while Will does the dishes. She stands in the darkened glassed-in porch overlooking the lake, speaking to Ted on Will's old black phone. Ted sounds tired and accusatory.

"Peter asked every ten minutes where you were," he says.

"Can I speak to him?"

"I put him to bed early."

"Anna, too?"

"Yes."

"I wanted to say good night to them."

"Too late."

"They're usually not in bed until eight-thirty," she says, realizing that her sadness is translating to a whine.

"I needed a break," he says.

"I stay with them when you're out of town."

"Well," he says, "I go on business. What you're doing is hardly business. How was Bobby?"

"What?"

"Bobby Kennedy. Who else?"

"He was great."

"Well, you've had your thrill. Now come home. When will you be here?"

"Late afternoon."

"Can't you come sooner?"

"No."

Ted is silent for a moment.

"I've been pretty good about all this," Ted says. "You wanted to have this selfish little freedom," he says. "But now I need you here."

"I'll see you at three or four."

When Lily hangs up, she's shaking. She goes over to Will, whose hands are bubbly with dish soap, and lays her head on his chest.

"Something wrong?"

She shakes her head. He rinses off and dries his hands, then hugs her for a long time.

Later, he lights a fire and shows her his prints, of the Indians, the lake, the cabin at dusk. They are exquisite. Masterpieces in her eyes.

"Take one," he tells her. "Tell Ted you bought it." She chooses one of the cabin at dusk, the lights inside spilling across the lake in the foreground. Will says he did the original sketch this summer, sitting in a boat with a Coleman lantern. She packs it carefully beneath her clothes. At least she will have something of his.

At midnight, they go to bed but don't make love. There is no desire left. But Will holds her spoon style all night. When she wakes up, her ear is sore and swollen from lying on it so unrelentingly. He is still sleeping, and she draws away from him and goes out to the glassed porch to look out at the lake, sparkling now with the first rays of light. She wonders if she will ever be here again. Probably not. Where else can she find an excuse like Bobby Kennedy? But at least she's seen it. She's seen Will's life, and now she can imagine it when she speaks to him or thinks of him. She's seen his life and now knows it is empty, waiting for her.

She leaves earlier than she planned. Her conversation with Ted nags at her, and she can't help thinking that she must go home and claim her children. The intensity of her feeling for Will somehow jeopardizes her hold over her children, and that frightens her. So, after breakfast, they lie together on Will's bed for a while, talking, without desire, still recovering from last night.

"I'm leaving soon," she tells him.

"Okay."

"Wasn't it good just to have this night?"

"Don't sleep with him," Will says.

"With whom? Ted?"

Will nods. "It's the only way I can own you."

"Okay," Lily says. "I know you want to own me. But do you love me?"

He looks at her and shakes his head. "I've told you I do," he says, and she searches his face but finds only annoyance that she's asked. All the way home, she nurses her doubts.

• • •

When Lily arrives home, she feels utterly changed. She feels she will burst if she doesn't tell somebody about Will, as though until she shares her secret with somebody, her relationship with Will won't really exist, will all be in her mind.

So she tells Polly she wants to come over. While the boys play and Anna sleeps on a quilt on the floor, she says, "If I tell you something, can you keep a secret?"

"What?" Polly seems full of herself these days. Smug and overly happy. Lily suspects it's because she's been smoking marijuana. She's offered it to Lily a few times.

"Want to turn on?" she always asks. And Lily is curious about smoking this weed that everyone is talking about. But she doesn't feel it's right to even have a drink when she's in charge of the children. And she is afraid that marijuana will bring about a loss of control, the sort of laissez-faire that will make her blurt out things about Will or the way she really feels about her life.

But now that she's about to reveal her secret, she wishes she were high. She is afraid Polly will be shocked, reject her, hate her for what she's doing.

"So tell me," Polly says, sipping her Tab. "You obviously came over to tell me."

"I'm having an affair."

Polly sets down her soda with a thunk.

"Who?"

"You won't tell Ted?"

"Why should I? I can't stand the man. Who? Who? This is great." Lily takes a deep breath, realizing that Polly's on her side. Polly, meanwhile, is licking the edges of two cigarette papers to join them, shaking pot out of a little leather sack she takes from the cigarette box on the table.

"He's an old lover of mine," she says. "Before Ted."

"So it's no one I know?"

"No."

"Too bad. I was hoping it was. It would make it so much more titillating. Like if it was Leonard." Polly's face puckers in an impish sort of way.

"Lois's husband, Leonard? I wouldn't do that!"

Polly lights the joint. The fragrance fills the room. "He's not so bad. Except I have no idea what he ever saw in Lois. What's this guy's name, anyway?"

"Will Sternhagen."

"What kind of damn name is that?"

"Scandinavian."

"So are you in love with him?"

"Oh, God. I guess he's the love of my life, or something."

"Or something?"

"I'm in love with him. I just never feel . . . I can trust it."

"Trust what? Are you going to leave Ted?"

"No."

"Why not?"

"Polly!"

"Well, it's not such a remarkable thing to suggest. You don't particularly love Ted anymore, do you?"

"Sometimes I do. He's the father of my kids. Would you leave Rob at the first chance?"

"Chance," Polly says thoughtfully, setting the joint in the ashtray and sipping her Tab. "Now there's the operative word. It sounds like you've been just waiting for this opportunity. But in your heart you're not really certain this Stern-cloggen guy loves you, right?"

Lily sits there on Polly's shiny black vinyl sofa, shaking. She even draws the afghan around her shoulders. "How did you know that?"

"It's just something I've learned about you. You don't think anyone can love you." Then Polly stretches, catlike, perfectly content. "God, I feel good," she says. "You really should smoke this stuff."

"I guess I don't," Lily says, seeing that everything Polly's said is true.

"You don't what?" Polly says, lifting the joint again to her lips, clearly having lost all interest.

"Think people can love me."

"Yeah," Polly says. "Ain't life a bitch? Come on. At least take one hit." Lily takes the joint in her hand and inhales, holds in the smoke just as she's watched Polly do. But after a few more drags, she just feels like sleeping.

The spring thaw comes, and the gutters drip, making Lily's little bungalow sound alive. All night long, when Ted is out of town, she listens to the rush of thawed water along the eaves. Will has come to visit her four times since she told Polly, and each time, she feels closer to him and more afraid.

"If we were married," Will says, "we'd exhaust each other," he says. Each time together, their sex becomes more violent, more out of control. Sometimes he bites her or pushes her down or makes her do things that feel degrading but so exciting. He likes to leave marks on her so that she won't undress in front of Ted. Blue hickeys on her breasts, a long scratch down her spine he inflicts with a jagged fingernail, on purpose. He wants to watch her masturbate with a candle, then breaks a tiny piece from the candle and tells her she must wear it inside her all the next day, after he leaves. He calls her around two the next afternoon.

"Is the wax soft?" he asks.

"I don't know."

"Feel it. Take it out and find out."

"The children are here."

"Go in the bathroom and find out. I'll wait on the phone. I need to know if you're thinking of me."

As she draws out the marble-sized piece, the candle wax is soft and malleable. It crushes down between her fingers and for some reason makes her want to cry.

And yet other times he is so loving, so worshipful, she drowns in his feeling for her.

"I can't leave you," he will say. "I can't do it." And she really thinks he might cry. He is clutching her as though he may never see her again.

"I don't want you to."

"Then why are you doing this to me?" he says. "You're killing me. I don't even like my life anymore. I can't find any contentment."

"What would give you contentment?" she asks him.

"I don't know."

"And if I said I wanted to marry you . . . ?" she asks.

"I don't even want to talk about it," he says. "I couldn't live with that," he says. "Being the cause of you breaking up with Ted."

On this last visit, Anna awakened in the night, and Will had come to her bedroom with Lily, stood in the shadows as she soothed her. Lily vaguely wondered then, as she focused on her child, whether her maternal side seemed attractive to him. Then she asked him:

"Would you accept her as your child?"

He'd blanched, become silent.

"I don't know," he said. "What are you saying?"

"I'm just wondering if you could ever be serious about taking on my family."

"I guess it would entail that, wouldn't it?"

"I'd say so."

"I always wanted my own children," he said bluntly.

"I see."

She doesn't know what he wants from her. She doesn't know how to help him. And her feelings for him are so desperate and confused, the joy seems to seep from their feeling for each other.

Yet despite the uneasy nature of her relationship with Will, Lily begins to think seriously of leaving Ted. He is sweet as ever with the children. Sweeter than she wishes he would be. He sings them to sleep. He carries them on his shoulders. He talks to them in silly voices and tells Peter jokes only three-year-olds would consider funny. But it is now pure acid between Ted and Lily. After the children are in bed, a silence descends. He goes to the study and shuts the door. When she thinks more seriously of leaving him, she realizes she can't do it unless she is sure she's done everything she can to save the marriage. She needs to feel if she leaves Ted, she's leaving him because there is no hope between them. She reminds herself daily that her decision can have nothing to do with Will, although she can't help dreaming of moving to Wisconsin with the children, finding a bigger house on the lake, waking to the sound of the winter birds in the trees. But she is clear her feeling for Will must be extraneous, another fact altogether. Her marriage must break up because there is simply no way to keep it together.

"I think we should go to a marriage counselor," she tells Ted one night as they undress for bed.

"What for?" He turns full-faced to her, studies her, giving her his entire attention, something he rarely does.

"Well, for one thing, we never make love anymore." She is surprised how shy she feels discussing the subject with him. She really doesn't know him at all, she thinks.

He shrugs. His shoulders look stooped and fatherly in his too-big striped pajamas. "I just figured we were past that."

"What does that mean?"

"It means that adults don't have to act like wild children. Passion can't last forever," he says. How military he looks. How severe and closed.

He stares at her. When he gets nervous, he stiffens, and his hands clasp behind his back.

"Is it religious guilt or something? That you can't like sex?" Lily says. "You seemed to, once. Is it since you started going back to church?"

"For heaven sakes, don't bring the church into this." He turns away, starts toward the study, even though she knows he had intended to go right to bed.

"So you don't want to see a marriage counselor?"

"I don't see the point."

"If you don't want to sleep with me, you don't imagine I might want to sleep with someone else?"

"What is this? Some kind of threat?" He stares at her, and she gets a chill so sharp down her spine, she visibly shivers.

That night, Lily lies in bed, and it is as though the ceiling is filled with stars. She is so stirred up, so uneasy, there is nonstop sparking against her retinas. No rest at all. Her hatred for Ted spills out, drowns her. She gets up at two in the morning and checks the children's rooms. Their mussed innocence wounds her. She doesn't want to do anything that would harm them. And yet to suffer through this perpetual emptiness is unbearable.

She tries to imagine their divorce. She tries to think of what Ted would try to do. He could never find out about Will. If he did, he'd snatch custody from her. She is sure she would lose the children. Then that would mean if she asked for a divorce, it might be two or three years before she'd see Will at all. Even if they were legally separated, it would be too risky. She imagines calling Will from pay phones. She wonders if he would grow angry or impatient. She thinks, somehow, he would not be there when she finally freed herself.

Then, she thinks of the oddest things. She thinks about how she would miss ironing Ted's shirts. She loves the thick oxfords he buys. Blue and white only. He is thoroughly out of fashion these days, when men are wearing burgundy-colored shirts with French cuffs, Peter Max ties as wide as bibs, Nehru jackets. But blue-and-white oxfords are what suit him. And on the ironing board they are so starch loving they crackle with certainty. She thinks how she would miss the smell of his deodorant on the sheets. And how lonely she would be in the night without his even breathing. And she thinks of losing Edith and Hal and the sense of stability they have brought to her life. She has felt so often that they have become her parents, the parents she always wished she had. Together, the thought of losing them and the small, insignificant details that have made up her marriage momentarily overwhelm her, and she weeps loudly on the couch in the living room.

And then Ted wanders in, looking truly annoyed.

"What is this?" he asks. "Menopause? Will you please come to bed." And she finds the idea of divorce not unattainable, after all.

The next night, when she can't sleep again, she tries to call Will collect from the phone in the basement. It is two in the morning, and she expects him to be angry, but no one answers. "Ring again," she tells the operator. She wonders if he could possibly sleep through the ringing but knows in her heart it would be impossible. Her hands are shaking, and she's in a cold sweat. There are three phones in the little cottage. All ring loudly enough to wake the dead. She knows he isn't there at all.

The next day, when she asks Will where he was, he says, "What is this? Are you spying on me?"

"Hardly that. I was worried about you."

"Worried. Worried about what?"

"Where were you, Will?"

"What does it matter?"

"You weren't there?"

"Well, obviously I wasn't here, Lily."

"Oh, my God," she says, thinking of the night she found out he'd slept with Louise Lewis.

"I love you," he says. "But what right do you have to expect me to be faithful to you?" She does not cry or scold him. She knows he is right, and it is a burning, bitter truth.

But she can't help being flippant.

"You ought to find out if Louise Lewis ever married," she says. "Maybe she's available to fill your lonely nights." And then, before he can answer, a further conversation that will be bitter and unresolvable, she hangs up.

The day she plans to tell Ted she is leaving him, she decides to make a really special meal with wine to give her courage. She has said nothing at all to Will, who is beginning to feel dangerous to her heart. They have never spoken again about it, but she thinks all the time about how Will might be with someone else, that he might be falling in love with someone else. She feels a panic sometimes so intense, it makes her feverish, makes her heart pound. She knows now, she will never trust him, not really trust him. Not if she wishes to protect herself. For he hides his fears in infidelity, in emotional distance, and she doesn't think that will ever change. Even before she felt this way, she's always known leaving Ted was something she must do only for herself.

She has asked a neighbor, Mrs. Hanksman, to watch the children for the morning so that she can shop quietly, thinking about what she will say to Ted tonight. She has used Mrs. Hanksman more since Anna has learned to walk, because she is restless in the shopping cart, wants to toddle down the aisles. Then Peter wants to get out, too, and in the end she is disciplining them, barely able to remember what she planned to buy. At the sight of Mrs. Hanksman, Anna bursts into tears, wails until she is reddish purple, but Lily, knowing this is one morning her plans must not be altered, hands her over stoically and gets out the door before she is overcome with guilt.

At the store she buys sirloin, though she's planned beef Stroganoff and it could take a lesser cut. Knowing she will soon be leaving Ted makes her tender toward him, makes her want to give him the best. She feels wistful as she buys the sour cream, the tin of real Hungarian paprika. In the vegetable aisle, she has chosen fat, sweet onions and is sorting artichokes when she sees him: Jack. She recognizes the golf sweater instantly, the slouch, the silver hair. Why today? she asks herself. Her first instinct is to run. Her heart betrays her with a thumping so loud she is sure the other shoppers will stop their carts and stare. She pulls her thin gray coat around her, hoping it will silence the sound.

In her panic, in an instant, she knows the time has come to face her enemy. Preparing to leave Ted has empowered her, and she is startled and pleased by her rare new strength. Armed with this sudden certainty, she turns and starts down the aisle, pushing her cart right at Jack.

As she comes toward him, he looks both left and right as though searching for an exit. But he is trapped and knows it. He has aged severely, grotesquely. His skin is wrinkly, with a sick yellow cast. And she can see that he has shrunk. He is just bones now. Bones and a cigarette. The pumpkin-colored sweater hangs on him as though he's a child in a hand-me-down.

"What are you doing here, Jack? Why are you following me?" she says, and her voice is the voice she would use to chastise a child. She could never have confronted him if her children were there. But now she stands before him, and she feels so much stronger than he appears to be. Her mouth is not dry, as she might have expected, but flooded with saliva. Her heart is not beating hard but steadily, intently. She has come to face the enemy with the unfailing ammunition of being right. This is how Saint George felt, poised in front of the dragon. The only sign that she is stressed is that her feet are so damp, she might be standing in a puddle.

"Why are you following me?" she asks.

"I . . . no . . . Lily . . ."

"Why? Why would you bother?"

"I knew I couldn't see you by calling you. I needed to see your children, your life."

"Why?"

"Because you're all I have left." Every syllable he speaks is a labor, suffused with the sound of pained breathing. His emphysema, Lily thinks. And the yellow cast is his bad liver. Smoking, drinking, guilt. She sees it on his face.

"But you've always hated me," Lily says angrily.

"Hated you? Hardly that. It was always you I loved," he says.

Lily looks at him and feels she sees him for the first time. He is lost. In purgatory. A lovesick boy grown old. He will die soon, she is sure. The inappropriateness of his wanting her has sickened her, frightened her for so long. But now she sees it not as evil but weakness.

"I'm not afraid of you," she says.

"Okay."

"What do you want from me?"

"To be part of your life," he says. He is so weak, he would fall over in a breeze.

"No," she says. "You can't be part of my life. I'm sorry. I'm sorry for you, but you can't. You forfeited that when you forgot I was supposed to be your daughter."

"I didn't expect you to say yes."

"Please stop following me," she says.

"Do I have to?"

She looks at how shabby his sweater is. Where has all his money gone? Or does he just no longer care about his appearance. She looks into the watery green of his eyes. Just a few years ago, the longing in his eyes could evoke such fear in her, she shudders remembering.

"I'm dying," he says. "I've been in the hospital . . . a few times."

"We're all dying," she says.

"I have no one. No one came to visit me."

She turns to walk away, and he calls after her.

"Your children are beautiful," he says. "Beautiful."

"I'm sorry, Jack," she says. "I'm sorry."

"Can I call you?" he is shouting, with his unfamiliar old man's voice. "Can't I?"

"No," she calls back. The aisle is remarkably long. The objects in the cart tumble with the speed of her walk. But she is no longer escaping. She is pushing forward purposefully. In the car, she sits silently for a long time, her head resting on the steering wheel. When she looks up, she sees Jack leaving the store with two grocery bags. He takes them to an old beat-up Rambler, and she watches as he drives away.

Lily doesn't tell Ted about Jack. She has something more important to discuss with him. She feeds the children and puts them to bed early. They cooperate as though they are part of the conspiracy. Alone in the kitchen, she simmers the beef Stroganoff, snips and steams the artichokes, melts the butter. Ted comes in about a quarter after eight. The kitchen is a perfumed trap. He kisses her his same perfunctory dinnertime kiss. He sits at the kitchen table, reading the evening paper, while she stirs and seasons. They eat in silence for a long while before she tells him. She realizes then that he rarely comes to her with something to say. She has carried this relationship on her back entirely. Like a turtle, she thinks. She'd thought of it as protection. But now she sees the shell as a burden.

"I want a divorce," she tells him.

He looks up at her, his fork loaded with beef Stroganoff. There is a faint sheen of butter around his surprised mouth. He takes the bite before he answers, chewing carefully.

"Is that what you want?" he asks.

"Obviously."

"But the kids."

"There are always weekends," she says.

"You bitch."

It is the first swear word he has ever said to her. In all these years, he's never yelled at her. Always at household objects instead. He's never beaten her except for his reaction the time she hit him. He's never imposed on her. In fact, he's treated her like a good but not very usable piece of furniture. She begins to cry. She wants to call Will, but she can't. If Ted followed her into the bedroom, if he found out about Will, her custody of the children would no longer be a given. The last thing she sees before he smashes a flowerpot and leaves is a dark gleaming light in his eyes so cold and calculating that it rips through her like a laser. A pent-up hatefulness that is finally being exposed to the air.

She lies down on the bed. She doesn't think Ted will be back tonight, though she can't imagine where he'll go. She sits up, lies down again, sits up, looks at all the objects in the room as though she's never seen them before. It will be months until she will really be able to read a book, to concentrate, to go through life with a sense of reality. But she doesn't know that yet. All she knows is that there is a lot new to look forward to, and she feels fifty pounds lighter.

Chapter Seventeen

Andres is shaving when he hears the news. He thinks for a moment the radio is playing an old tape, remembering the blackest moment in modern American history. But the sound of panic goes on and on. He turns up the transistor. Lather drips from his razor right onto the speaker. But he can't move.

"Kennedy shot. Pool of blood. Ambassador Hotel." The facts repeat themselves again and again, and he listens again and again, as though only in repetition will he believe them. Bobby, too?

Andres was looking forward to this election. It is not the first time he's been able to vote, but as a converted American, he holds the option to vote as a gift. He'd planned to vote for Kennedy. His allegiance toward him was swayed by Lily. Does she know of the assassination? He picks up the phone to call her but sets it down again. He is afraid to be the bearer of news so painful.

In these past two months, he has called Lily nearly every day. She needs him now, he thinks. She has finally sent her husband away. He knew she would. And sometimes Andres thinks he will ask her to marry him again. But he is tired. And her presence these days is like shards of glass. She is sparkling, reflective one moment and the next, wounding him with sharp edges. She exhausts him.

What makes him most impatient is her relationship with Will Sternhagen. If she chose to step out of her marriage, why did she have to choose Will and not Andres? He's surely loved her better over the years, stood by her, cared for her more. He no longer wants to love her from afar. He no longer wants to be safe from his feelings for her.

"Sometimes I think if I don't see Will soon, I won't be able to go on. I feel like I've lost a limb," she tells him. "I'm afraid he's sleeping with someone else. I know he is. It's killing me, Andres." Andres feels so hateful toward Will, he finds it hard to swallow.

This is his last year of teaching. The print department is not so popular anymore. People are finding bolder expressions in painting these days, it seems. Print looks to some of the students to be a tired medium. And the students who are in his classes are more interested in cold depictions of soda bottles or soup cans or Op Art than in-depth expressions of life. His prints are still valued, but not like they used to be. His gallery is respectful, but the checks grow smaller each season. They call less often.

He has not had a lover in over a year. The women look hard and impassable to him these days. And he is too old and fragile for rejection. But there is a quiet acceptance in him now that he's never known before. Sometimes it scares him how easily he can deal with disappointments. Sometimes he thinks it must mean he is near the end of his life.

He has begun to look for apartments in Chicago, and when he goes into the city, he takes the train out to see Lily. And this is when she wounds him. Sometimes she will snuggle in his arms and tell him she loves him.

"When you hold me, Andres, it's the only time I feel safe. You're the only man in the world I'm not angry at," she tells him. And it's the only time he feels completely threatened. Too hopeful for his own good. This afternoon he is planning to drive to Chicago once again. He's heard there's a studio open at the Cliffdweller's Club on Michigan Avenue, the very place he's set his heart on. And he called Lily last night to tell her he's coming to see her. Now he wonders how upset she'll be with Kennedy's assassination, if she will want to see him at all. He is bringing a new print as a gift for her, but he looks over at it now, leaning by the door so he won't forget it, and it seems pale and weak compared to the work he used to do. He is a man whose passions are draining from him like meat hung from a hook.

Lily turns the TV on about noon so that Peter can watch "Bozo's Circus," and when she hears a reporter's serious voice coming out of the TV before the picture solidifies, she gets a chill. The first thing she sees when the picture fills out is a portrait of Bobby Kennedy, one of those graduation-type portraits where the eyes are too hopeful, the chin too weak. Beneath the picture are the year of his birth and the year of—" She sits down in the chair Peter usually occupies every afternoon in front of the television, and he pushes at her.

"Hey, Mommy. Where's 'Bozo's Circus'? Get up. That's *my* chair!"

"Oh, my God," she says, and her own voice seems as if it has come from someone else. Anna comes over and butts her head against Lily's stomach. "He's dead," Lily says. "He's dead."

"Who's dead, Bozo?" Peter asks, starting to cry.

"No. Bobby Kennedy."

"Who's he?" Lily closes her eyes and remembers Ted's words when Jack Kennedy died: Our hero's dead. It makes her want to call Ted, to find comfort once again in his undemanding solidity. But Ted never liked Bobby Kennedy anyway, and besides, Ted is gone. The day after she asked for a divorce, he returned, and clenching his jaw, he packed some clothes in his Samsonite suitcase, took a few pictures of the children, and left, finding a pay-per-week apartment in Niles. And then his face changed. It frightened her how different he suddenly seemed. So angry she couldn't bear to be in the same room with him. Peter told her that when Daddy took him to the park the day before he left, Peter thought he saw him cry and that in the car he screamed at another driver who veered into their lane.

"Daddy said lots of really bad words," Peter reported.

The children are traumatized by Ted's leaving. But less than Lily feared. To them, his absence must seem like an extended business trip. They often ask when's Daddy coming back. Peter especially whines for Ted at night. And one night, Lily goes out with Polly and Rob so that Ted can put the children to bed.

How can Ted be silent when, despite their distance from each other and her love for Will, Lily's heart is breaking? Sometimes she just wishes he'd cry or ask her to start over or hold her in his arms and mourn the loss of their marriage together. When she tries to cry to him, when she tells him she misses his presence in the house, he looks at her with the eyes of a predatory animal.

And then there's Will. The day after she told Ted she wanted a divorce, he called at his usual time, and she told him that she was ending her marriage, that they mustn't talk again until the divorce is final.

"How could you?" he asked. And he seemed truly angry. "We didn't even discuss it," he said.

"It isn't something for you to discuss. It's about me," she told him. "Just about me. My husband. My marriage."

"But are you expecting now that I'll marry you? I didn't say I'd marry you."

Lily is silent. Her rib cage feels as though it's shrinking.

"I'm expecting nothing," she says. But, of course, despite all her best intentions, it's a lie. She had believed in time she'd be with Will. Even though she will never trust him. The more she thinks of it, the more she is sure that that was entirely her intention. Why has she been so dishonest with herself? His passion holds her as cruelly as that bug under a shoe.

"I'm making no promises," Will says, and his voice is annoyed and hard. And, at the same time, he's equally furious they can't see each other.

"How long will this be?" he asks.

"A year," Lily says, "maybe even two."

"Oh, great," Will says. "I'm supposed to wait two years to see you. And this is okay with you?"

"Maybe we'll find a way. A little espionage," she tells him, but doesn't believe it. She won't risk her children, even for Will. And though Ted isn't likely to contest the divorce, she can't take any chances. She begins to look at her relationship with Will as a fruitless obsession. She feels better not seeing him. Safer. He'd made her feel so good, but it was the kind of good feeling that could last only a precious while.

Early evening. The grass smells both of spring and old leaves. The little bungalows all up and down the street are lit up, though the days are longer now, and there is still a silver glow in the sky. Lily is rocking in the rocking chair with Anna in her arms when she hears the bell, wishing she were still nursing her, could still feel so close to another human being. Her heart does not just ache. It feels as though it's been beaten. It feels black and blue. And her body is so filled with longing it impedes her, drags behind her, embarrasses her.

Andres stands at the door nervously, a print leaning against one leg. His eyes seem to spill with sadness.

"Such a day for me to come," he says. "I do not know if this woman needs the company or if it is best not to disturb."

"I'm glad you're here," she tells him. "Come on. Sit down." She takes his arm, and he winces. Her touch burns him. His feelings for her frighten him. She rouses both the tenderness he rarely uses and the sexuality he's been repressing. But to her he is the father she never had, the comfort, the strength, she always sought in people who couldn't possibly give it to her. Even Ted. And he is the sweetness, the gentle tenderness, she cannot find in Will.

She sits by him on the couch. So close he can feel her breath on his neck. It is clovelike, sweet.

"Well, is that print something you just wanted to drag on the train, or is it for me?" she asks.

"For you, of course," he says.

"Come on, show me." He gets up wearily and brings it to her. It is beautiful, but not as intense as most of his prints, a little wistful. It makes her sad.

"Beautiful," she says. "Really, Andres. I love it."

"It's not so good," he says.

"Don't you think so? You're just being modest."

"With Kennedy gone, this is a year of sadness. I don't know." He sighs. "Maybe my next print will be about that."

"You always liked sad things," she tells him.

"Yes. You, too. In your art. Are you making art these days?" he asks her solemnly.

"The art of being a mother only," she tells him. She despises the defensiveness in her voice. He has tapped her most vulnerable spot.

"I've already bought your Christmas gift," he tells her. "Maybe it will inspire you."

"Five months early?"

"I thought if I gave it to you without a holiday, without a reason, you would not be one to take it. So I wanted to buy it while I was thinking of it, but you will have to wait until Christmas for me to bring it to you."

"But I once accepted a piano from you, and it was no holiday at all."

"That," he says, "is because the world was coming to an end."

"I can't even remember what it was like to paint or make prints anymore," she says. "I used to lose myself in my work. Now I can't even seem to focus long enough or find the energy to make a little sketch. And I feel so critical of anything I do."

"You must find your way back," Andres says. "You will again 'lose yourself' in it and, I think, find yourself as well. It must be your . . . your quest. This is the word? Quest?"

Lily nods. The thought of "questing" for her art exhausts her. It makes her think of a time as a child she went hiking with her friends and realized that five miles back, where they'd stopped for lunch, she'd left her hat. It was a yellow sun hat with pink roses on it. No one wanted to walk back with her so far, and it seemed too dangerous to take the hike alone—it would be dark before she got back—so she imagines that the hat remained forever under an elm tree, glowing yellow even in the thick shade. It must have been rained on, must in time have faded from its startling yellow, turned to earth under autumn's elm leaves. Her art feels like this: a sad, bright, lost memory, faded, irretrievable. Still, as she readies the children for bed, she wonders how she might begin the journey back. She wonders if she could possibly find her way.

Andres helps shepherd the children to the bathroom, to load their toothbrushes with toothpaste. They know him now but are shy, cautious, around him. Peter speaks of him in the third person. "Mommy, will you ask the man to tell us about the horses on his farm?" Peter asks. It is a story Andres shared with Peter before: his childhood, when each child had a nanny and a pony, the latter being much more exciting than the former.

Anna points and tries to tell Lily that Andres is silly. She giggles at him and flirts up from her dark lashes. "Silly guy," she says, or Andres thinks she says. Someday she will break hearts, he thinks. He is glad it won't be his. He'll be dead by then or incapacitated. He has been filled with dread of dying lately. Morbid, they always called him. Yes, he is morbid.

When the children are sleeping, Andres and Lily eat at the dining-room table, politely, looking into each other's eyes constantly for clues, and suddenly there is an intensity between them, a leaning forward, a touching of hands.

And as they talk about their lives, Andres says softly, "For all the years that I have known you, I have wanted to know one thing, my Lily, one question. In the beginning, I asked you often, but you gave me no answer. For a long time now, I am too afraid to ask."

"I'll answer it," Lily says.

"Why are you so sad? From the first day I saw you, I could see this sadness. Sometimes I see you as a bird, hurt. Your wing is not just broken; it is torn."

"Oh," Lily says, and she feels afraid. Will he still care for her when he knows?

"It's how my mother died," she says.

"How she died? Not because she died?"

"Yes. How she died. She committed suicide."

"Oh, blessed God," he says.

"But it isn't even just that. It's why she did." Already Lily feels the tightening in her throat.

"You must tell me, Lily. Even if it is hard. Even if you are afraid." How did Andres know she was afraid? She feels his large, warm hand enfold hers.

"My stepfather . . ." And she falters. How encouraging his eyes are, how patient. Somewhere in those patient eyes she finds the courage to go on. "My stepfather was a selfish drunk. And sometimes, when he thought I wouldn't notice, he would touch me. Touch me, wanting me. But it was always so little, so careful. I hated him for it. I felt so wrong about it. But I thought if I said something to him, we'd both be embarrassed . . . I thought if I pretended it didn't happen, then it wasn't really happening.

"Then, one night, I was home from college; my mother was out playing bridge. He'd been drinking a lot. He liked to drink a lot. And that night, he came into my room, and he was so drunk he stunk of it . . . and he started to grab me, to kiss me and press me against the wall . . ." And as she tells it, she is reliving it, every moment, the crush of her shoulder blades, the desire to flatten, to flatten.

Andres closes his eyes. She knows he is feeling her pain. "What happened?" he asks.

The shame of it overwhelms her now, spills like poison into her blood as she remembers that single moment of desire. She is wailing now. Wailing for help as she has never cried before. "I wanted him. For a moment, Andres, I wanted him. How can I ever forgive myself for that?"

Andres comes around the table and kneels by her, holds her tenderly, pressing his face into her neck.

"You are human, Lily. You do not have to be forgiven for that." How solid is his hold, how unwavering. "It is he that cannot be forgiven. He raped you."

"I kicked him in the head, Andres. Somehow I got him to leave the room before he did."

"My God, I am glad."

"But then I did what was truly unforgivable: I told my mother. I told her the next day. About all the times he touched me, everything. And that afternoon she got in her car, drove to Chicago, and jumped from the top of a building."

"It was right to tell her, Lily."

"She killed herself for it. I thought I had to tell her, to stop him. But there must have been something else I could have done."

"How angry you must feel toward your mother," he says.

"Angry?" she says. And there is the shrill in her voice right now, though anger is not the emotion she has ever named in relationship to her mother.

"After all," Andres says, "she left you to face Jack alone. You must, in the smallest way, hate her for being so weak. For not staying to defend for you."

Hearing Andres's words, a rush of feeling jars her. "She should have protected me. A mother's supposed to protect—Andres . . ." But her throat closes around her tears, and she finds no more voice at all. Andres pulls her tighter to him. "Cry, my Lily," he says. He smells of chamomile and tweed. Of the leather patches on his sweater. His embrace makes her reach up, pull him closer. Has she ever felt so close to a human being? She is weakened with realization, with feeling, with feelings for him.

"We are both survivors," he tells her, and kneeling by her, stroking her hair and neck with care, with a cherishing touch she can never remember feeling before, he slowly kisses the tears from her cheeks, from her chin, from her lips.

When she has quieted, when a warm silence between them makes her lay her head on his shoulder, she says, "Now tell me why you are so sad. Now you must tell me."

His voice is deep and even at first, like a storyteller's, hypnotic, as he recites the history of the constant turnover of regimes in Paraguay, all so inconsequential to his family, and then the rise of General Stroessner. But emotion starts to flood his words. She pulls back so she can see his face, his sad blue eyes.

"My parents know they must go quickly," he says, and she sees their panic in his face. "They begin to pack all the things they care for," he says. "Too many things—they plan their escape to Buenos Aires. But they are fat with the things they think they must have. They pack for two days, or three. My brother calls to say good-bye. Come, Andres, he says. But my wife is the daughter of a man, a favorite man of General Stroessner, and I am maybe safer, we think. Do you know the safety that young people feel? It is a lie, this safe feeling."

"Yes," Lily says, nodding. Once she felt safe. Once she did.

"Their car, my parents' car, is stopped. My parents are murdered right there, in my father's Buick, with over a hundred bullets, I learn from my wife's father. Who counted these bullets? I wonder sometimes. Who, please, counted the holes in my parents' bodies? My brother, he is tortured . . . to death, I cannot even tell you of this . . . all because my father once gave money to another regime so that they will not take any of his farmland and ruin his view. It is true. For this, my family dies."

"Andres."

"So many nights, it is me, it is me who knows my brother's torture. It is my nightmare, even today. In the end, I ran away. My wife, she will not come, and I am glad. Maybe they do not want to kill me, after all, these ugly soldiers of General Stroessner, just because my father paid for a good view. I do not want to know. I ran."

"Andres." She touches his shoulder, his craggy face. How she wishes she could make over the past for him, reknit the torn memories, remove the violent sadness that marks his face.

"I think the survivors suffer most," he says, looking into her eyes now. "The survivors who have to say, Why? Why? and Why not me? Lily, you know this. You know." Andres holds her arm so tight, it heats beneath his fingers. "Every room I enter, I search for the closest door. Everyone I care for . . . I search for the door in my caring. Everyone but you."

And Lily nods and feels what he is saying to her core, for she is her mother's survivor. She endured all her mother endured, the hateful men her mother chose to rule and ruin their lives, the life she herself could no longer suffer, and here Lily sits, here she breathes, and all these years has known an emptiness in her core like a hollow tree that could collapse on itself with a single rap of wind.

"Andres, I wish I could spare you even one second of one bad dream," she says. As she looks into his eyes, he reaches up and kisses her. His kisses are desirous but careful. His hands are respectful as a sculptor's. Every touch of his fingers leaves a print, a shadow, an indelible mark of feeling.

"I want to take you to bed," he tells her finally. "I cannot go through my life and not know you this way. To give you pleasure. To draw pleasure from you. If it is not too hateful for you. Please. I want no more. I know you will never marry me," he says.

She looks into his face and sees herself. It is magical how his expression mirrors her fears, her hopefulness, her loneliness.

"Yes," she tells him. "Please."

There is a rich silence as he takes her hand and leads her from the table. Lily does not think of Will or Ted. She is enwebbed with only Andres. How has she kept him so distant from her heart? The only man who can really know it?

In the bedroom, he undresses her carefully, slowly, and with great interest. His hands are as exquisite as driftwood, and she kisses them, opens his palms to her lips. He tastes herblike, of the woods, of leaves. His wrists are delicate in her fingers, his arm, the strong arms of a man who controls a drawing instrument, an etching instrument, with insane exactitude. She savors him, cannot know him until she unwraps every mystery with her lips, her tongue, her eyes, her hands.

"Andres. Andres."

She lets him leave the lights on. She is not afraid of revealing her flaws to him. She knows he loves her without judgment, that he will love her imperfections as he discovers them, that in his very touch he will bless them and make her see herself transformed.

How sexual his caresses, how graceful his embraces, as though they are underwater, swaying together like seaweed, flesh to flesh, their skins wet with desire, a slickness brought to the surface by years apart, by the electricity of their sameness. He is an old man. An old man. The hair on his chest is white, and his long fingers lack the pad of youth. But his caresses are searing and yet familiar, so familiar. Why? She has known him. Known all along she would find him, in the ugliness of her life. The goodness of him, the pureness of him. He is old, and he has embraced and bedded a hundred young women, but she knows, she knows with certainty, he has never loved any as he loves her.

He kisses and caresses the length of her body, whispering at the fullness of her breasts, sucking her nipples to fat buds, remarking on the glossy darkness of the hair between her legs. "So dark. So dark," he says as he opens her legs and parts her with his tongue. "Like honey," he says. She is so excited, his single finger enters her with the intensity of a penis, and she cries out. She is liquid, she is changed, and then she is losing control, feels herself quickening.

"Don't," she says suddenly, not wanting to come without him, alone. "Wait . . ." He raises his head, looks at her with worry.

"Come into me," she begs. "Please. Come into me, Andres."

"Now?" he whispers, moving up to lie beside her. "But this must last, please, Lily . . . our only time."

"It's not, Andres. It can't be. It's only the first time."

"The first?" he asks.

"A hundred times. Days and nights. A hundred times."

"Oh, beloved girl. Beloved girl . . ." When he enters her, she is shocked by the swollen fullness of him, the perfection, the throb of him. They both make a sound, deeper than a sigh, a sound of discovery, of relief, as though it is the balm they have been seeking always. Their bodies move as one. No violence. Butter melting. Clouds opening. And yet she is crying, calling, with an intensity of feeling she has never known. No man has opened her this way. Made her feel so excited while making her heart so safe. This is too good. She must never turn from this feeling. She must never lose him. She begins to climax, and it is so intense, so surprising, she wraps her legs about him at first, to stop it, to numb it, but in doing so, she draws him even deeper into her, which thrills her more, and there is no slowing it. She is falling, plummeting, arching with it. She bucks him, spreading her legs as far as they will spread, and the motion makes him gasp, press fully into her, cry out that he loves her. He is lost—she feels it in his whole body—and she welcomes the throb of his semen splashing into her, full of healing, full of life.

"I didn't know I could love you this much," she tells him. She is still coming, feels it could last an hour, this rhythmic embrace of his spent penis.

"Andres." She closes her eyes and feels safer, more happy, than she can ever remember. Finally, her body is quiet, and she lingers in the liquid connection of their bodies. She thinks it might be the first time in her life she has ever made love to a man without anger. The only time she has ever felt worthy of that love. She revels in the sound of his breathing, his whispering that he loves her, loves her, loves her.

"Lilla, all my life," he says, "I have waited for this."

When he withdraws from her, her body for a moment startles, longs for it not to end. But he settles, heavily, warmly, beside her. Lying on his stomach, his arm encircles her. She takes his hand and brings it up to her lips, kissing the smooth driftwood skin, the calloused palm.

"I can't stay awake," he whispers.

"Shhh . . ." she tells him, finding pleasure herself in the lullaby familiarity of the sound. "Shhh." In moments, he is asleep. She remembers the night he stayed awake to watch over her, so many years ago. Now she is watching over him, over the vulnerability of his face, with his childlike arc of closed lashes, his lips innocent, the sound of his breathing. And yet it is his presence that comforts her, asleep or awake. I am safe, she thinks. I am safe.

They do not hear the key in the lock. They do not hear the footsteps. They are so sated, so peaceful in their sleep. And even when Lily does awake and realizes that Ted is in the room, she cannot move or respond. He is only a dream to her. She sees every detail of his face, and yet it is so flat, so without feeling, she is not sure he is truly there, standing in the doorway, looking giant-sized, framed in the shadows of the hall behind him. That is why she doesn't call out to wake Andres. That is why she cannot understand at all when Ted picks up the model of the Skink and she sees his trophy, clutched so calmly in his hand, as he comes forward toward the bed. Why does he have it? she wonders.

She opens her mouth to speak, but no words come out.

"I never thought it would be him," Ted says as he brings down the brass nose cone savagely into the back of the only man that ever loved Lily the way she needed to be loved. Andres gasps. And then there is a trill in his voice that sets all the air in the room screaming. Lily tries to pull herself away, to stop Ted, but Andres, in agony, grips her, and her motion and Ted's rage cause the model to rip down, tearing through Andres's back like scissors through silk.

Ted sits in the chair while Lily presses the sheets to Andres's torn back. She does not know if he is dead or alive. She has tried to find his breath and cannot, and yet she thinks every now and then she hears a gasp. She has called the ambulance. Ted's head is down, and he is saying nothing. She's taken the bloody model from him, but she would not be afraid, anyway. If he killed her now, she doesn't think she would care. And she doesn't think he would be capable. He is weak. He is limp. She dresses clumsily, still trying to stanch the flow of Andres's blood with one hand. The blood climbs the sleeve of her shirt. She watches it as though it is someone else's arm. The paramedics will know what happened when they see Andres naked and facedown, when they see Ted catatonic in the corner, but she doesn't care. She is weeping but cannot feel her tears. In the end, she gives up on the blood. There is so much blood, she will never be able to stop it.

"Why did you come?" she asks him, her own voice husky and unfamiliar.

"I came," he says, "because I missed you. I came to watch you sleep."

For a moment, Lily closes her eyes and feels so paralyzed with his words, she might be made of stone. Then she rests her face near Andres's, kisses his cool brow, and lies motionless, staring at her bloody sleeve until the doorbell rings.

PART THREE

Iowa City

Chapter Eighteen

Lily is driving across the Mississippi River alone. Polly has agreed to keep the children for the weekend, and Lily feels anxious without them, as though she's gone somewhere without her purse and keeps feeling for it, panicking. Both her children have been clinging to her lately. They are too young to know what happened, and they heard nothing the night the ambulance and the police came. But they know they no longer get to see their father on weekends, that Lily is now silent most of the time, and that Grandma Edith cries and will not look into their mother's eyes. And maybe they notice that Lily will not eat. She has lost so much weight her clothes are pinned to stay on, and she is pale and listless.

"Smile, Mama," Peter said to Lily last week. "Please." And the fact that he noticed Lily's sadness hurts her, so she has been making an effort for them. She reads them books. She tells them jokes. She helps them draw pictures and rubs their backs to ease them into sleep. But she has been able to do nothing to take away her own pain. It is only now, as she crosses the significant barrier of the Mississippi into Iowa, that she can find the distance to breathe without each breath burning her with acrid, clinging regret.

At first, she couldn't do this: face the life Andres led for so many years without her, pack his things, learn him better after his death. But she can no longer pay the rent on his apartment. And the school has written her impatient letters saying they would like to give his studio to a man named Habling who casts figures in acrylic and paints them so realistically, people try to speak to them in art galleries.

Andres left a trust fund for his sons and everything else to her, as he told her he would. Andres's executor sent a Xerox of the will for her to see. The part about her was handwritten, and she ran her fingers along the letters and kissed the paper, as though she could bring him back to her for just a moment. "For my Lily, who gave my life back to me," the inscription reads. She has pondered this acknowledgment of his love for her and wishes she understood it better. How ironic that she feels she took his life away.

Lily has felt since Andres's death that if she looked in the mirror, there would be no one there. And it is not just the pain of his loss as her lover, as the lover she always wished for, that reduces her to nothing. That pain alone is drilling, relentless. There is no escape from it. Even in her sleep it stays with her. She has awakened many nights, weeping. She has barely been able to get out of bed many mornings.

But more than that, it is the loss of him as her guardian angel that is, for her, unbearable. Andres was always there for Lily, to love her, to remind her of her value. Without him, there is only emptiness.

And now there is no man in her life. Andres is dead, Ted is in jail, and Will—since she told him about Andres—has hardly spoken to her. He was silent when she told him that she and Andres were making love just a few hours before Ted came in. He was cold when she cried over the phone. She could not blame him. He would surely see her making love to Andres as a betrayal, though he was not being faithful to her for perhaps a very long time. All the men in her life are gone, even Andres, even the uncle of her soul. Like her mother, she has always looked to a man to give her value, to define her. Where shall she look now?

She has not been in Iowa City for more than eight years. Since it is late summer, the town is empty. Heat seems to burn upward from the streets, and the trees have a brownish gleam to their leaves, as if they couldn't live another day in the searing heat, as if they cannot wait until autumn comes.

In the streets this summer, there has been such violence, the whole country has felt like a bomb ticking. The melee at the Democratic National Convention. Race riots in Detroit and Chicago. Bloody faces appear each night on the national and local news and make Lily cry. But the streets of Iowa City are echoing, and clean, as though there could never be violence here or any noise at all.

Lily drives through them and remembers. She remembers her initial resentment of Andres, her coffees with him, and then their date at the fancy restaurant, with champagne and the art student–waitress who made her so uncomfortable. And as she drives, she thinks of Will and the beginning of their love. Looking back, her years in Iowa were equally delicious and lonely. There was the sex, and then there were the times with no sex. Except for her art—yes, her paintings and printing, there was nothing more. Even with Will. She had nothing of Will except the time they spent together. She had no commitment, no avowals. Just the sex. So intense, it sears her now to remember. If love came out of that, it was perhaps a lucky aberration. And now the out-of-control rage of their love for each other is gone, like a fire burned to the ground. Just the charred, exhausted ashes remain. But the art, she remembers now achingly, like sex, defined her. If she could find it again, would it do the same for her now? The night he died, Andres told her it could.

Andres's apartment is in a small, modern apartment building, just two stories tall, with a parking lot. She takes the key his lawyer sent to her and holds it in her hand for a few minutes before she has the courage to step into his life. She wonders if there are other women who should know about his death. But then surely they already do. The Iowa City papers must have carried the story: "Popular Artist/Professor in Tragic Slaying." Just the thought of it brings an iodinelike heat to her face. If anything in her life was wrapped in purity, it was the way she and Andres felt about each other. It enrages her to think of the taint this casts on it.

She is shaking when she turns the lock. But there is a familiarity about the room that comforts her immediately. Many of his prints are framed and hung on the walls. Others are rolled into a wall of black cubes he must have built himself. It is a simple room. Besides the prints, it is almost stark. There is a large bed, a dining table, a bookcase. In the closet she looks through his clothes. As she draws the hangers along the rod, Andres's herbal scent surrounds her, and she begins to cry. She does not believe he is dead. She feels somehow he is there watching her.

"I'm doing the best I can," she tells him out loud, and she begins to take the prints off their hooks. One by one, she stacks them against the wall. Pictures of tragedy, loneliness, hunger, despair. All hers now. All hers.

These many years, she accepted Andres's love, giving him nothing in return. Yet that last night of lovemaking, when they came together like two people who had been searching for each other for years, in that single night, she gave him everything.

If she could do it again, she would still make love to Andres the way she did, for she is certain it was the most significant moment of her life, and maybe his. And, at the same time, she cannot escape the unbearable guilt, the certainty that it is *she* who killed him. Why must she live with this guilt again? Now she is responsible for the deaths of two people. She's gone over again and again in her mind why no words of warning ever left her lips. "The survivors suffer most," she remembers him saying. "They ask Why? and Why? and Why not me?" All because Ted still had a key, because he wanted to watch her sleep.

There are few people in the art building. She tells the secretary in the art office that she is going up to Andres's studio to take his things. The secretary stares at her. She is a woman in her fifties who must have been there even when Lily was in school. She looks familiar. Lily thinks she recognizes the big hoop earrings, the dyed black hair.

"Are you a relative?" the woman asks.

"No. I'm"—she pauses and cannot find the word—"his heir."

"Your name?"

"Lily Nicholson." Ted's last name, though she has worn it for the last six years, feels false to her. Can she really once have been Ted's wife?

"Wait. I'll have to ask Professor Tunney."

Lily remembers Tunney. He was head of the art department even then.

"Must you?"

"It will only take a minute."

She speaks on the phone, and then the door to the office behind her opens, and Professor Tunney comes out. He is a tiny man with little hair on his head but a tuft of white hair in each ear.

"Lily Beach," he says, and by his use of her maiden name, she knows he remembers her.

"Yes."

"Come in." She bites her lip. She doesn't want to come in, to talk to anyone about Andres. What if Tunney thinks she was just one of the thousands of women Andres must have slept with over time? What if Tunney hates her for what happened to Andres?

"We are very sorry about Andres," he says gravely. "He was the pride of this department."

"He was a wonderful man," she says. His respectful tone throws her, worries her. It was not at all what she was expecting. She is close to tears and swallows continuously, hoping that the tears will run down her throat instead.

"There is department life insurance," Tunney says. "He left it to you."

"Oh."

"Why you?" Tunney is staring at her as though trying to see something that isn't there. She is housewifely, unassuming, she knows. Not overweight anymore but tired. She is wearing jeans and a sweatshirt for the mess of the move. She knows he is thinking, Why would Andres die for her? Why would Andres love her at all?

"We loved each other," she says.

"He didn't speak of you."

"He kept to himself mostly, I guess," she says.

"Yes. That's true. The thing I remember most about you was the way he put you up for the Breckner seat. He campaigned for you. Of course, your work was wonderful. I remember it still. But he wouldn't let any of us ignore it. And then, of course, you turned it down. He was crushed about that."

"I know."

"Knowing Andres, it's surprising he wasn't killed years ago by a jealous husband. He was a ladies' man, you know. He didn't just wait around and pine for you." Tunney has a cruel face. A mean mouth.

"I know that. Everyone around here always knew that. Look, you don't know anything about him and me. No one does."

Lily gets up to leave, and Tunney rises, too.

"May I have something of his?" he asks, suddenly tender.

"Were you friends?"

"I guess. As much as anyone was with him."

"Is there something you have in mind?"

"Just any print or drawing. I always admired his work. I thought he was the best artist we ever had around here. I still do, even though he's kind of lost his following. I don't even know what his stuff is worth anymore."

"I'll give you something," she says, touched by the request. "I'll give you something nice."

Lily climbs the stairs to Andres's studio, dragging a load of flattened boxes with her. She aches all over, hurts inside. She will never feel pure or simple again. She will never get over this memory. It is as though tragedy has introduced a new skein to her life that ever after must be woven into the fabric, that alters it forever. A brown or black thread muddying a bolt of pale blue. A color that will be woven through her experience every day from now on. In the most innocent, joyful colors of her life, these threads will appear, dark blots, mistakes, that will never again allow simplicity or clarity.

But the mere fact that life *can* be woven after what happened to Andres astonishes her, that bolt after bolt is made at all, that day after day life presses forward and goes on—this is a miracle.

Though it has been months since Andres was in the studio, it still reeks of turpentine, ink, oily pink hand-washing gel, acid. Here there are unfinished prints, other copies of the last one he gave her, scraps of notes, calendars. She sighs as she looks around her. There is no one to call to help her. No one else she can commiserate with.

She opens two, three boxes with purpose, stamping them into shape, snapping open the final, reinforcing flaps. When she fills them, she is not certain what she will do with their contents. She doesn't know how to throw away squashed tubes of viridian green or Thalo blue that once belonged to Andres, that once inspired him, that allowed him to create. In the end, she knows they will fill the basement of the many houses she will occupy.

There is only one thing in the studio she is certain she will never store in a basement: a mahogany paint box filled with new oil paints, exquisite brushes, glass and silver turpentine bowls, a mahogany palette. On the outside of the box are the initials LBN. It is the Christmas gift Andres spoke of. It is his last gift to her. She touches each tube of paint with a reverence and mourning. The box is exquisite in its own right. How had he ever imagined she deserved it? And the colors with their brilliant bands—will she ever have the courage to exploit them, to harness them for her own use? She thinks of Andres telling her to find her art again. She thinks of the yellow hat beneath the elm tree. Does she have the strength to journey back for it? For a moment, touching the contents of the box, it seems a cruel discovery: He is asking her to go on without him, He is asking her to find what she has lost without a map, without his aid. He has left behind only his belief that she has it in her to do it.

Glencoe

It is July 1969. The hottest July in Lily's memory, over a year since Andres's death. Lily and the children have been living in a little English Tudor house in Glencoe. There are green awnings in the summer and a rose garden with blush roses that make the bees dizzy with desire. In the backyard, the children swing and laugh well into the evenings. And there is a ceramic fish pond Lily's stocked with goldfish the size of trout. But the goldfish are listless in their pool, and the roses are bowing their heads this summer to the gluey heat.

For not quite a year, Lily has tried to make a new home here, a new life, in this house that she bought with Andres's money. There was more money than she might have imagined, and it worries her, the morality of taking it, when it is because of her he died. Yet, there is not a day that she doesn't think of Andres, wondering how things might have been different. She does not think often of Will now or of Ted. But her feelings for Andres never waver, never leave her. And in her emptiness and pain, she feels an odd duty to him to find herself in her art again. It is all he would ask of her. It is what he would be telling her now. Still, as the months go by, she is too shocked with loss, too weary. Some nights in bed she closes her eyes and thinks, Andres, if you are watching me, don't be too disappointed. Remember that I am human. Remember that I am flawed.

On this July day, it is Lily's desire to fend off the emptiness that has her looking for order in her life, that has her doing her spring cleaning, months late, in weather far too hot. The desire to leave the bungalow where Andres died led to a hurried move late last summer. She did not sort or throw away, and now, when she suddenly finds herself with the energy, it seems imperative despite the hot weather. While pulling out old hatboxes of long-out-of-style sundresses and maternity clothes, she finds the paint box that was Andres's last gift to her. She draws her finger along the lush mahogany and leaves a trail in the dust. A gift too beautiful for her, too fine for her, she thinks. And what has she done with it? Let it gather dust. Carrying the box tenderly down the stairs, she brings it to the sink, where she wipes it until it gleams. She sets it on the table and tells herself, Tonight I must use it, though she wonders if she'll have the courage.

After the children are asleep, she opens the box and sorts through its contents, imagines Andres individually selecting each tube of color; and this image, the clear hope he must have had as he took each tube in his hand, strengthens her to hunt down some of the canvas and stretchers she brought from his studio, his old tacking stapler, rusty and squeaking.

Her hands are steady as she pulls the canvas taut until it thumps like a drum, as she pours turpentine into the glass bowls and lays out the jewel colors along the rim of the too-beautiful-to-dirty palette. It is a ritual that resonates in her, that reminds her of the many times she has done just this. But when she brings the brush to the canvas, the ritual dissolves, and she tastes the metallic flavor of fear. Can she remember how to use the brush, to make it an extension of her eye? Can she make it an extension of her heart, as he would wish her to?

She opens a *Life* magazine and finds a picture of a female car mechanic, posed casually, her male cohorts looking on. The woman is slender and strong and nearly beautiful. Her arms are bare, the sleeves having been crudely ripped from her overalls, and there is something in the woman's face that touches Lily: a sadness in her eye, a determination in her mouth. Lily lifts the brush and begins to paint the light on the woman's arms, the shadow of her neck. The brush delivers its paint with arcs and curves that delight Lily, surprise her. In a few minutes the canvas begins to hum with color. Color spills from the woman's shoulders, radiates from her eyes. Greens that hiss, magentas that seem to valley the canvas with their depth. Yellows that flirt with orange. Blues as translucent as seas. Lily loses all sense of time, all awareness of herself. She lets the brush load and dance, as if by itself. She is lost in the rhythm of the brush to palette, brush to canvas. She is lost in the fat strokes of color, the shapes, the thrill as the colors collide. And she is lost in the woman's purposeful face.

She is shocked when she hears Peter's call, for it is morning. She has not stopped working all night. She scrubs the paintbrush in its glass of turpentine, dries it on the chamois, stretches, and turns to leave the room. But from the door she turns back to see what the night has come to. And what she sees is a painting more beautiful, more detailed, more fully realized, than any she has ever attempted. What she sees is a painting she has painted just for herself.

About the Author

JENNIE FIELDS was born in Chicago in 1953. She received a B.F.A. from the University of Illinois and her
master's degree from the Iowa Writers Workshop at
the University of Iowa. She is presently a senior vice
president of a large Manhattan advertising agency and
lives in a 108-year-old brownstone in Park Slope, Brook-
lyn, with her seven-year-old daughter.